The Beauty of Bond Street

Jacqueline Navin

BERKLEY SENSATION, NEW YORK

THE BERKLEY PUBLISHING GROUP
Published by the Penguin Group
Penguin Group (USA) Inc.
375 Hudson Street, New York, New York 10014, USA
Penguin Group (Canada), 10 Alcorn Avenue, Toronto, Ontario M4V 3B2, Canada
(a division of Pearson Penguin Canada Inc.)
Penguin Books Ltd., 80 Strand, London WC2R 0RL, England
Penguin Group Ireland, 25 St. Stephen's Green, Dublin 2, Ireland (a division of Penguin Books Ltd.)
Penguin Group (Australia), 250 Camberwell Road, Camberwell, Victoria 3124, Australia
(a division of Pearson Australia Group Pty. Ltd.)
Penguin Books India Pvt. Ltd., 11 Community Centre, Panchsheel Park, New Delhi—110 017, India
Penguin Group (NZ), Cnr. Airborne and Rosedale Roads, Albany, Auckland 1310, New Zealand
(a division of Pearson New Zealand Ltd.)
Penguin Books (South Africa) (Pty.) Ltd., 24 Sturdee Avenue, Rosebank, Johannesburg 21960,
South Africa

Penguin Books Ltd., Registered Offices: 80 Strand, London WC2R 0RL, England

This is a work of fiction. Names, characters, places, and incidents either are the product of the author's imagination or are used fictitiously, and any resemblance to actual persons, living or dead, business establishments, events, or locales is entirely coincidental.

THE BEAUTY OF BOND STREET

A Berkley Sensation Book / published by arrangement with the author

PRINTING HISTORY
Berkley Sensation edition / June 2005

Copyright © 2005 by Jacqueline Navin.
Cover art by Tim Barrell.
Cover design by George Long.

ISBN: 0-425-20356-5

BERKLEY® SENSATION
Berkley Sensation Books are published by The Berkley Publishing Group,
a division of Penguin Group (USA) Inc.,
375 Hudson Street, New York, New York 10014.
BERKLEY SENSATION and the "B" design are trademarks belonging to Penguin Group (USA) Inc.

PRINTED IN THE UNITED STATES OF AMERICA

10 9 8 7 6 5 4 3 2 1

Prologue

"I believe I liked it better when I was your secret lover," Lord Marcus Roberts said to Lady May Ellinsworth Hayworth as he flipped through the newspaper spread over his lap. It was a Tuesday morning, a rather typical day. They sat in companionable silence in the sunlit coziness of her informal drawing room in the elegant town house in London's ritzy Mayfair district.

May sighed, frowning through the spectacles perched on the end of her nose at the delicate fringe upon which she was working. Her fair hair, still untouched by a single strand of gray, fell in disarray about a face that appeared much younger than her four and forty years. "That was because all you did was sneak into my boudoir at night."

"Which I enjoyed," he admitted. "It was something to look forward to, even if it did give me a crick in the neck to climb through the basement window."

She smiled, her green eyes crinkling in the corners. It was a slight admission of her age, the laugh lines etched by a merry temperament.

Her trysts with Robert when she was staying with her niece while her house was being refurbished were a fond memory for her as well. Wildly romantic, *and* the tantalizing element of adventure.

"You did nothing but complain. 'I am too old for this,' you kept saying, and, Robert, you are only six and forty." She leveled a well-manicured finger at him. "And if you say that is old, then beware, for I am only two years younger."

His name was Marcus Roberts, and he was a peer, but she still called him by the name he had used when he'd posed as a commoner and seduced her. She had met him when he was Robert Carsons, the owner and operator of the finest carriage works in London. She had not known of his noble blood, then. It was with rough hands and silken kisses that he'd made her fall in love with him, a lowly stable master.

But she'd never really completely believed the ruse. With his aristocratic good looks, she had always known he was not what he seemed.

"But you look a score my junior," he replied with a diplomatic sparkle in his dark eyes. She loved the roughish way his hair, a distinguished salt-and-pepper, fell straight into his eye when it was uncombed. Robert was a man who could look like a duke when dressed, but she preferred him unkempt.

She smiled whimsically. "It was so lovely when it was just the two of us in our own world."

"And now," he said, pulling a face as he snapped the paper to fold it neatly, "we have to be respectable." His mouth thinned disapprovingly.

"I thought you liked spending leisurely hours with me. And, after all, it was you who came out in public first. That disguise . . ."

She fell into laughter, which he observed impassively. She smoothed the pink feathers frothing around her neck and composed herself. "You said you did it so that you would be able to squire me about in public."

"See, then, it is your fault. You drove me mad, running

about with that silly lord who was in love with you. I had to do something."

"You risked everything for me. And I love you for it."

He pretended not to be moved by her sweet declaration, but his bluster lost some of its blow. "It was worth it. But I still say that we have lost a good deal of our precious privacy. Now, I must depart and dress for the evening in a few hours. You will go upstairs and bathe—without me, which I find intolerably bothersome. And then I must return to escort you to the rout tonight. It is all so much *work.*"

"I see." She lowered her head to her fringe again, her lips tightly twitching. She had a good idea where this conversation was headed.

"If you would but marry me—"

"A-ha, now we have the meat of it. This is your ploy." She put down her needlework and stood. Her petite frame was slender, wrapped in a stunning gown of silk—in pink, her favorite color. "We have been through this. Can you not accept and be happy with how things are?"

"No," he countered sharply. "I am most dissatisfied."

She saw he was not in a mood to be charmed. Crossing to the jumble of supplies strewn over the settee, she fetched some threads out of her sewing box and turned the topic of conversation. "I hope you are not trying to beg off of the Hastings' rout tonight. Need I tell you how important this is? Tonight of all nights."

He held up a hand. "Do not trouble to explain. I know you must go for Sophie's sake, and I am not meaning to make complaint."

"It is her first large gathering, a debut of sorts." She returned to her seat. "When I bring one of my brother's children into society, I feel close to him. With the two others, I could look into their faces and see him. Michaela—well that one is obvious. And Trista, as well, in her own way had his manner, that aloof way he had."

She sighed, picking up her work. "I admit, it is a bit more difficult with Sophie. Perhaps because she is so beautiful. She is so . . . formal. Once she is over her nerves, I am confident she will do fine."

Her words were meant to shore up her own confidence in the latest of her departed brother's children. She'd devoted the last few years, since his death, to finding the illegitimate children from Woolrich's many affairs and restoring them to their inheritance. But Sophie had proven much more challenging than the first two young women who had slid so easily into her family.

She frowned as she contemplated the cool beauty of Sophie Kent. What was it that made her so difficult to warm up to? As she puzzled on the vague unease she always felt in the company of her newfound niece, her needle slipped, causing her to prick her finger. She made a small exclamation and put the wound immediately to her lips.

Robert came to his feet. "What happened?" He took her hand and examined the tiny wound. "Poor May," he purred and slid the tip of her finger into his mouth.

May laughed softly. "You are naughty. I must go . . ."

"Upstairs?"

"We cannot . . . Sophie . . . is . . . My maid will be looking for me soon to dress my . . . hair . . . I . . ." She could hear the breathy weakness in her own voice. After all this time together, he could still do this to her.

Tiny jolts of excitement shot from the slender finger he was now plying with his tongue.

"Stop! You are wicked."

"I thought you'd forgotten. You've been so wrapped up with your latest protégé."

"You cannot be jealous," she scolded, taking her hand back so that she might claim the normal functioning of her heart.

"May, darling, you know I would never make issue with any of your efforts to reunite yourself with your family. I know what it means to you and my aim is to help you in all ways possible." He grimaced and added, "Even if it means going to the Hastings' rout tonight."

She softened. "I know you love me, and I know you understand, Robert. But admit it, you do not like Sophie."

He thought on this a moment. "I have no objection to Sophie. It is only that she seems to frustrate you. It is in you I sense some discontent with her."

"She is unique," May admitted. Still, she was glad to have Sophie in her life, at long last. She'd been looking for the young woman for more than a year. Her solicitors had sent out letters upon letters, trying desperately to track down her whereabouts. Then, Sophie Kent had suddenly appeared at the solicitors' offices five months ago. May had been overjoyed.

Initially, they had been awkward. May had not worried, certain that would pass, as it had with the others. Sophie was pleasant and most appreciative of all May provided. Her manners were flawless and she was very compliant and eager to please. But she was reserved, even cold in some way. She held herself back. It was true, she did frustrate May.

"Perhaps it will come in time," Robert reassured her. "You have to consider that her life might have been a hard one, making it difficult for her to be open with someone until she knows them well."

"Yes. I shall keep hoping." She allowed him to lead her to the settee, clearing away the jumble from her sewing box so that they could sit together. She curled comfortably beside him. If a servant were to come in, it would be unseemly, but really, when had she cared for such things?

She lay her head on his shoulder. "How is it you always know just the right thing to say to soothe me?"

He wrapped his arms around her. "Because I love you."

There was an interval of silence. "You feel it, too, with her, do you not, Robert?"

He considered this. "To my mind it seems . . . as if she is hiding something."

May twisted in his arms and looked up at him. "Can you always tell if a woman is hiding something?"

"I have rather keen senses. From all those years as a

spy, you understand. It gives one a preternatural sense about things."

His stare seemed a bit too intense, and a ripple of uncertainty fluttered in her heart.

He said, "When you love someone, then nothing can break that, May. So, I suppose there is nothing to do but wait patiently for trust to grow."

Was he only speaking of her newly found niece? She remained silent, reminded sharply of her own secret.

She longed to tell him. What a relief it would be to unburden herself. He had possessed a hidden past, and she had helped him expose his true identity and clear his name. He had trusted her. . . .

But, no, her circumstances were far different. Robert had been a hero, a man who had done a great thing to protect an innocent. He'd sacrificed for honor, for some ultimate good. She could claim no such thing.

Some secrets could not be born, not even with love.

They were interrupted at that moment by a sharp rap. The pocket doors were opened and Johnson, dressed smartly in his footman's livery, entered the room.

May straightened, giving her servant her attention.

"Madam, pardon me for intruding so abruptly." He was flustered, which was unlike Johnson. She was instantly alert. "A man just arrived with a most disturbing request, and bade me give it to you with all haste. He is waiting in the hall."

He produced a letter, holding it out for her on the salver she used for her correspondence. The fact that he'd taken the time to observe this formality seemed incongruous to his manner.

May picked up the letter and read swiftly. She handed it to Robert and turned to Johnson. "Bring Lord Farnsworth to me."

Robert looked up after reading the missive. "Gideon?"

May called after Johnson. "And fetch the physician at once!"

The servant went out swiftly, returning with a rather

bedraggled dandy with a worried face and a wrung hat between his clenched fists. May stepped forward, forgoing all courtesies.

"Is he hurt badly?"

"Yes, my lady, he is. I have come to you in all desperation. I dare not take him to hospital."

"Good God, no!"

"But we have only bachelor's quarters in St. James."

Robert stepped forward. "Is his injury mortal?"

"I know not. But it is grave. Please, you must understand this. When the disaster occurred, my thought was of you, as he mentioned he'd seen you from time to time in Town, and spoke of you so highly and with a fondness I'd scarce heard from him before. I believe you are related, although I do not know how."

"My dead husband's brother," May clarified in a rush, "and beloved to me, although we have barely kept in touch these years past. I spoke to him only recently when we met at the Park." She brushed aside the explanation when she realized she was babbling a bit from the shock.

"He did not wish to come here. He was . . . I think it was humiliating to him to beg charity, but, my lady, I hardly know where else to take him."

Shifting to a tone of authority, she said, "Of course you did exactly the correct thing. He must be here, with family. Have him brought here at once, but in secrecy. Dueling, in case you did not know, Mr. Farnsworth, is not legal. He could be arrested, as could you for serving as second. Bring him through the mews, then in the servants' entrance. And do not worry yourself that he will protest. You must tell him that I insist, if he gives you any trouble over it."

"In any event, he is in no position to argue," Robert said, placing a comforting hand on Lady May's shoulder. "I will go with Lord Farnsworth, my lady, and fetch my lord to you. Do not make yourself anxious. He will be brought here, I assure you."

The command in his tone reassured her. She grasped his hands, holding his gaze for a moment to communicate to him her thanks. She had come not only to love this man, but to depend on him in a strange way. She was a strong woman in her own right, but she did not object to his taking charge and comforting her at times when she needed it.

When he was gone, she thought of Gideon, of how he had looked when she'd seen him last. He had possessed a devil-may-care air, a grin filled with wickedness and eyes full of such sadness. . . .

She thought, then, of him small and staring at her with those same impossibly gorgeous eyes filled with adulation. Inevitably, she came to remember Matthew, and her heart gave a painful wrench.

She reflected how strange it was to have thought of her bitter secret only moments before and then have the one living reminder of it so soon after land on her doorstep.

ℑ Chapter 1

Sophie's first thought when she'd heard running footsteps, shouts, and then the low, urgent voices was that they'd come for her.

Poised frozen in the midst of the exquisitely furnished room that was her bedchamber here at Lady May Hayworth's ultra-fashionable home, she waited for the sound of feet pounding on the stairs and for the magistrate and his constables to burst in and announce that she'd been caught dead to rights impersonating a person of quality.

The sounds died down, fading into a quiet she thought ominous. After a significant interval, she relaxed.

Not the constable, then, nor the magistrate.

In degrees, her breathing returned to normal. She sat calmly at the dressing table and schooled her thoughts away from anxieties.

She had her toilette to make for tonight's rout—her first large party and a debut of sorts. At two and twenty, she was far too old to be a true debutante, so Lady May had decided on a gradual introduction into the elite circles of the bon ton.

She took in a deep nourishing breath. Now *there* was anxiety. Yes, it showed in her reflection, in the clear, sparkling brown eyes staring back at her with the alarm she could not quite shake off. She was to enter society proper at last. The beau monde—the beautiful world she had always watched, envied, and craved—was to get its first real look at her.

She was still in her wrapper, her hair loose and long, twirling haphazardly around her shoulders in a golden cascade, awaiting the attention of her dressers. She put the time to no good use, simply going round and round again with her nerves, until Sally entered, breathless and waving her hands excitedly.

"So sorry, miss," Sally said. "My lady has not yet come upstairs for her toilette, so I thought I would get started with your hair. There is a to-do downstairs."

"Oh?" Her heart beat crazily against all the logic she could muster. "I hope it was not bad news."

"I wouldn't have a clue, miss," said Sally with enough of a pout to communicate how dearly she would have liked one.

Jeannie, the other maid whose chief responsibility it was to see to the gorgeous wardrobe May had purchased for Sophie, came in and set about her work. "The gold brocade, miss?" she asked.

"No, Jeannie. That one. Ah . . . Aunt May picked it for tonight."

It never rolled off her tongue. *Aunt May.* Because it was a lie.

Jeannie pulled out an eggshell sheath embroidered intricately with white and pink designs. Lace and pearls were used sparingly to compliment the dress's elegant simplicity.

It was stunning, the work of Lady May's prestigious and exclusive modiste, Madam Bonvant. Like all of the clothing May had purchased for her, it was a creation beyond any woman's dream.

Sophie marveled, as she so often did, that this was her life now. Dresses in the latest fashions, exquisite shoes and gloves of the softest kid, hats of spectacular design, and undergarments so delicate and sheer she blushed whenever she slipped one on. She had servants to pin her hair and care for her wardrobe and generally fuss over her.

She had not exactly been poor living with her mother, but she'd never enjoyed this degree of wealth, this absolute extravagance. It overwhelmed her sometimes, the thrill of it always weighted with the heaviness of righteous guilt, for all of it, every stitch of clothing, every minute spent in this luxurious home, was stolen.

"Did you get a look at what all that going on was about?" Jeannie asked. "All I heard was a great deal of shouting and there were men at the kitchen door."

Sally did not take her eyes from Sophie's hair, her hands moving quickly. "My lady rushed back to the mews with Lord Roberts after Johnny came in with some sort of message. I couldn't catch him to get him to tell me what it was all about."

Jeannie frowned as she fussed over the dress, brushing it out and inspecting it closely to make certain each fold was perfection. "The mews? Is it a new horse, then?"

"Surely not. It has the mistress overset, whatever it is."

Sophie was keenly aware that a lady of quality—which was what she was supposed to be—would never tolerate gossip such as this in her presence. But then, she considered practically, one would never find out what was going on. She wisely stayed silent and listened.

Jeannie, seeing she was not going to be admonished, went on, "I heard Cook mention something to Mrs. Hanover to ready one of the guest bedchambers upstairs. Do you think it is a visitor?"

Sophie started. "Why would a visitor be arriving in such a manner?"

The two servants exchanged glances. It was one thing to gossip in front of a lady, quite another to gossip with her. Sophie silently admonished herself. She had to get used to the habits of the nobility if she were going to be successful impersonating one.

"I don't know, miss. I don't think we should be saying all this," Jeannie said as she searched for the correct pair of stockings. Finding them, she laid them reverently on the bed, next to the dress.

"Don't be such a stick, Jeannie," Sally said petulantly, and yanked on Sophie's hair to make it nice and tight before twisting it artfully.

Jeannie pursed her lips as she selected some rouge powder and tint for Sophie's mouth.

"Thank you, but no," Sophie said in the nicest way she could manage when she saw what Jeannie was doing.

Regarding her with dismay, Jeannie said, "You will be peculiar if you are not enhanced. All the other women will be."

Sophie did not like wearing the cosmetics. True, they looked exceedingly smart on Lady May, elevating her fair prettiness to absolute glamour. However, the overly flushed cheeks on a rice-powdered pallor, replete with reddened lips that were achieved by the use of the rouge paste, reminded her too much of her mother and her aunts. As dear as they were, she wanted nothing of their trappings.

"I think the pink for my lips, then," Sophie said, trying to be accommodating.

Jeannie glanced at the dress laid out on the bed. She saw at once Sophie's suggestion for less color was a good one. Pressing her lips together, she assembled the correct shades and began to dab them on.

"A light hand, please," Sophie cautioned, and Jeannie nodded curtly.

If there was one thing Sophie knew, as the daughter of an actress and courtesan, it was how to create an alluring effect. Her mother and her two best friends, whom Sophie had called Aunt Linnie and Aunt Millicent, had been renowned in their day and enjoyed a significant amount of acclaim both for their talent on stage and their gay lifestyle. Many men had felt privileged to have any of the three beauties grace their beds.

This had led to a string of wealthy "protectors," and a busy life of parties and amusements. But when age had stolen their looks, the adulation had faded, and the premier demi-monde had moved on to younger, fresher faces. The three women had been all but forgotten.

They had lived together in Aunt Millicent's house, a tidy town house in Fitzroy Square, and Sophie, the only surviving child among them, had been their pet. And all three had equally been her mother.

She had mourned each one as they had fallen ill and died. First, Aunt Linnie, who was petite and rather vapid but as sweet as a child, then Mother, who had been distant and vaguely bitter at the loneliness of her later years. The last to go was wise, strong Aunt Millicent, who had succumbed to influenza last fall. With her passing, Sophie had been left penniless, defenseless, quite alone. And desperate. Most of all, desperate to avoid the inevitable course that would take her life along the same path as her aunts.

That of a whore—

"These shoes, miss?" Jeannie asked. "I know they were made to match, but there are these pink ones as well that will look splendid with that gown."

Sophie barely looked at the slippers. "Yes, the ones made for the dress, please."

Whore was a crude way of putting it, but it was, after all, what she was used to hearing. It was what the others had called her mother and aunts away from their hearing, but not from hers. It was what the children whom she had tried to play with at school said, what the ladies who passed them on the street hissed just loud enough for her to hear.

Oh, Aunt Linnie liked the term, *courtesan.* Practical Aunt Millicent had said they were mistresses, which, she insisted, was a fine tradition and not dishonorable in the least. Mother had clung to her past as an actress, stating there was no disgrace in being a fashionable demi-monde.

But there had been deep disgrace these women had chosen not to acknowledge. Sophie had felt it every day of her life.

Perhaps someone who did not understand her feelings might judge her harshly for the action she took when Aunt

Millicent's death had left her alone, penniless, and without
a single prospect for a respectable life. If it had been possible, she would have done anything else; she would have
gladly taken employment, even the meanest position, but
who would hire her or take her into service? She was far
too comely to work as a governess or companion. She was
too educated to be considered for employment as a servant
or shopkeeper's assistant. Caught between the carefully ordered strata of English society, she was lost, drifting toward what she feared, in her more anxious and irrational
moments, was her destiny.

Such was her state when she'd discovered the letters
Aunt Millicent had hidden away, letters from Lady May
Hayworth requesting information on the child she had
given birth to some twenty-odd years ago.

Sophie had not thought about it twice. She'd gone to the
solicitors who had sent the inquiries and told them she was
that lost child.

"Miss? Are you angry with me? Did I pull too hard?"

"No. No, Sally. It's fine." She was startled at herself for
being so lost in thought. "I was just . . . oh, woolgathering."

"I'll try to have a care," Sally promised. "Jeannie, please
bring me the curling tongs from the fire."

Sophie braced herself. She dared not breathe while
Sally tortured her locks into tamed ringlets. It was ironic,
really, that she submitted herself to these machinations to
catch a man when she'd spent so many years avoiding any
sort of male attention. But then, this time, she was Sophie
Kent. And as Sophie Kent, she could reach for the one
thing she could never aspire to as Sophie Temple: marriage
to a respectable man.

"All right, miss, now let me put these pearls in . . ."
Sally frowned at her creation, calculating the right spot in
the artful arrangement of curls for ornamentation. "Just a
bit longer."

Sophie's fingers toyed idly with the expensive bottles
glittering like prisms on the vanity as she ticked off the

commandments she'd broken. Thou shalt not steal. Thou shalt not bear false witness.

Thou shalt not covet a dead child's wealth and family, a tidy inheritance all ready and waiting for just the right girl—of which you are not, but you could be . . . you could, with some clever artifice and a bit of luck, since the right one, born to Millicent Kent and Lord Woolrich, had died all those years ago and would not suffer for the lie in any case. . . .

Ah, but her falseness ate at her.

She sighed, and looked at the mirror again. Such a pretty face, Mama had always said, holding Sophie's chin to keep her still so that she could admire the beauty she'd produced.

Sophie was her jewel. She'd cooed over the almond-shaped eyes, the straight, fine nose, the sculpted cheekbones. She'd sighed in pride and envy at the full lips. Sophie's evenly spaced white teeth caused her mother to beg her smile more often and to add a beguiling twinkle to her eye when she did so, in order to captivate a man. She'd expected to see Sophie settled with a wealthy protector. An earl, a duke!

A violent shiver jerked her spine.

"Do you have a chill?" Jeannie asked anxiously.

"No," she said quickly. A shawl was fetched for her anyway.

She refused to think on these things any longer. She had work to do—that was how she thought of tonight. She had one season—this was all her conscience would allow her to take advantage of Lady May—to make the best marriage possible.

That was how she was going to make certain *her* children would be welcomed by good families. They would not be hissed at on the street, nor cruelly cut by others at their church school. They would be invited with the other children to each other's houses for tea and playtime, not left behind, lonely and bitter. Her sons would sit in the drawing rooms of polite society and go to school and be well-thought-of among the quality. Her daughters would dance at assemblies and not be shunned or, worse, propositioned. They would not draw the lustful eyes of young men who thought them an easy tumble for the fact of who their mother was and what she had been.

The world did not dare hurl insults or make rude comments, or sneer at anyone who was tied to an important family. The rich, the powerful were immune to all she had endured.

She closed her eyes, concentrating on her goal. It was simple, clear, and finite. One season. And when she was wed, she would find a way to repay May for every pence she'd taken from her. She would. Every pence.

"Well, open your eyes, miss. Do you not like it?" asked Sally.

Sophie obeyed, and stared at her reflection. Her beauty surprised her. She was used to her face, used to the reaction it got, but Sally had outdone herself. What she saw surpassed all Sophie's hopes to make a good impression on this most important of evenings.

She rose and went to Jeannie, who, with Sally, held out the dress. She slipped into it, her body beginning to hum with excitement. She felt it, like a charge in the air, the way the air snaps before a bolt of lightning hits nearby. Tonight . . . there was magic around her. She felt it in every part of her.

She would find her husband. Maybe tonight. Maybe . . .

Moments later, one of the footmen knocked on the door to give her the startling news that their evening's outing was canceled.

In her disappointment, she quickly forgot the sensation she'd felt only a moment ago. About tonight holding her destiny.

May gazed at Gideon Hayworth, the Earl of Ashford, and thought him as beautiful as Lucifer in repose. Her throat constricted. Feelings clashed inside her. She was overcome by memories, of love, of self-recrimination, and above all, of fear.

His blond hair was as pale as wheat, curling rakishly in a style so effortlessly fashionable it made her ache at his fine beauty. When he'd been a boy, his head had been covered in fat curls, always tousled and unkempt.

Nothing else of the boyish Gideon remained. He was nearly thirty years old. His body was hard, fully muscled. The body of a man. He was devoid of his shirt, for it had been in tatters and the physician's assistant had had to cut it away. Gideon had been carefully washed, and his right hand, arm, and shoulder were bandaged, as well as a good portion of his head on that side.

He'd been dueling this morning. Pistols at dawn, somewhere in the park by Lord Farnsworth's report. The pan had been overloaded, which had been the fault of Farnsworth, who had beaten his breast and pulled his hair at the mistake. When Gideon had shot, the gun had misfired. The powder exploded, seriously injuring him.

The smell of charred flesh and hair had been replaced by the acrid smell of the medicines the physician had used to paint the wounds after he'd cleaned them. He was not bleeding his patient, which May had insisted upon. She could not tolerate leeches. She would rather die of bad blood than endure those disgusting things affixed to her skin, and she would not consent to submitting Gideon to such treatment. The physician, a serious fellow with wiry white hair and a full beard named Daley, had relented with trepidation.

Her willpower gave out, and she reached out a hand to Gideon's sweating brow and touched him. He felt clammy.

His eyelids fluttered open, revealing vivid blue irises. She was startled at the familiarity of them. They had been lit with a wicked gleam for as long as she'd known him. But his eyes appeared flat now. His mouth was tight and pale.

"Rest," she told him. "I know you are in pain."

He shook his head as if to deny this, but said nothing.

"Daley just left. You were sleeping." Unconscious. It had frightened her how he had lingered in unnatural slumber. "He says you will make a good recovery if you behave."

His mouth twitched as if he appreciated the unlikeliness of his doing such a thing.

Then he began to speak in a tired, husky voice. "I used to dream this."

She leaned forward. "What?"

"When I had to go away. After Matthew died. I dreamed I'd wake up and you would be there. And then you'd take me with you."

Emotions dammed painfully in her throat, preventing speech. Patting his hand, she could only nod, and in a moment it was all too much—seeing him, touching him, having him sleeping and looking so much like the little boy she had loved.

She rose. "I shall not stay with you if you insist on speaking. It is not good for your recovery. The physician said rest. I will leave you."

His hand closed over her wrist with surprising strength. She pulled away, fighting a dizzying feeling of drowning.

"No . . . don't go." He could barely make the words and his eyelid was already falling to pull him back into the sleep induced by the sedative Daley had administered.

"Rest well, I shall return," she managed. This seemed to relax him, or else the drug took hold, for his grip loosened and May extricated herself and fled from the room.

Gideon's eyes fluttered. "Don't go," he whispered, and his loose hold on consciousness slipped. He fell fitfully into sleep.

ॐ *Chapter 2*

Gideon's dreams were strange, visited by ghosts — Mother and Father, Matthew, and May. No . . . no, May had been real. This was her home. He remembered now. And . . . she'd been here, in the room with him. He realized this as he surfaced, rising in degrees out of unconsciousness to the deep pull of breathless pain.

He shrank away from it, trying to sink again. He dozed, the aftereffects of the sedative giving him ease for a short while longer. When he opened his eyes once more, he had forgotten where he was. He had no recollection of the morning, of the duel, nor the explosion until the awareness of how much he hurt brought it all back.

He sighed, settling himself, determined to make his peace with it. If he could keep himself from thinking about the burns, he could bear them easier.

Taking stock of his situation, he studied his surroundings. The room was nice, but nondescript. The tick of the clock felt like a hammer striking his head. He could not move his upper body much. The right side was tightly bandaged, his chest, arm, and shoulder, as well as the side of his head swathed in pungent-smelling linens. His eye was throbbing and he could not open it very much.

He refused to acknowledge the fear that flirted with his thoughts. If he had lost sight in his one eye, he would adjust in time. No use worrying over it.

He noticed his breathing was short, and forced himself to lengthen each breath. Had May returned as she'd promised? Perhaps she'd come in when he'd been sleeping. He was disappointed that he'd missed her. He was lonely and feeling the sting of his foolishness. Or perhaps ashamed was more to the point.

It surprised him that he was not irritated. He'd threatened Farnsworth with all the curses of hell if he brought him here, but now the thought of being in her home brought a sense of calm.

He'd been very attached to her as a child, being only seven when she'd married his brother, and he'd lived with them at Ashford Manor. She was the woman who had been like something close to a mother to him for a good deal of his childhood. But he'd lived without her, or indeed any tie to family of any sort, for a very long time since.

He felt weak, and as much as he did not like it, a bit afraid of the pain should he push his body too far, so he did not dare try to move. He longed for a distraction.

Predictably, he ruminated over the stupidity of the actions that landed him here. A duel. He'd fought a dozen or more with no harm done. With swords, all one had to do was pink his opponent. Pistols were even easier. A shot fired in the general direction of the man standing twenty paces away. It was understood, the entire thing fairly harmless. Except when one managed to really make a challenger irate.

He should have known Selwyn would demand satisfaction for the insult to his wife. It seemed rather a waste to go to the trouble for Abigail, who was a ridiculous bagatelle if there ever was one.

The damnable nuisance about it was that Abigail Selwyn had proven to be not all that exciting in the having, certainly not worth this. Oh, she'd made the chase enjoyable. But wasn't that the way of it? Women were never as much fun as they promised to be. The chase . . . that was the thing. After that, no woman held his interest for very long.

He'd tired of her and the woman had cried foul. Perhaps Selwyn wouldn't have minded the affair so much if Abbey had behaved herself properly. But all that weeping and sulking. She had even taken to her bed to "wane," as she put it. Her hysterics only turned the matter into a great bit of nonsense, and Selwyn had had no choice but to call him out over it.

He sighed, thinking perhaps he would try sleep again. But his mind would not quit its remonstrating. God, for a book. But what would he do with it? He could not see clearly enough to read.

Perhaps he had handled the affair with Abbey poorly on his end, too. He simply could not make the woman understand that he was not cut out for love. And he had no patience for petulance or tears. She'd accused him of having no heart, and that was true enough.

It made him sad to hurt her, but there was nothing to be done about it. He hadn't loved anyone in a very long time, and didn't think he was likely to. He rather thought that this part of him, the capacity to care for another above himself, was broken. Irreparably, like a shattered vase. Not enough glue to fix those kinds of breaks.

What he would not give for a flask of wine. No. Whiskey. Scotch whiskey to burn pleasantly on the inside and distract him from the throbbing wounds.

A shadow passed over the doorway. Thinking it might be May, he came instantly alert. He rolled his eyes against the deep stab of his headache to fix on the shape. It was not May. He could see that she was taller. She was slender where May was fashionably curved. She held herself differently, too, and the pose spoke of confidence and hesitation.

A woman. Nothing like a woman to restore the humors. . . .

"If this is heaven, I must be looking at a true angel." His voice sounded like a rusty hinge. He cleared his throat.

"But, no, there is this pain. So I must still be alive. And you are real."

Her head tilted. The creature was bemused.

"So much better," he murmured.

She looked behind her with a gesture of uncertainty, and he was suddenly afraid she would flee. He reached out a hand. His arm felt like it was made of lead, and he couldn't hold it up. It fell with a thud onto the covers; ignominious defeat. But it got her attention. "Please. Do not go."

That sounded pathetic, although effective. She hesitated. "Come. Come in," he said. "I am restless."

When he smiled, the pain increased under the bandage over his eye and cheek. But he did so because charm was instinctive, and he couldn't help himself. He was an intolerable rake, after all, and everyone knew it.

And even if it hurt, it made him feel better because she did not seem to be leaving.

Sophie hesitated in the doorway.

This was absolutely wrong. A lack of personal discipline was what it was, a fault of hers.

Gently bred girls did not creep about in the night to steal a look at a man in his bed. But she was not gently bred. She was the love child of an actress and an artist, and although she wished very fervently to behave herself . . . she just could not bring herself to move back into the hallway.

His eyebrow rose very slowly. She wanted to melt into the floor, humiliated at having been caught.

"Do not go," he said quickly as she took one step backward. His voice was low, a gravelling baritone that scraped the air. "Please."

His expression was almost pleading. It embarrassed him. She could tell, the way he'd said, "Please," like that, then shook it off.

He seemed to fill the bed in which he reclined. His face was obscured by his bandages, but she saw one side of a clean jaw, a high brow, blond hair lying in crisp wheat-colored curls against the snowy white of his pillow. His nose was large, strong, too patrician, his mouth sensually curved. The eye not covered by bandages regarded her steadily. It was thickly lashed, and vibrant blue.

"I . . . I just looked in for a moment," she went on, embarrassed to have no good explanation for trespassing. "To see . . . I . . . Do you need anything?"

She was stammering, to her humiliation. He was a very good-looking man, she realized. Blue eyes and soft blond hair—angelic touches on an otherwise hard face, a masculine face comprised of strong bones and sharp angles; the high cheekbones, the sharp jaw, the long, elegant nose all chiseled into startling handsomeness.

"Stay," he repeated. "Miss . . . well, would you be good enough to give me your name."

"I am Sophie Kent." When would she cease to wince when uttering that lie? "I am a guest of Lady May's." She took a step inside, drawn by him despite all the sense she'd cultivated in her twenty-two years. "And you are Lord Ashford."

"You have heard of me," he replied with a sly grin. "Ill or good?"

"Both," she said.

This seemed to be a different response than he expected. "What a forthright person you are. Well, then you are forewarned. Forearmed . . . and all that."

"Indeed? Am I to take warning?"

"A practical observance. I am a man not prone to self-control. It is not in my nature to behave properly in the presence of a woman as beautiful as you are, Sophie Kent."

He lay on his back with the sheet drawn up to his chest, physically imposing, despite the fact—or perhaps a bit magnified by it—that he was in bed. Much of him was covered in bandages, but that did not prevent tantalizing glimpses of naked masculine flesh from showing. This did not appear to trouble him, however. He certainly demon-

strated no modesty, seeming quite at ease, like a pasha reclining on cushions and presiding over his guests, sure of
his dominion.

"But you are injured," she observed, surprised that there
was a touch of coyness in her words.

"So I am," he agreed, shifting slightly. The discomfort—probably a very inadequate word—registered around
his eyes, and at the slightly downward turn of his mouth at
the corners. "And so you are quite safe. Come closer."

"May I get you something? Is there anything you
require?"

His eyelids dropped just enough to give him a threatening air. "Do not get me started."

Her skirts rustled crisply in the quiet room as she advanced. "You are being provoking."

"I tell the truth. Which, of course, some find provoking.
But you seem made of sterner stuff, Sophie Kent, than to
flee because of a bit of repartee."

He was staring at her. She'd always reacted with alarm,
even defensiveness, at a look like this, warm and sultry
with male awareness. But this time, she felt a small thread
wind down in the pit of her stomach. It was a nice feeling,
something that made her want to do as he asked. Stay.

"You tell the truth, do you? All the time?"

He lifted one shoulder. "No one tells the truth all the
time." Again, that smile. It was a heart-stopper, and
he wielded it like a weapon. "We all have our faults," he
added.

"A man who admits faults. I believe this is a night of
some moment. I have never encountered such a beast."

"You call me a beast," he murmured, "when you hardly
know me. You are immeasurably astute, Sophie Kent."

At his self-irony, she laughed. He chuckled, too, then
winced.

Concern altered her instantly. "Are you suffering?"

He did not answer, but his lips pressed into a tighter,
whiter line.

She turned away, looking at the bedside table. Her

hands trembled as she picked up bottles and tumblers. "And here I am, talking away at you when you are in need of medicine. Is there a tonic here for pain? Who is to tend you?"

He extended his hand, strong and broad and darker hued than hers, to cover her questing fingers. "No. Leave it. It is not so bad as yet. Besides, the medicines make me feel strange and drowsy, and I do not wish to sleep. You provide me with all I require right at this moment. Distraction, companionship."

He shifted, sitting up. The sheet covering him slipped to his waist, revealing more of a magnificently broad chest that was absolutely . . . it was decadent.

The sight of it affected her profoundly. He was *male,* and for the first time in her life, she was struck forcefully with all that meant.

She could not keep her eyes from the way his body was so differently made. The muscle was defined by intriguing cuts in the hard flesh, and the soft, warm glow from the lamp cast a velvet sheen that made her mouth go suddenly dry. And the worst of it was, she was drawn to want . . . to . . . touch him.

He saw her looking. She averted her eyes.

"I've interrupted your evening," he said, his gaze taking in her gown, her hair.

Smoothing her skirt self-consciously, she replied, "We were to go to a rout, that is all."

"I am sorry for the inconvenience, and yet I am glad you have come." He seemed to relax. "Things were getting quite bad in here. I was actually beginning to have penitent thoughts."

"Perhaps they are useful for you," she said with both primness and a smile. "A dollop of penitence is good for the soul."

He nodded. "Every now and then." He settled himself with an effort. "I was rude, wasn't I? I did not mean to be. When I see a beautiful woman, I get flirtatious."

"A reflex?" she asked, doing a poor job of hiding her amusement. "To flirt? Is there such a thing?"

"It must be because I do it all the time."

"Do you need any water?" she asked, turning quickly to the bedside table.

He nodded. "You must be disappointed to have gone through all that trouble only to have the night cancelled."

"It simply does not signify. Lady May explained what had happened." She poured a glass of water for him.

"Did she?" He took it, bringing it to his lips without breaking his gaze. "Did she explain that it was by the consequence of my own folly?"

"I suppose she believes that is your own business, and not to be bandied lightly."

He made a small sound that might have been mistook for derision if his face had registered any bitterness. "What *did* she tell you about me?"

"Only that you are the brother of her late husband and that you had been injured dueling." She thought he was growing worse by the sour expression on his face. "If you are growing tired, I should leave you in peace and quiet."

"But I hate peace and quiet," he said, his voice sharp. "So you had to come and see for yourself. You could not resist a peek, eh?"

She rolled her eyes. He was growing mischievous again. "I had only thought to look in for a moment. I was . . . curious."

"You are a woman of impulses. Why does that please me so? Ah, do not look at me with so much wariness. I am wicked, I admit, but I am quite tame now, with half of me near done away with."

He did not seem harmless to her, but she did not tell him this. He would no doubt take it as a compliment. "Whatever impulse drove me in here tonight, I should quit now that I am satisfied you are doing well, at least inasmuch as I see you are in fine possession of your wits."

"Oh, but I am not well at all. I am in pain. Most horrible."

He meant to tease her, she knew full well, but she paled with horror nonetheless. It made her faint to think of him suffering. "Very well. I will stay a few more moments, until your nurse comes. Is she due?"

"I do hope not. I like it perfectly well with you and I alone together."

"Now, that is what I am referring to. You are impertinent."

"I?" He donned a look of innocence, or at least tried. His face could never be completely without a touch of mischief, she thought.

She gave him a lofty look, full of reproach. "You must not . . . flirt."

"It is second nature, I assure you. And doing so normal a thing to me as breathing is restoring my spirits. Come. Sit by me. I can barely see you in the gloom."

She laughed softly. "The light is sufficient. No, sir, I will stay here."

"You disappoint me." He threw it out like a challenge.

"Are you never pleased?" she said.

"Let us not get into the topic of my pleasure."

"It seems to consume you," she countered, "and has proven unavoidable in all your innuendoes."

"You are not missish in the least." He chuckled. "I find that so refreshing in one with such arrogance."

She smiled blithely at the ambiguous compliment. "I am so glad you approve of me."

"Yes, I do. I see myself in you. Like recognizing like, as it were . . . that look in your eye. Do not worry, I shan't give you away."

She pretended not to react, but a hard thumping of her heart beat painfully in her breast. *I shan't give you away.*

"I fear you are becoming delirious," she said.

"It's the damned medicines. Fogging up my brain."

"That is good. It dulls the pain."

He shrugged as he sipped at his water, his gaze dropping to her bosom. Sophie experienced something very strange. She grew warm and the flesh above the plunging neckline of her gown tingled with tiny pinpricks of pleasurable sensation.

"Come closer, Sophie, for it maddens me not to see you well."

She tsked, giving him a wry look. "I am close enough."

"I am infirm," he reminded her, "would you have me vexed as well? My eye . . ."

She almost laughed. He was insupportably exasperating. "You have one perfectly good eye. You can see me well enough."

"I give you my word I will behave quite honorably. There, you are safe. Now, come closer. I truly cannot see. My vision is blurred from this infernal . . . laudanum or whatever."

"You are incurable, sir." She sniffed, but shifted slightly closer to him, hating that she was allowing herself to be manipulated, but he did not play fair, after all. She could not wholly disregard his wishes. He was suffering with burns, for goodness' sake.

And he was charming. He was blatantly outrageous, but he had a gentleness in him. And vulnerability. Yes, that was the thing, wasn't it? He was hurt, and that made him irresistible.

"You are by reputation a horrid rogue," she said softly.

"Oh, but I am." His smile was slow, and absolutely charming. "I admit it freely. But still a good man, that I promise."

"But is the promise from a rakehell a worthy one?"

"My promise is always good," he said, and his voice was strong. It sent a ripple of chills through her. "I am not without honor. I would not touch any woman who did not wish it. But . . ."

"Ah, there is a 'but' to qualify your guarantee of safety."

He chuckled softly. "I was merely thinking on the fact that sometimes women deny what it is they really want. Have you noticed that?"

"No. I am shockingly direct, myself."

He grinned, his head falling back. "I like that in a woman."

His strength was indeed flagging. The volume of his voice had lowered. She could barely hear him. And so she did move closer.

Just a little.

"A man likes to know where he stands. But I wonder if it is possible to change your mind."

She smiled back at him. "Indeed, sir, when you are well, you may try."

He lifted a corner of his mouth. His eyelids were heavy with fatigue. "A challenge. How quaint."

"It may console you while you recuperate. You seem like a man who thrives on challenge."

She could not help it, she touched him. Just to smooth the hair from his brow where small droplets of perspiration had formed.

He closed his eye, and she was glad she had done it, even if she hadn't really meant to, because it seemed to soothe him.

"Please tell me you are not married," he said.

"Of course not."

"Thank God. I am not up to any more duels."

She chuckled softly. "No. No husband to burst in to demand satisfaction."

"It is stupid, playing with other men's wives. But it is also so damned convenient. Only *in*convenient when they carry on when the thing is over and their husbands are forced to call you out." He opened one eye and pinned her with a curious glare. "And how is it that you are unmarried?" He drew in a deep breath, rallying his stamina. "You are not so young, you know."

She withdrew her hand as if he'd bitten it. "I am not an ancient, either."

"Oh, dear. You are not waiting for the *grande* passion are you?"

"Heavens no!" She drew back. That was what she got for her moment of weakness.

"Ah. You say so with convincing disgust." He nodded in approval, a soft smile curling his sensuous lips. "What is it you want? Do you even know?"

"I do," she said quickly. "I want security, a steady life."

"Marriage?"

She pursed her lips, sensing he was mocking her.

"Ah, dear," he murmured. He tilted his head up, bringing his good arm up to tuck his hand between his head and the pillow. The pose did interesting things to the muscle in his arm, and thick cords of vein stood out on his skin.

He continued in a thoughtful manner, staring upward so that she was free to look her fill. "What we desire, deeply desire, is not so easily answered," he mused. His words were beginning to slur. "It might be that we do not know ourselves what that is."

"Do you know?" she managed to say.

The question seemed to surprise him, perhaps unnerve him a bit as well. "Sometimes I do," he said after an interval.

"Well, I always do."

He chuckled, as if it were so simple to read her, as if she were an unimaginative chit who clamored to lose herself in mediocrity.

"You are tiring."

"Do not leave me yet." He said it quickly, and with enough appeal to stall her.

She settled back and he issued a long sigh of satisfaction.

Taking advantage of the quiet moment, she broached a topic that had made her curious. "May mentioned you have not seen one another in a great while—"

"May and I," he cut in sharply, "have a history that is too lengthy, and far too complex, to discuss."

"I was only curious why your friends brought you here. May was very grateful to Lord Farnsworth, I believe, who was rather beside himself with concern."

"He is probably more concerned about the inconveniences to himself while I am indisposed. He does enjoy tagging along with me."

"That seems unkind."

He frowned contritely. "Perhaps it is. And unjust. I . . . People have proven unsteady in my life . . . Unreliable. At best. I do not expect much from them, you see."

She was fascinated at the shadow that crossed his features. Then he smiled, and it was gone and he looked at her. "I enjoy my freedoms, and, yes, my pleasures. My philosophy of playing light and fast has served me well."

"And yet here you lie," she observed pointedly.

This caught him, and he gave her a wry grin. "Ah. Yes, well, not my finest hour to be sure."

"Was she worth it?"

His face froze, his expression pricelessly stunned. "No, actually. She was not."

"It was her husband who called you out," Sophie said. "May learned how he challenged you to pistols."

He nodded, and settled back. He seemed to be tiring. "He had the right."

"Then you feel remorse?"

"I feel pity." His eyelid lowered slowly. "I do not have a great respect for the institution of marriage."

"But surely you concede marriage brings happiness to many people." She felt defensive, though he was not attacking her beliefs, merely stating his own.

"I do not believe that happiness is a state."

"Of course it is. When you have what is most important to you, all the things you've dreamed of, then certainly you are happy."

"Do you think so? I've only known a moment, small, precious and for that time, you are happy. It does not last." He laid his head back on the pillow, his eyelid falling shut. "It does exist. It seems long ago, but I remember."

"You are tiring, so I shall not argue with you."

"You are not one of those women who equate marriage to *happiness,* are you, Sophie Kent? There is so much else out there beyond silver tea services and fine linens and a housekeeper waiting for her instructions each day."

His body seemed to melt a degree into the mattress. His voice thinned. "There is art, there is music, there are brisk rides on an open moor, or the deep shadows when you lose your way in a forest path and the thrill when you find your way out again. An entire world, a whole and complete life. The small things."

For some insane, infuriating reason, she felt herself quiver. The set of her heart, steady all these years, wavered just a little . . . like the faint shimmer on a still lake in the deep heat of summer.

His hand crept to hers. It was warm, but it didn't disturb her to touch him. Indeed, she drew strength from the feel of his strong grip. She let her fingers do what they would, curl around his and hold on.

"I suppose I should rest now," he said creakily. "I think I'm quite done in, blathering on like a fool."

She leaned forward. "Hush. I will stay, if you wish." Laying her free hand against his forehead, she felt once again for fever and was relieved to find none.

"Do something for me, please?" she asked.

"Anything within my power," he replied weakly.

"Sleep."

The sound of someone entering brought Sophie instantly to her feet. She whirled to see a servant coming in at a brisk pace.

"Oh, miss!" she exclaimed, laying a hand over her heart as she caught her breath. "You gave me a fright."

She rushed straight to the medicines lined on the bedside table.

"Hurry, please," Sophie said as the woman fussed with the bottles. "He has been fighting his pain."

"I will. I-I am. I am not sure what . . ."

Ashford opened his eyes. His face was tight. He could no longer hide his agony.

"That one," he said, raising his hand with an effort to point to a brown flask.

"Why are you so long at coming to check on your charge?" Sophie demanded.

She glanced at Sophie, but turned her reply to the man lying in the bed. "I'm Candace, sir. I beg your pardon for being late. I am sorry, I truly am. It will never happen again—never, I swear!"

Sophie retreated to the doorway. He deserved his privacy, but she was not quite happy to leave him to the questionable care of his nursemaid. Candace cast her a resentful look.

"I *will* do better. See, my man and I, we got into a tiff, and I . . ." She blushed scarlet and clamped her mouth shut. It seemed to take considerable effort.

Ashford took the draught she mixed, nodding when he'd swallowed and Candace took away the glass. "Love. It's such a bother, isn't it? Do not fret, Candace. Your delay gave me more time with Miss Sophie."

Sophie fumed that the woman had neglected him, even for a little while. That he had to endure one moment's pain longer than necessary was not to be forgiven!

She opened her mouth, but Gideon turned his head weakly. "Do I have your word, Miss Sophie, that we shall tell no one? After all, everyone deserves a second chance."

She did not have any intention of doing so, but suddenly she remembered her own blemish. A larger trespass than this.

She ground her jaw against her annoyance, but nodded. "If you wish."

"Will you come again?" he asked groggily. His words began to slur slightly, but with his tousled hair and relaxed state, it made him all the more attractive. What a revelation. Men were very appealing rumpled and sleepy.

"I will be tiresome bored," he wheedled with an impish grin.

"I . . . I could read to you."

His laugh was dry and grating. "Do you imagine I am a

literary fellow, reflective, prone to deep contemplation? I assure you I strive for the absolute opposite." He hesitated, his face twitching into a dark look. "Very well. You might . . . read to me."

She hesitated, wondering if she had made an error in her impulsive offer. Too late she realized that she was a lady now, an unmarried woman, and he was a man. A man who was an unpardonable reprobate—he even said so himself. She had to have a care for her reputation.

And then she saw that his expression was anxious. He was waiting for her to say yes. And she realized that he was asking so prettily for her company to save him from being alone. And it dearly mattered to him.

She might have made mention of it, and scored a point. Instead, she said, "Only if you promise you will behave respectably."

He frowned. "If I must."

He closed his eye, grinning faintly, and would say no more.

 *Chapter 3*

Sophie joined Lady May in the drawing room the follow-
ing morning. She found her still in a state of anxiety, her
lovely face lined and full of unhealthy paleness.

"I am so sorry about missing the rout. Are you terribly
disappointed, Sophie dear?"

"Of course not. Please, do not concern yourself with
that." Sophie felt a powerful rush of affection. She hated
that she liked May so much. She hadn't thought she would.
May was one of *them,* those who had cut her when she had
been out with her mother and aunts.

But May had turned out to be wonderful. And her kindness had been difficult to accept. Sophie's only consolation
was that she was absolutely, positively, if-it-took-her-until-
the-day-she-died-she'd-do-it committed to making some
sort of restitution. When she was married, she would find
a way to give back all she had taken.

But there were some things, like affection, one could
not repay. That bothered her.

"Dr. Daley, the physician, is seeing him again this
morning. It was kind of him to come first thing." May
twisted her hands together.

Sophie extended her hand, placing it on May's arm.

"What is it?" A terrible thought occurred to her. "Has he taken a bad turn? Has he come down with fever?"

"No. It is not that. He was fine, for all of his injuries. He makes no complaint. I . . . I am just so overset by all of this." May took four quick steps, then stopped. "It was a duel. A duel! What has Gideon come to? I want to give him a piece of my mind for being so careless!" Her shoulders slumped. "And the next moment I am not angry at all. I am just so happy he is alive."

Sophie took May's hand. May seemed touched, and Sophie was surprised that her own eyes stung. It was infinitely rewarding to be able to do something in return for all she'd taken, even if it was as insignificant as holding May's hand.

"Come along then," May said. "We'll go in my sitting room. Lord Roberts arrived early and is with Daley and Gideon. He will let me know when there is news."

They waited in silence in May's plush boudoir until the footman showed in the physician and Lord Roberts.

"He is no worse this morning?" May asked anxiously.

"It is early," Dr. Daley said. "But the skin looks healthy. But I must stress he is to be kept quiet. He must stay in bed. He is already balking at this, but please understand that exposure to infection is our greatest risk. With burns, it is always a frightening probability."

Lord Roberts stood protectively at May's side. "He will do all he needs to do to make a full recovery. We will make certain of it," he said, and May seemed comforted by the quiet assurance in his deep baritone.

Sophie was as well. She was desperate for every drop of news of Ashford. It seemed to be good, and she realized only after she relaxed that she had been taut with worry.

"Well, then, let us go have our breakfast," May said after Daley took his leave.

"I will return later," Roberts said, giving a bow. "I have some business of my own to see to today that cannot be postponed. I will call on you later. Send word immediately if you have need of anything."

He held Lady May's hand longer than was seemly. Sophie turned away, almost certain that if she were not present, they would have kissed.

She heard Lady May murmur, "Thank you so much."

They returned to May's private parlor where they always took their breakfast. This was May's favorite room, where she spent as much of her time as possible when she was not entertaining. It was unaffected by fashion or any particular design of the day, cluttered with pretty arrangements of the personal memorabilia collected over her life.

Thick Persian carpets lay underfoot and the plush material of the furniture was worn soft. Everything in here had the patina of fine things aging well, which was an apt description of the handsome middle-aged woman herself.

Sophie went to the small table set with a chocolate pot and accoutrements and poured herself a cup.

She brought it to the round table in the corner, where the windows had been opened to admit a soft breeze. Breakfast here was usually modest, a coddled egg, rolls, a slice of toasted bread with jam. Sophie had been pleased by this when she'd come here.

Her mother and aunts had taken great pride in slabs of bacon and trays of kippers and fried potatoes laid out, and feasted liberally enough to thicken their waistlines considerably. It was a habit from many years of overnight guests, and having a gentleman leave one in the refreshing light of day with a feeling of satiety in every realm was a mistress's best trick.

She snapped her mind back from these thoughts. It was a trap, thinking too much on her past life.

"I am so pleased Gideon is doing well," May said. "I saw him myself before the physician arrived."

"I looked in on him last evening," Sophie said, feeling a flush of embarrassment. "I suppose I was curious. And concerned. I found him awake and we spoke for a while. He . . . he was in need of diversion."

"How extraordinary." May blinked, as if refocusing, for she was seeing Sophie in a new light. "Oh, dear . . . well, I

hope he was not in a foul mood. I am certain he gave Dr.
Daley a devil of a time. He was not very gracious to me,
either. It is the medicine, no doubt."

Sophie poured another cup of chocolate and brought it
to May. May refused it sweetly. "How thoughtful. But no,
thank you."

Sophie went to her chair with the cup still in her hands
and placed it on the table next to the one she'd poured for
herself. Both remained untouched as did the jams and
plates of warm toast.

May mused, "Daley is the finest in his field. I do not
know why I cannot stop worrying. Gideon was quite lucky
in his injuries, Dr. Daley said. He admitted that the burns
are bad, but they will heal. And there will be some scarring, I am sad to say, though how much he could not pre-
dict. What a shame. He was always so beautiful."

It was strange to hear a man called beautiful, but Sophie
found it fit him. Strength and virile beauty . . .

She had a thousand questions about him, but she should
really mind her own business. In fact, it was *best* if she became involved as little as possible.

But for some reason, she asked, "Has it been long since
you've last seen Ashford?"

May made a sweeping gesture. "Well, I see him in
Town, of course, although he is not of first society. Casual
sorts of things, you know . . . on the street, in a shop, dining out. We spoke briefly each time, but no more. But we
do not run in the same circles. We were once so close. So
happy."

Again, that frown, as if she could not help her thoughts
from turning to whatever it was that preoccupied her.

Sophie knew that May had lost her husband to suicide,
and the tragedy still marked her. It was obvious that the
memories of those times pulled her into morose thoughts
and the arrival of Lord Ashford brought all of it to the fore.

If Matthew Hayworth had been anything like his
younger brother, Sophie could imagine the pain that lin-

gered after her loss. One would never forget a man like that.

May said, "He was not only my brother-in-law, you see. He was truly a treasure in my life. I have to say, I adored him from the moment I met him. Not to be seen and unheard, that one." She rolled her eyes, then smiled. "He was full of life. And mischief. But boy-mischief, you know. And charming!"

The first trickle of laughter in two days came from her as she relaxed into her recollections. "He had this fringe that was always too long and hanging in his eyes, and this sweet pointed chin. His lashes were as long as a girl's, and he had the reddest lips. He was like a cherub—but not in his nature, mind, which was more of an impish nature. Just in his looks. We doted on him, and the three of us . . ." She faltered. "We were quite a family."

"But he did not stay with you," Sophie asked, "after your husband's death?"

May's mouth whitened. She put the cup of chocolate to her lips, then took it away without drinking. "He was taken off to live with relatives. I did not wish it, but I had no say in the matter." She fetched her handkerchief from her sleeve and dabbed one eye. "Oh, my, this is too difficult."

"If you would rather not speak of it," Sophie said, trying to keep the reluctance from her voice. She very much wished to hear about Gideon. Lord Ashford.

May used her handkerchief again. "His guardian, Reginald, wished Gideon to live with him, but Gideon had never even met him. It was rather awful, sending him off, but I had no legal recourse. He was but fourteen, then. Almost a man, but still so much a boy. You should have seen the look on his face."

Sophie did not want to imagine that, but she could.

"Oh, he was very stalwart as he climbed into that dreadful black carriage Reginald sent. He appeared like a soldier, he was so stiff, so brave." May's voice broke slightly, and she paused for a moment until it was steady. "He was tall for his age, already wearing that handsomeness that he has. I thought I would die to let him go. He kissed me good-bye, and I promised him I would be with him soon. I said . . . I said I would visit all the time."

The handkerchief went to her eyes. She took a moment to compose herself. "I was not allowed to, however. Reginald hated me, and I him. I should have fought—fought with everything I had, but I didn't. I couldn't, really. So I just let him go."

"But why did Reginald want to keep you apart?"

May collected herself. "Reginald Hayworth was a severe man. He did not approve of me. Perhaps he disliked Gideon's affection for me. He had no sons, and I think he had it in his mind to take Gideon and mold him. It meant cutting all ties. I can tell you I did not like Gideon going to him, not at all. But I wrote several times. I tried. At first, I did try. All my letters were returned with crisp reassurances that Gideon was well and I need not concern myself any longer." She waved her hand helplessly, the soaked handkerchief fluttering sadly. "So I gave up. Oh, Sophie, that was so wrong of me!"

Clasping May's hands in her own, Sophie exclaimed, "You cannot blame yourself!"

"It is the same as Robert said, but you simply do not understand. Can't you see what Gideon has become? He is a rakehell. He cares for nothing. He has a dreadful reputation and no decent family would receive him."

"But it was his choice, my lady. I believe he rather disdains 'decent' society."

"Yes, it is true. But where did that disdain come from? He was not that way as a child."

"Lady May, I know it is sad for you to see him like this. The duel, the reckless living, but you cannot think you are responsible."

She thought she heard May say, "It is because of what I did," but it was spoken so low, she couldn't be certain.

Suddenly, May sat up straight. She wiped her face and took in a swift, sharp breath. "Enough of this blubbering. I don't know why I am being so silly, burdening you with all of this. Lord, Sophie, you are kindness itself to put up with me."

Sophie smiled, hoping May knew how grateful she was to be able to do some service in return for all she'd received. "I wish I could do more."

"Just listening to me has helped. My mama used to say a good chat and a good cry were a worthy remedy. That and two fingers of brandy."

They laughed.

May said, "I confess I am not completely unhappy by this turn of events, as strange as that may seem. It might be a chance to get to know him once again, reconcile. I would like very much to be more than cordial strangers."

"I was wondering," Sophie ventured, "since you usually receive on Wednesdays, and that is today, will you be doing so?"

May's hands fluttered at the neckline of her dress. "Goodness, no. I had quite forgotten about that. We cannot have visitors. I will leave word with Johnson to say I am not seeing anyone. Except Lord Roberts, of course."

Sophie had already known Roberts would not be counted among the others who might be turned away. He was at May's side nearly every day.

May was most certainly not his mistress, not in the kept sense that her mother and aunts were bound to the men who were their patrons, but neither was the relationship between May and Roberts simply a friendship. They were . . . united in some way, joined by a bond Sophie had never seen between a man and a woman. It was a quiet, steady connection, felt more than seen or heard in any single action, any significant word.

It fascinated her, attracted her curiosity and wonder. And . . . and made her envious. Because it made her wonder what it might be like to have a man's eye rest gently on her in that way Roberts had of looking at May, as if she were the single and most central aspect of his entire world.

She thought it would be uniquely pleasant. Then she thought of Ashford for some reason . . . *Gideon*. What a unique and unusual name. It sounded mythic, and noble. It suited him.

"Sophie, there is something I might ask of you," May said. She was hesitant. "As you had such a pleasant interview with Gideon last evening—"

Sophie started. Had she said it had been pleasant? Had it been? Pleasant was a benign word. It had been tender, disturbing . . . and *yes,* pleasant, too.

"I was wondering if you would not mind looking in on him today for me. I would go and sit with him myself, but I am afraid I would be poor company."

She was afraid of being emotional, Sophie guessed. "Why, I am happy to do it. You rest. I will take care of anything that needs tending."

May was grateful, but that subtle melancholy remained.

Sophie thought about this as she returned to her room to tidy her appearance after whisking into the library to grab a book, and wished she knew what it was about Ashford that so deeply affected Lady May.

꒰ Chapter 4

Gideon had been fed, washed, and tucked into fresh linens, all of which made him miserable.

He despised this helplessness, felt unmanned by this infernal pain and the infirmity of it all. Lying in the bed with half his body wrapped and boredom coaxing bone-deep yawns that pricked tears into his eyes, he tried to fend off the tide of thoughts.

He hated to think. No good ever came of it, at least not for him. He was a man of action. Action brought reaction, and reactions were, invariably, interesting. Amusing sometimes, annoying at others, sometimes resulting in a nuisance—consider the wretched duel that had landed him in this spot—but always *not* boring.

When Candace came in, he was glad for the company.

"So what is the trouble with your man?" he asked her.

She startled at such a bold and blatant question, then proceeded to protest, just as he knew she was going to, then relaxed into a game of resisting and then confessing increasingly intimate details about her rather risqué relationship with the under-footman of a neighboring house.

"But, of course, you should demand marriage," he told

her. "The fellow is deceiving you with these protestations of needing more time to find a better paying position."

This disappointed Candace mightily. "Do you really think so?"

"Indeed, for it is exactly what I would do were I he. There is always something in a man's head telling him, 'Wait, not yet. Someone better might come along. Someone prettier, richer—whatever, just different!' You see, the idea of saying yes, which is so appealing to a woman, means to a man only a lifetime of saying no."

"But why does he need someone better?" She all but wailed.

This was actually quite fun. He'd never waxed philosophic about the nature of men and women. He was surprised to hear his own thoughts on the subject. They quite impressed him.

"The lack is not in you, my dear, nor in any woman. The lack is in the male. In his constitutional inability to commit."

Commit suicide by marriage. He kept that particular jewel to himself.

While an indignant Candace digested this, he became aware of a shift of atmosphere. Some sense—did he hear it? sense it? see some unregistered motion out of the corner of his eye?—made him turn his head just then to look toward the door.

To find Sophie Kent, in just the spot that he had found her last night. But there were no shadows now, only bright, revealing sunlight, so he could see her quite clearly.

God, he'd thought he'd exaggerated it in his mind. Fever-fed imaginings, drug-induced visions of a tall goddess with tumbling curls and a voluptuous mouth . . . She was real, she was here.

She was not happy.

"Damnation," he muttered. Of course, she had to have heard him. He actually flushed, slightly embarrassed. It annoyed him a bit. Why should he feel like he'd retract any of it if he knew she was listening?

She looked measurably different today than she had last evening. Her hair was down, tumbling in a riot of tawny curls, reminding him of twining lovers, limbs wrapped around each other. God, he'd chop off his foot for a chance to sample the texture. It looked soft, springy. He wondered what scent it held.

His body reacted to the wayward direction of his thoughts, and he resisted further sensual imaginings.

"How are you feeling?" Sophie asked.

Her eyes were steady, regarding him with no quarter. Where did she get such poise, that mingling of amusement and disgust that told him she saw him for the silver-tongued fake he was? And yet he had the distinct impression that she did not disapprove.

But perhaps that was just his fancy.

"There is a devil trapped in my head, using an ax to whack his way out." Turning to Candace, he said, "Thank you. That will be all." He wanted to get rid of her quickly now that Sophie was here.

Sophie acknowledged the servant stiffly before she left, then turned her gaze back to him. "I heard you were in foul spirits."

"Odd. And I am usually so cheerful after being nearly mortally wounded by a misfired pistol."

She smiled and moved forward. "I see your cheek has not lessened."

He touched his bandaged face. "I am relieved to hear it, as I was much afraid that it had."

She pulled his hand away from his face. "I know you are quite capable of comprehending my meaning. I cannot be the only person to refer to your inimitable nerve."

"True. One can find much to fault me with, but never say I am a dolt."

She regarded him. "No. You are, I imagine, quite clever."

"And you are brave." His flesh tingled where she had touched him. He resisted the urge to rub the spot. "I did not think you would return."

"Did you not? Then you do not know me very well. I gave my word."

Her lashes were long. Peering down on him, they threw spiked shadows over her eyes, obscuring the color and making it impossible to read her expression. He said, "I do not know you as well as I would like to. . . ."

"I did not come here to resume our flirtation," she pronounced firmly. She held up the book she'd brought with her. "If you wish, I will read to you."

He squinted to read the cover.

"Sir Walter Scott," she explained.

"What? Not Byron? Is he not all the rage with the women of fashion these days?"

She was surprised. "Do you prefer Lord Byron?"

"I only thought it would be better suited . . . something from his *Hours of Idleness* would be perfect for the occasion."

She stared at him, lips pursed.

"Irony," he explained patiently.

Shaking her head, she sighed. "Would you like me to read?"

He tried not to look pleased. "If you must."

She sat down on the chair. He had planned to make a fuss to have her closer, even get her to the edge of the bed where he'd managed to coax her last night, but he could see her well this way. He liked looking at her, so he was content.

"If you do not like Scott, I could choose something else. Not Byron, however. He is too risqué. And far too florid for my tastes. I could retrieve the sermons of Cotton Mather if you prefer a more substantial—"

"I am ready and waiting for medieval adventures with Sir Walter. Besides, I have no doubt Cotton Mather's fire and brimstone speeches would worsen my condition."

"Rather like the devil is weakened by the power of scripture," she agreed cheerfully. She opened the book, pointedly ignoring his damning look.

He settled back as she began to read:

> *The Ladye forgot her purpose high*
> *One moment and no more*
> *One moment gazed with a mother's eye*
> *As she paused at the arched door.*

"What an image," he intoned. "A beautiful woman poised just at the door. I can see it in my mind's eye. I have only to think on last night, when I looked up and saw you—"

She interrupted him to read on, drawing a snort from him when Scott introduced William of Deloraine.

> *Five times outlawed had he been*
> *By England's King and Scotland's Queen.*

"Ah, so he is a rascal," he said with some satisfaction. "Even Sir Walter understood that women love a scoundrel."

"He is a hero. Now hush and listen."

She had not read for but a few minutes when he cut in. "I am unsatisfied with your answer last night as to why you are unmarried. You have many fine qualities. Surely your looks alone are enough to render men stupid and start polishing up the love prose."

"Perhaps it is something to do with their aversion to commitment," she said, sweetly.

He paused, giving her her moment of triumph. Then he shrugged. "A man would part with far more than his freedom to look at that face until the end of his days. Not to mention a wit like yours, those scathing powers of observation—honestly, you quite give me the chills—and that terrifyingly quick, unpredictable mind."

"A woman's mind should be that of her husband's," she said, her tone absolutely flat.

But she was flattered. It was in the way she held her head. He knew women. This one was not easy to read. Still, she was not completely unaffected by the fact that he'd *noticed* something beyond her looks.

"Hah. Your mind will never be anyone's but your own,"

he pronounced with satisfaction. He ran a single finger along the line of his jaw as he studied her.

"And you approve of free-thinking women?"

"Why should it matter if I do or not?" he challenged.

"It does not signify, I assure you."

"So you have no care for others' opinions?" His tone communicated his doubt.

"I am not adverse to the good opinion of others," she replied.

"But it is so tiresome. And what does admiration bring?"

"You are laughing at me."

"You mistake me. I could not laugh at you. A man laughs at a woman for many reasons, only one being for comedy. Delight, that is another. And pleasure in her company."

"Do you wish me to read to you or not?"

"You don't read Sir Walter Scott normally, do you? You chose that for me. Thoughtful of you. Let me see . . . romances, I think. Ah, Mrs. Radcliff? And Miss Jane Austin."

"I read all manner of books."

"But you like the romantic books best, I'll wager."

She closed the book and laid it on her lap. "I am not a romantic sort of person. I am practical minded."

"You would like to think so. But you sighed when Darcy and Elizabeth Bennett wed."

"I did, as it was an advantageous match for them both."

"But what did you think of Lydia and her Wickam? That was quite . . . racy."

"I daresay the reader got a solid sense that Lydia would come to regret her rash elopement. Wickam was a scoundrel who used her cruelly to gain financial advantage."

"You object? Then how is it not equally as objectionable when a woman weds a man in order to find herself in an advantageous situation?"

She bristled. His words came far too close to what she planned. "That is different."

"Indeed, you must be joking. How is it different, pray?"

She leaned forward, fully engaged in the debate. "Because a man has the ability to earn a living. He makes his own fortune. He gambles, he sells, he buys, he spends. But a woman's fortunes are inexorably bound and, in absolute terms, are determined by the men in her life. A woman's existence is one of dependence, not self-determination. A woman has only the good luck or the clever stealth to find someone trustworthy. A man stands or falls by his own merit."

"That is rubbish," he said. "A woman has powers on this earth no man can approach, no matter how rich or influential he might be."

She was fairly steaming now. "Indeed, sir, it is you who must explain yourself now. How do you see it so?"

"Because every woman has what every man wishes." He paused, watching the question gather on her features. "She has the power of pleasure. No, not merely carnal delights—do not think me a lecher. What I mean is that it is in their very nature to appeal straight to the heart of what men most desire."

He had her now. She was interested, her chin lifted, her head tilted as she listened.

His own heart was beating faster. His body was aroused, and this amazed him. Imagine being aroused by wordplay.

"Their softness makes a man feel stronger," he went on, lowering his voice. "Their pliant flesh, their pleasant laughter, their feminine affectations bolster the perception of his own masculinity. She makes him feel better—best when he is in the company of the only woman, the ultimate woman who maximizes all these perceptions for him. What man, given this great gift of self-esteem, would stint on any price to have her?"

She surprised him by saying, "In his bed, you mean."

"In his bed, at his table, in his drawing room, up in the nursery presiding over his progeny. To possess this creature whom he has only to look at and be better in his own eye than he could ever be without her, this is what draws a man to think he is in love."

She seemed to be struck momentarily dumb. Then she smiled. "Why, Lord Ashford. It is *you* who are the romantic."

Gideon flushed, feeling caught, exposed. He had gotten snagged in his own game. "By God, you cut me! Indeed, you mistake me, I assure you."

He was sputtering—actually sputtering. Damn her.

"I see. But I am puzzled." She was gloating. That was not a good sign. He felt his defenses rise. "That earlier speech, with Candace, seems to be inconsistent with this analysis of the nature of love."

"Not at all. There is no inconsistency. What I have described is why a man seeks to possess the female—which we cannot argue is in evidence by the fact that men do marry. But no man, dear Sophie, has any desire to *be possessed himself.*"

There. He felt much better now.

She was annoyed again. "I hope you are very wrong, sir. Some men do, I sincerely hope, strive for the same things women want. Family, marriage, a happy, contented life."

"Some men, I grant you. But not sweet Candace's man."

"And not you."

He lifted his good shoulder. "I daresay, it goes without explanation."

"I have known men like you," she said, shifting into a haughty pose.

He laughed. "I would say, dear Sophie, that you have never met anyone like me, but that would be braggadocio, and I never stoop to such tactics."

"And yet you cannot resist."

"I merely observe a truth I know to be so. As for your own opinion . . . well, you shall find out for yourself."

"You think quite a lot of yourself," she observed acidly.

He laughed then. "Oh, dear Sophie, I said you have never met anyone like me. I did not say that was a *good* thing."

Her eyes narrowed and she stared at him for a good

long time before he was forced to ask, "Are you going to read?"

She bowed her head, opened the book, and resumed the tale of the swashbuckling Scot.

He settled back, disconcerted in some way he could not define. There was a vague sensation that he had failed some test, some measure of character. But the soft intonation of her voice was pleasant, and he allowed himself to be lulled out of his annoyance and relax.

Strange the presence of a woman, even one annoyed with him, would prove so soothing.

ॐ *Chapter 5*

Sophie closed the book when Ashford's soft, even breathing told her he had fallen asleep. She should have left then, but last night's late hour had left her fatigued. There was a monstrous crick in her neck. She leaned her head back to gain some relief, just for a moment, and closed her eyes.

There was a slight buzz along the length of her body, a hum riding her skin. She guessed it was annoyance at Ashford. His behavior today was just as irreverent as it had been last night.

She was not one to suffer disrespect of any kind, and yet she couldn't really say it was disrespect exactly. He was completely uninhibited, unconventional. So why did she persevere, when she had promised herself that if he stepped out of line as he had done before, she would take herself out of there instantly?

He was infirm, she told herself. That was why she'd stayed. Besides, she had promised May. . . .

Breathing in deeply, she felt her body slipping into the tingling numbness just before sleep. She would not doze, she was sure. Just thinking.

There was a certain degree of pity she had for Ashford,

although his predicament was certainly one of his own design.

But he *was* injured, regardless of the circumstance. How much he was suffering was hard to tell, but it had to be substantial. He did not make complaint of it. She supposed that made her admire him as well.

Her mind slowed as sleep took her despite her confidence that it would not.

She dreamed of a tiger—not a real dream, but flashing images scrolling through her mind as she dozed. Wanting to touch it, she reached out and felt its thick, luxurious fur, all the while watching its eyes, which held no sentiment, and knowing this was very dangerous, yet not able to move, to flee to safety.

When she awoke, she was startled to find she'd nodded off. She stood, forgetting about the book on her lap. It thumped to the floor. She froze, fearful that Ashford would awaken. He did not.

She could have slipped out then, but she paused. Gazing at him, she felt a lessening of her tension. There was so much pleasure in seeing him like this, without the dreadful self-consciousness he made her feel. The always watching, assessing, looking for . . . purchase. He wanted something from her.

The idea was exciting, not alarming at all, which it should have been. There was a quality about him that stirred her like no man ever had. As he lay on his back, all expression wiped from his face, his chest rising and falling in gentle repose, she felt a stirring, a rising awareness of her own body.

He had said a woman's softness made a man feel stronger. The words rang true, because she was experiencing the inverse. Just gazing at his physique made her feel softer, terribly vulnerable. She wanted to put her hand where the nightshirt gaped, flat on the firmness of his breast where taut skin stretched over warm, firm muscle, and feel it under her palm. Feel flesh and the thrum of life's blood beneath.

She makes him feel better — best when he is in the company of the only woman, the ultimate woman who maximizes all these perceptions.

What would it be like to be that one woman for him?

My God! My God — that was it! He had made her *want* him. She had never, never wanted a man. She looked down at him, amazed now that she had identified what it was that was so different about him. He tempted her.

He was . . . Well, he was beautiful. So much so she could not resist touching him. She laid her hand on his shoulder, just where the neckline of his shirt gaped, and it *was* marvelously warm pliant flesh with hard muscle and bone underneath. It did something strange to her. It made her feel a little weak.

His eyelid opened and she gasped in surprise. Before she could pull away, his hand closed over hers.

She wanted to say something, some sharp retort or demand to get him to release her, but she was mute, her indignant words washed away in a flood of humiliation.

He did not gloat. He did not let go. He regarded her calmly, impassively, as if it were no shock at all to find her leaning over him with her hand on his person. But there was energy seething from him now, a heat that made it impossible for her to do anything but watch as he took her hand from his shoulder to his lips. Very slowly, very slowly, he pressed it to his mouth and kissed the palm.

Only he didn't just kiss it. He . . . he *caressed* it with his lips. Right in the sensitive cradle of her palm. The feeling that shot up her arm was incredible. She felt herself sway, felt the world tilt and dim.

She began to pull her hand away, frightened at what he was doing, or more rightly what effect it was having.

He wouldn't let her go. She pulled harder.

"No," he said.

At last she spoke. "You are kissing me."

"I am kissing your hand." He rose, not without some pain judging from the way his pallor washed lighter, but he did it. She didn't shrink away as he came nose to nose with her. "This is kissing you."

He released his grip only to snare her hair, holding her hard by the back of her head while his mouth came up to hers. She caught her breath, one ragged rasp of shock as her whole body went stiff.

And waited. She did not break away. She didn't even think of it.

He kissed her without any tenderness. She angled her head and let him. And then she kissed him back, forgetting everything but the closeness, the fire, the splendid feeling of her blood shooting through her veins, her head swimming without thought, her mouth invaded by his tongue, and the way the knot in her womb responded to the demand with tiny tremors of pleasure she had never experienced before.

He broke the kiss and fell back onto his pillows, his chest heaving and his face white. He'd hurt himself with that kiss. But that was nothing compared to what he'd done to her.

His eyelids were heavy. Pain flickered on his face. His eye—such a gorgeous blue; a man's eyes should not be this beautiful—stared at her accusingly, as if he were the one who'd been caught off guard.

His hand still held her, but she twisted away easily enough. Or he let her go. She backed up, afraid to turn her back on him. You don't turn your back on the devil. Everyone knew that.

"Will you come again?" he asked in a reedy voice. "Or have I frightened you away for good?"

"No." She shook her head. "No. I shall not return. I do not think I should."

"Then you consign me to this void," he said. His voice was hard, touched with a bleakness that affected her despite herself.

"You will make me feel guilt to get me to come back here, and then you will do this again." She waved her hand at him accusingly. "This is a game to you, some vapid amusement to pass the time."

"If you read to me," he replied steadily, "then I promise I shall not kiss you."

"You cannot be trusted!"

"Untrue. I am as good as my word, always. I never promised not to kiss you, but now I have. I always do what I say."

"You would ruin me for your amusement. If anyone had come in just then . . ."

"I will not kiss you," he said again. "I will expect you tomorrow. I find Scott not at all the bore I had feared. I am looking forward to hearing more."

"I do not know." She shook her head.

He settled back on the pillow more comfortably, turning his face up and closing his eyes. The matter was settled. "Yes, you do."

She opened her mouth, reflexively wanting to reply. But she had nothing to say.

She left. Fled? She went out the door, not knowing at all if she would ever return. But of course she did.

The very next day she came back armed with new resolutions to make certain she did not give him any opportunity to take advantage of her again.

These she did not need. True to his word, he did not kiss her again.

"Do you mean to say Lord Ashford is here in this very house?" Mrs. Milton, sister to Lady May's dear friend, Lady Viola, was aghast. Her large frame recoiled as she stared at May with a blend of horror and reproach.

The ladies were the only callers May had received since Gideon's arrival. This was because Lady Viola was an especially close friend and Mrs. Milton's daughter, Margaux, had struck up a pleasant association with Sophie.

Before May could respond, Sophie said, "I admire Lady May's kindness and charity in taking such good care of a treasured friend."

May's smile was full of mischief. "He is quite harmless, Eugenia. He is upstairs, confined to his bed."

Mrs. Milton gasped and looked protectively at her daughter. "Lady May, please!"

"The man was injured. Of course he is in bed. It is not unseemly to say so."

"Injured *dueling*." Her retort was ripe with disapproval. "Under circumstances I will not repeat in the presence of my daughter."

"I do not debate his reputation. Indeed, Viola, have I not bemoaned the very same to you?"

Lady Viola turned toward her sister. "Indeed she has, Eugenia. It is such a shame. All that money, and the title. And he is handsome, isn't he? We saw him at the coffee house, May, remember? That was last September. He swept a bow in front of you. Oh, my. He was odd, though. I was not certain at first that you were on good terms."

May's smile faded. "The word is sardonic. He is always that way when he sees me these days." She brightened. "But it is my hope that his stay here will bring us closer."

"Surely, you do not mean to *keep* him here," Eugenia Milton said. Her eyes swerved to Sophie and swept up and down her frame, as if newly assessing her suitability as a companion for her Margaux.

"Indeed I do," May said calmly. "It is my dearest wish that our friendship be fully restored. What's more, I have decided to sponsor his re-entry into society."

"But his reputation! And you have Sophie here. I say this only because Sophie is unmarried. It would be disastrous for the two of them to remain under the same roof."

Sophie knew Mrs. Milton had no concern for her reputation. She disliked Sophie, mainly because she served as competition for her own daughter, although there was no need to fear Margaux failing to attract male attention. The young Miss Milton was quite pretty, with glossy dark curls and dark eyes that snapped with a barely checked exuberance for life. She had a curvaceous figure in contrast to Sophie's slimness.

She was interesting, as well, and quite fun to be with. She had a secret passion for the scientific and cultural discoveries currently being imported by the Regent. Although Sophie did not share this interest, she never failed to find Margaux's discussion of the topic fascinating. This she did always out of earshot of her mother, as Mrs. Milton did not approve of ladies having intellectual interests.

"But I am here," May observed, her voice as sharp as glass, "so there can be no reproach. Everything is amply supervised, you see, and there could be no better chaperone than a relation to both of the parties."

"Of course," Lady Viola pronounced happily, eager to dismiss the tensions.

"Can we see him?" Margaux whispered to Sophie. "Just a peek!"

"Heavens no! He is not a curiosity." Sophie kept her voice low. The three older ladies were busy talking and took no notice.

"I am deliriously curious. What is he like? Is he so handsome, as they say?"

"He is a devil," Sophie said, her lips curling. "He is no companion for a young lady. I doubt your mama is anxious for you to make the acquaintance of Lord Ashford," she reminded her.

"She had better not forbid me coming here," she replied darkly, a surprising spark of rebellion flashing in her eye. Her creamy complexion flushed a becoming shade of rose. Sophie thought how pretty she was when she came alive. Unfortunately, when she was in the presence of her mama, that didn't happen too often.

She was often subdued, so much so that she barely spoke. She never played music in public, despite possessing what Sophie regarded as an astonishing talent, for fear of not measuring up to Mrs. Milton's exacting standards.

Lady Viola and Mrs. Milton rose to leave, and Margaux gathered her shawl. "I shall see you at the Lady Bassingstoke's ball?" she asked.

"Yes. Lady May says I am to go, even with Lord Ashford here. She does not wish me to postpone my entry into society any longer."

"Isn't it exciting!" Margaux declared. "Our first ball."

Sophie assured her it was very exciting, but she didn't feel the anticipation she would have thought. Her mind was on Lord Ashford these days, and even as she realized this, she thought of Mrs. Milton's warning. Would others also look with aspersion on Ashford's presence in the house?

She could afford no whiff of gossip if she were to achieve her goal of a respectable marriage.

She had to trust Lady May, who seemed unconcerned that Ashford would present any sort of complication to her reputation. To this she clung, relieved to abdicate her worries to the more experienced woman. Besides, she was not certain she could resist seeing Ashford again, even if May saw fit to forbid it.

Chapter 6

"*I heard some news of Selwyn,*" May told Gideon one morning during her usual daily visit.

Gideon was distracted. In his hand he held a letter, and his mind was on it, not the conversation with May. He turned it around and around in his hands until May snatched it out of his hand.

He started, and stopped himself just as he was about to leap to his feet and take it back forcibly. Steeling himself to calmness he raised one eyebrow in question.

"Did you hear what I said?" she asked petulantly. "Selwyn. I was talking about Selwyn, the man you dueled with? Gideon, my goodness, where is your mind today?"

He rose slowly and reached for the letter. She handed it to him with a humph of frustration.

"I beg your pardon. I had some rather disturbing dreams." He dropped the letter on the table, setting a half-full glass upon it. "Now what is this about Selwyn?"

"Well, he is not making a fuss, that is the first thing of import. I was worried he might not feel satisfaction had been gained. But he has been silent on the matter of you, and that is indeed a good sign that this matter will be resolved without further nonsense."

"Why should he not be satisfied? My own mishap, the faulty loading of the pistol done by my own second, did the job for him. He got the result he wished."

"Gideon, another man might still be enraged, still demand that honor be met. As it is, no one is hearing any complaints from Selwyn how it turned out. Although that twit of a wife of his nearly fainted the other afternoon when speaking of it, I heard. She still carries the torch, I suppose."

"What a muddle," he complained. The entire affair bored him now. "Though I am glad to know Selwyn is not keen on demanding I show up at Wimbledon Commons anytime soon. Well, at least until I get rid of this." He pointed to the bandage over his eye. "I can hardly sight him accurately with this in the way."

"Do you not take this seriously?"

"May, if Selwyn is quiet, perhaps it is so the magistrates will not arrest him for dueling. I doubt he has turned saintly in such a short amount of time."

"Gideon, really, you are being obtuse and absolutely disagreeable at every turn. What is wrong with your mood today? Can you not understand that one great concern is at rest, that Selwyn is not pursuing the matter of the unfinished duel *or* his wife's infidelity? I for one was thrilled."

Shrugging, Gideon went to his chair. "It does not matter. But if you are pleased, then I am pleased."

"You are a monster today. I will see you tomorrow, when I hope I will find you in better spirits."

He went to the window and looked out into the middle distance. He was aware of that damned letter at his side, within reach.

At the sound of Sophie approaching, he closed his eyes and took in a deep breath. May was correct, he was in a terrible state today.

He looked over briefly at Sophie as she entered. There was a loosening of the tension in his shoulders that told him he'd been waiting for her, despite his preoccupation.

"I hope you have brought a novel," he said. They had

completed Scott quickly, and he had insisted on a novel next.

"I have something else, which you might like." She held up a slim volume.

He reached for it, and read the title with a twisted smile. "Ah. *Hours of Idleness*."

"I believe you requested it."

"You make a concession, for I recall you do not care for the florid poetry of Byron." He tucked the volume beside him. "I thought I heard voices earlier. Were there callers today?"

"It was Margaux." She took the book with her to her seat. "I believe I've spoken of her before."

He nodded. "The one with the dragon matron for a mother."

Sophie laughed. She would never have told anyone else of her opinion of Mrs. Milton. "Who was in full force today, I must say. In fact—"

"I am not in the mood for conversation," he said. He stared moodily out of the window. "Just read."

"You are not feeling weak," she said, concern in her voice.

"For God's sake, stop fussing."

She drew back, stung. "Very well."

Although sometimes he was thoughtful, he was not usually abrupt like this with her. Sophie did not ask after his mood, however, guessing it would only irritate him further.

He was very still, staring out of the window with a faraway look in his eye. His profile was hard as granite, framed in the gray light where beyond the thick panes lay a low-lying sky hung with fat clouds of charcoal and blue.

She had passed some pleasant hours in his company with her sketchbook. She thought of it now, lying on the bookcase in the corner. This was a portrait she wished to capture—Ashford at his most unfathomable, his most compelling.

Instead she opened the book and began reading.

"I think I should like the colonies in America," he said abruptly after she'd read only a few lines.

"They are not our colonies any longer." She was used to his interruptions. They would often launch into intense discussions in the midst of a chapter. It was the restlessness of his mind, half listening to the story, half wandering. "Our king managed to lose them. So, why would you like to go there?"

"The idea of an egalitarian society appeals to me. I never did like the entire concept of the nobility. From what I can see, they are all a bunch of self-important jackasses. What I cannot figure is why you wish to marry one of them."

She laid the book down. Not this again. "The idea obviously puts you out."

"I am not put out. I am shut in." His voice rose, grew sharper. He paused and peered at her. "How is it you've achieved the advanced age of twenty-two and not been kissed?"

"What? What sort of question is that?"

He leveled an accusing finger at her. "When I kissed you, it was your first kiss. Do not deny it."

"It is unseemly for you to mention that. You promised you would not."

"I promised I would not kiss you, not that I would not speak of it. Now, why was that your first kiss?"

She sighed. "I am not the sort of woman who kisses men."

"You kissed me," he observed.

"No," she explained patiently. "You kissed me."

"And," he countered, his eyes burning into her, "you kissed me back."

A flush of pleasure warmed her at the recollection. She averted her gaze, suddenly annoyed. "I believe we are finished for the day," she said. She closed the book with a snap.

He gave her a heavy-lidded glare. "You are in a snit."

She remained seated. "You are in a monstrous mood. What is wrong with you?"

He smiled, and she knew he was observing that she did not rise to leave. She stared back calmly, daring him to relent and have her stay or continue this and she would, her gaze promised, quit him immediately.

"Of course I am being rude. I am a cur," he conceded with a shrug, looking for all the world as if he'd won. He returned his gaze out the window. "Which is something you are already quite well aware of. Could you light the fire? It's already laid. The flint is in the box there on the table."

She rose to do as he asked. It was very damp today, a fine mist from the outside putting a chill in the air, and the dry warmth emanating from the hearth was welcome.

She studied him, his face impassive, and wondered at his thoughts. Every day, he was shaved and dressed before she arrived. His clothing was always casual. He might be a scoundrel, but he was not a fop. And he was careful to dress properly, if not fashionably. He liked to wear loose-fitted breeches, which did not look as if they were made for him but he preferred them for sitting for long stretches as they afforded more comfort, and a billowing shirt tucked in to his waistband, but not cinched with any waistcoat. These were clean, of good quality, but not fussy. He tied a cravat loosely at his neck and always kept the studs fastened in his shirt.

It had surprised her at first, for it showed he'd taken care to observe elements of propriety for her sake. In his appearance, if not in his conversation, that was.

"I am not in the mood for reading after all," he said.

"May I sketch you?" she asked, laying down her book and reaching for her paper and pencils. He usually did not object, but she always asked.

"I will drive you away from me one day," he said softly, not looking at her. "I do not know why you come here, except for charity." He shifted, his face twisting on the last word. "Do you know what it is for a man like me to beg for charity from a woman?"

"I suppose," she said gently, "it is as hard as it is for any man."

"You do not think highly of men, do you, Sophie?"

"I like them well enough when they are not making jackasses of themselves."

"Ah." He looked pained. "And how do I fare in that department?"

"It depends on the day," she replied lightly.

He grinned and for the first time, the darkness on him fell away. "I do not frighten you. You are incredibly brave when I am . . . Well, sometimes I think of us as beauty and the beast. Why are you so different from other women, Sophie Kent?"

She opened her sketchbook and propped it on her knee. "I am a survivor, my lord. That is what I see as my distinction."

His eyes flared, intrigued. She liked the pose and swept her grease pencil in a broad stroke to catch the way his shoulders curved his body forward. "And what have you survived?" he asked in a low baritone.

It was difficult not to drop her gaze. "Humiliation. Dissatisfaction, the sort that goes deep and lodges in one's mind. I have known what it is to want, and I have determined to prevail and not ever experience that again."

"Is that it? That fierceness in you . . . that guardedness. Lost little girl."

Was he mocking her? He had to be, and yet his eyes were warm.

"But why—that is what I ask myself," he mused. "Was it your beauty? Were the other girls jealous?"

Her hand moved quickly. His moods were so changeable, she would not catch him if she did not work fast. There was a frustration in him that always fascinated her. He was not a man to ever do anything in half-measure. And always, with it, was the subtle tragedy that she never quite understood. Today it was more pronounced than usual.

"I was a gangling, unsightly thing until I was fifteen. I was too skinny and I had a hideous neck. It was like a giraffe. And my nose was enormous."

"Well, your nose is regal, quite in proportion, if a bit strong. It is what makes your face commanding. And I will say your body has filled out rather nicely. Slender . . . round in the right places."

"My lord," she warned.

He continued unperturbed, "And that neck, it is like a swan's. Ah, you are getting that tight look again. I apologize for noticing such things. No . . . I do not. But I do apologize for my bad manners. I will amend my conversation to your pleasure. To return to our dilemma, you were not outcast because of your looks."

"No. It was . . . If you must know, my mother was an actress. It is something I do not like to bandy about loosely, for obvious reasons. I grew up as the child of a woman whom most of society considered not to be a lady."

"Are you ashamed of her?"

She avoided that particular question. "She was a good woman, a good mother. She and my aunts were wonderful and fun and generous and caring and many other good things. But they were not good *society*."

"Well, then, now I know how you can stand me. You've had plenty of practice with the unconventional." His eyes pinned her deftly. "So . . . I understand the great wish to marry now. You did not wish to follow in your mother's career?"

She flushed, enough of an answer for him.

"It is not a disgrace," he said softly.

Ducking her head, her hand traced furiously, that anxious curious expression on his face, the lively interest in the eye.

"You are not so intent on your sketching that you did not hear me," he observed. "So I can deduce you will not discuss this with me." His forehead creased as if an unpleasant thought came to him. "You are using this time to attract a husband. I recall that word you used—utter blasphemy to my ears but apparently music to yours. *Respectability*. And yet, day after day, you sit with me. I, Sophie Kent, am not a respectable man. Nor am I the marrying kind."

His hand came up to his chin, rubbing thoughtfully. "You are wasting your time with me when there is a man to catch. It troubles me, Sophie, I must admit, why you attend me so well."

She began to fill in some shading to her sketch when he suddenly leaned forward and closed his fingers around her rapidly moving hand.

She snapped her head up, startled. His skin was hot, spreading its warmth up her arm and across her chest. Her breasts tingled, and the sensation was delicious, stealing her breath. It frightened her, and for the life of her, she would not show her disconcert. Yet neither could she remove her hand from his.

He was smiling casually, as if the contact was nothing. "You will soon be too busy to bother with me any longer once you are properly inducted into the realms of the polite world. How I shall miss you. I do not know if I can bear that."

His grip tightened. His thumb slid over the back of her hand, exploding sensations that rattled her to the core.

That he was dangerous burst suddenly into her thoughts and she snatched back her hand with a flash of fierceness that surprised them both.

She pulled herself into prim lines, closing her sketchbook. "As long as you behave the gentleman, I will still visit you."

"Ah," he said, his tone far away and melancholy, "you would change me."

She wanted to deny it, but she bit back the words. It was indeed what she had said, but her mind rebelled against the thought.

There was something tragic in a tame tiger. All that

brutal wildness gone, the broken spirit reflected in resentful eyes.

No, she would not change him. She played the shocked virgin when she was secretly delighted with him because that was what she was *supposed* to do. It was what good, well-bred young ladies did.

But it was not what she felt.

Sophie spent a pleasant day with Margaux, shopping with their aunts and taking luncheon out. She was determined to shake the growing obsession with Lord Ashford, so she schooled her thoughts away from the man languishing in his sickbed.

It was not easy, but Margaux's lively companionship was a good diversion. They meandered through the book shop, her friend taking advantage of being out from under her mother's disapproving eye and purchasing several pamphlets on the exotic imports beginning to flood the country from the Orient.

"Thank goodness I brought my large bag," she said, stuffing the finds deep into the tapestry shopping pelisse.

"You act as if it were contraband." Sophie laughed.

Margaux made a face. "Well, it is. Ladies do not have intellectual interests."

"But of course they do!" Sophie exclaimed.

Shaking her head, Margaux hitched her voice in an imitation of her mother's stern tone. "Not well-bred ladies. One will never find a husband that way." She sighed. "So, it must remain my secret."

Sophie was chagrined. For one thing, she realized how little she knew about the expectations of the elite world. These were clearly understood by Margaux, something Sophie did not share. Her background was coming back to haunt her again.

Yet it angered her to think of her friend needing to secret her interests. What was objectionable about a woman with interests beyond serving a proper tea and gossip?

The words Gideon had spoken—very much along these

same lines—came back to her, mocking her pursuit of respectability. As they exited the booksellers, she pushed the recollection away determinedly. Why did the man always invade her thoughts?

"Let's look in here," she said, directing them into a shop that featured ribbons and lace.

"Just look at this cording!" Margaux exclaimed, holding up a length of fringe. "Mama will be pleased if I bring home something to decorate my dresses. A day well spent, she'll say, and she will not frown, nor look too closely in my bag."

Sophie thought this not a terribly interesting pursuit. Her hours spent with Gideon were filled with challenge and delight. But it was not how a lady spent her day. This was.

Her inability to evict the man from her thoughts made her cross when she saw him the following day.

"I was a beast yesterday," he said as soon as she entered his room. "Please forgive me."

His apology surprised her, and the built-up annoyance fled. It would be churlish to refuse his request for pardon, and yet the steady regard of his eyes made Sophie uncomfortable. "Of course," she murmured.

He watched her. She could feel his gaze on her skin, pricking it hot. "You are a good woman, and I am not always a good man."

"But you do keep your promises," she reminded him.

"That I do, to my sometimes regret. That I do. But do not think it does not come at a price."

She did not know how to take this. Or perhaps she knew exactly what he meant and did not wish to confront her own reaction.

Taking her seat, she picked up the sketch she had done yesterday and pretended to examine it. "Well, I am here, am I not?"

He leaned back. His stamina was growing day by day, but he seemed tired today. She half rose, putting her book and pencils aside. "Gideon?"

He looked at her, registering her use of his name. She hadn't meant to. To cover her dismay, she took her seat once again and picked up a pencil. Rubbing it between her fingers, she forced herself to study her work.

To her relief, he said nothing more about her slip.

"Indeed, you are here. Every day, just like May," he said. "Each morning she comes in and tries to smile and make conversation. A quarter of an hour, no more. Then she flees."

Laying his head back, he rubbed his hand over his eyes, wincing when his fingertips touched the bandages. "She hates to come here."

Sophie reached for him. "Are you hurting?"

He caught her wrists as she reached for the bandages. Their gazes locked, and she felt a sharp tremor of excitement trip pleasurably down her spine.

"I am talking about May. I notice. All right? I *know* she sends you to me. Just tell me . . . is that the only reason you come? For her, so she won't feel she has to?"

"No," she said quickly. Her hands grasped his, held. "I'm calling Candace. You are obviously in pain. The physician told us to watch for infection."

He sounded suddenly weary. "Candace is probably reclining quite pleasurably under her lover. Leave her be."

She had grown used to these ribald references. They did not rattle her. "Surely you know that Lady May is deeply concerned for your well-being."

"It is the past. It is like a wedge between us. But what I cannot seem to understand is why." He looked at her tenderly. "I am afraid you only pity me. You are the finest thing I've known, Sophie Kent. The finest thing in a long, long time. You've made these interminable hours bearable. I don't suppose I can complain too much over who you did it for."

She almost said *I did it for you.* But she stopped herself in time.

She watched his eyes drop to her mouth and she was suddenly aware of her parted lips, the way they were strangely sensitive to the brush of air as she drew in and exhaled rapid breaths.

Perhaps he would break his vow and kiss her, she thought. The idea made her feel weak and warm.

It was he who averted his gaze, he who sighed and pulled back slightly, leaving her blinking away the after-effects of the potent moment.

Holding out his hand, he asked, "Let me see your sketch."

She turned the paper so he could see it. It was not very good to her mind, but she was grateful for the chance of a diversion while she gathered her composure.

He smiled and nodded, obviously tiring. "It is a master-piece," he pronounced. "You never fail to amaze me, Sophie." His eyelid drooped and he relaxed, as if contented at last.

She stayed with him until he slept. She did not know why, only that the brittleness in him made her reluctant to leave until after he had found peace. As soon as his breathing was even and deep, she rose and placed the book they had been reading on the bedside table, ready at hand for to-morrow. Her hand brushed an opened letter, and it fell to the floor.

If not for seeing the signature at the bottom as she returned it to its place, she would never have presumed to look at it. But it was signed in a neat, precise hand. The name: Reginald.

Picking it up, she perused it quickly. Of course it was wrong to pry, but his moodiness of late—this had to be the reason.

Reginald wrote: *It is of no surprise to me to find you have come to such a disgraceful circumstance. This I foresaw in your very first days with me. As I warned you then, and repeatedly, and still maintain, you are of a weak nature prone to pleasure-seeking and devoid of the elements of character that befit a man of the aristocratic status to which you were born. Your many disappointments should prepare me to expect any loathsome behavior from you,*

*and yet I find you can always find new ways to induce my
abhorrence of your nature. Perhaps now you will realize
that there is no reward in your continued habits of disso-
lution and disgrace.*

Sophie felt rage as she read it. She recalled May's
telling her of a happy child. That child had lost a beloved
brother, then gone to the care of this horrid man?

A painful lump pressed against her throat. She didn't
know if she was more angry or aggrieved by reading this
piece of vituperative prose.

She folded the letter and placed it back where it had
been. She had no business reading it, and should have felt
guilty for having done so. But she did not. The weight on
her heart stayed with her long after she left, yet she felt
somehow closer to Gideon.

And she liked that.

 *Chapter 7*

Gideon suspected Sophie had seen Reginald's letter. Upon her arrival the following day, he challenged her.

"Yes," she admitted, barely blinking. He loved that, the way she met challenges head-on, no wasting time with theatrics. "It was lying out in the open. When I saw the name, quite by accident, I could not keep myself from taking a look. That is no excuse, I know, and I am sorry. I had no right."

He observed, "You do not appear penitent."

"I invaded your privacy, and I am clearly not in the right on that matter. But I cannot say I regret it, no."

He stared at her, trying to make her squirm. She did not. God, she was something.

Waving his hand at the table where he'd folded the paper neatly, he said, "Cheerful, didn't you think? I mean the letter."

"I thought it abhorrent." Her chin came out. "My only regret is that I do not know the man. I should dearly like to tell him what I think of him, and that he is an awful snob and a first-class rotter—pardon the term."

"Not at all," he said, amazed.

"And that if he thinks himself so superior, then I would

like to advise him that in the matter of character, he is most
assuredly your inferior, and all his airs and posturing will
not change the simple fact that he is vile."

The vehemence, the passion! His face split into a smile
he realized must appear alarmingly absurd. He composed
himself immediately.

Still, he was pleased to the marrow of his bones. "Well,
I have to admit, I share your low opinion, but then Reginald and I never did not get on, from the very first. Actually, that is a mild way of putting it. He was a twit in my
estimation, and I . . ." He waved his hand. "I, apparently,
was a tragic waste of his time."

"He is a hateful, horrible man," Sophie said softly.

He liked the soft compassion in her eyes. Was he growing weak, sentimental in these days of confinement? He
normally would have none of this sort of thing. And he
never spoke of Reginald.

It had been more than eight years since he'd even laid
eyes on him. When he'd come of age and his trust fund
was turned over to him, he had gone out on his own, and
never looked back, not to Reginald's drafty house in Suf-
folk, not to the warm fires and pleasant comforts of Ashford Manor.

Reginald, however, still felt it his duty to advise Gideon
on his low character. The occasional letters of complaint,
to which Gideon never replied, were the only communication.

"Well, do not feel too bad for me for having to endure
him," he said, "for I did not do so for long. He sent me
away to school, thankfully. Perhaps some of the blame
goes to myself. I think he'd hoped to make something of
me, something that resembled himself to an alarming
degree—at least I found it alarming. As I was quite clear
from the first day I was ushered into his barren home that
that was not going to fly, he did not have much use for me.
In fact, he used to say I was the kind of man who would be
nothing but a blight on society, and, after all, that has fairly
well been the case in many a person's estimation. So, in

effect, he was right. A point, no doubt, that gives him great glee."

Her eyes sparked annoyance. "Gideon, what a dreadful thing for him to say! And at a time when you were no doubt still grieving and missing your home. Even at fourteen, you were still a boy."

"I grew up quickly," he said, and was surprised at the quiet savagery in his words. He had meant to make light of it, but something was happening. All the intentions to show her how little Reginald mattered to him any longer seemed to fail him. Instead, he'd tapped into emotions he would not have chosen to show her for all the world.

But they would not quiet. "It suited us both for me to stay at school at all times, even during holiday." He tucked his chin into his chest, feeling the words burn on their way out of his throat. He should shut his trap and leave it be.

But then she said, "You must have missed home so terribly. Your brother, and . . . and May."

Oh, Lord. The sting of those words.

"She was not allowed to see you," Sophie explained calmly.

He shrugged. "It was not so bad, just the nights, really, those early nights right after I was sent away, when I was alone in the dormitory when all the others had gone home for holiday. It was just so very empty. It got to me then, I confess. It was very dark at night. Harrow is well out of the city, so there were no lights to soften that blackness. If you've lived in the country, you know what I mean. There were only the stars and they . . . are so far away. I was miserable, I admit it. What was worse, I had this unfortunate habit of feeling sorry for myself."

He tried to laugh, but the sound was so dry it sounded like a foot scraping against rough stone. Sophie blinked, and she looked innocent, so accepting.

"So, to distract me," he continued, "I'd tell myself that she was on her way, that very night. Mind, every night was 'this very night' in my fantasy, and the only way I could sleep was to think that I'd just get a bit of rest before she arrived. I'd close my eyes, sure I'd awaken to the sound of her footsteps coming down those vast, empty halls, coming to take me away with her, and it would be as it had been."

He stopped himself, horrified at having said so much. Yet, somewhere, some part of him unclenched.

To his utter shock, there were tears on her cheeks. "Oh, Gideon," she whispered.

"What is this? I did not mean to make you weep." He reached out, then paused. It would be dangerous to touch her now. Her tears would burn him, burn him deeper than the flashing pan of his pistol had burned him, and those scars would never heal.

Sophie seemed to realize she was crying and swept her cheeks dry. "I am not weeping. I am furious. I would dearly like to track that horrible, wretched man down and plant my heeled slipper firmly on his rear!"

She clapped a hand over her mouth, shocked at what she had said.

His brow shot up. "Miss Kent!" he gasped, and broke into peels of laughter. "You are like a Valkyrie. A noble, beautiful, and wickedly vengeful Norse spirit."

"Indeed." She sat down primly, recovering herself in a way that was so charmingly Sophie, he had to hold himself back from grabbing her. "Am I to be forgiven for reading your letter?"

"How can I not when you champion me so well?"

"Thank you." She reached for the book. His hand stopped her. "I do not suppose I could ask you to keep the letter a secret. From May especially. It would distress her to know how it was with Reginald."

"But of course I will. I should not have read it in the first place." She studied him. "I thought . . . well it seemed to me that you were angry with May in some way."

"So? That does not mean I wish to hurt her."

A smile crept across her face, full of admiration. It embarrassed him. To divert her, he said, "Are you going to finish your sketch today?"

"No. I want to do a new one." Her eyes shone. She was looking at him differently, and he had a sense something had changed between them. "Something more cheerful."

"Flowers, then? Or a landscape from the window?"

"No, you," she announced, picking up her pad and turning to a fresh page.

"Me? Again? I would think you would be getting quite bored with that subject."

"You are in quite a different mood today. Let us see if I can capture it. That is the ever-renewing challenge to the artist."

Sophie's response was astonishingly satisfying. He did not have to put any of those black feelings he harbored for Reginald into words. She had done it for him, as adeptly and effortlessly as though she'd been his champion all of his life.

It did not escape his notice that she did not once ask if he might *deserve* those criticisms leveled in Reginald's letter. That he knew he did—at least to some degree—did not detract at all from Gideon's pleasure at having her so sublimely take his side.

He had never before experienced such contentment with a woman, while at the same time the escalating desire for her edged him to the brink of madness.

Making love to Sophie—the thought, the imaginings were enough to boil him in his skin. But he'd given his word, hadn't he, that he would not kiss her, and, after all, how did one seduce without the kiss?

And so he would not, not even when his blood burned like acid inside him because then he *would* be just a rake, a scoundrel without scruples. She would despise him, and perhaps he would despise himself. The price of one kiss would be the rending of their relationship forever and for good.

And he simply could not do without her. How was that for a decadent reprobate?

He must be losing his touch.

"How did you know I read the letter?" she asked as she readied her pencils.

"I did not," he said craftily. "I saw I had stupidly left it out and wondered if you'd looked at it. I assumed, and correctly, that a direct accusation was the quickest way to assess not only if you'd peeked, but what you thought of it."

"You are no gentleman, sir," she cried, aghast at his trick.

He smiled. "Which is what I keep telling you."

"Oh, dear," she said, waving her grease pencil threateningly. "I am considering giving you horns and warts."

"Do your worst." He relaxed back into his chair.

She sketched idly. "This conversation is no good. It has me thinking too much. Thinking is not conducive to art."

"All right then," he said. "How do I facilitate this . . . art?"

She angled her head, studying the sketch. "Hmm. Tell me something, something about yourself. I want to know something good about you, something you value. What was your happiest moment?"

"Waking up the first night here and seeing you in my doorway."

"Stop flirting. The best memory of your childhood, I meant."

He look a while to answer. She watched him as he pondered this, his gaze drifting off to the far distance. A smile curled slowly after a moment's pause. Yes, that was what she was after.

She tried to replicate it with strokes of her pencil. Her inadequacies frustrated her. She did not fancy herself a great artist, but there was something about his face, his nature, that made her want to capture it.

"Tell me," she ordered, as she worked.

"Summers. Riding my pony. We would go on long rides, Matthew and May and I. We'd pack luncheon—cold ham and crusty rolls. May would read to me, then I to her. I remember *Ivanhoe*. And . . ." His smile broadened. "My secret place in the woods. It was really just a pair of fallen trees bucked up against each another. I wouldn't do much there, just sit and marvel that I had a clandestine place all of my own."

He leaned forward, resting his forearm on his knee. "And I remember the smell of grass. Do you know how sweet it is when it is newly cut? Whenever I smell that, it takes me back to all the summers of my life."

Stopping, he said, "You aren't sketching."

She'd quite forgotten about his portrait. "Oh."

"So tell me yours."

"My happiest memories?" She thought for a moment. "We had picnics as well. My aunts and I used to go out of the Town some days in the summer. We'd take a barge to Greenwich, or sometimes to Windsor. They would bring some of their friends, and we were a gay crew. We would have all sorts of amusements. Sometimes a few of them who were musicians would play a concert. The women danced—it was quite hedonistic by society's standards."

She laughed suddenly, remembering. "And we would do dramatic presentations. All the time, not just on these outings. Each aunt would take a scene from one of their greatest parts. Aunt Millicent loved to do Lady Macbeth. And my mother was so proud of her Beatrice in *Much Ado About Nothing*."

She paused, suddenly remembering that her "mother" was Millicent Kent and it should have been "Aunt" Annabeth who had been Beatrice.

But Gideon would not know the particulars, names and such. Her slip did not register.

"It was a scandalous play to be performed on stage," he observed, his eyes dancing with pleasure.

"Indeed, yes," Sophie replied, then warmed to his smile. "Aunt Linnie *loved* the raucous comedies and would act out *all* the parts in different voices of the farces that were so popular in her generation. Then they would give me the key lines for each of them. How kind they were— all the great moments of their seminal roles and *I* would steal them. How they'd applaud!"

"Did you have talent?"

"Absolutely none. But that did not stop them from doting on my every performance. Sometimes we would mount
a full production. I have played Juliet and Portia . . . I can
still recall my lines. *The quality of mercy is not strained. It
falleth as the gentle rain from heaven upon the earth beneath* . . . And Antigone—poor Antigone. How I loved
doing her death throes. I have been them all, but only in the
drawing room."

"Sophie," he said softly.

She blinked and looked at him. He was regarding her
with the most curiously tender expression on his face.

His hand reached for her. She did not draw away.
Dazed, she let him touch her cheek.

"You are crying," he said.

"I know. I cannot imagine why."

"Perhaps because you miss them." He smiled at her, so
full of understanding it hurt to look at him. "That is not so
unnatural."

"I never did before." Her face broke, and she felt a swift
and hot flood of grief. She gasped twice, catching the emotions before they flooded out.

"Shhh," he said, and grabbed her hand. She still held
her pencil. He brought her knuckles to his mouth, and
kissed them.

"You said you would not do that," she whispered.
Why was she objecting? Her hand felt as if it had been
filled with lightning. And that awful swell of sadness
was receding.

"A slip." He dropped her hand and she was disappointed in herself for having reminded him. "It was meant
differently from before. It is merely the affection I hold for
you, Sophie. As a friend."

"Yes. We are friends, aren't we? That seems so strange.
Why is it I can tell you all of this? I've never had anyone
to confide in before. All new. So many new things at once.
Sometimes, I lose myself."

"You do not have to pretend with me, and maybe that

makes all the difference. And I do not have to pretend with you. You've seen me at my worst, and maybe it gives you the freedom to be less than your best at all times. And isn't it such a relief to be less than your best—anytime?"

He made her laugh. She nodded, giving him his due. "You are certainly thoughtful for a rogue."

"Well, when a rogue is kept from his debauches by infirmity," he said wryly, waving a finger at his bandages, "he has to come up with new diversions. I am finding I have a penchant for philosophy. And who would have thought it, I am turning out to be very wise."

"Very wise indeed," she replied with a smile, "if not terribly modest."

He shrugged. "No one is perfect."

Chapter 8

*On the night Sophie entered society at the Bassingstoke
ball, Gideon chose to be alone.*

Candace had offered to stay with him tonight. They
sometimes played draughts in the evening, to pass the
time. They gambled on cards, which she liked better but
she was dreadful with it, which was why he insisted on
playing for penny pots. He tried to let her win, but sometimes she caught him and scolded him, and he had to play
straight.

But he'd sent her away tonight, thinking he was in the
mood for a sulk. It was the night of Sophie's debut, of
sorts.

God he would have loved to have seen her.

So that was why he was feeling sorry for himself. Normally, he was not the type to sit and brood. In fact, it made
him quite dodgy. He'd outrun his emotions for most of his
life. It was more his style to get out of here and raise hell.

But this evening, Sophie was dancing. Laughing up at
men whose cravats were impeccably tied and pantaloons
were pressed to crisp creases.

Respectable men—gentlemen. Husband types.

The itching on his wounds was maddening. He wanted

to rip into the fresh skin just knitting together at the tender edges of the burns.

It might scar. Daley always evaded that direct question. The dratted man was supposed to have come this evening, but sent word he'd been delayed. Something about delivering twins.

Sometimes it frightened him, thinking of being disfigured, especially his face. That was normal. Who would not find the idea of facial scarring alarming?

Sometimes, though, he didn't care. He was more comfortable with this reaction. It was always better when one did not care too much—about anything. It saved wear on the nerves.

Yet when he thought about Sophie Kent, he did care.

And that made him laugh. The hollow sound chased the silence, sounding mournful and not at all cheerful.

He cared. What a twit he was. It was actually too funny.

Sophie gasped as she stepped into the sumptuous glitter of the Bassingstoke mansion. It was like walking into a dream, Sophie thought, as May shot her a bracing smile. Trembling, Sophie kept telling herself, *This is it. This is what I've come for.*

She thought of her mother, her aunts, and felt a swelling of emotion. How proud they would be of her.

"Look at the cut crystal," Michaela Khoury said. Dark-haired, green-eyed, a near replica of her father, the Earl of Woolrich, Michaela had been the first of the earl's children to be found by Lady May. She had been quick to try to befriend Sophie, and despite getting a cool response initially, she'd been unflagging in her efforts.

This time, Sophie did not shrink from the contact as Michaela, escorted by her husband, took her by the arm and led her farther inside. She even pressed a bit tighter next to this "sister."

"It is a beautiful home," Lady May pronounced in practical tones, sweeping beside them. She was dressed in a stunning dress of lavender with pale pink touches. She always managed to appear soft and feminine. "But it is no more so than what you're used to by now. It is merely dressed up for the ball. And, of course, all the candles. Andrew . . . that is, Lord Bassingstoke knows how to show his wealth. Come, do not be intimidated. You are going to have a wonderful time. Just wait until all of society gets a view of that face."

Michaela caught her eye and giggled as May cupped Sophie's chin and beamed at her. "Ah. I think so often of Wooly at times like this. Your father would be so proud."

The reminder of her "father," which immediately plucked her guilt, was nearly enough to send Sophie fleeing back into the carriage. If not for May on one side and Michaela on the other, she might have done just that.

Lord Roberts took Sophie's hand. "You will do wonderfully. Try to enjoy it. Now, ladies, if you will excuse me, I have a wager waiting for me."

May frowned as Roberts bowed to her and went off to one of the rooms off the large circular hall. "Billiards. I despise that game. Why did they have to invent it in the first place? It is such a nuisance—all the men going into one room. It has absolutely killed the more lively conversations at these things."

"I completely agree," Michaela said, adjusting her gloves and checking her reticule. "My chief complaint is that it steals the men from being available to ask ladies to dance."

Her husband grinned at her. "Not that it has deterred you from filling your card."

Major Adrian Khoury was a rather famous war hero, a favorite of Wellington, and had fought at Waterloo. He had been badly wounded and now walked with a limp, requiring the use of a cane. The injury meant that he rarely danced. He did not, however, mind that Michaela occupied herself with friends in the quadrille or a reel.

Michaela laughed happily. "I only do so to make you jealous."

Major Khoury's eyes warmed as he gazed at Michaela.

"It is effective. But I do insist on saving any waltzes for me. I may not be terribly graceful, but I am determined to be the only man who holds my wife in public."

Michaela gave him a melting look. "I would have it no other way, Adrian."

Sophie glanced away. It always gave her a start to witness these kinds of exchanges. They were normal in her new life. In fact, men and women had much different attitudes toward one another than she had been led to believe was typical of the aristocracy.

"My friends are usually in the card room," May said, bustling Sophie away from the others. "I have gotten Lady Melbourne to promise me she would introduce you to her nephews when we arrived. That should get your evening off to a fine start. And, of course, you already know Viscount Eastleigh. And his cousin, Mr. Rochfort. My, that is quite a contingent of beaus and should keep you occupied. You will not have a moment to rest your feet, I'll wager."

Sophie thought of Ashford, of his amused contempt for all this. He would laugh himself silly to see her now, shaking like a feather in a gale. Ah, but if he were here, how much easier it would be.

He would likely tuck her hand into the crook of his elbow—regardless of whether that sort of thing was "done"—and march her through the proceedings with his particular brand of irreverence to distract her from her anxiety.

She silently chastened herself for such thoughts. She had to face this alone. And face these people, the very ones who had judged her ill all of her life, and found her so lacking in breeding, in morality, in character.

"There you are," Lady Viola Carraway exclaimed, rushing forward to greet them. "Just in time, too. I am losing most dreadfully."

"I told you not to play whist," May scolded sweetly.

"I should listen to you more often," she replied.

May smiled, smoothing a fluff of feathers artfully placed at her shoulders.

Lady Viola then turned to Sophie. "My dear, I cannot imagine anyone looking lovelier.

"Thank you, Lady Viola. Is Margaux here?"

Waving her hands in the direction of the dance floor, Lady Viola replied, "She and my sister are somewhere out there."

May gauged the crowd, identifying who was here and calculating how to make the most of the evening. To her, society was done with precision.

"Very well," she announced after taking in every detail and every face around them, "let us go into the ballroom, Sophie. It is time you began entertaining requests for a dance."

Sophie found Margaux quickly. They embraced while Mrs. Milton glared in alarm at Sophie's graceful beauty fitted next to her daughter's plump prettiness.

"Have you danced already?" Sophie asked.

"I have three promised. When the orchestra plays, I must go to the first one. Lord Milford!"

"He could barely wait until we were in the door," boomed Mrs. Milton, "before he was at my side, begging an introduction." She nodded, supremely pleased. "He is very wealthy, you know. Has four thousand, at least."

"But he is rather peculiar," Margaux said under her breath. "He twitches."

They giggled together for a moment, until the outburst was quelled by Mrs. Milton's stern look. May ducked behind her fan to hide her smile.

Margaux pulled Sophie a short distance away. "This is the one I wish to show you. Look, there. Do you see the one with the dark hair? He is not so tall, but he has those large eyes. Isn't he wonderful?"

Sophie glanced over at the man Margaux indicated. He was slender, the kind of elegant figure prized so highly in fine society. His tailored coat fit impeccably, and his dark good looks made him stand out in the crowd.

To her mortification, he caught them looking. Margaux

made a small squeak and struck an adorable pose of indifference while Sophie looked away as quickly as she could.

Sophie was pleasantly surprised to find she and Margaux were immediately besieged by men begging to be presented. Her dance card filled up quickly. Margaux was kept similarly busy. As the evening progressed, the pair often sought each other out in order to sit together in between dances to rest and sip lemonade.

"This is wonderful!" Margaux pronounced after they had dispatched a pair of young gentlemen to refill their glasses. "Of course, you are so lovely, it was assured. But I was very nervous. When Mama insisted I come to London to make my debut, I thought it was a very bad idea, as we did not know many people. But Aunt Viola was such a sweetheart, and well thought of, and I took heart. When I met your aunt, however, I knew it was going to be perfect. How lucky we are to be paired together."

Sophie laughed. "I can have no doubts as to the success of anything Lady May undertakes. She may look like a confection in her pink feathers, but she must never be underestimated. Still, I can't imagine what it would have been like without you along with me. I was quite nervous, and it is so good to have a friend."

"You were nervous, really? But you never seem so. You are very cool."

"I have been accused of being . . . reserved."

Gideon had teased her mercilessly about it, actually, with that wicked gleam in his eye as if he were enjoying every moment of baiting her—which he probably was.

"But your aunt watched over you. Look, here she is bringing another man for you to meet. Ah!" Her hands fluttered in front of her face. "It is him, the one I showed you before!"

She squirmed in her seat, flustered. When May arrived with the gentleman, however, Margaux had magically composed herself.

"Allow me to present you to Lord Burton," May said to them. Sophie could tell by the tight control of her excite-

ment that she considered this one a great catch. "My niece,
Miss Sophie Kent, and my good friend Miss Margaux
Milton."

Lord Burton appeared to be close to thirty years of age,
a blade of a man with a soulfully serious look about him.

Margaux gave Sophie's ankle a little kick, a sign of her
excitement. Outwardly, however, she appeared perfectly
calm as Lord Burton bowed low over each woman's hand.

He addressed himself to Sophie. "Do you like the
party?" he asked in a pleasant baritone.

"It is quite nice, thank you."

Poor Margaux's pretty flush deepened to scarlet when
Burton did not turn to her to ask after her. Sophie was at a
loss as to what to do to help her. Matters became worse
when Lord Burton requested a dance.

Sophie hesitated, not wanting to hurt her new friend.
Margaux tried very bravely not to appear crushed. With no
other choice save being outright rude, Sophie wrote in the
dance and Lord Burton removed himself with the promise
to come collect her later.

"I am sorry," she said to Margaux when he had gone. "I
know you liked him."

"Oh, do you think that is the only man I will admire?"
Margaux said, tossing her head. "La! Already I am looking
forward to my quadrille with the young Earl of Pentworth.
And Lord Burton, while handsome, seemed rather *serious*,
don't you think?"

Dubious, Sophie let the matter drop.

When it was time for Lord Burton's dance. Sophie was
surprised to feel a start of excitement. He was so elegant.
There was undeniable breeding in every line of his slender
male form, in the shadows and strong bones of his face.
She, however, could not help but compare him to the
harder, broader form she had grown used to seeing every
day.

She scolded herself; she was very firm in her intention
not to compare every man she met to Gideon. The virility
he exuded would be out of place here, in the gracious hall

filled with people whose great ambition was to appear ultra civilized. There was something distinctly *un*civilized about Gideon.

She followed Burton's lead as they took their places on the parquet floor, feeling a bit bemused at her good fortune. She was surprised to see Michaela and Major Khoury also waiting quietly for the music to begin. Major Khoury caught her eye and gave her a wink. It was then she realized this must be a waltz.

Lord Burton placed his hand on her waist, the other grasped hers, and he began to move with the opening strains of the gentle music. He was a masterful dancer, but she was not. The slight pressure that was meant to guide her in the correct direction did not seem to translate into the proper movement of her feet.

Lord Burton was kind enough not to make anything of her lack of grace. Even with such generous tact, she could not say she enjoyed the dance. Her nerves were too tightly strung.

They chatted amicably, but even his easy conversation did not ease her tension. She felt conspicuous, an imposter, more so because she did not seem to be able to find the lead the gently bred women around her followed with such ease.

Then the dance was through, and Burton led her back to the edge of the floor, where her next partner was awaiting her with a beaming smile.

Burton bowed, and asked, "May I request the privilege of being allowed to call on you?"

"Yes," she stammered, taken aback. The fact of Lord Burton's interest buoyed her for the rest of the evening.

Later, Margaux approached her with a smile. "I suppose it is only my fault to have made a friend with your face."

"Pardon me?" Sophie asked.

"You are very beautiful. Lord Burton preferred you. I am regretful, but not angry. I wanted to make certain you knew that."

"Of course we shall neither of us ever be silly enough to squabble over a man. Did you enjoy your dance partners?"

"Not so much. They were all very dull. But this is only the first ball, yes? Oh, here is my partner for the reel."

A tall blond man approached eagerly. Sophie gave Margaux a teasing glance. "My, he is handsome. Do enjoy."

Margaux gave her a playful tap with her fan. "I will see you later."

As Sophie turned, she smiled politely at a man passing her just then. She froze, a thin cold thread of fear catching around her throat. The man paused, too, his gaze resting for a moment on her.

She knew him. What was his name? She could not remember. But she knew the face. She had seen him in her aunt's drawing room.

"Miss Temple," he said, inclining his head.

Temple! She could barely speak, barely move.

When she found her voice, she managed to say, "I believe you are mistaken. Have a good evening." She hurried away, fighting the impulse to run.

Chapter 9

The physician arrived late, having spent the better part of the evening delivering twin sons to a duke and duchess, and he was worse for it. Daley peeled away bandages and probed the new skin, making soft "hmphs," and "ah-has" under his breath that had the nursemaid wringing her hand.

"I've decided to wrap your wounds lighter," he pronounced when he was finished, "and exposed some of the skin that is ready. Also, I am leaving the eye undone. You can wear a patch over it, which I recommend. It will be sensitive, and too much light too quickly will damage it."

"Hand me that mirror," he told Candace.

Daley held up a hand to stay her. "It is not wise to look at this stage."

Candace looked to Gideon.

"Do it," he told her. She cast a frightened look at the physician, then brought the small looking glass.

"There is still a good deal of healing to be done," Daley said. "Remember, it is hardly finished."

Gideon saw his skin was pink and puckered around the wounds. His heart lurched as he examined his eye, his temple, his cheekbone. To him, it seemed impossibly ugly. He wondered what Sophie would think.

"The eyebrow is growing back," Daley said encouragingly.

Putting down the mirror, Gideon asked, "What more healing can I expect? Will it always look like this?"

"It will improve, as I've told you repeatedly. But gradually. Burns are not always predictable. You must give it time."

It was a strange thing, but he somehow felt he had no time. A hoard of sweating suitors would arrive at their door to pay their respects to Miss Kent. More nights like tonight, which was the first of many big nights for Sophie, and he felt impotent, trapped, caged by these damned burns.

With a sigh, he fell back on the pillows and allowed Daley to wrap his wounds as he pleased. He wondered why he would begin to regard any ball with longing, but the idea of Sophie there made him nearly dizzy with frustration.

He wondered if he were a man like those of the ton, the kind of man she wanted—respectable, polished—would he have the courage to show up at her door and beg an audience with her? He rather thought he would. He rather thought he might do anything to win her heart.

If he were a different sort of man.

Daley startled him, his face pursed into a complex network of deep grooves as he frowned over his work. "I can release you to return to your apartments," the physician said. "Although I must say that I do not recommend it. The areas that are ready should be exposed to air. The skin must toughen, but I do not wish you to be out and about in public. There is still a slight risk of infection. And . . . well, there is no way to put this delicately."

"It will disgust people," Gideon supplied.

The man responded with patience. "There will be curiosity. Staring. It might distress you."

Gideon thought about going back to his fashionable apartments in St. James. He had very much valued the solitude of a bachelor's life overseen by a discreet housekeeper who did not disapprove of late hours, the smell of spirits, or the sight of an ample bosom displayed prominently on a female guest when she came across one creeping out of the building in the early hours of the morning. His valet, Stephens, did an excellent job of making Gideon's life of leisure and pleasure as effortless as possible.

He did not think of it as home, however. That was Ashford Manor, a place he had not seen in more than a dozen years.

However, he rather liked it here. There was something comforting about the place. Although he and May retained a strained relationship, he was not ready to abandon his proximity and the hope that they would rediscover a portion of their previous affinity for one another. He still cared for her a great deal, and he'd missed her.

Morcover, he liked Sophie. He liked her. He found her uniquely fascinating. From her soft blond curls to the muted light of her eyes, to her smile. He liked her look. He even liked the strong nose that she had said once kept her from being beautiful. It added a dimension to her beauty, a regal quality.

He could not imagine leaving.

Daley packed his instruments back into his bag. "I will speak to Lady May. You may begin to resume activities, but slowly. You may move freely about the house from time to time, but there should be frequent rests." Daley looked toward Candace to make certain she understood his orders, as if he already doubted Gideon would follow them.

"What about outdoors?" Gideon asked. He longed for fresh air.

"The air will do you good, but avoid the sun." He paused at the door. "Take a walk in the gardens where it is shaded."

Gideon frowned, going deep into his thoughts. The physician exited, but Candace remained, watching him with speculation in her eyes.

"You are going to stay here," she said in that way that made it a question.

"I have got to make my escape," he groused. "Lady May confided in me the other day that she is determined to make a gentleman of the first cut of me."

Candace stared at him. "Good for her. I don't know why you insist on going on pretending otherwise."

Pretending otherwise? The statement left him thinking as Candace bid him good night and went to find her bed. Or her lover.

Sometime later, after a period alone with himself and the long silence of the house, he resolved to send for his man, Stephens. If he was staying on here, he was going to need his valet.

There was a message waiting for Sophie when she arrived home. Gideon wished to see her.

She was faintly alarmed, knowing the physician had been due. Stopping only to doff her cloak, she made haste to his room.

He turned as she entered, and she could see his gaze move over her, rapt with approval. Sophie felt a thrill at the slow, appreciative smile that spread across his face.

He angled his head at her, holding up a finger and twirling it, indicating she was to turn around. She did so, giving him a full view of her gown.

"You are stunning," he said softly when she was finished showing off her finery. "Forgive my cheek in summoning you here. It is unconscionable of me to disturb you tonight. No doubt you are tired. But I had to see how you looked." Waving her into her usual seat, he added, "And I confess I wished to hear all about your very first ball."

It pleased her that he was so interested. Then she noticed—his bandages were different. "Doctor Daley came—there has been an improvement!"

Gideon touched the wrappings. "He said it was time to expose the new skin to the air. Only the few places that were still blistered were wrapped."

"Your eye . . ."

"It needs shielding," he said, tapping the patch he sported. "I will not lose my sight."

Happiness surged inside her, and for a moment she forgot herself. She surged forward, her hands out, as if she meant to embrace him.

It was an impulse, and damn her lack of breeding, because it felt so natural. He took her hands and with that contact, she stopped dead, realizing what she'd done.

His eye was dark. His nostrils flared, and his lip touched with a sultry curl.

"Well," he murmured, his eyes fastened on her mouth, "I am moved by your excitement on my behalf."

Shocked at her indecorous behavior, she made to retreat, but the slight pressure of his hands kept her tight.

She could smell him, detect the hint of soap and sandalwood, a slightly spicy scent that made her light-headed.

"I . . . I just am so pleased," she said weakly.

His hands released her, but she did not move at first. It was impossible to break eye contact, not when he was staring at her like that.

Then she recollected herself and rose, blushing wildly. "Really. And May will be thrilled. Absolutely . . . I mean, it's wonderful, Gideon."

"Now, enough of me, it is you and this grand soiree I am anxious to talk about."

"I will tell you in the morning," she replied.

"Ah, then you are anxious to be abed? To your dreams? Anyone I know?"

"As a matter of fact, I probably would not have been able to sleep." She took a post by the window instead of sitting. "Maybe I've been looking forward to telling you."

He steepled his fingers and peered at her. "Of your conquests? The bucks and swells no doubt fainted when you walked in the place."

She arched her brow and peered down at him, amused. "Indeed. Many had to be carried away to hospital."

He laughed, a flash of white teeth catching the firelight. Her stomach gave a pleasurable wrench. He was so appealingly handsome. She had seen no one like him tonight, nor would she, she thought suddenly. Well, of course she wouldn't. Men in polite society didn't . . . *smolder* like that.

"I presume you danced?" he queried. "With whom? Anyone twice?"

She relaxed, tilting her head. "It was the world I had fantasized about all my life. It was, in a very real sense, a dream come true. Everyone was so beautiful. All the colors of the gowns . . ."

"Yes, yes, I am aware that everyone dresses to the limit of their purse for these things."

She leaned forward. "The silks. Honestly, the rustling as the ladies walked about was incredibly loud. Nearly everyone had on stunning jewels. And I thought, 'Oh, Lord, I am not supposed to be here.' But Lady May kept pulling me along, and I—"

"Why the devil would you think that?" he fired. His vehemence caught her off guard. "You have every right to be there. Your father is an earl."

She ducked her head quickly to hide the flush of shame. Her father was a painter and an art instructor, not the Earl of Woolrich. "I . . . It was just . . . new. Different. I don't really belong."

He waved this off. "You must not think this way in the future. You have to hold your head up, stare them straight in the eye and dare them to snub you."

"Is that what you do?" she inquired.

"Of course. And do you know something? As wicked as they think me, none dare cut me."

The comfort she derived from his fierce defense suffused her with warmth. "I do not know if I can master your arrogance."

"You are becoming quite adept at it," he replied drolly. "And so . . . the gentlemen . . . the dancing, the fetching of the punch, the running about with plates of petit fours and other sumptuous offerings . . ."

"You cannot be interested," she protested, sinking into the chair at last. Her feet were aching terribly. She surreptitiously slipped her shoes off and flexed her arches. "I thought you hated such affairs."

"On the contrary, my thoughts refused to focus elsewhere all evening."

To her shock, he leaned down and brushed aside her hem to grab her foot. She balked, almost coming out of the chair, but it would have sent her into a tumble. "What are you doing?"

"Do not worry. Just relax."

"I will not!" She tried to pull her foot back, but he only chuckled. "Release me at once—"

"It is not wicked, I promise." He placed her foot on his knee and arranged her skirts so that her legs were covered. "Very respectable."

"It is *not* respectable."

Her voice was breathless. Drums of warning pulsed in the back of her mind, but she could not seem to focus on the escape they urged.

She did not wish to. Just as she did not wish to stop this shocking liberty of his hands on her, touching her with electric fingers.

"But it will feel wonderful." He watched her with blazing concentration. "You will see."

She opened her mouth to protest, but his hand enveloped her ankle and squeezed gently. It felt so good the breath went out of her.

"Now I have your attention," he said in a soft voice. "Relax, Sophie, and stop making a fuss. This is nothing more than a task a servant might perform."

But he was not a servant, and she was acutely aware of it. She wished she could summon some will to protest what was incontrovertibly a very inappropriate manhandling of her person by him . . . but, *God*, it felt so good. His hands had her slender foot in their grasp, kneading gently, and the will to resist seeped out of her.

"And the gentlemen tonight," he said. His voice was as smooth as silk rasping over flesh. "Did you find anyone of interest?"

"My lord, can it be you are jealous?" she said, appalled that her own voice came forth throaty with pleasure.

"Madly," he replied quickly, his gaze challenging and unapologetic. It burned for only a moment before it dropped away, and he became suddenly occupied with her arch. He pressed his thumb into it from heel to toe. "Do you know what I would have given to have been there?" he murmured.

She was silent, and so was he. What was she to say to this?

Very gently, he tucked her foot under her skirt and brought the other onto his lap. "I keep interrupting you. Continue." His eyes narrowed. "Did you make . . . promising connections?"

"A few," she answered coyly. She was reluctant to tell him about Lord Burton.

"They will call, of course." He grew thoughtful. "I should be up and about very soon. I shall look forward to meeting them."

This shot a bolt of panic through her. Seeing her face, he laughed. "I only tease you, Sophie. I would not dream of interfering."

She gave him a look that made him laugh harder.

"Why are you so curious about all of this?" she asked, ruffled by his amusement, which she suspected was at her expense.

With an effort, she pulled herself up straight, retracting her foot. He surrendered without comment.

"Everything about you interests me." A half smile played on his mouth. The crisp curl of his hair twining over his brow, and at his neck to touch the collar of the dressing gown, caught the light from the fire and gleamed rich gold.

"I am tired of talking about the ball," she said, rising. She'd gone too far, allowed him too much freedom tonight. He was making grand sport of her, plying her with some dark intent she could sense just below the surface. She'd let her guard down, a dangerous thing to do. It was because she'd missed him.

He propped up one eyebrow at her cooling mood. "All right, then. We could converse about fashion. I was curious about the latest style of cravats. Tell me, how are the gentlemen of the ton tying their neck ligatures these days?"

"Very tightly," she said in clipped syllables. "I would be very happy to demonstrate." She folded her arms over her chest. "Good night, Gideon. I am going to retire. It has been a long night."

His sigh made it apparent he was disappointed. But he said, "Yes, go on then." He held his hand out for hers.

She hesitated. He'd been impossibly forward with her tonight, and she was afraid to touch him again.

But he only brushed a quick kiss across her knuckles. "Dream pleasantly," he murmured. "Of silks and chandeliers and a queue of beaus begging for your hand. Good night, Sophie."

The way he said her name sent a rash of chills over her flesh, and she escaped the room feeling breathless and bemused. Something had happened, she thought, but she could not understand what it was that had changed.

Chapter 10

"Gideon, I woke you!" May cried as she entered the bed-
chamber to find him still sleeping.

Gideon shot upright, momentarily disoriented. "I over-
slept," he croaked. Clearing his throat, he eased back onto
the pillows.

"Only nine o'clock. You are always awake by now.
You've complained you could not sleep at nights."

He rubbed his face, raking his hands through his hair. "I
was able to sleep last night. Like the dead. I can't remember the last time I did that."

"I shall come back later," May said, giving him a fond
pat and heading for the door.

"Why? It is your usual time. Fifteen minutes in the
morning, nine o'clock, every day faithfully."

She stopped with a short gasp.

He raised his brows in response to the glance she threw
at him over her shoulder. "Why don't you open the drapes,
get some light in here to unglue my eyes."

Gideon was never his most cheerful self in the morn-
ings. He arranged his coverlet and grabbed the shirt and
old trousers he had tossed onto the floor when he'd
climbed into bed last night.

He pulled the shirt on and then took a long drink of water from the glass on his nightstand as daylight spilled into the room.

"You are not feeling ill?" May asked, her back turned while he slipped the trousers on under the coverlet. What indignities the infirm suffer, he thought morosely as he fastened them in place. "Doctor Daley was emphatic that we should keep a strict watch for infection. Although he is really very happy with your progress."

"I am well. Better than ever. You can turn around now."

She did so with a renewed smile. "Gideon, are you happy here? Well tended, well fed? Do you like it here? I mean, a house is so much better than some rooms let in St. James, and I have the whole of the staff available for you."

He was a bit suspicious of what she was after. "It is immensely comfortable here. You have been quite generous in allowing me to stay so long."

"Well, that is my point, you see. I noticed you had your valet come, and it encouraged me. I would like it if you would continue to stay." She stammered, and this surprised him. Of course, she had been skittish, even evasive, during her visits since he'd come here, but today she was altogether undone.

"I always meant for my house to be yours. It was just that we did not see each other for so long." Her hands picked nervously, first at the froth of rushing at her throat, then at the glass on the table. "I can almost look upon the accident as a blessing of sorts because it gave me that chance to have you here. It was almost like it was meant to be."

"I am not sure that is the best idea." He raked his hair. "I believe my being here is . . . well, it seems to be hard on you."

"You must stop that. It makes you look unkempt." Almost absently, she pulled his hand away from his hair, then stopped, a bit shocked at herself. "Oh, my. That came so naturally. Well, I suppose it is because I am determined that you are going to grace the best drawing rooms in London. So you had better brush up on deportment."

He was stunned. "I do not plan to grace the drawing rooms of London."

"I have plans for you," May said, excited. "That is all part of it. Gideon, please hear me out." Taking a breath, she paused for dramatic effect. "I want to sponsor your re-introduction into society."

"I believe we have discussed this. It is a kind offer— but no."

"It is not an *offer.* I am simply giving you the courtesy of telling you what I am going to do. Oh, Gideon, do not be put out. It is only what I would have done had I been allowed to when you were of age."

"But why would I wish to be bored silly in society's drawing rooms? I am having much more fun in the bedrooms."

"Are you?" She had that look, the one she would get when he was younger and losing an argument to her. Taking a long, steady, and very pointed look at his bandage, she said, "Are you indeed?"

He scowled, touching the clean linens Candace had replaced yesterday. They still smelled of the potent unguents. The flesh underneath stung and itched, sometimes to the brink of being bearable.

"I was not able to be there when I wished to be," May said, moving closer.

He forced himself to look at her. He said, "Of course, you were very busy. Society has such arduous demands."

Sometimes it got to him, seeing her. She was older. The signs of aging were subtle. Time had been kind to her. Her beauty was not untouched, but it was not much lessened, either. God, how he used to love her.

May crossed her arms. "Without a woman's influence— and women, of course, are the force of civility in society— you naturally became unruly. Enamored of the things that bring quick reward, and quick pleasure. Just like a man." She huffed a short laugh of exasperation. "And you were angry, weren't you? You still are, even if you will not admit it. Anger makes a person reckless."

"Why do you suddenly care? You've not bothered all this time."

He immediately regretted what he'd said. He never wanted to hurt May.

"I failed you, Gideon." She said it simply, yet the words were weighted with emotion. He felt it inside himself, too, as hot as the touch of a branding iron. He had never *blamed* her. He'd only missed her, damn it.

She said, "But I want to mend that as well as I am able. Now you must let me help you take your place in society. You are Lord Ashford. It is time you began acting like a member of the aristocracy. Please, *please* consider it."

He was quiet for a few moments before taking her hands and folding them in his. "Let me ask you something, and then I will decide."

She seemed to sense what was coming. He could see her brace herself. He said, "Do you think about Matthew, about those days?"

The change in her was severe and abrupt. She recoiled, snatching her hands from his. She blinked rapidly, trying to keep her composure but he still knew her well enough to detect the rage of feelings running rampant across her face.

He nodded, seeing what he had suspected. "This is why it is not a good idea for me to remain. You have been kind to me, at a time when I needed someone, even if I resisted it. But really, we barely knew each other. Let us not pretend that it is all pleasant reunion and happiness. My staying here . . . you can hardly bear it."

"You are wrong, Gideon. Why would I beg you to stay if that were the case?"

Gideon remained nonplussed. "I suppose it is because I look like him. It must bring it all back."

May reacted.

"When we would come across each other in Town," Gideon continued, his voice soft and steady, "I knew it bothered you. I have memories of my brother. I know I resemble him. I could tell you saw it. You could barely stand to look at me."

She shook her head, as if trying to deny it, but there was no vehemence. "Gideon . . . it is so complicated."

"Why?" He was genuinely surprised. "Matthew shot himself. That was no one's fault. Was it because you quarreled right before?"

"You knew?"

"I heard it, muffled. I was young, but even I saw something was wrong with him in the weeks and months before. Leading up to . . . well, everyone calls it 'the accident,' but it wasn't an accident. But it makes it more palatable, I suppose. Let us be honest, though. He was not himself."

"Yes, Gideon." She barely choked out the words. "He . . . he was not himself."

"And he was getting worse. He was angry, irrational all the time. That is why he killed himself. He was ill."

She nodded jerkily. "That is right. He was. It was a terrible time. I should have shielded you, but I did not know what to do myself."

"How could you shield me?" A thought occurred to him. "Is that why you think you failed me?"

She bowed her head, taking a long time to gather herself together. "I used to think of you all the time. I would have come, Gideon, had there been any way."

Gideon closed his eyes. He did not like the welling of emotion that threatened, rising like a swell just below the surface. May was holding tenuously to her emotions and he . . . he was filled with feelings he had not experienced in a long time.

She said, "Reginald was a bastard to me, but I always hoped he was kind to you. He wanted you so badly, fought me to get you. Was he a good guardian to you, Gideon?"

Gideon waited a moment before responding. "He was not unkind."

He was glad that this fragmented truth seemed to give her some relief. It was not a lie, strictly speaking. Reginald had not once beaten him, after all, nor had he deprived him

of food or been stingy in providing for his board—anywhere but in his home.

She rose. "I should let you get to your morning ablu-
tions. Doctor Daley said yesterday that you might begin to
come to the parlor, take your meals with the rest of us."

"Ah. The banishment is over."

She paused at the door, hesitant, then squared her shoulders. "You did not give me an answer, Gideon. Will you
stay?"

"I will remain. For the time being."

It made her happy. It made him miserable, for as he
dressed, examining the new bandages the physician had
given him along with a fresh black eye patch to wear over
the tender skin of the damaged eye, he wondered why the
hell he would want to be on hand to witness Sophie Trent
wooed and wedded to another man.

Other than the fact that he wished to be no other place
than right here. Damnation.

When one plays with fire, one can expect to get burned.

That was what Sophie kept thinking over the following
days. Something had happened, had been happening, between Gideon and her, and she could not deny it to herself
any longer. It was fire, but it didn't frighten her. It was dangerous, but it didn't send her fleeing.

And the burning was getting hotter.

It was disaster if she were infatuated, this she absolutely
knew. He was a famous—or rather infamous—rake, and
she was a woman with origins that would not bear up
under close scrutiny. So far, Lady May's breezy explana-
tions for her appearance in society had not been examined
too closely. They thought she was the daughter of the Earl
of Woolrich. . . .

Her stomach twisted sickly. She hated the lies she'd
told, but they'd been necessary. However, they were still
lies. Any lack of injudiciousness could bring notice, and
perhaps inquiry, and that would assuredly be her undoing.

She would not be brought down by an indiscreet passion, she told herself over and over, hoping to strike caution to temper the rising temptations. But how could she resist?

Her body still tingled when she remembered how he had touched her. What was even more impossible was that she wanted to go back in there, see him again. She wanted to feel the strange shivery delight.

The more she knew of him, the more drawn to him she became, until she no longer cared if she were walking into the mouth of the dragon each and every day. She could hardly wait to get there.

He did not attempt to touch her again. She was grateful for his restraint, but it only seemed to increase the tension. Each day, she began with resolutions of propriety, but soon he would coax her to lay aside the book, and they would talk.

He could lull her out of herself as no one else had ever done. She told him about her aunts and their heartaches and about herself living in such a strange and fascinating home. She told him of the slights she'd endured. To all of this he listened, his eyes missing nothing, hiding depths neither one of them openly acknowledged.

But it was there. And it boiled to the surface on an occasion that began innocently enough with her asking him why, to May's great frustration, he insisted on refusing her efforts to gain his entrance to the polite world.

"I learned a long time ago it was not for me," was his initial answer, spoken curtly so as to discourage any further inquiry.

But she was too curious. "But did you *always* hate balls and such? When was the last time you were out among the ton?"

"The kind of gatherings I went to were hardly gay. Reginald's friends were not ones to kick up their heels. And the last time— Is that what you wish to know? I can tell you about it for I remember it well. I was nineteen and with a friend during holiday from school. That was a night of infamy, for I took the young Lord of Carrollton, John

Essex, and dumped him upside down in the fish pond installed in the dining room."

She gaped. "Gideon, are you joking with me?"

He shook his head. Rising to his feet, he said, "I cannot sit for too long."

Sophie was not petite, not as May was. Oftentimes, with the older woman, she had felt large and uncomfortable, for Lady May's neat smallness was the height of femininity. Now, with Gideon standing next to her, she did not feel tall or conspicuous. She felt as if she had only to take one step and she could tuck herself in the tidy space made just for her under his arm. The notion of sheltering next to his large, broad body was immeasurably attractive.

The direction of her thoughts should have brought alarm, but they did not. These sorts of musings never did these days.

"What was your question?" he asked. His voice was softer now, almost teasing.

"The pond. Why did you do such a thing?" She watched him make his way to the window, just where she'd found him so many times. That caged-tiger look assembled over his features, the one she could never capture with her pencil.

"He insulted someone. I took offense."

"Who did he insult? Ah . . . it was a woman, was it not?" She was surprised to find herself annoyed at the thought.

"She was a young lady, perhaps your age. Her brother was in our circle and I knew her. She had as sweet a disposition as one can find. She was not blessed, shall we say, with the type of figure men find appealing, and her face was plain. Now, I have no complaint of any man who finds a woman too fond of tea cakes and a complete lack of bosom—my apologies, but you must be used to my plain speech by now—not to his taste. However, I do when he accosts the woman with his opinion in a way no one can find pardonable."

"He insulted her publicly?"

"Among the men, he made some comments—very

loud, very specific. It got them laughing. I could see by the way she looked over at us that she suspected she was the recipient of the jokes. She was mortified, and I took exception."

She was touched. "How terrible. The poor creature."

"Look, Sophie, as much as I enjoy seeing that glowing admiration in your eyes, do not think I did this out of some Robin Hood–style heroism. His boorish comments against the woman furnished an excuse for doing what I'd been itching to do since I'd met him."

"Oh," she said, disappointed.

"And the girl's family did not appreciate the gesture, as it only drew more attention to the disparagement Carrollton was spewing. The gossip in the aftermath of the . . . uh . . . dunking, was as much about her as him. The family did not think I did them any favors and my friend never spoke to me again."

"It seems rather ungrateful." She was indignant.

"Well, that is the aristocracy for you. Fairness and virtue pale under the need to—above all things—*avoid scandal.*" He made a production of a feigned shiver. "They never did forgive me for that."

"Oh, Gideon, you cannot tell me that they did not thank you for defending their daughter."

He paused, looking at her strangely. "I am afraid I cannot in good conscience lead you to believe I did this deed for the sake of virtue. It was quite the opposite. I dunked the fellow purely for my own pleasure."

She would have liked to think well of him. "And why did it please you to punish him?"

He winced. "Because the man was a self-inflated idiot. He reminded me of Reginald. He wore that particular expression that was so similar—you know that way people have of looking at you as if you are some particular and disgusting form of insect? I took some delight in letting him know exactly what I made of his airs and mistaken superiority."

She waited a moment. "I do not imagine that dunking a peer's son results in a great deal of invitations."

"Surprisingly, no," he answered wryly. He smiled down at her, and she had that sensation again of wanting to sway into him.

His eyes were on her face. She wondered what it would be like to stand full against him and have his lips seal over hers again.

He brushed his fingertips against her cheek where one spiraling tendril rested. She should not let him do that, she thought distractedly, but did not move.

Stepping back abruptly, he looked to the ceiling. "You are a temptation, Sophie Kent."

She was a temptation? Dear Lord, he was the devil himself.

"Do not look so disturbed," he said. He moved to the other end of the room, walking slowly. He was much better on his feet than when he had first arisen, but he was still stiff, slow but purposeful. She imagined when he was at his full strength, he possessed that particular brand of male grace that indicated a love of athletics.

He turned to face her. "You fascinate me, Sophie. And, yes, there is the physical attraction. I won't deny it. The truth is, I would give anything to take you to bed, except the one thing it would cost. You would hate me. You might quite possibly even hate yourself. Besides, I gave my word, remember?"

She could not look at him. "I remember. You promised you would never kiss me."

He nodded. "Go on, now," he told her. "Your young men will be calling soon. You must make your toilette."

There were so many things she wanted to say, so many things she felt. In the end, she only said, "Gideon . . ."

"I like the way you say my name," he said softly. Then his face snapped into a bracing smile and he wiggled his fingers for her to go.

She stood for a long moment, uncertainty freezing her in place. She did not wish to leave. There was nowhere else to go, only dull diversions to be endured until the next time she saw him.

But in the end, she did go, disturbed and reluctant and not even caring if it showed.

"I must think of a way to make him agree to stay permanently," May told Robert as she paced a wide circle in the drawing room. "He only promised for the time being. What does he mean by that? I will not have him leave me again.".

"You can always tie him to the bed," Robert replied from his chair.

She shot him a look. "I am extremely upset. I do not appreciate your humor."

He raised his hands. "I apologize. I simply wished to make you smile."

"I am quite put out that Gideon may leave and you are being insufferably unsympathetic."

He sighed. "You said he agreed to stay."

"But not for good."

"He is not a child, May. Gideon is not ignorant of society. He simply does not care for it. He views it with intense disdain. Frankly, I am amazed that you so heartily disapprove of him simply because he has attracted gossip in the past. Your own brother was cut from the same cloth and you were remarkably tolerant of him."

She pulled a face. "Wooly was different. It was in his nature. He was never serious about anything. Oh, I loved him, of course I did, but he had no depth to him. Gideon is different. He is sensitive, intelligent."

"Perhaps you must accept that he is simply different from the man you would like him to be. Look at what it is doing to you, this constant worry. When is the last time you ate a meal?" Robert asked. "You pick at your food. You take Sophie to routs and balls and you play the part, but your heart is not in it. You pace—see, you are doing it now. May, I do not know why your conscience plagues you like this. You have not done anything wrong."

If he knew, he would not be so understanding, May thought. Gideon's life had been ruined by her hand. She had sent him to Reginald—her act had sent him to that dreadful man. And he'd hated it. He couldn't lie to her, she knew Gideon had hated it.

It was in the guarded way he spoke, in the droll way he pretended not to care about anything. If she hadn't known him as a boy, she would not torment herself so much. How could she make Robert see it was her fault?

"Your nature is changing. It is almost as if you are being drawn into something inside yourself. Something very unpleasant. It is him."

"I am worried for the man. He was injured."

"I mean Matthew," he said, the words falling like stones. "I believe it is your first husband who is at the heart of this tension. Look at you. You flinch when I say his name."

She gaped at him, feeling suddenly trapped. "I will not discuss Matthew with you."

His face twitched, a sign of his annoyance. "I've known almost from the first days and nights we spent together that you keep a secret. I've never asked you about it, never wanted to. But it has something to do with Matthew, and with Gideon. It is ripping you up inside."

Her throat closed and she thought for one awful moment that she was going to faint, her shock was so great. How had he known? How long?

As if plucking the questions from her mind, he said, "My former profession, remember? It is second nature for me to notice the things that give you away. I do not mean to do it, it simply comes to me."

"You have been analyzing me like one of your marks?" She meant to be indignant and ended up sounding shrill.

She could not move as he rose from his chair and came to her. Even with the shocking revelation that he knew so much, she still found comfort in his touch. He ran a gentle knuckle along her jaw. "I love you. Nothing you tell me will change that."

"If you love me, then you will stop pressing me for details I have made obvious I have no wish to talk to you about."

"Gideon's being here is not good for you," Roberts said, dropping his hand. "He is becoming an obsession. I will never stop wanting the best for you, fighting for that, even against you if I must."

May knew he had meant it to be reassuring, but it made her afraid. The last thing she needed was Robert prying into the affair.

Chapter 11

Sometimes, Sophie thought as she labored over her sewing, being respectable meant doing some awfully boring things. Lady May, whose hand worked swiftly at her square of linen, was amazingly adept at needlework.

"Ouch!" she exclaimed, putting her finger to her lips. She'd stuck it again.

May chuckled. "Patience. Keep your eyes on what you are doing."

"I did not know you liked sewing."

"It helps me think," May said. She held her head at an angle so that she looked down through the spectacles she used for close work. "I've no talent for it, but it keeps me from madness when my nerves are riled."

"But you do a fine job. Why, look at your handkerchief. The roses are all exactly right." Sophie held up the tangle of thread woven into hers. "Mine is an absolute disaster. Of course, I've never sewn before. My mother had no interest or knowledge of it."

May's needle paused, and she gave Sophie a close look. "Your mother was of a different sort."

Sophie could not keep the tightness from her mouth. "Yes. Indeed."

"That was meant as a compliment, Sophie," May said with quiet force.

Looking down at her sewing, Sophie replied stiffly, her tone making no mistake of her feelings. "My mother was an actress."

May's face registered surprise, and not pleasantly. "But your mother is to be envied. She led such an interesting life. She was on the stage. Imagine." She said this with such admiration that Sophie was taken aback. "She had talent, and that is always to be admired. To create something, as a character in a play, or what you do in your wonderful sketches, it is something very special."

"It is thought a tawdry profession."

"And yet we trot off every season to be entertained by thespians. A stage actress has each and every man in the audience in her thrall. They project a heady spell over an entire audience. I am sure poor Wooly was quite besotted. I wish I knew more about his romance with your mother. Do you know anything?"

"Mother never spoke of such things."

Sensing Sophie's mood, May clucked. "Sophie, I suspect there were some who were not kind to you because of the life your mother led, but if you allow it to sour you, then you are only giving them the means to succeed in making your life miserable."

Sophie's needle missed and she pricked her finger. Setting her jaw, she attacked her square of linen, frowning with concentration. She was determined to master this.

Sighing, May said, "That brings me to mind of Gideon. How the injustices done to him in his life have turned him."

"You mean Reginald Hayworth?"

"Yes, Reginald." A strange look came over May's face. "And other things. It was difficult for him to lose his brother. They loved each other very much."

"And you. He loved you. He still does."

"Does he?" She sounded troubled. Pausing for a moment, she seemed to forget what to do with the needle. "I hope there still is affection there. It makes me so sad, So- phie, that Gideon is not in fashion with the ton. He's ca- vorted openly with men's wives, dueled . . ." She shook her head sadly. "It is such a waste, and so wrong for him. Gideon is unhappy, I know it. And soon, he will leave me, and I fear he will return to his feckless diversions, and I will lose him forever."

Sophie felt a bump, a single, powerful bang of a heart- beat against her ribcage. "Did he say that he plans to go soon?"

May tried to shrug, but her brow knitted into a frown and it was not so much a gesture of dismissal as one of de- feat. "It is inevitable. I know that when he is well enough, he will not hesitate."

Gideon leaving. Well, of course, he would not be here forever. Sophie had known that.

A slow frission of panic began to quake inside her. She couldn't imagine losing the hours with him.

"He is coming down for luncheon. I've asked Adrian and Michaela, as it is something of a celebration, being Gideon's first meal taken outside of his room. I think I will plan something very special for Cook to prepare." May rose and took a moment to stretch.

May came to peer over Sophie's shoulder. Her eyes widened. "Goodness, Sophie." She held up the mauled linen. Stitches were placed in a haphazard pattern despite Sophie's best efforts to emulate May's meticulous instruc- tion. "Oh, dear. Perhaps you should stay with sketching."

When Sophie gave a quick knock, then entered Gideon's room, she caught him in mid-stride, as if he'd been pacing.

With the eye patch on, more of his face was exposed. She'd grown used to that, but today he'd combed his hair differently in the absence of most of the bandages he had worn since the accident.

He was different. Less of an invalid, a man nearly re- stored.

"I told the maid to give my regrets." He stalked to the

hearth and crossed his arms over his chest. "I am not inclined to join the family today."

"I would have thought you would be looking forward to taking advantage of your new freedom. Lady May even planned a surprise for the meal."

The wariness did not leave him. "I do not like surprises, generally."

"You will like this one. It is lamb. With mint jelly. She said it used to be your favorite."

He turned away, a signal that he was unmoved.

She asked, "Is it because Major and Mrs. Khoury are to be here?"

He scowled, and at that moment he looked like a recalcitrant little boy. "I look like a Corsair," he said, touching the eye patch.

"It is quite dashing, you know."

He did not look pleased. Muttering something under his breath he avoided her gaze.

It touched her that he was so self-conscious—he, the brash, devil-may-care rogue. He was much less of a blackguard at heart than his reputation would allow.

She approached him and reached out. He stiffened, then allowed her to lift the patch. He didn't flinch as she inspected the skin underneath, but she saw he wanted to push her away.

"Why are you wearing this? The eye was not damaged. You said your vision is fine. The scars are healing."

He pointed jerkily in the direction of his brow. "The physician suggested it. As it heals . . . Do you not think it will repel people?"

"Not any of the people who would be received into this house. May would never stand for that."

"Are they to be given a list of rules when they enter the house: Do not stare, do not gasp, do not faint?"

"You are making much more out of it than it warrants," she told him emphatically. "You have to come out in public sometime, and this is a good way to ease the transition. Come, it is not so bad."

"I have a mirror. I can see for myself."

"Then you know that it will hardly send small children running in fright from the sight of you."

He shook his head. "You are cruel in the extreme. You make a mockery of me when I am hideously deformed."

"That is not from the scarring, dear Gideon," she said with polite sweetness.

He stared at her, shocked, then broke out in laughter. "Lord, you will give me no shelter."

"I shall. I will assure you that it will heal," she said more soothingly. She pushed aside a lock of hair. "And in the meantime, you should enjoy the mysterious bent this patch lends you. Why, you could be a pirate, and, after all, pirates are quite appealing. All you need is a gold ring through your ear."

His fingers closed over her wrist. They were strong, surprising her. She felt a thrill go up her arm. "I will not play for pity this time," he said hoarsely. He removed her hand and released it.

Why had she done that? She could not seem to stop herself from touching him.

She straightened. "Then you will receive practicality. Now, come."

He stepped away. "All right then, pitiless angel. Tell me how I go about walking out of this room when I know everyone who looks at me is going to see this." He indicated the patch. "And the worst part of it is, they will think to themselves that it is justice."

"You just do." She ushered him out of the door. She cast him a quizzing glance. "Justice?"

He scowled. "The stupid pan was too full," he mumbled as they descended the stairs. "I should not have left that to Farnsworth. He had been drinking. Ah, but we all had. It was not his fault. My own stupidity. That is what they will say when they see my mauled face. And they will be right. So tell me, what do I do with that?"

She paused, and as she was on the step in front of him, he was forced to stop as well. "You have to hold your head up, stare them straight in the eye, and *dare* them to snub you."

"Ah. My very own words used against me. Very good." He inclined his head. She felt the tension leaving him. "You are too clever by far. I shall follow my own advice. I shall simply brazen it out. To hell with their distaste."

"Indeed, when have you cared for other's opinions?"

"I am slipping. I am out of practice, being too long under the care of your tender ministrations."

"Tender? I rather thought I was hard on you at times."

He seemed to be having a private joke, for he tried to hide a smile. "You could not do so if you tried."

"I shall have to apply myself more assiduously to the task."

That made him laugh, too. "You are good for me," he said quietly. "You chase all the shadows away. All right then, I will come down. I suppose I must face the curious sooner or later. Come with me to the drawing room. We'll shock them all. Beauty and the beast."

She fell into step beside him. "They are lovely people, you know. Nothing to fear."

"You would think so, them being your family."

She covered the fluster she could not quite control. She had to stop reacting when May's relations were regarded as her own. She must have a care, for she would give herself away. Gideon saw far too much. "And yours. May still regards herself as your sister."

His jaw set in a hard line. "And Lord Marcus Roberts— is that his name? I don't know if I like him. He has such a keen look in his eye."

"Afraid he will see into your black soul?"

He paused, and gave her a lazy look. She didn't even notice the scars. His face was mobile, pleasant. One tended to look at his mouth, the way it moved and flexed with each expression.

"If he could see into my mind, dear Sophie, I guarantee I would have been tossed out of here a long time ago." He spoke in that enigmatic way so that she did not know if he were serious or teasing. "I am wicked, you know. It's all over Town."

"You are not wicked," she said sensibly. "You just like to pretend you are. I wonder why."

He grinned and nodded. "Perhaps some day I will tell you."

They continued down the steps. She reflected that these unexpected flashes of flirtation never repelled her as other men's had. Sometimes he amused her, sometimes he surprised her into breathless shock. But she enjoyed it either way.

He hesitated outside the parlor door. Voices could be heard from inside.

Giving her a doubtful glance, he warned, "If Mrs. Khoury flees in terror, I will be put out with you."

She patted his hand. "Michaela is not the fleeing type. However, if she lets out an involuntary scream when she sees your hideous disfigurations, then surely she will desist eventually, so just be patient. Ah, lucky for us there are two men on hand who can carry her away until she can collect herself."

He pursed his lips thoughtfully. "I just realized something."

"What is that?"

He turned toward the door and squared his shoulders. "You are a great deal more wicked than I." Expelling a long, loud breath, he said, "Let us go in, then."

Chapter 12

When Gideon entered, Michaela cut off in mid-sentence. She smiled, extending her hand. "Lord Ashford," she said, "I have been looking forward so much to meeting you at last."

She smiled warmly as he took her hand and bowed over it, issuing an effortless compliment that made Michaela blush becomingly.

Two men sat apart from the women, hunched over a chess board. Major Khoury looked up at the sound of his wife's voice. Lord Roberts rose to come stand behind May, his hands resting lightly on her shoulders.

May reached out her hand to him and Gideon went to her next. "Oh, Gideon. You look wonderful." Her eyes shone, her face full of beaming pleasure. "Just wonderful, doesn't he, Robert? We've been awaiting you. Come. Sit here with Michaela and me. I have been so anxious for you to meet everyone."

Sophie beamed at her. How did she always know the right thing to say? It amazed her how goodness just seemed to flow out of May, and Sophie felt a pang of pride and softness, and realized that she loved her.

It was a good feeling, so she would not dwell on the fact

that she had no right to have any attachment to her. She could ponder her sins at her leisure, but for now she would allow herself the luxury of enjoying this company of people she had come to care for very much.

She had to admire Gideon as well. He was so smooth, slipping into urbane tones and charm of such sincerity it was impossible to resist. He bestowed his attention on Michaela, using that singular way he had of staring at you until you wanted to shout out your confession, and Michaela was utterly pleased with him.

Admiration and exasperation mingled as Sophie observed him. Jealousy? Oh, just a dash.

It was Michaela who said what needed to be said. "You seem to be healing well, my lord. I trust your wounds are no longer troubling."

There. The subject of his injury had been brought up, and in the gentlest way. Michaela could not have found a more compassionate and tactful manner of getting the matter dealt with.

Sophie found she was waiting for Gideon's reaction. He hesitated only a second or two, then shrugged and smiled. "They get better every day."

The men resumed their seats and took up their game. May selected a pile of drawings made on thick paper and handed them to Sophie. "I was just telling Michaela that I am in the worst possible predicament. Will you just look at these fashion plates?"

Sophie obligingly flipped through a stack of sketches as May shook her head. "I usually adore all of Madam Bonvant's designs, but these are so unlike the styles I prefer. She *knows* that."

Michaela put down her cup and sat forward. "Let me see." Taking the sketches, she frowned. "I think Madam Bonvant will tell you, 'Zee fashion, zey change, *oui?* We must go along or we will be seen as gauche.'" She handed the pages to Lady May, who chuckled at the expert impression of the modiste.

Sophie held her hand out. "May I see them again?"

May passed them to her. "And she knows pink is my trademark. Now, I do not expect to be decked as a confection, but none of these designs are soft enough for that touch, that *look* that is distinctly me. I detest this empire waist. It is a hideous silhouette for someone of my height, but I can hardly order a fitted bodice."

Roberts cleared his throat, angling an amused glance at the ladies as the major frowned in concentration, studying his next move. Sophie glanced at Gideon. He observed everything, his eyes darting from person to person as he reclined in a rather dashingly tranquil pose.

"I am meeting with her tomorrow to tell her what to do, but I do not think she will listen. She is rather opinionated."

A snorting sound came from the chess table. Lady May shot Lord Roberts an arch look. "Did you say something, my lord?"

"Nothing, my lady. I merely heard your characterization of another as opinionated, and it struck me as irony."

"Rather the pot calling the kettle . . ." Major Khoury murmured.

Roberts waved his hand at the women. "Carry on."

Sophie sent for her sketch pad and pencils. When they arrived, she opened the book to a fresh page. "Let me see those," she said.

May handed her the plates. "I need some fitting up top, dear. And not so blousy coming from under the . . . um, *bosom*." She whispered this last with a sly look at Gideon. He obligingly gave her a wink.

Sophie's hand worked swiftly, drawing a quick silhouette of a dress. "Like this?"

May peered at it. "Why, yes. That is more like it."

Sophie added a few strokes to suggest feathers at the bodice. May laughed. "What a clever girl. May I take this to my appointment tomorrow, Sophie? At least it will give me something with which to illustrate to Madam Bonvant what I am talking about."

"May I see your sketchbook?" Michaela asked.

Sophie hesitated. She had not meant to make a spectacle of her drawing, but she had never been bashful about it. She handed the book to Michaela.

"Naturally, you would have artistic talent," said May, leaning forward to peer at the book. "That sort of thing goes through generations. We Ellinsworths have no ability in the arts. We appreciate them, of course—perhaps more for the wonder of seeing someone do something so grand and, for us, impossible."

Sophie put the pencil back in her tin box. Her father had been an artist, giving instruction to several young ladies as a means of employment. His affair with her mother had ended when she was three and she never saw him again, but Mama had not minded when she asked about him and had often noted how she took after him in so many things.

"I quite agree," Michaela said. "These are wonderful. You really have an eye."

Sophie flushed and thanked her. A surreptitious glance at Gideon won her a smile.

"Come and have some tea, gentlemen," Michaela called. "Aunt May said luncheon will be served within the hour."

The major rubbed his chin. "In a moment. I am about to vanquish Lord Roberts."

Roberts chuckled. "You best take the break now, Khoury. If you think to hold tea until after you've bested me, it will most assuredly be cold."

The major, whose intense concentration now belied Sophie's earlier impression of him as an easy-natured man, appeared startled. He studied the board all the harder.

Sophie could feel Gideon's eyes still on her. He watched her with an intensity that made her glow.

How different everything was with him here. She'd enjoyed Michaela and Major Khoury's company many times, but today held a special happiness, as if something had been missing and was now complete.

Lord Roberts came to sit with the women and a nervous Major Khoury followed. Michaela shook her head in amused exasperation. "Really, Adrian, you are taking this all too seriously."

"It is war," he replied. "Chess is a war game."

Now Sophie understood his intense concentration on the game. His pride was on the line.

Roberts removed his spectacles and rubbed the red marks on the bridge of his nose. "It is not war. It is art. It is strategy."

"But Adrian was known as a tactical genius," May reminded him. "Strategy is his forte."

"It is only a game!" Michaela declared. "Aunt May, tell them."

"Tell men not to take their competitions seriously? Impossible. Sophie, you talk some sense into them. You possess such a practical mind."

"I daresay I am hard put to think of anything, Lady May." Sophie grinned. "They seem quite determined."

Lord Roberts was amused at the ladies' teasing. Adrian Khoury managed to look a bit sheepish, and Sophie expected he had been on the receiving end of a hot look from his wife.

Gideon put his cup aside and stood. "May, if I might, I would like very much to take a turn in your garden, if it is private."

"Very private, Gideon."

He turned to Sophie. "Will you accompany me? I have not been out of doors for so long, and it is a beautiful day."

She accepted and dispatched a parlor maid to fetch her shawl and hat. When she was ready, they exited through the library door and walked down a flagstone path to a tiny garden laid out with precision.

"Well, was that so difficult?" she asked.

"Don't gloat, Sophie," he said pleasantly. "You know it was not trying."

She chuckled. "Very well, we shall have a more neutral conversation. Do you prefer formal gardens or a more natural design?"

The air was thick with moisture from an earlier rain.

Overhead, the clouds were being chased away by a steady wind.

"I prefer gardens with convenient nooks to retire to when one wishes to have a private moment with a woman."

She sighed. "You do not attend balls, so why do you care if the gardens afford opportunity for debauchery?"

"Kisses are not debauchery, Sophie." His glance was enigmatic. "Is that what you were raised to believe?"

She flushed hotly and hoped he didn't see it. "Public displays of things that are meant to be private are not good manners. That was what I meant."

"I agree. Hence my partiality for garden nooks." He managed to look triumphant without a trace of smugness.

A wild wisp of discontent flittered across her thoughts. She would not mind at all if he pulled her into a nook. She shivered at the idea. "You take such pride in being rogue."

He was the one who paused this time. "What gave you the impression I was proud of that?"

"You all but brag."

"You mistake me. I only endeavor to be honest."

She faced him. "Why is it so important for you to be honest? It does not trouble most people as much as it seems to do you."

"One reason is that it is one of my few virtues. A man must believe himself to possess at least some in order to live with himself. And two . . ."

"Two," she prodded.

"I abhor liars," he said.

She knew, of course, that he could not suspect that she was herself a most grievous deceiver, but the comment struck so close to home, it was difficult not to wonder if he did.

He turned and proceeded up the path. Sophie followed.

She could not disagree with anything he had said. It was the ultimate insult to lie as she was doing. But did he not understand that sometimes, it was necessary? Wasn't it like stealing—not as wrong if it came from need and not greed? When you are starving, is taking a loaf of bread a crime?

"Truth is not absolute," she said, and was somewhat startled to find she wanted to confront him.

"How can you argue this is so?"

Her conviction grew. "Because sometimes, people have secrets for good reason. And sometimes, we are not qualified to judge those reasons simply on the absolute measure of truth or lie. A person's heart must be their own judge."

He walked thoughtfully for a few moments. "Do you deny that lies hurt?"

"So does truth sometimes," she replied softly, and that won her silence for a short space as they took in the garden at a slow pace.

"You are a strange, fascinating creature, Sophie Kent," he mused. "I like the way you challenge me. It makes me think. I don't believe any other woman I've met has pushed and pulled at my intellect the way you have."

She smiled, warmed by the generous compliment. His eyes shone as he stared at her. "Did I mention that you look especially lovely today? That dress is very charming. The color makes your eyes look so very bright. And that prim décolletage does wonders to draw attention from the grotesque length of your neck."

She gasped and laughed, her mouth open in amused shock. He wagged his finger at her. "I did owe you that. You were quite cruel to me earlier."

She shook her head and rolled her eyes as he chuckled.

When they arrived at the folly, Sophie agreed to sit. She found herself quite contented as the mild air ruffled the grass and lifted earthy scents.

"It is good to see the sun," he murmured.

"This is a beautiful garden. Lady May has such flair. I do not know how she can say the Ellinsworths have no talents. She has great fashion sense and putting together décor is so second nature to her, she does not see it for the wonder it is."

He nodded. "I remember when she came to Ashford

Manor. Matthew was proud as a peacock of his new bride, and she swept into that place and transformed it. Within a year, it was almost unrecognizable, and alive with activity. The rooms were always buzzing with conversation with friends calling all the time. Then . . . I do not remember why, but it changed." He broke off with a grimace and readdressed himself to Sophie. "I noticed you do not call her 'aunt,' as Michaela does."

She blinked, taken off guard by this abrupt change of topic. "She has had more practice. She was reunited with May several years ago. A thing like that takes time."

"You had a happy family, I assume. A family of women—aunts. Perhaps you miss them and it feels wrong somehow to look upon May as your family now."

If he only knew how close he was to the truth, though not for the reasons he surmised. She had to fight not to think upon May as her family, not because she didn't want to, but because she didn't deserve to.

They rose and circled around the folly, wishing to enjoy more of the soft spring day.

"Why did you want me to come outside with you?" she asked him.

"Because there is no one else I would rather spend time with than you."

She angled a look at him. "Were you at ease in the drawing room?"

"Everyone was very polite," he replied.

"I think it went splendidly, and, indeed, Michaela did not scream, not even gasp."

He made a face, shaking his head. "Wicked, wicked, wicked."

"But that did not end your nerves."

He gave her a look, apparently insulted.

"Everyone was taking part in the conversation but you," she supplied. "It was quite obvious."

"Drawing room conversation is something I am not used to," he answered quietly. "That sort of thing with the chess, the dress sketches, the easy chit-chat. I was never good at it."

"I suppose it all seems very boring to you."

"Boring?" He was genuinely surprised. "It could not be more so. It is so real, so ordinary, so *comfortable,* that it seems the most exotic thing I've seen in many years. It reminds me of times I'd almost forgotten." He studied the sky, but his gaze was farther away than the clouds.

"Of Ashford Manor?" she ventured.

He nodded. "It is family. I have not had one for a long time." He shrugged, and his mood lightened with an effort. "I suppose I should try to do better to be sociable. I do not wish them to think me aloof. Bored? Really, that is what you thought was wrong? I suppose I've led my bachelor life too long, done what I wanted, when I wanted. I can be moody."

"No," she said with false surprise. "Moody? You, Lord Ashford? I've never seen evidence of such a thing."

"Indeed," he replied smoothly, as if he did not pick up on her facetiousness. He rose and so did she. "It is sadly so. I suppose I am going to have to be . . ." He paused and rolled his eyes. "Cheerful."

She laughed at him. "You can be charming. I know you have such skill. You have even told me so on numerous occasions. And as you *always* tell the truth . . ."

He laughed, pulling her hand through his bent arm. Her body was close to his, close enough that she felt the warmth along her side. Her fingers touched the new skin knitted over his burns. She pulled away, but he said, "It does not hurt. Your touch is soothing."

So she let her hand rest where it was as they went back inside.

❦ *Chapter 13*

After luncheon, the post arrived. May was excited to find a letter from her niece, Trista. May and Michaela hurried to a settee to read it together.

"She writes about the baby," May gushed. "Trista says the little angel is awake every two hours and wailing to rouse the dead."

"But she doesn't mind," Michaela said, a bit wistfully. Sophie noticed the sadness in her smile, and thought perhaps she longed for a child. She and the major had been married for a few years and had not yet produced a baby.

May scanned the letter anxiously. "Andrew is doing well. He is so happy in his new home. Oh . . ." She sniffed as she read silently, then clapped her hands. "She says that Andrew and Roman and Roman's sister, Grace, took a short overnight visit to see an old aunt, and that they all had a marvelous time."

She exchanged a happy glance with Michaela. "I told her that Andrew would adore his papa in time."

Sophie had never gotten the full story, but she surmised that Trista and Roman had had a love affair, which produced their son. Some circumstances had parted them.

Then, shortly after Trista had been found by May and brought into the upper echelon of London society, Trista and Roman met again and eventually married.

They read the letter several times, then May passed it to Lord Roberts, who had returned with Major Khoury to their chess game immediately upon returning to the drawing room.

Sophie noticed Gideon had pulled up a chair to the chess board. He was reclined in it as he watched the play, his forefinger tapping on his top lip. He made a quiet observation to Major Khoury, who murmured something back. They began to point at the pieces.

Lady May sighed as she finally laid down the letter. "I adore correspondence. When a letter arrives from a friend, it is like getting a small present. If you will excuse me, I am going to write her back right away while everything is fresh in my mind." She went to her desk and opened the drawer.

"Must you do that now?" Roberts called after taking a bishop with his knight. "I am almost finished trouncing the major and am coming to join you. Do leave that. Enjoy your company now."

"Oh, you are right," May said. "I just get so excited. I miss Trista, of course, but I want to see that baby! And Andrew, my little love. It makes me miserable not to see him. Oh, look. I'd almost forgotten these."

As she opened the drawer to place the letter from Trista inside, she pulled out a packet of letters, old ones judging from the yellowing parchment. They were tied with a red satin bow.

"I meant to go through these for you, Sophie. I came across them in your father's things and brought them down here to look at them more carefully. The dates seem to be around the time he was courting your mother. I think he mentions Millicent Kent, and I thought some of them could actually be letters from her. It occurred to me that you might wish to read them. I promise, I will get to it immediately and give you anything pertaining to your mother."

Letters. Sophie froze, not knowing what to say. She had no voice as her mind flew over a sudden groundswell of worries.

Letters from Aunt Millie . . . What could they say that would incriminate her—was there anything?

"Sophie?"

She jumped. "Oh. Yes. That would be wonderful."

"Look how happy she is, May," Gideon drawled. He had stood and moved now to stand at May's desk. "Imagine, letters from your mother to your father, Sophie."

He was so damnably observant. It was impossible that he would know anything. But she had spent so much time with him, debated, fended off all of his probing questions and close observances . . . Was there something she had said in one of their many extraordinary conversations that had given her away?

"Yes, imagine," was all she could manage.

From the table where the men sat, Major Khoury made his move. "Checkmate."

Lord Roberts's mouth dropped open. He stayed seated, staring incredulously at the board where his king did indeed sit in mortal jeopardy.

Gideon rubbed his chin, catching Roberts's eye. "Sometimes one does not see it coming."

He glanced at Sophie, and in her sensitive state, she wondered if that were a warning.

But Gideon seemed immediately distracted, idly moving pieces to set up the board again, and she thought that she was being foolish. She was not quite rational when it came to her twisted conscience, so she had probably imagined the entendre.

Khoury rose and stretched, saying, "Come, Ashford. I'll take you on."

May welcomed a disgruntled Lord Roberts onto the settee with a comforting pat on his thigh. "You will best him next time, darling," May whispered consolingly.

Lord Roberts grunted, then shrugged. "I was distracted," he complained, and May bit the inside of her cheeks to keep from smiling.

"Good God!" Major Khoury exclaimed from behind them. "What kind of opening gambit is that, Ashford? Reckless, reckless!"

Lord Roberts rushed to see this wonder of chessplaying strategy, bending over the board with his brows furrowed.

"That is either brilliant," Roberts pronounced admiringly, "or the stupidest play I've ever witnessed."

Gideon smiled, looking crafty. "I suppose we shall see. In approximately eight moves."

"Or less!" Major Khoury growled, hunkering down on his elbows with murder in his eyes.

The women began to laugh and the men were bewildered at what in the world was so amusing. And the matter of the letters was forgotten.

*At breakfast the next day, Lady May was dressed for rid-*ing in the park. Lord Roberts was to bring round his carriage.

"Are you certain you do not wish to come with us?" she asked Gideon, hope detectable in her eyes.

"Another time," he replied. His hand itched to reach up and touch his eye patch. He hated the thing. He thought he must look absurd, like some Bluebeard.

"But you love the park. You used to ride the Row."

"Yes. But . . . not today."

Sophie said, "I think I will stay behind as well."

"Your poor admirers will be disappointed," he said.

It was getting harder and harder to be with Sophie. He wanted her, but he could not have her. She wanted marriage, a husband, respectability, and he wanted sex.

No, not just sex. He already saw that was not possible. She was different from his other women. One time would not be enough. He wanted to make love to her, many different ways, in many different moods.

He would think of these sometimes, putting himself through such delicious torment until he thought he would scream in frustration.

When Lord Roberts pulled up in a handsome brougham, Lady May placed her hat on her head and hurried outside.

"I know you wanted to go," Sophie said.

"I'd rather stay here with you."

That pleased her. She was so easy to read. But she was uncomfortable, too. And he wondered why he said such things to her. He couldn't seem to make up his mind what to do with her. He flirted with her because he couldn't help himself. It was a valve, taking some of the pressure of his mounting desire away. He would not seduce her. If he did—whether she succumbed to him or not—he would lose her.

He had to learn to be contented with friendship. But that was becoming more and more difficult.

"It is a shame to be inside when the weather is so favorable. I have an idea," she said, and went to speak to the housekeeper. She returned and told him they were going to spend the morning outside, in the garden folly.

The day was overcast, the kind of clouds that might spit some rain now and then but did not threaten a downpour. Sophie pronounced it safe enough and they sat under the shelter of the classical structure.

They talked idly. A hamper was brought out to them, containing food and freshly brewed tea. Sophie announced cheerfully that they were to have a picnic.

She brought her sketchbook and began to do some landscapes. Inevitably, she turned to him.

"No," he said before she could ask. "Draw something else for a change."

She made a disgruntled face. "You are becoming a grouch."

"You should have gone with Lady May and Lord Roberts today."

"I just thought we had not had a chance of late—"

"I am not an invalid any longer. I am not desperate for companionship."

Oh, but he was. Desperate for every moment she spared, but he did not wish her to know.

She laid down her pencil. "Have I become a nuisance?"

"No," he said, refusing to be caught in that ploy. "But your friendship with me must not interfere with having fun."

She wrinkled her nose. "Having fun." She sighed. "I am afraid that is not the case. I keep forgetting not to walk too fast, to smile in that way that makes me look intelligent but not too much so, to laugh softly, to remove gloves at this time, keep them on at another . . ."

"Dear, dear, what a terrible burden."

"Do not laugh! And I am a horrible dancer. I can never remember the steps. During the quadrille, I begin to do a promenade when I should be crossing over."

"Sophie," he said, "it will get easier."

"That is what May says. She is kind. I like her friends, but so many parties! I am afraid I am a recluse at heart."

He should not like to hear this as much as he did. Dare he think for a moment it was his company that drew her home?

He almost laughed at his own conceit. She was a young woman from a different world suddenly thrust into the highest circles of polite society. It had nothing to do with him that she was overwhelmed and sometimes wished to take quiet times to gather her energies before venturing again into the demanding world of the bon ton.

"You will be a great force in society once you find your sea legs," he told her. "Already you are all the rage, at least according to May. 'The Beauty of Bond Street.' That is what they call you, you know. I have never seen her glow so well with pride."

She blushed, feeling more ashamed than she wished to allow. "It is because May is forever taking me shopping. I keep telling her that I need nothing. I already have more than I can ever use."

In fact, Sophie hated shopping. Nothing grated her prickled conscience more than to have May spend large amounts of money on her.

That was when she felt most like a horrid cheat. The first time she'd walked down Bond Street with Lady May, she had harkened back to the times she had strolled those shops with her aunts.

"Hold your head high, Sophie dear," Aunt Millicent had said, her voice projecting as if she were still on stage. "You are just as good as they are."

But the stares of the people around her had told her she was not, at least not in their eyes. Their lips curled, their eyes narrowed, beaded, held her in contempt as she strode along with her aunts with their eccentric clothing and boisterous manners.

And though strolling with May she was given the greatest of courtesies, it still felt no different, not when she felt the interloper.

Well, after all, she was. A fraud . . . God, would her conscience ever abate?

"It makes her happy," he said. "May enjoys giving. It is her nature."

"You admire her a great deal."

Gideon shrugged. "There is much to admire," he told her. "And as you recently reminded me, she is family. All the family I have left."

He rose, brushing aside these bruising thoughts. The day was too glorious for such deep musing. "As for the dancing," he said, holding his hand out to her. "Let me show you."

"Here?"

"Come. I happen to be an excellent dancer."

"You are joking."

"Indeed, I am not." He grabbed her hand and pulled. She scrambled to her feet, laughing.

She collected herself, fluffing her skirts as he bowed to her. She groaned.

"The music begins . . ." He began to hum and took the first steps of the quadrille.

She did not move. "This is impossible."

"Go to your left. Point your toe. There. Come, you know it."

"I feel ridiculous."

He ignored her, humming as he guided her through the steps of the dance.

She obeyed his lead, studying her feet as they moved in the patterns. He shook his head. "Look at me, not down. Glide. Act as if it is effortless."

"But I have to think about everything I am doing. I had no dance master as a girl."

"I am your dance master. This way, now."

She fell into a fit of giggles when she misread his lead and they collided.

"You are right," he told her solemnly, leading her forcefully in the correct direction. "You are atrocious at dance."

"I told you so."

"Do not think so much." He turned his back to her, executing the next portion as if they had switched partners. "Just let the dance move you."

"It will move me to my seat," she said, flouncing down into a chair.

"Giving up?" he teased.

"I am a failure, and I admit it."

"Never." He yanked her to her feet again, this time more forcefully, and she careened directly into his arms. It was a neat, well-executed maneuver.

Her smell was a blend of scents, a potent concoction that bled the strength from his knees. She laughed in his arms and he laughed, too, the sound of their voices mingling pleasantly.

His arms moved around her. The need to have her close erased all reason. His body shook and he clung to the fading powers of thought.

The look on her face was rapt, her eyes alight, and he

could talk himself into an unspoken invitation written there, releasing him from the bond of his word.

He could justify it. He did not even have to try that hard.

His hand moved, and he felt the delicate curve of her back. His body pulsed with sudden awareness, painful in its intensity, as he put the slightest of pressure there to shift her hips forward.

Her thighs settled nicely against his arousal, and he saw the moment she registered the pressure by the way her eyes flared, her mouth dropped open. His blood rushed through his veins, leaving him light-headed.

She still watched him. Her breasts rose and fell with her rapid breathing. She would not object if he kissed her. She wanted him to, he knew it.

The stupid girl should flee. Didn't she have any sense?

Crooking his forefinger, he touched the back of the knuckle to the trembling swell of her breast. She did not balk, did not back away.

Her skin was on fire. He only meant to indulge in this one tiny little transgression, but he moved his hand so that all four fingers lay against that tantalizing glimpse of flesh. His palm up, he moved his hand down, stroking with the back of his fingers. To the neckline of her dress.

Her eyelids drifted closed, an invitation. Surely an invitation. *Permission.*

He dropped his hand. His chest crushed hers, and he could feel her breasts thrusting against his rib cage. He moved his mouth to cover hers.

He stopped. With his breath tearing in and out of him, he stopped somehow.

He'd said he would not kiss her again. He'd *promised.* And that meant something.

Besides, she wasn't for him. She was pure, was Sophie, and what could he do but taint her? She was for the likes of Burton, her polished good friend who knew his way around a drawing room and could squire her to any soiree in the Town.

And he was a rogue, poison to a respectable woman, but he did have his pride.

Barely.

She waited, and he thought maybe his pride was not worth it.

A rustle on the walk drew their attention. It was a maid from the house, standing at the foot of the folly steps and appearing quite uncomfortable. "Ah, Miss Kent, Lord Burton is waiting in the drawing room."

Sophie went still. She did not move out of his arms.

Gideon felt his throat close, making breathing suddenly difficult. Perhaps it was a sign, significant that it was Lord Burton waiting for Sophie. Had he not just thought that it was with the distinguished lord that Sophie belonged?

It was he who stepped away from Sophie, he who told the maid that Miss Kent would be in momentarily.

"Go on, Sophie. I know Lord Burton is a favorite of yours."

"Indeed, he is." She seemed rather confused, disoriented. He understood the feeling. "He is a fine gentleman."

She sounded rote, her voice holding no enthusiasm.

He tried to smile, but the corners of his mouth refused to turn up.

Suddenly, she started, "I cannot entertain Lord Burton. May is not in. I have no chaperone." She looked at him, as if he might rescue her. "Will you come and meet him this time? I think you would like him."

But it was beyond him. To watch her sit while a dandy paid her court was too much to ask. "Keep the door to the hall open. It should serve until May returns. I believe that will be shortly." He could not resist touching her cheek. It was smooth, like cream kissed with a hint of rosy blush.

He watched her as she composed herself, then entered

the house, glancing back at him once. He made a shoo-ing motion with his hand and smiled encouragingly, but the moment she was inside the house, his smile died quickly.

Chapter 14

"Lord Burton, what a lovely surprise," Sophie said. She thought of what Lady May would do, and tried her best to emulate it. She allowed him to bow over her hand.

He looked dashing today, yet unlike her friend Margaux, her heart did not skip a single beat at his pleasing appearance. She made an effort to be welcoming, for a trace of her reluctance might come through if she were not careful. She did enjoy Burton's company usually, but his arrival today had been . . . most inconvenient.

"Miss Kent. How good of you to see me. I hope I have not interrupted."

"Not at all," she lied, smiling her Lady May smile. "I was out in the garden, taking the air."

"I could have joined you," he said as they took their seats.

"No!" Sophie exclaimed. "No, I mean, I was coming in when it was announced you had come to call. See? Perfect timing."

He gave her a doubtful look, then shrugged it off. "I am on my way to a lecture at the Society for Oriental Studies, and thought I would ask you if you would care to join me.

I apologize for the late notice, but it only occurred to me that it might be a pleasant diversion."

"Oh, thank you. How thoughtful. Unfortunately, we have an engagement this evening for dinner."

"Ah, of course. I should have known. Your social calendar cannot allow for such whims."

"Oh, come now. I often can, and I would enjoy an outing very much at another time."

The maid came in with refreshments, and they sat back cozily. "Marie," Sophie called as the maid took away the tray, "leave the door open, please."

Marie nodded and made her exit. "So tell me what is so fascinating at the Society for Oriental Studies today."

"A lecture on the new Indian imports funded by the Prince Regent. He is building his folly out in Brighton, and the antiquities he sponsors are rarities that have inspired a rash of interest in Indian and Chinese artifacts." He stopped short and laughed. "Lord, I am a dullard when I get going. Forgive me for boring you."

"What? I will have you know I am quite acquainted with the wonders of the Marine Pavillion and all of its marvels. I even know a thing or two about the Egyptian treasures Napoleon collected."

His eyes lit brightly. "Do you indeed. Why, Miss Kent, this is intensely surprising."

"Allow me to clarify, my lord. It is not my interest, but rather the vivacious enthusiasm of my friend Miss Milton. She talks often of the latest scientific discoveries, and she makes it so fascinating that it has intrigued me." She paused, sipping her lemonade coyly. "Perhaps you will see her at the lecture. It is my understanding that she often drags her maid to clandestine adventures away from the disapproving knowledge of her mother."

"But why should Lady Milton disapprove? It is a singular and fascinating course of study."

"She thinks it unfeminine."

"But nothing could be more so, a woman with a mind

for knowledge and an appreciation for the aesthetic wonders of these ancients."

Hiding her self-satisfied smile as she took another sip, Sophie murmured, "I am glad to hear that you think so, Lord Burton."

When May arrived home to find a visitor sitting with Sophie in her drawing room, she did not hide her surprise.

"I hope you do not mind," Sophie said, rising to speak privately to May as she took off her cloak, hat, and gloves. "Gideon said it would be all right for me to play hostess until you arrived home."

"He did?" She paused, giving Sophie a startled look. "He did not object?"

"No. He was actually quite charming about it."

May seemed perplexed. She swept toward their guest, leaving Sophie to follow.

Out of the corner of her eye, Sophie thought she saw a shadow. But when she turned, there was nothing. She could not escape the feeling that someone had been there. And that the someone had been Gideon.

He'd been watching over her, she thought, retiring after May returned to act as chaperone.

She felt a flood of emotions. Guilt and pleasure and sadness.

How she wanted to go to him. Instead, she took her seat next to Burton. Her urge for the respectable, secure life she'd always coveted was now fully at war with the dark, exciting feelings Gideon elicited.

However, Burton was a pleasant guest. With May present, the two younger people could relax and enjoy conversation. Burton was urbane, with a dry wit and an uncanny ability to express his observances in an amusing manner.

The visit passed quickly, and Sophie realized that she liked the gentleman very much. She might even marry him if he asked. He'd make an excellent husband, and she would be envied, admired, granted the dignity among the peerage she'd always been denied.

Everything she always wanted. Wouldn't that bring the happiness she so desperately sought?

It wouldn't, she knew. Because she would never love him.

"Farewell, my lord," Lady May said a short time later as Lord Burton bowed over her hand, about to take his leave. "You must call again soon." Casting a covert look to Sophie, she added, "We have both enjoyed your visit so much."

Sophie knew what she was thinking. He was no sooner gone, when May asked, "Do you favor him, Sophie?"

"He is a good friend," she replied.

"Ah. Like Gideon?"

Caught off guard, Sophie could think of no response. She had not realized May would see that, too.

With a secret smile, May settled on the settee. "I have finally found the family connection to you. It certainly is not in looks. With Trista, with Michaela, I always saw their father in them. With you, I see so little of my brother. But I suppose it is that way with some children."

Sophie pushed aside the mild pang of disquiet. She was actually getting used to it. It disturbed her less these days. She supposed that should alarm her that the painful bursts of conscience were lessening, but she was more interested in what May was saying than in sinking herself into doleful self-rebuke.

"You have a sense of social conversation. You never seem ill at ease, although I know that you were today because you were unsure of the protocol. That cannot be taught. It is instinct," May went on. "I daresay you will attract too many who wish to use you as their confidant if you are not careful. People love a sympathetic ear."

"Ah, so that is the problem," Sophie said with a laugh, eager to take the conversation away from what hereditary traits she might share with May. "I had to sit with the Duchess of Tewsbury at Lady Viola's tea the other day, and she talked me deaf. I made a bit of a game of it. She was speaking of her son's marriage, bragging actually, and I was watching all of the ways she belied the perfect picture she was painting."

"Oh, dear," May said, laughing. "Yes, indeed, I imagine things are quite different between her and her new daughter-in-law than she wished to depict."

Sophie agreed. "They are undoubtedly at odds. What is worse for her, I gathered from how she gave herself away that her son is in sympathy with his wife."

"How delicious." May was easily distracted by this interesting morsel of gossip. "She forced that boy to marry that woman, and he was a sweet boy. Man. Lord, I am aging. He is three and twenty, a man full grown, and I am still calling him a boy."

"You are not old."

May preened. "Thank you, dear. In any event, I am glad that he is finally standing up for himself with that old baggage. Oh, dear, my language . . . Shocked you, did I? Well, I do not normally speak so, but with my intimates I am quite different."

Sophie was bewildered. An intimate? May considered her thus?

"You know me well enough by now to realize I am not unkind in my attitudes as a rule, but some people are an exception. Do not mention this, please, but my dear friend Lady Viola's sister, Eugenia, is one of those people who try me. She is a horrible snob and I do not like her."

"I agree on Mrs. Milton's character. Margaux has confided to me that her aunt and mother quarreled bitterly about allowing her to come to call at the house."

"How horrid!" May was instantly incensed. "She dares to presume to hold her nose up at me and my family? It is Gideon, of course."

"Yes. His reputation, you see."

"It is in the past," May pronounced firmly.

"Not far enough in the past for some, I am afraid."

May was disturbed. "I was not in any way doubtful that I could mend Gideon's respectability, but could I have misjudged?"

"Please do not let this worry you or I will be sorry I said anything."

"I am mainly concerned about you, Sophie. I would never do anything to harm you, and perhaps I am not being honest with myself about the potential for that with Gideon under the same roof. Perhaps I should send him away for your sake. Robert insists I should, but I cannot. For reasons I will not explain, I *will* not. Failing Gideon again is simply not something I can live with. I hope you will understand."

Sophie rushed to reassure her. "The ton respects you. You have not misjudged your influence in the least. It does not seem to have limits as far as I can see."

May seemed relieved.

Sophie continued, "And I am very happy here. I feel so blessed . . . more than you know. I appreciate so much the opportunity you've given me and would be so unhappy if you felt you had to turn Gideon away because of me."

"But, my dear," May said, blinking with astonishment, as if this rush of gratitude were unseemly, "we are family."

Sophie wished she had not said that.

"There it is," May said quietly, relaxing into her chair with a soft sigh.

"Pardon me? There what is?"

"That look. It is the way you used to look every day since you arrived. Here we are, having such a good chat, and a marvelous time, and then the look comes over you."

Sophie did not know what to say. May held up her hand reassuringly. "I know you are happy to be here, and I know you appreciate what I've done—you've told me many times, too many to count. But you put it between us, Sophie. And that is no way to repay kindness, with distance, with formality. And I thought we were making such excellent progress."

Sophie stammered, "I am sorry. I do not mean to be rude."

"Oh, darling, you are never rude. You just . . . oh, dear, it may sound simple to say this, but you *hide*. Sophie,"

May said gently, "you are a great joy to me. I am only try-ing to be your friend as well as your aunt. I think you like me as well as I like you. We do get on well."

Sophie looked down at her hands, thinking. Her mind was taunting her with the clear, seductive thought of lay-ing it all out. Truth—that which Gideon held so sacred. What would happen if she just told her—admitted every-thing right now? She felt a rush of dread, and an under-current of longing. How she wished she could, but fear stopped her, clogged the words in her throat.

But she must say something. She opened her mouth. What came out surprised her. "I may disappoint you some-day."

"Oh—" May, who was probably ready to reassure her that this could never possibly happen, stopped. She con-sidered Sophie for a moment. "Perhaps you will. People do not always live up to others' expectations, and yet we for-give them. Sometimes more than once. Sometimes without end." She seemed thoughtful, as if she were discovering this for herself. "And . . . perhaps one day, you might find something in *me* that will make me less than what you thought I was."

"I do not think that is possible. You are already estab-lished quite high in my estimation."

May reached out her hand to cover Sophie's intertwined fingers sitting on her lap. "Just as I do not think it is possi-ble that you could ever be less in my eyes than what you are now."

Sophie shook her head. "There are some disappoint-ments that cannot be borne. They are too great. They break a friendship."

"Love can mend a great deal. And I have come to love you, Sophie. For you, not just because you are like me or have Wooly's chin or any such. Your companionship is a great delight to me. We are friends, are we not? It is much more than mere relations, for some relatives cannot stand one another, but it only makes it so much better that you are my brother's daughter, and all the more precious because of that fact."

Sophie closed her eyes. She felt the confession pressing in the back of her throat. It was almost as if it were fighting to be free, to find its way out of her.

She nearly wished it would. If she but parted her lips, she could blurt it all out and then it would be done. Would she be sorry?

But she was a coward. Her lips pressed tight, and she opened her eyes and smiled at May. "Thank you. I feel the same way about you."

That, at least, was the truth.

*Gideon lounged in May's drawing room, submitting him-*self to the anxious perusal of his friend Lord Francis Farnsworth. He had felt it only right to accept the man's call over the others who had left cards and requested visits. He supposed he should be flattered that the hellions he ran with were willing to wake at noon, don morning clothes and sit calmly in a lady's drawing room for his sake, but he could muster surprisingly little enthusiasm for their visits and had, in the past, turned them politely away.

Farnsworth was different. He had perhaps saved his life and he'd shown good judgment in bringing him here. It had been out of character. The man was the type who took his cues from others, but he had been surprisingly decisive when the situation had deteriorated. Gideon supposed he owed him something, and for this reason had consented to see him, but had no more enthusiasm for it than he did for the others.

"They don't look bad, not bad at all," Farnsworth pronounced with forced cheer as he peered closely at the scars. "That patch will have the ladies swooning. By God, you'll be good as new in a few weeks, and I daresay up to your old tricks, eh?"

He laughed and rubbed his hands together. Farnsworth had always been something of a voyeur with Gideon's affairs. He'd taken great pleasure and pride in his good friend's prowess with the ladies.

Gideon knew this was as much a matter of opportunism as admiration. By attaching himself to Gideon, Farnsworth could avail himself of any disappointed women who might hope to catch Gideon's eye. He was an expert at offering a steady shoulder, sympathetic ear, and agile hands that could undo a corset with breathtaking ease.

"I hope you've been raising hell in my absence." Gideon swirled the port in his glass. Farnsworth had drained his glass in three gulps. Gideon hadn't offered him more. "I would not want this slight incapacitation of mine to have hindered your fun. Tell me what I've been missing."

"Well, Selwyn has been quiet. Afraid of the magistrate." Farnsworth snorted. "So, he seems to be satisfied with your little mishap. Honor served, even if it wasn't at his own hand. He is a coward, after all."

No, Gideon thought, he was a man who had been wronged.

Farnsworth was going on. "And his wife 'went away,' which means he sent her off to the country until she regains her head. That could take a long time with Abigail."

Gideon felt a momentary pang. Pity for Abigail? Had his dalliance caused so great harm that she was irreparably disturbed?

Farnsworth's next words banished his guilt. "I have it from a fellow who lives up in those parts that she's already found consolation with no less than the parson's son!"

He fell into guffaws. Gideon did not so much as crack a smile. It disgusted him, the entire domestic mess. But people like Abigail Selwyn and her enthusiastic appetites had been his way of life.

"Enough of the Selwyns, what of our group?" The words were wooden, spoken without any real interest.

Farnsworth took no note. "Stripped Buckley and Broadwick of three hundred each last night at White's." His chest puffed for a moment, then deflated as he went on.

"Then I went to Boodles's with Charleton and lost half of it. I got potted after that. Blast, but I've never had the luck in cards, not like you."

"I went home with empty pockets many a night. The trick is not to let anyone see it broke you."

"You always had them thinking you left because you were *bored!*" Farnsworth seemed to find this very funny and collapsed into gales. Gideon smiled and let his gaze wander around the room.

This was May's formal receiving room, not the one she used with family. He'd only been here once before when she'd made him meet some society twits who had come to pay her a call. He'd left quickly after the presentations to a countess with a pretty face and frigid disposition and another, Lady Pickering, who barely inclined her head to acknowledge him, were concluded. He had seen they were anxious at being exposed to his bad reputation, as if it were something contagious.

And a bad reputation was actually a kind of contagion. In London, the unwritten rules were strict and a man like him was worse than a typhus victim.

But Farnsworth didn't think it a drawback. With the band of rascals he had run with, the worse the reputation, the greater the attraction.

How appealing that puppylike admiration had once been.

Why did it now grate? And why had he thought just now of Farnsworth as a *former* bow?

"How is Roth?" Gideon inquired.

"As obnoxious as always. He is bursting his waistcoats, and those were already let out. He has immense appetites, that one." A broad wink, and he added, "In many areas. He won at Madam Gilford's the other night. He bought drinks all night long, then he and Margaret got a bit carried away. On the divan, you know the one, by the curtained alcove. They pulled the curtain only halfway, being in too much of a hurry and we laughed ourselves sick at the sight of Roth's pink arse."

The comment, Gideon found, was distinctly repulsive. And yet many times he, too, had laughed at the portly man who had a penchant for ladies as round as he was and was not too particular about privacy.

He felt impatient for the visit to be over. Sophie might return from the park where she had gone riding with Margaux. He would have enjoyed accompanying them. He was frustrated with being housebound, but the physician had warned him against the dangers of the sun on his skin.

He would have forgone the cautioning—he had never been any good with authority—if not for his fear of venturing into public before the scars were completely healed. Damn his own pride, he did have some vanity after all, and he would avoid being seen as unsightly.

The worry brought his fingertips to touch the smooth skin high up on his cheekbone. He would never grow a beard or long mutton chops no matter how fashionable it became, for the stubble his valet wiped away with the razor every morning grew uneven around the burn sites and would probably never be restored.

Just deserts, Reginald used to say. A wicked end for wicked ways. Oh, Reginald had many ways of expressing disapproval, and dour predictions of Gideon's doom.

Why the hell was he thinking of Reginald? He was out of sorts, that was it, which was also why Farnsworth seemed a bore to him today.

What Sophie would think of this band of rascals with whom he had associated filled him with a fresh hot flush every time he thought of it.

She might return any moment. He wanted Farnsworth out.

Farnsworth lounged in his chair, his legs spread in a crass fashion. Gideon had recently been reminded that gentlemen in a drawing room did not fling themselves haphazardly in a seat. And say what one would about drawing-room manners, but no one could accuse either Roberts or Khoury of being fey. Rather, they both held the fashionable manners of their class comfortably. He liked them, too. They were far more interesting than Farnsworth.

"So, when are you returning to St. James? God, you must be ready to run out of here, although that depends on what the ladies look like. I have heard that Sophie Kent is a beauty, and Lady May, of course, is well-known."

"They are taking care of me," Gideon corrected tightly. "They are as family."

"I'll say, lucky bastard you are!" Farnsworth guffawed. "You've got to be bored, though. Come on, admit it."

"The physician is still concerned." Gideon fought the urge to shout at the man but continued in his forced reasoned tone. "He warned me that most victims of severe burns do not die from the actual wounds, but from infection that strikes while their bodies are weakened by trying to heal. So, I shall not be rushing to my bachelor life."

Farnsworth appeared alarmed. "Good God. Then take your time, by all means. Just know that when you are ready, we will spend a week celebrating. That should brighten up your spirits."

Strangely, it didn't.

Farnsworth continued. "And you, of all men, Ashford, know how to celebrate. I can hardly wait."

"I do not think I will be doing much carousing." He motioned to his face. "Some of this will be permanent. The physician could not tell me how much."

"Nonsense. You still have that way the ladies love. The women will probably think it dashing, and you'll have more of them than you know what to do with. Which shall be a benefit to me." His eyebrows waggled. "I mean it, by God, it adds to your wicked air—wounded in a duel. The suffering rake. Lud, they'll swoon."

He chuckled, and Gideon thought him a simpleton. Who the devil would wish to have a bevy of women about who got impressed by such things?

"You should be going," Gideon said abruptly. "I have to take my dose now, and it brings on a tremendous fatigue."

God, he had no shame—begging off using the excuse of being too *tired*.

"Potent stuff, eh?" Farnsworth rose. One good thing about the man, Gideon reflected, was that he never refused anything Gideon told him to do.

He was trying to rush him out the door, his mind ticking off the seconds against Sophie's return. Farnsworth paused in the hall to put on his hat and don his gloves, chatting amiably while Gideon silently willed him to hurry.

A footman opened the front door and stepped aside as Sophie entered the house.

"Oh. Hello." She blinked, surprised to see Gideon's guest. She smiled, and Farnsworth gaped idiotically.

Gideon closed his eyes for one moment, just long enough to curse the fates for their perverse pleasure in thwarting him.

Then something shifted in the air. Farnsworth grinned.

Farnsworth's smile was unapologetically lascivious. His eyes gleamed with an almost malevolent fire, and Gideon's hand instinctively knotted into a white-knuckled fist.

Sophie, too, was wide-eyed, but the recognition he read in her stricken look was one of horror.

The truth dawned on him, flushing the heat from his bones and leaving him cold.

They knew each other.

In the silence, he had no choice but to make the proper introductions. "Lord Farnsworth, may I present Miss Sophie Kent."

Inclining his head, Farnsworth said, "Miss . . . *Kent*. What a pleasure." He swiveled his gaze to Gideon. "I am beginning to understand your attraction to the gentler aspects of society."

Sophie blinked rapidly, making no reply.

At the look his friend shot him, Gideon nearly let fly the violence building up inside of him. It would feel uniquely satisfying, he thought, to smash that grinning head and rattle it sufficiently to rid it of the very objectionable thoughts it obviously entertained.

How dare he defile Sophie with his leering smiles and lurid glances? Rage rattled inside Gideon as he struggled to maintain his composure.

"Farnsworth was just leaving," Gideon said with force. "Good-bye, Farnsworth."

The other man was surprised and greatly disappointed to be bustled out, but Gideon did not care. The red haze of his anger made him rough as he urged him to the door.

Farnsworth blustered, "I was leaving, yes, of course, but I could—"

"No, you could not."

He resented Gideon's handling of him, but kept a tame exterior. "Ah, well, good day to you. A pleasure to meet you, Miss Kent, an honor, really." He kept his gaze on Sophie as he stepped toward Gideon. "Ashford, I shall make certain to call again. Soon." He leaned in close and spoke under his breath. "I believe you are on to something here. I swear, you have inspired me."

"Not too soon." Gideon gave him another shove toward the door. "I am still recovering, and visitors take a good deal of effort. Good-bye, Farnsworth."

He slammed the door and turned to a startled Sophie with an affected look of nonchalance. "Come in, Sophie. There is still a chill in the air today. I am certain you could use a cup of tea."

Sophie complied, bemused. She stared at the door he had just shut so rudely. "Was that a friend or foe?"

"A friend who overstayed his welcome." He would not bring up the matter of their having known each other if she didn't.

She composed herself swiftly. "He reminds me of someone I met once, at one of my aunt's parties," she said at last. Her voice was light in an effort to sound unconcerned. "He might have been a young man whose father brought him to the town house once."

Wrinkling her nose, she smoothed her skirts. "As I recall, he was a rather disagreeable fellow."

"It sounds as if it were none other than Farnsworth. He can be . . ."

What could he say—rude, obnoxious, lewd? And what did that say of him to have such a bosom bow?

"But, of course, I do not mean to speak ill of your friend."

"Do not concern yourself. It does not insult me."

"It must have been good to see a familiar face."

He wanted to heatedly deny this, but instead he offered a mere shrug. Farnsworth's visit had brought unwelcome reminders, the smell of that wild life, a life he no longer found attractive, granted, but *his*. He'd made it, forged it, reveled in it . . .

That did not please him.

What the hell had happened to him?

Sophie said, "I recognize the name as the man who brought you here the night after the duel, is that right?" Gideon nodded as she removed her pelisse. "He was a good friend. I heard you were not keen on the idea. He was a brave soul to go against you."

He grunted something, not wishing to malign Farnsworth. He didn't want to talk about his old friends, his old life. It was as if two alien forces had collided today, and the result was a certain rawness inside him he did not know how to contain.

"I always wondered something," she said. "Duels are, I believed, fought at dawn. And yet it was much later than that when you arrived, in fact it was almost evening."

He shrugged as he strode purposefully to the family drawing room. "The injuries did not seem so serious at first. When it became apparent they were, I was adamant that I did not want to come to May's door, begging for succor."

"Then why not make other arrangements?"

"I did not intend to lose." He smiled at her pointedly.

"Which, strictly speaking, I did not. I thought the burns were superficial, the kind a little whiskey could cure."

The thought horrified her. "You doused them in whiskey?"

"It kills infection, you know. It probably saved my life. Hurt like the devil, though."

The memory of the pain could still bring on a wince. "Which was why I doused myself with it as well. Between that and the laudanum I was well out of it and ranting like a demon, I suspect." He shot her a smile. "I thought I'd died, and that you were an angel, remember?"

She flushed and turned away. "I am possessed of an excellent memory, Gideon. For example, I believe you promised me tea."

"So I did. Sit here, and I'll stoke the fire while we wait for the tray."

"It was brisk today. Invigorating. So good to be out of doors." She stopped and shot him an apologetic look. "Oh, I am sorry. That was thoughtless."

"Why should you not enjoy the day?" He told a footman to find the housekeeper and inform her that Miss Sophie wanted tea.

"Where is Aunt May?"

"I have no idea. Aunt, did you say? I am certain that makes May happy to hear you call her aunt. And I am all for anything that makes May happy."

"You are fond of her." She lifted one of May's shawls she had left draped over a chair and wrapped herself in it. "I was not always so sure."

"I adore May, except that she has this appalling notion to save me. Would you mind telling her I do not require her to?"

"Tell her yourself." She sat and pulled on each finger of her glove to loosen it. He watched as she slid it off, finding it very erotic.

That was a bad sign, if the vision of a woman removing a glove could leave his mouth dry and his heart thrusting blood to parts of him he'd rather not be noticing right now.

Something was wrong with him. It was Farnsworth's visit. It had stirred dangerous emotions in him. He felt perhaps he should not be alone with Sophie right now.

She began to work on the other glove.

He told himself to look away, but didn't.

"I do not believe you have completely settled the past," she observed.

It was true. The past.

He took a seat, crossed his legs and leaned back. "We have reached an agreeable state between us."

"You told her Reginald was kind to you. She is not reassured, however."

"I told her he was *not unkind*. Quite different, and not untrue. True, he was an ass, and, yes, I hated him. But he was not a monster, so smooth the stubbornness from your jaw."

She raised a delicate brow. "Are you certain you are not toying with the truth?"

The truth—she wanted the truth, did she? The very truth that had been brought so starkly to his attention this very day.

Very well. For the first damned time, he'd tell the truth.

He shrugged, studiously calm as she continued to study him. "I found ways to cope, a certain sort of comfort, so to speak. It was not too difficult, so do not feel too bad for me. You see, when a school chum of mine brought me home with him on holiday, I discovered a wonderful distraction. Women. They were plentiful at his home as his parents liked to entertain. And they had the prettiest maids. I found, to my delight, that the fairer sex could prove marvelously useful in diverting my . . . eh, energies. And, voila! I was no longer lonely. No more listening for footsteps in the dark."

He got the reaction he was looking for. Her eyes flared, just for a moment, and her back went ramrod straight.

Regret mingled with satisfaction. Good. Let her see him for what he was. Let her see the *truth*.

And then, suddenly, he could not bear it. He turned

away, and tossed out a question. "How was Mademoiselle Margaux today? Has she a special suitor yet?"

She shifted, taking her time to answer. He figured she was a bit bemused by his abrupt change of subject. "She is much in demand."

"As are you. Do you have anyone special?"

She threw her hands up in the air. "Gideon, why are we talking about this?"

"Because I am finished talking about maudlin old me. And I did not think you'd wish to continue to converse on the topic of the many uses I have found for women."

"Uses?" She sounded as if she were choking.

"Surely, you are not surprised. Did not May warn you about me? Did you forget what I was? A libertine, Sophie."

"Who beds other men's wives," she snapped bitterly.

He strode up to her boldly, wanting to make her turn away. He stared her down and yet she met his glare. "There is a certain joy in freeing the promise of a woman who is not quite innocent and yet unworldly in those ways where men keep their women sheltered. Fleshly pleasures being chief among these. I consider myself to be doing a great service to these misunderstood ladies who merely are in want of a patient hand and willing spirit to release the pent-up desires they do not know how to express."

She was indignant, apparently speechless, flushed prettily with red-stained cheeks and soft little breaths from her temper rising. "You are being unpardonably rude. Have I done something to deserve this in your eyes?"

"Of course not. But do you think life is just? This is the man I am, Sophie. I am not one to dance attendance upon matrons or point my toe and sweep a courtly bow. I have a horrid reputation, and it is time you realized that it is well-earned. You have not seen me at my best."

"Do you not mean worst? I suppose Farnsworth's visit reminded you of all the diversions you are used to and miss so much. Is that what is to account for this sudden disrespect?"

"I do not disrespect you. I merely—"

"Yes, tell the truth."

"Above all, truth. But you know, the man's presence brought to mind much in the way of reminders of what I am. It might be that it is time I went back to that life as it is all I know." He might have added "the life I miss," but he couldn't.

"My goodness, I hadn't realized," she said with a blend of prim arrogance a matron might use. He found it as adorable as any of her other moods. "I see we must be a dreadful tax on your patience. Of course, all of this time in the society of gently bred women, which you detest, shut in without your usual . . . *diversions,* did you call them?"

Bitterness dammed a painful lump in his throat. That was not it. But it *should* have been, damn it.

He blew out his breath, hoping to gain command of his mood. He was confused. Why had he lashed out at Sophie, but for the fact that perhaps it was she more than anything else that held him in this suspended state, clamped to her side with invisible irons he was powerless to break? She, even more than his temporary infirmity, held him here, because, damn it all, *he did not want to go back to his old life.*

But that was not her fault, but his own. He was suddenly sorry. "Sophie, I've upset you," he began.

She shooed her hands at him, cutting him off. "Oh, but do not trouble yourself on my account, Lord Ashford. My feelings are the least of your worries. What we need to concentrate on is all those poor married women suffering right this very moment, neglected and aching all this while as they await your return, for who else is available to liberate them?"

He was angry with himself for doing it, but he could not help it. He laughed. He tried to stop, thinking she would be offended if she thought he was laughing at her, but the more he tried to sober himself, the more heartily he laughed until he was doubled over.

It really was funny. Such arrogance on his part, more so because he *had* actually taken pride in servicing certain women who were looking for someone to show them the way of pleasure, and here he was, nothing but a cuckolding rake with delusions.

When he looked at Sophie, she was trying to remain sober, but not quite mastering the twitching of her lips. It was, sometimes, as if she could see inside him.

The housekeeper arrived with tea, but Sophie asked for the pot to be brought up to her bedroom, as she wished to change. "I have a gathering tonight, and I must not be late," she said. "I have been reminded recently that I need to tend to matters I've put off for too long."

"Indeed, Miss Sophie, I'll have the tray sent up."

She wheeled the tray out, and Sophie followed her. Gideon stopped her. "Sophie."

She turned to him, her color still high, and her temper as well despite the laughter they'd shared. "Thank you, Lord Ashford, for your honesty. I can always depend on you for that."

She left him, the smart click of her heeled slippers fading into silence.

Good, he thought. That was good. Now he was free of that particular entanglement. It would not be long before he would be leaving Park Lane. Whether he wanted to or not.

He did not belong here. That was what he realized today. Farnsworth's appearance had brought a clear understanding. He was no different from the man, his intentions no better. A fox in a henhouse.

He had best realize he was going to have to do without those things he'd grown used to. Like Sophie.

Especially Sophie.

Chapter 15

May welcomed Robert into her boudoir. He gave her a lingering kiss. His hands were warm on her back, and she felt a sudden urge to lead him to her bed.

She began to do so, but he hung back. "I need to speak with you," he said in a low voice.

"My. You sound so serious." She turned away, immediately on alert. "I hope you are not going to make another tedious complaint about Gideon."

"I was not aware that I was being tedious."

She immediately regretted her snappishness. He was worried for her, she knew that. And she had to admit, this was comforting in some respects, the warm envelopment of steady and uncompromising love.

Taking a deep breath, she shook off her irritability. "Do you require anything? Scotch? Wine? We could go down to the drawing room."

"Dinner is soon." Used to his surroundings, he went to a chair and took a seat. "I will wait until after. And this is a much better place to afford the privacy I wish for what I am about to say."

There was a tautness she could see around his mouth.

His eyes looked harder, too intent. She had another moment of alarm.

"May," he began softly, "it is time you and I talked about Matthew."

The jolt of fear was white-hot, zinging from stomach to heart. She replied quickly, "You know I never discuss my marriage."

"May," he repeated, his tone maddeningly calm, implacable, "it is time to tell me."

She felt each nerve flame in blinding fear. She wanted to flee, but her dignity kept her rooted on the spot.

"May," he said a third time, "I want to know why you killed Matthew."

The room spun and faded. She thought she might faint. A hand at the small of her back prevented her, and a voice at her ear called her back as she fought the bleariness closing in.

He was beside her. "I am here, May. I love you. I can take whatever it is you have to tell me."

He guided her to a chair. He knelt before her, holding her hands in his as she breathed in deeply.

"How did you know?" she whispered.

"Look at me."

She was afraid to, but she did.

His eyes weren't hard any longer. They were kind and filled with love, and that, of all things, brought on her tears.

"I know you," he answered simply. "And I know human nature. Equipped with this knowledge, it became increasingly obvious when your guilt over Gideon did not abate that there was something permanently rooted in you. You had changed. It was just a hypothesis, but you've confirmed it."

He kissed her hand and smiled at her. "Now don't trouble about it. The hard part is over. I know you shot Matthew. All you need to tell me is why."

Shot Matthew. The words were cold, implacable and

condemning. She'd feared ever speaking them to anyone, and it was not easy to sit calmly and discuss this.

She tried to pull away. "I cannot believe you are so cool about this."

"On the contrary." He held her gently, denying her the distance she sought. "I believe completely that you had good reason to do what you did. Trust me, May."

She took in a trembling breath. All right then.

Yes. It was time.

"I did kill Matthew. I . . . God, I shot him in the garden." She closed her eyes for a moment, trying to gauge what it felt like to finally admit the terrible truth she'd hidden away for so long. "It was ruled a suicide, as you know. I never contradicted the inquest verdict. Do you think I should have?"

"It depends why you shot him."

"I do not know where to start. When have you ever known me to be at a loss for words?"

"Tell me about Matthew, May," he commanded softly, folding her hands between his rough palms. "Start at the beginning, perhaps, and then it might come a bit easier."

She felt a gurgle of panic in her throat, threatening to choke off her words. "We chose each other. It was a love match. You know that. And we were happy for a time. We lived at Ashford Manor, a lovely house. We filled it with friends. And Gideon was like my own brother, but like a son, as well. It was a very special relationship. He thrived with us."

She swallowed. Robert nodded encouragement, and she continued. "Matthew was always volatile. It was one of the things that fascinated me about him. But as the years went on, he grew moody, frustrating. Sometimes . . ."

"Go on, darling," he coaxed in the softest voice.

"He began to be violent. The black moods increased. He was impossible to be around at those times, with him imagining all sorts of things and blaming everyone, including me, of preposterous conspiracies. Infidelity, mostly. He would not be disproved, despite all persuasions of logic. Then, just as suddenly as they came on, the moods would clear and he would be so sorry. I made excuses for him, covered for his behavior. I thought it was what a wife should do."

She stopped, gathering herself for a moment in an attempt to clear away the mists closing in on her thinking. "But it only grew worse in time. I came to a point that I wanted to leave." She shrugged. "I had my own money, many friends. But there was Gideon. I could not take him by rights."

"So you stayed and tried to protect him."

His grip on her hand tightened. She squeezed it back. "I would see the signs that a mood was coming and make certain Gideon had someplace to go, a neighbor to visit, a servant to take him on long, exhausting walks or riding deep into the forest to get him out of the house. I had my own ways of avoiding Matthew, but I could not always do so. It became impossible to escape his rages."

"What happened the night he died?" Robert asked.

May flinched, the memory hitting her like a sharp blow. She calmed herself with an effort, stared Robert straight in the eye, and spoke. "We quarreled. Matthew was at his worst. I do not know why I said it, but I told him I was leaving. It just came out. It surprised me. But . . . it did not frighten me for once. I began to think of how I could escape him, take Gideon with me. He was so ill at this point, I began to hope he would not even have the power to stop me.

"He saw it, the way the idea grew inside me, and I was suddenly braver. This was a mistake. He began to . . . to strike me and I was afraid, truly afraid for my life. He grabbed me, his hands around my neck, and he squeezed so hard I began to pass out. He said he would kill me. I fled and ran out into the garden and hid in the darkness."

"Did he follow you?"

May nodded. "He brought his pistol. He . . ." She shivered and suddenly Robert's large hands were cupping her jaw. His face was earnest, close to hers. The compassion she saw in his eyes gave her courage. "He was going to kill me, Robert. There was nothing of the man I loved left, only the sickness. He had seen that I was sincere in wanting to leave. He would never forgive me. I knew I had made a terrible mistake. He was going to kill me."

"Shhh," Robert said, kissing her fingertips. "Hush, love. It is in the past. He cannot hurt you now."

"But can you believe me? Can you know what it was like to know the man I loved, the man I married and lived with for years, was determined to see me dead?"

"I believe you, May. Do not forget I've seen the worst of humans in my career working for His Majesty's government. Men like Matthew degenerate and often the women they hurt refuse to face the horrifying fact that someone they love truly means them harm. Thank goodness you realized what was happening."

May nodded, breathing deeply. It felt good that he understood. "I knew I was running for my life, but he found me and we struggled. We fell to the ground, then I got up, managed to get my feet under me, but he grabbed my leg. He was trying to pull me back down. He . . ." Her hands fluttered, batting away a memory of that hand. "I do not know how, but I was suddenly holding the pistol. He laughed, Robert. He *laughed*. He thought I would never use it. He had this look on his face, so cold. He came for me, and I knew he would take the pistol from me, and if he did that, I was dead. So I closed my eyes and I fired."

There was sudden quiet. It felt like wet wool over the two of them, dragging down May's shoulders under its burden. "I killed Matthew," she said, just to hear it for the first time.

He grabbed her, held her tight. "My poor girl. Oh, my poor girl."

"I dropped the gun and ran inside," May murmured, brushing her cheek against his shoulder, nesting there. "The servants called for the magistrate. It was he who called it a suicide."

"I suppose it looked that way, with the gun right there and the wound consistent with close range." He smoothed her hair.

"He never asked any questions, never doubted Matthew had done himself in. The servants were forthcoming about his malady, the deep depression and violent outbursts. Not one of them spoke a word against me."

"They loved you."

"They were loyal, yes. I wonder if any of them had heard anything, if they knew. I never spoke of it, of course, and no one else did."

"And this is why you blame yourself for Gideon?"

"Reginald took Gideon, and you know the rest of it. Poor Gideon. His life was irrevocably changed, lost. All he knew, everyone he loved was taken from him."

"May, you have to relinquish this guilt." He pulled back to look at her. "You killed Matthew in fair and rational self-defense. It was the right thing to do, of course it was. You cannot think this was anything less than necessary, and perhaps even good. Yes, good. Matthew might have gone on a rampage and killed you, then Gideon and then himself if you had not stopped him. I have seen such things."

This was something she had never considered. She began to shake her head and stopped. She could not deny what Robert said was possible, as much as it pained her to think it.

"When men are in the madness of great despair," he said, "it drives them to think they are taking their family with them into the next world."

"But he would not have hurt Gideon, he loved him so."

"He loved you, but he would have destroyed you. He was not rational, depressed so deeply he was not himself. He might have even been truly insane. In any event, he most certainly was dangerous."

He pulled her into his arms again and held her. They sank together on the Aubusson carpet, not letting go while they rearranged themselves like children curled around each other.

"It chills me even now to think of you in so much danger. How glad I am that you are so brave and so strong."

"I am not sure if I am."

"There, there," he said, kissing her temple.

"I wasn't sad, Robert. He was dead, and I didn't even mourn." She began to sob. He curled her tight, kissing her hair. "I was relieved."

"Poor girl. My poor, poor girl."

That made her sob the harder. She clung to him and cried her tears. It was a long while before she was quiet.

He released her enough to smooth her damp hair and smile down into her face.

"Now I know. Now you have told one other person," he said. "You must listen to me. This is not a crime just as when I killed de Nuncier, it was not a crime. Killing to save a life is not murder. You must put this out of your mind at last, May. For your sake, for mine. For the sake of all who love you."

She hiccoughed and nodded. "I feel I can now. I can try, now that I have told you."

He smiled, wiping his thumb over her damp cheeks. "If you need to speak of it, if you have any trouble, you must come to me."

"But . . . I should tell Gideon. Then I think I can truly place it all behind me."

"No!" He was harsh, startling her.

May twisted to look at him. "But his life was altered by what I did. He deserves to know the truth."

"It cannot help him. Rehabilitate the man if you must, cart him to parties and present him to the finest society you can persuade to tolerate him, but do not tell him this, May. It is not useful." His gaze was penetrating. "Trust me in this, please. This is between us, no further."

She did not have the heart to argue. She relented, curling into the comfort of his body once again. She felt spent, exhausted, but content. A great weight was lifted from her soul.

Robert's words of comfort made sense, but there was still a great sense of loss inside her. If she could tell Gideon, explain to him that it had been an accident and that she had never meant for anything she ever did to harm him, she thought she could find the last bit of peace she sought.

Robert's arguments were not so much persuasive as an excuse for cowardice. She was afraid, yes, for Gideon was so close now, and she loved him still. She wanted him to stay.

If she told him, he might hate her.

Robert remained with her a long time, sitting quietly. When they decided to go down to dinner, he asked her, "Dare I hope that you will finally consent to marry me? I know all your secrets now, and I accept them fully. So there is nothing else to hold us back."

She sighed. "You are relentless."

"I need you," he said simply, smiling because he saw she was not really resisting him any longer. He held her. "And you need me, you little fool. I will never harm you, May. You know that. It is time to give yourself again. I will not fail you. Have faith, love. Have faith."

She smiled up at him. "I believe you. Just . . . Give me time, Robert."

He hesitated, then inclined his head. "I'll wait as long as you ask."

At dinner that evening, everyone was surprised when May announced that she was taking the lead in mentoring Gideon's emergence into polite society and having a small informal soiree.

His response was predictable. "I regret I will not be able to attend."

May clearly anticipated this. "I expect you to be there, Gideon, as you are the reason I am having the rout."

"But there is no need. I do not require the society of dowagers and debutantes."

"You are wrong," May countered firmly. Her smile was pleasant and implacable. "You are a young man of title and nobility. It is your place in society that you are undertaking, the one you would have had had I been there at the right time to see to."

She glanced at Robert. He gave her a nod, and this appeared to buck up her resolve. "Now I am doing so," she continued, "and I would appreciate it if you would not make a fuss."

"It is far too late for all of this worry over my reputation." He waved his fork as if the matter was settled.

"Nonsense. I hold great sway in society."

"A blessing from the pope could not save me." The fork was now directed to his temple. The scars were nearly faded, but faintly visible. Probably they always would be, to some extent. "I doubt—"

"Not to mention," May went on, "you are in a household with a young lady who is unmarried. If you remain unacceptable society, it will reflect badly on Sophie."

Sophie rolled her lips between her teeth to hide her smile. She had to admit, it was an excellent ploy, stalling Gideon quite effectively. His displeasure was apparent.

From the other end of the table, Lord Roberts spoke. "I do not think you would wish to give anyone the wrong opinion, Ashford. A prolonged absence from society after your accident, considering under what circumstances it occurred, might be seen as a lack of backbone."

That backbone stiffened on cue. Gideon looked appalled that his valor should be called into question.

"As tedious as it may seem, May's idea is an excellent one." Roberts finished with a sly look to his hostess, who smiled warmly back at him.

Gideon's jaw worked as he assimilated these very excellent arguments.

May said, "Then you will attend, Gideon, dear?"

"Of course he will," Lord Roberts said, his tone both

congenial and commanding. "If for no other reason, I am certain Lord Ashford would do anything you ask just to please you, my lady. For all you've done for him these last months, I do not think what you request is beyond Lord Ashford's ability to grant."

There was nothing he could say to that, so Gideon nodded graciously.

Sophie ate with pleasure, loving that Gideon had been bested. She was still angry at him for his cruel words to her. He had no business flaunting his many affairs, almost boasting of them. It had stung unmercifully.

She had been having a difficult time not thinking about the things he'd told her, his *penchant* for "tutoring" women who wished to experience passion. She could not get the idea out of her mind. And the images . . . The images were shocking.

She knew that he'd only chosen the one area that was exactly the right one to get her goat. She was jealous, plain and simple. Tutoring married women in pleasure— she could scream every time she thought of it. Indeed, did he think himself some toiling missionary to neglected wives? Was he that arrogant, or had he said it only to goad her?

She hated that a part of her was intrigued. Pleasures?

Her mind was rampant with curiosity. She was, of course, not innocent of what sex was. Her mother and aunts had explained the act very thoroughly. It was all done in good taste, and she had accepted the information without undue shock. The women had felt there was dignity in their profession, and they conveyed this along with respect for one's self and one's body.

But they had not spoken of female pleasure. That part, she supposed, had been strictly personal. She knew, of course, that the act of sex was exceedingly enjoyable to men, and that women might enjoy it as well, if the right man were the partner. These were referred to as "good lovers." Gideon's artless boast might be crude, but it did ignite the question in Sophie's mind as to whether or not he was a good lover.

The possibility excited her. She had no idea what one was, but there was all that confidence he had in himself, that sly perception, as if he knew things he had no business knowing.

And she had no business wondering about.

They finished dinner and adjourned to the parlor, the men joining them after a small interval. Sophie was consumed by her thoughts, reflecting on her foolishness, her complete misapprehension of Gideon's character.

She had forgotten what he was. She had almost come to believe the worst of what was said about him was not true.

But it had to be. Farnsworth was his friend! She had a clear recollection of that man, now that she had a chance to think about it. He'd been one of the bucks to think she was easy prey, being the daughter of an actress and courtesan. On the one occasion when he'd been at a gathering she'd attended, he'd caught her in a corner and it had taken a swift kick to his shin to convince him to leave her alone.

And, as she'd been so brutally reminded, Gideon was of the same ilk. What had she been doing harboring romantic notions for a man who called himself a rake and a reprobate with smug satisfaction? The thought had sobered her. In recent days she had stayed busy outside the house as often as she could.

Lord Burton called often, and they never failed to pass pleasant hours in each other's company. Their relationship had deepened to a comfortable and enjoyable association. Sophie appreciated the man's dry wit, his cool reserve and intellectual interests as an antidote to the sultry confusion that overcame her in Gideon's company.

If his intentions were marriage, she told herself firmly that she would definitely take into serious consideration an offer. He was calm, steady, admired, and firmly entrenched in her circle of friends. He was an excellent candidate for the kind of married life she had always envisioned.

"Oh, Sophie," May said suddenly, "I have been meaning to ask you if I happened to give you your mother's letters."

"No," Sophie replied, rattled at the mention of the letters from Aunt Millie. She dropped her fork, which clanged against the china plate. "Pardon me. No, Aunt May. You did not give them to me."

"My heavens, what did I do with them? I cannot seem to find them anywhere. I went through them, as I promised I would, and set aside the ones from your mother. There were several. I wanted us to read them together. I must have done something with them, because they are not where I thought I left them."

"They will turn up," Gideon said. Sophie shot him a look, and he smiled back at her, raising his brows and adding, "These things always do."

Her chest burned, for she knew he was taunting her. The creases that appeared in the corner of his mouth when he smiled were starting to show, holding secret amusement.

He had them. He must have sensed her reaction to the letters and taken them. What was more, he *wanted* her to know he had them. Dread formed like ice crystals around her pounding heart.

She tried to calm herself—why would he take the letters?

His change of mood lately, almost as if he were angry with her—was this the explanation? Did he know something? Most of all, if he did have the letters, what did he mean to do with them?

Her answers came swiftly. When she entered her bedroom that night, she found the letters tied with a ribbon sitting on her dressing table with a card laid on top. It was Gideon's card, his name neatly printed in simple block letters. Gideon Hayworth, Lord Ashford in plain black ink on cream colored stock. Handwritten in a bold hand with little flourish was the message, "I did not read them. Keep them safe."

Sophie grabbed the letters, a stack of perhaps five or so, like she was snatching damning evidence out of the hands of an accuser. Sitting with a plop on the dressing table chair, she felt a wash of relief followed very swiftly by dawning astonishment.

Gideon knew her secret.

Chapter 16

"I have a few questions for you," Sophie said from the doorway to the library.

Gideon jerked, almost spilling the scotch he was about to pour from his decanter into his glass. "Jesus, you startled me!"

She entered and took the decanter from his hands and placed it back on the sideboard. He was mute, holding his empty glass.

"In polite society," she explained, "a gentleman does not drink in the presence of a lady. Besides, I would have all your faculties at their utmost until I have gotten satisfaction."

His eyebrow jerked, and he looked like a mischievous demon. "Satisfaction. Is that what this is about? Praise lord, at long last."

The innuendo annoyed her.

Tossing her head back, she said, "You cannot frighten me with tasteless innuendo."

She did not move, remaining close enough to smell the faint hint of spirits, to feel the slightest emanation of heat.

"What a shame. A clever girl would be frightened of me."

"You will not hurt me." She held up the packet of letters. "You've already had an excellent chance. Why did you take these?"

He sighed, as if put-upon by her demand to explain himself. "I thought it would make you happy."

"What is it you are after?"

"After?" He shook his head, as if not comprehending the question and repeated, "I thought it would make you happy."

She looked at the letters she held, thinking. She was suspicious.

"Sophie," he said, "why can you not simply take the gift and go?"

"I want to know. What game are you playing?"

"People see what they know," he said patiently. "You could have a hundred people around you and none would think it strange or odd in the least, how you deflect certain questions, how your gaze falls away or you look down at your hands when you are uncomfortable. But I see it. To me, it is as plain as all that fine golden hair on your head. There is some great mystery in you, Sophie, something that holds you apart. It is like red meat to a starving dog, that aura. To me, anyway. I cannot seem to fathom what it is behind those shadowed eyes."

She flushed, pleased and frightened at the same time. "I think you have been reading too much Byron. What fanciful thoughts you have."

"Little girl lost, and who best to notice than a man who's not found his way straight in fifteen years? I glimpse it in you, some misery you hold in secret. I saw it when May spoke of the letters. I knew something about them made you afraid."

She wanted to say something sharp to make him stop. His words were having a strange, very powerful effect on her. Her heart raced, her heartbeat drummed in her ears.

She felt a pulsing of confused emotion. Part of it was realizing that he did not know she was an imposter. That was relief.

But this was far less than knowing that he had seen so much, and had never challenged her. He'd accepted the mystery, trusted her.

He jerked his head, indicating the letters. "You can tell her you've found them if you like. I just thought I would give you the choice."

"I thought . . . you seemed like you were going to threaten me with them."

He gazed at her softly. "Sophie, I would not hurt you."

"Would you not? Then why are you flinging about your detestable past, as if I wish to hear about all of your women?"

"Would you have me pretend, or worse, to ignore what cannot be changed? I am not the sort of man who will sit tamely at your side and hide my nature. It is a carnal one, a nature of drives and desires you would not care to know of. See, you look away. Let us not pretend anymore that we are friends. It is a joke. Friends? What is a friendship between a man and a woman who desire each other? You know full well what is between us. It is in your eyes, in the way your lips part and your breath hitches slightly when I move close. And if I touch you," he added, extending his hand. She skittered away like a wary cat. "If I touch you, your whole body reacts."

"Is that what you think? Must you see everything in light of carnality? All those fawning wives have spoiled you. So, in your estimation I am no different from those women you take such tender pity upon and grace with your generous tutelage in love?"

"Oh, Sophie, you are different from every other woman I've met." He paused a moment, then grinned. "And I never said anything about love. I am not a man to talk to about love."

"Do you think yourself immune?"

"Not immune. Incapable."

This annoyed her. What did he mean—did he see himself with some deficiency? She resisted the urge to ask him. "I am not a dreamy-eyed miss with any thought of love. You do not have to worry about me. I know what I want."

"I wonder if you do. It seems to me it is more the case that you know what you do not want."

"What an odd mood you are in since your friend came here." She broke away, glad to put some distance between them. She tried to fill her lungs, but the air seemed too thick. "You seemed to dislike your friend Farnsworth. The trouble started with his visit."

"The trouble started the day I set eyes on you and saw something I wanted very much but could not have. But Farnsworth, yes, he reminded me that we have been in an isolated world, you and I, and a false one." He gave a small laugh, one both sad and amused. "I was doing a fair job of this pretty little pretense. I had even deluded myself into ignoring the fact that we come from completely different worlds, and mine is poison to yours, Sophie. Then Farnsworth came and that which was so familiar, so ordinary before seemed foreign. And, yes, unwelcome. But a reminder of what is real, nonetheless."

"Are you so afraid you will forget?"

"I know I *will* forget myself, because I already have. *We* already have. I even kissed you, and you kissed me back, and I never had a kiss like that one, Sophie. Never. I want you. You know that, you've always known that. We pretend we don't realize it, but it is always there. And, dear Sophie, you want me."

She stiffened. He gave a short, gruff laugh. "Oh, don't worry. It's not fatal. Like many infections, if you catch them in time, you can be saved. I'm catching you in time."

"I do not know whether to be insulted or flattered." She chose her words carefully. "You say these things and . . . and it is almost as if you cared for me."

"And what if I do?" he said. The words were not a challenge. They were spoken softly, and their effect was astonishing. She felt almost weak, then light as air.

But he shook his head, and if she had some hope in her breast—a surge of exquisite wanting that swept her up so swiftly it alarmed her—it was quickly dashed. "I am not a gentleman. I never wanted to be."

"I don't believe you like being scandalous." The thought burst out of her. "You use it like a barrier to place between yourself and everything you care about. You do it with May, and now me."

"Believe what you will," he shot quickly, but she could see he was disturbed. "I will go to May's soiree. I'll sit nicely and behave myself, but I am not going to make a future balancing a teacup on my knee and nibbling scones, Sophie. This . . . this, what you see, this is someone else's life. Me, docile and necessarily tame. If not for the colliding of a host of improbabilities, it would be unthinkable, impossible that you and I would be in the same world. We never should have met."

"I think you are wrong," she said. "Why do you insist on trying to convince everyone you are dedicated to being as wicked and unprincipled as that loathsome Reginald always predicted? The shame of it is, you've given him the great gift of thinking he was right all along. Do you think you spite him? Is that what rules you? Then he has won, Gideon."

He made a dismissive gesture with his hand, as if to ward her off, but she ignored him.

"But it is you who suffer, you who deny all the good things to wallow in depraved relations. You stay in this house, complaining all the while of your lost freedoms and missed opportunities for debauchery, and do you know what, Lord Ashford? I believe you like it here. And perhaps that is what has made you so prickly all of a sudden."

He glared at her. She felt the currents of his anger, and something else. Something infinitely exciting. She stood firm.

"Sometimes, Sophie, I wonder at your sense."

"Do not pretend you are a danger to me."

"But I am. I am the worst kind of danger. Here we are, in the middle of the night when the house is asleep. And me, being what I am, I can destroy you simply by association, yet you trust me with such liberty. You wish a re-spectable life, marriage and children and moving in the cir-cles of first society—I am your nemesis, Sophie. You should run."

"I do not wish to run.". She was finding it difficult to breathe. Her chest rose and fell in shallow inhalations that came too rapidly.

His eyes begged her to stay. "Run, Sophie. Run now."

She moved forward. "Do you know what I think?" she asked softly.

His eyes had darkened, their pupils large. His mouth was parted, and she saw he, too, panted lightly, as if there weren't enough air in the room. The heat must have taken it all, for she felt as if she were on fire.

He said, "I have heard far too much of your opinions."

"I think it is you who are afraid of me."

He nodded slowly. "And so I am. God, I am, and that is the truth."

She stood so close to him, her breasts nearly touched his chest. He looked down at her, as stiff as an armored knight. His hands remained at his side.

"You are a man of honor, you once told me. You've never lied to me, you've never compromised one iota on that score. And yet you are a scoundrel, a scoundrel with a code of conduct far beyond the most admired gentleman in any lady's parlor."

"I have so precious little to take pride in."

Her body trembled and she wanted him, wanted his kiss. She waited, knowing he would not. Her dignity re-belled, but even that could not prevent her from reaching out to touch him.

His hands moved quickly, darting like striking snakes to ensnare her wrists, keeping them from him.

"Don't."

She wanted to lash at him. Frustrated, humiliated, she swallowed the hard lump of emotion burning in her throat.

Her flesh burned where he touched her. She wanted to run, wanted to weep.

"I release you from your promise," she said.

He blinked. His nostrils flared and he stared at her. He shook his head. "Go to bed now, and don't ever tempt a devil again."

"I said I release you from your promise. You once vowed never to kiss me again. I tell you now that I do not wish you to keep that vow." She reached for him, her hands grasping his face. His skin was hot, smooth, and hard. Her fingers trembled. Her palms burned with the feel of him.

Still, he did not move. She felt alive, her nerves pulsing with sensations that surprised her, thrilled her. "Very well," she said after a moment. "Then I shall kiss you."

She closed her eyes and surged forward before she lost her nerve. His mouth was unyielding, but his hand touched her at her waist, then tightened.

She paused and pulled away, her breath soft and quick in the silence between them. Her eyes opened to look into the inscrutable darkness of his. He seemed to be making up his mind. She was afraid he might push her away, but his grip held fast. He pulled so that her hips pressed against his as his head slanted and he leaned in to kiss her just as she'd been wanting him to do.

Her breath caught at the gorgeous feeling of his lips on hers. His arms wrapped her tight, and she twined hers around his neck, arching to be closer.

The hunger took hold, the one she had felt all along but had tried to pretend she didn't.

He took hold of her with powerful arms. Bending her head back, his hand thrust in her hair to hold her steady while he kissed her hard. Their tongues met, mated. His cheek rasped roughly against her cheek and she reveled in the sting. His teeth found soft flesh and scraped tantalizingly until shivers rolled over her back and down her arms. She quivered, falling into a dizzy well of feelings that were more wonderful than she could have ever imagined.

"God, Sophie," he murmured, his lips feathering softly along her jaw. "What you do to me . . ."

She ran her hand over the breadth of his shoulders, felt the texture of his skin on his neck and the crisp hairs that curled at the nape of his neck. He smelled of spice and soap. It made her head swim. Or maybe it was the relentless kiss that drove her senses to their limit until she shook in his arms, weak and yet straining with a strength and drive she did not know she possessed.

He twisted, bringing her with him, then pushing her until she fell softly on the long divan by the window. Bracing himself over her, his one arm on the sill, the other on the curved back of the divan, he stared at her and she reached for him, making a soft sound of pleading. He flexed his arms, his muscles bunching into thick cords as he lowered himself to kiss her once more.

She shifted to the side as he settled next to her, supported by one arm while the other went around to scoop her close, holding her so that every portion of their bodies touched. He was flame, and she could not get closer than she was, yet she wanted to. She pressed shamelessly against that terrifying warmth, needing it.

He ran a palm down the side of her waist, making her feel so tiny. Her breasts tingled as he splayed his hand over the back of her thigh. She felt his touch through her skirts and curled her leg, liking the intimate possession. He shoved the material upward, boldly running his hand up the undercurve of her bottom.

His mouth played with hers as he grasped her, held her. His powerful legs flexed and brought his body to slide against hers, hip to hip, and she heard a soft, unintelligible groan. She felt him, knew the hardness that burned against her thigh was him aroused. He was ready to take her. The thought pulsed a numbing throb of pleasure through her, and a dreadful, delicious emptiness ached to be filled.

She quivered under the passionate kisses he rained down her neck. His hand captured both of hers and held them over her head. She squirmed underneath, her body arching to make contact with his.

She welcomed the weight of him. When he touched her

breast, she let out a moan. Biting her lips to quiet herself, she fought a flush of embarrassment until she heard his answering sound, wordless encouragement of passion. He pulled at the neckline of her dress, exposing her shoulder. His tongue traced the roundness of her upper arm, then lower to where the swell of her bosom began to rise.

The heat of his mouth settled on her, and she cried out. Her body strained. It was like a fever in her, this wild sensation. She was hot, burning, craving.

His mouth claimed hers again and as they kissed, his hand quested under her skirts again, this time encroaching on the secret, aching place between her legs. His breath tickled her as a gentle stroke of his finger ignited innate need.

Her first thought was to push him away. But when her hand went to his wrist, she arched against his hand, and he stroked again. The sound she made drew an answering groan of pleasure from him. "You are so hot," he said quietly.

She felt no shame now. Her nerves were pulsing, wildly demanding this thing he was offering. With Gideon, she had a kind of freedom she'd never experienced before. She needed him, needed something. He gave it to her with another slick caress.

Rolling her head, she murmured, "What . . . ?"

"Shh. Just feel it, love. Just feel."

Her nerves screamed for something she didn't understand. He curled his finger into her a fourth time and she felt heat burst inside her, dissolve her, and thrust her up into spasms of sensation.

She made a sound, too loud. His mouth claimed it. His hand touched her lightly, knowing what she needed right at that moment. Riding the waves that came to her over and over, one surge after another, left her breathless, gasping, grasping him desperately as sated warmth replaced the storm.

In the end, she still ached for him. Dazed, her body utterly limp, she yet yearned for what she knew was true sexual union. She heard his breathing next to her ear, a heavy, grating rasp.

"That was quite a kiss," he said with a lopsided grin.

Her mind felt hazy, as it did when one first awakened, sorting sluggishly through what had just happened.

Her hand slipped to his hips, pulling him close.

"No. Not here."

Her eyelids would not open fully. She was barely capable of speech. "But you . . ."

"Shh. I will not take you here. Not like this."

She let her head fall back, confused still. "What did you do to me?"

His lips sank into the soft flesh of her neck. She moaned. "There are various terms for it, however I know none that are not in some part vulgar, so we will just call it a caress. A very intimate caress."

She pushed against his chest and he sat up. She scrambled to a sitting position.

"Do not tell me you are going to get indignant now," he drawled.

She shook her head, running her hands through her hair. It was a mess. She began to shove the parts that had come undone back into place. "You sound like the tutor. Is that what this was? You were merely instructing me, as you so often do, in the delights of womanly pleasure?"

"Sophie," he said softly. She stopped.

He caught her hands and tugged so that she turned toward him. She did not raise her head. "I suppose you think I am just another of those women."

"I told you already. You could never be like any other woman." His voice was tender. "Perish the thought. Pleasure is not just for my devotees, my dear," he added wryly.

She shook her head. She did not want him making light of this.

"I am sorry," he apologized. "Darling, what is the matter?"

"I feel like such an idiot!" she said, throwing her hands up.

•

He rearranged his long legs so that he sat beside her. "Oh, Lord. I thought you were sensible, Sophie. Are we now to have to sort through all the guilt?"

"Not guilt. Stupidity." She saw his confusion and tried to explain. "I never imagined it was like that. All this time, I thought it didn't matter."

"Sweetheart," he said kindly, "what the devil are you talking about?"

"Sexual intercourse."

"Ah," he said, although he did not have a clue. And she might have shocked him by being so frank.

She blushed. "I thought it didn't matter, all that sort of thing. Sex never interested me. My mother and aunts were the sort of women who took lovers. It seemed to be something quite important to them, taking lovers. They made no secret of it, but I just never felt . . . I just didn't think it mattered."

"Ah," he repeated. He wound a strand of hair absently around his finger.

"I never imagined I would . . . like it."

He felt a completely selfish burst of pride. "Aha. There we have it."

She shook her head slowly, amazed. "I could not have imagined anything like it."

He could not keep the smile from his face, although he did his best not to appear to be gloating.

"It is probably because you are so skilled."

"You are not by chance referring to that claptrap about married women coming to me for instruction in . . . Well, did you actually believe that rubbish?"

"You say you always tell the truth," she ventured. She looked like a doe, wide-eyed and timid. He wanted to gather her into his arms again.

The persistent thrum of desire in his blood, be damned, he was going to be as gentlemanly about this as he possibly could be.

"Sophie, I am not an ignorant man in these matters, yes,

I admit it. But I've never had a woman as exciting as you. Nothing before has ever been quite like this."

"But you . . . you didn't . . ." She knew there was more to intercourse than what they had done. There was his pleasure. A man's pleasure was foremost, and yet he had done nothing to find release.

"That is for another time. If you wish it."

"But what will happen . . . to you . . . to your?" She looked away, miserably embarrassed. "Isn't it painful?"

He sighed. "Yes. Excruciating, horrible."

She slapped his arm, reluctantly smiling.

"I'll live. I am contented, Sophie. Besides, I can hardly haul down my britches in Lady May Hayworth's drawing room. What happened just now was certainly not accept-able, but I was overcome." He paused, thoughtful. "I do not think I've ever been quite so overcome. . . . But you deserve more than a grope and a tumble."

He touched her face, holding her chin so that she could not look away. "You deserve to be made love to. And when I do make love to you, it is not going to be hurried on an uncomfortable divan. I want to take my time, undress you fully, feel your body against my own, show you—"

"Oh, God, stop!" she cried, falling against his shoulder as shudders of delight racked across her shoulders.

She was quiet as she took in a deep breath. "I thought that men needed to . . . you know. My mother told me that it was something that drove men mad if they did not have it."

He chose his words carefully. "Pleasure, I am finding out, can take many forms."

She did not know what to make of that. She settled in his arms gingerly. "But you do not regard yourself as my tutor?" She picked at the finely stitched seam of his shirt. "A tutor is cold, detached. I would not like it if you thought you were doing this as a kind of favor—"

"Good God, indeed not. Sophie," he murmured, kissing her forehead softly. "You mustn't listen to the wild things I say. Dear God, don't think . . . I would be the worst liar that ever lived to ever think I could be objective where you are concerned. Tutor indeed. It is you who teach me so much."

She turned her face up to him, and asked, "Then why did I let you do that?"

"Because," he replied softly, tracing the fine angle of her jaw, "in spite of all society's rules and moral demands, not to mention the discomfort of the furniture, it was right."

She sighed, appeased.

Gideon never felt the hypocrite more, telling her anything as if he had any more of a clue about what had just taken place between them. All he did know was that it was the most intimate encounter he had known as a man.

And indeed, despite the ache in his groin, it was enough.

"I suppose I must confess that our friendship . . . has developed a certain *affection*," Sophie said. "I trust that does not disturb you."

"Most profoundly. And most agreeably. And I assure you, Sophie, that your *affection* is more than adequately reciprocated."

"But do scoundrels reciprocate affections?"

"Ah. Excellent point. This might mean I'll be tossed out of the scoundrel's guild."

She smiled. "It pleases me. But it should not." She frowned. "I do not know where it will lead."

He had no answer for that. He closed his eyes and willed himself not to think about it. There were frightening ideas skirting on the edge of his mind, thoughts of domesticity he'd never entertained.

He was not a man for home and hearth. He was a wastrel . . . but that had become boring. He did not know what he was anymore.

Taking her hand, he held it palm-to-palm with his, then slowly folded his fingers down to intertwine with hers. He studied the way his broad palm dwarfed her slender hand, the strong, supple fingers encased with capable strength. He felt a stirring of protectiveness, of being larger, stronger. He had never cared about anyone more than himself, but he had the strange and distinctly medieval thought that he would slay a dragon for this woman.

Too much Sir Walter Scott, he thought, and smiled to himself. Her fault entirely, and he would tell her so. Later.

"Are you curious about the letters?" she asked after a while.

"I am interested in everything about you," he replied. "But I would rather you did not tell me. Not now. It would be all muddled with that . . . kiss. Besides, I rather like you as you are, a mystery. Just know that if you are ever in trouble, then I am your man. You come to me, do you hear?"

She was silent, but nodded. He didn't know why he had made her promise this, but he was glad he had.

"What?" he said with a short laugh after a protracted silence. "Am I to understand I am to be allowed to have the last word?"

She rested her cheek on his chest and sighed. "I find myself without a single one to offer."

Chapter 17

"*Sophie?*" *Margaux said.* "*You are woolgathering again.*"

Blinking, Sophie looked at her friend. "I am sorry. I suppose I was distracted."

"Is it the soiree?" Margaux asked in a rush. "I vow I am so excited. I am finally going to get to meet Lord Ashford. I tell you, I was very put out with Mama not allowing me to call upon you once Lord Ashford was released from his sickbed, and she was not at all keen on me attending the party, either. But my aunt Viola put her foot down. And with the guest list—imagine, Lady Jersey and the Countess of Melbourne, just to name a few—she can hardly object for any cause of propriety. Oh, your aunt May is very clever . . . Sophie? Sophie!"

"Aunt May is brilliant," Sophie said, snagging the last of her friend's comments and trying to cover her rudeness. Her mind was sponge today! "She maneuvered this entire soiree to maximize Lord Ashford's exposure to all the correct people. In one fell swoop, he is brought before a large number of major influences of the ton."

"And we are the beneficiaries. All those wealthy matrons make for wealthy heirs. Male heirs who could be suitors." She giggled.

"Margaux," Sophie exclaimed, pretending to be scandalized, "I thought you were looking to make a love match!"

The women were sitting on Margaux's bed, sorting her tangle of ribbons. It was something to do as they chatted pleasantly.

"I just have not found him yet," Marguax said with a shrug. "Although I did make the acquaintance the other evening of a very interesting man. *Very* interesting, Sophie. You would adore him. He is very dashing, a viscount! Not that *I* care at all about that sort of thing, but it made things much easier with Mama that he is so highly placed. We met not long ago at Lady Pembroke's dinner party. He was very attentive to me, and I admit it is quite flattering to have such a handsome man in attendance. Oh, Mama is delighted with him because he is rich."

She made to smile, but the gesture was tense. Mrs. Milton tended to be dreadfully overbearing and impose on her daughter her very exacting ideas of a suitable match.

"I am to see him tonight at the theater," Margaux added brightly. "He asked me if I have a box and promised to drop in."

"My, this is a quick development." Sophie was thrilled that her friend had finally found someone who interested her. This would ease her mind a great deal to see Margaux settled happily in romance. "Do you like him, too?"

"Indeed, I do very much. And, you know, when it is true love, it does strike quickly. No, no, do not frown. I intend to proceed very carefully. I know you do not believe in love matches."

"Not true. I just do not regard 'love' as a practical basis for marriage. For myself, anyway. Margaux, do not forget that I saw my mother and aunts fall in and out of love a number of times."

"But there is the one great love. The *grand passion*."

"For you, I have no doubt," Sophie said, then stopped as she realized what a prig she sounded.

Was she being a hypocrite? She was caught up in a passion herself. Obsessed with Gideon, considering taking him as her lover.

Considering? Was she fooling herself? Nothing about her relationship had any similarity to rational thought. She was sliding down a slope slick with emotions she could not get a hold of. Did not wish to get a hold of. It was too glorious, too thrilling.

Her mother and aunts had often teased her, most times gently, sometimes more sharply, that she was far too serious. What would they say to see her now?

She knew they would laugh themselves stitches in their sides. Just the thought of their great pleasure made her smile. Perhaps she *was* too serious sometimes. She certainly liked this part of her, the freedom, the excitement.

Since the incredible experience with Gideon, she'd been on a cloud. She'd wrestled with thoughts that brought her closer and closer to accepting the unthinkable. One grand affair, one indiscretion before settling into the respectable life she'd always wanted.

Or if she did not, she would end her days never knowing what their exalting encounter had promised.

She did not think she could consign herself to that.

Remembering Margaux, she said, "Just . . . do take care, please. Even great lovers must be sensible a little bit."

"Mama would not allow me to do otherwise." Margaux nodded, her glossy dark curls bobbing adorably. "But I am excited, Sophie. I do like him very much."

"I have an idea," said Sophie. "Give his name to Aunt May and she will make certain to include him on the guest list. This way, you will have something extra to look forward to at the soiree, and I will get to meet this wonderful specimen of masculine superiority."

Margaux squealed in delight, pleased with this idea. "Oh, you tease me. But you will see. Then you will be jealous!"

Sophie found herself drifting off again and again. She could not keep her mind on anything Margaux was saying.

Gideon seemed to be waiting for what she would do next. Every glance between them was electric, every touch—which they managed with alarming frequency—held a jolt. To others, she had no doubts they appeared as they had before. They were very careful about that.

But nothing could be the same again, that she knew. Not in her heart.

Margaux smiled at her and gave her a little shove, shoulder to shoulder. "Dreaming about Lord Burton, Sophie? I swear, you are quite overset today. Oh!" She grew excited. "Did something happen? Did he speak? Oh! Oh! Did he try to kiss you? Tell, Sophie, do!"

"No, no. It is not Lord Burton on my mind."

It was disturbing to realize how little thought she gave her most attractive and erstwhile suitor. Because of Gideon, her interest in Lord Burton, despite his patient attendance to her at every affair they attended together, could not grow beyond friendship.

Although she liked him, he was cool, aloof. But Gideon was fire, and it was an unfair perception because she could not help but compare the two men, and Lord Burton came up very short.

For now. When she and Gideon had spent their passion for each other, Lord Burton's steady reserve would be there. She would come down to earth soon. Her mother always did. An affair would start, flame, burn, extinguish. She should not make any rash decisions.

She and Gideon were still as far apart as they had ever been, creatures from different worlds. And yet . . . this was surely passion's insanity whispering in her ear . . . but . . .

In so many ways, they did not seem opposite at all. They seemed perfectly matched.

"It is the soiree, just as you supposed," Sophie said, seeking to provide some plausible excuse for her state. "It is much on my mind. So many details to consider. Did you decide on what you are wearing?"

"I think the white embroidered muslin with blue piping.

I wish to appear delicate and graceful." She laughed, then looked alarmed. "Or do you think it too innocent?"

"Innocent can beckon a man's attention," Sophie replied absently as she wrapped a black ribbon into a neat bundle.

"Perhaps that deep rose, the one I wore to the Cowden ball? It is much more mature. I think I would like to appear worldlier, more sophisticated. What are you planning on wearing?"

"I think the lavender dress. I wore it to a dinner party a few weeks ago. Do you remember it?"

Margaux declared she had loved it, and since Sophie had elected to go with a soft, delicate dress, then she would stay with the white muslin.

They descended to the drawing room moments later to join the older women. Sophie was curious at Margaux's sudden enthusiasm for her new beau and looked forward to meeting him at the soiree. It made her feel better about all the attention Lord Burton was showing her. She'd known Margaux had thought him handsome and been disappointed when he'd shown an interest in Sophie and not her, but they'd never allowed it to come between them. This reassurance that her friend had a new romantic interest reassured her that Margaux would find contentment.

She wondered if she would, as well. Things were changing so swiftly. She had thought herself a practical woman, but she was not.

She was a dreamer. What was more, she loved being a dreamer, loved not having to be engaged in the tight struggle for survival and the deep and frequent examinations of herself and her motives, or be suspicious about the world around her, no longer striving so hard.

For now . . . she was drifting so pleasantly in currents she was not sure of. For the first time in her life, Sophie just let herself go.

*　　*　　*

In the evening, Gideon suggested to Sophie that they take
a stroll in the garden.

Sophie tried to appear casual as she laid down the scrap
of lace she'd been working on—May had suggested she
give up embroidery and was trying to teach her some tat-
ting stitches.

"It will feel good to get a bit of exercise." Sophie rose
with a smile to her companions, trying to betray none of
the excitement rattling around inside of her. "I fear I liked
the dessert pudding too much and ate quite more than normal. Thank you, Lord Ashford."

The night was quiet and dark and thick with impending
rain. Invisible clouds blocked out the moon and the stars.

"Should I get a lamp?" Gideon asked.

Sophie said, "No. We know the path well enough."

They made their way without trouble. Once in the folly,
they sat together on the stone bench.

"What are we going to do, Sophie?" Gideon said to the
sky. "I think about you all the time."

"I think about you, too," she said.

"That should please me. It does. But it does not. I am
not the right man for you. And you are nothing I need. I tell
myself that a thousand times a day. You are not what I
need. But you are what I want. You see, everything is in the
reverse of what it should be."

She turned to him. "Maybe it is because we are looking
at it inside out."

He gave a short laugh. "Lord knows, I've not seen
much straight in my time. I am nearly thirty years old and
I haven't figured out a damned thing." He paused. "That
isn't true. I know what we are to each other is not what you
want. It is not marriage. It is not respectable."

Bowing his head, he seemed to draw upon reserves of
strength. "I said something to you the other day I had no
right to say. I told you that I would make love to you one
day."

Sophie shivered. She remembered that promise every
moment since, feared it, treasured it.

"That was unfair. You were unprepared for what happened. Sophie, there is a reason why I keep myself to married women, and it has nothing to do with what I told you. Married women are simple. They are convenient. They are even uneventful. And they are unavailable for real attachment. They realize what it is we are entering into. Women like you . . ."

He made a movement with his hands, as if to force the words he couldn't summon. "You don't know the game, darling. I may be a rake and a rat, but I always prided myself on one principle. I never hurt anyone. Sophie, I won't hurt you."

"You didn't," she whispered. "You did not take advantage of me."

"Yes, I did. I pretended I didn't want you, then I pretended I did but I wouldn't take anything from you, and now even that is gone. But you have to think about this flirtation, Sophie. You have to think about it now before it goes any further. I don't want to be your regret."

"I don't want to think about that," she replied quietly.

"You have to think about it sometime. You must face the unalterable fact that I cannot give you what you need."

"I will think about it. I will." He was frightening her with this kind of talk. "But not now, Gideon. Don't make me think about it now. And I must tell you, for a man with a black reputation, you have a very disappointing penchant for lecturing me."

"Am I lecturing? I am just trying to save myself from hating myself in the end. Purely selfish motivations. Do pardon me."

"You are a fraud. And I don't think you are a scoundrel at all." She sighed. "And I am not a blushing debutante out of the nursery, Gideon. You do not have to protect me. I have lived a very peculiar sort of life. It was a happy one in many respects, but it has held bitterness as well. I have made up my mind to have a different life for my future, for my children. But then, I met you. It is my choice. I know what I am doing. And I know what to expect."

"Indeed, you have the advantage, then. Please enlighten me."

"Gideon, lovers leave. They always leave. Husbands are permanent. You and I, we know what we want. For now. This is for now."

She felt his back go stiff. "Ah. So this is temporary. I did not realize you had made that determination."

It came as a surprise that he was annoyed. She heard it in the tightness of his tone. "I want you to know I understand that I do not have any delusions about . . . My mother was a woman of the world. I am not a romantic. And I will not have untoward expectations." She faltered. "I thought it would be a relief to you after all you just said."

"You just . . . amaze me," he said. "I see you are all straight on the matter. What a relief."

He did not sound relieved. He seemed to be looking at her with the same tender regret with which he had begun.

She wasn't sure what she had said wrong. Nor was she sure what she could do to set it right.

He sighed, then reached for her. His large hands cupped her face, and he kissed her, a gentle, thorough, lingering kiss. She leaned into him, treasuring his closeness. Inhaling his scent, she closed her eyes and let the languid feelings come over her.

Why did he not ravish her? Why had he not come to her room? What kind of scoundrel was he, when he never pressed a single advantage she offered?

No kind of scoundrel at all.

And what kind of woman was she becoming, to want him this badly, to wish to throw everything away to have him just once. And *that* was when she understood.

He *would* be her regret. Yes. She would slide easily into the tides that swirled around them, let herself go under and revel in the feelings, and then she would look at herself and know she had betrayed herself. She would have lied to May, cheated and stolen a life that was not hers, and it would have been for naught. In the end, she would find herself a woman like her mother after all.

She drew away. It was difficult. For all the sudden sensibleness that had just descended upon her, she did not wish to lose the comfort of his touch, his closeness.

"Let us go back inside," he said.

She felt a primitive stab of grief. She wanted to stay. She wanted him to do the things he had done to her before, and more . . .

Was he going to make her beg? She rose reluctantly. "Yes, come on. We certainly don't want to do anything that might tarnish your reputation."

He laughed, his voice a disembodied baritone in the darkness. For once, she wished he was not so good-natured. She wanted to hear in his voice some of the bitterness inside her.

✇ *Chapter 18*

It was the night of the soiree—May's designed introduction for Gideon to reenter fine society, and he was nervous. Actually nervous.

Outrageously, knee-knockingly, jaw-grindingly nervous.

The knowledge annoyed him. He stared at his image in the mirror, looking at the scars. He'd shed the eye patch a few days before and the marred flesh stood out starkly on his temple. It was much improved, but still noticeable enough.

He could almost imagine Reginald chuckling with that smirk Gideon could never stand—so much so that he had gotten very good at turning it to a glower in short order—floating like a taunt in his imagination. He'd always been an abysmal failure at these sorts of affairs. He was no good with the haute ton. They disapproved of him and he despised them.

He wondered what sort of reaction he would get among May's company of guests. And then he cursed hotly, drawing the startled attention of his valet. Why the hell did it matter all of a sudden what the dowdy matrons and pompous lords of society thought of him?

That it *did* matter, as much as he hated to admit it, did not please him. He suspected he knew the cause. Causes. Sophie was certainly one. Everything had to do with Sophie.

And May. It had recently become important to please May.

He accepted what had been growing in the back of his heart since the day he had crossed May's threshold. He did not want to go back to his old life. Her single-minded focus to rehabilitate him had annoyed him at first, but now he was warming to the idea. And the possibilities. He realized he would not be nervous about tonight if there were nothing at stake. But there was. A forbidden, ridiculous idea was forming in the back of his brain. He dared not allow it full birth.

But he might. He would have to see how things went.

When he descended the stairs, some guests had already arrived. Major Khoury joined him.

"Good evening," Adrian said.

Gideon replied, "It is good to see a friendly face." He glanced around the room to see who had arrived.

Sophie waved to him from the corner, where she was standing with Michaela and another woman. His breath caught.

She was incredibly lovely tonight. Her smile was brilliant and her eyes glowed. She wore a frothy dress of lavender. Her body was long, lithe, and graceful, the kind that suited the current vogue of Grecian fashion. The lines of her skirt fell softly about the considerable length of her legs. There would not be a man present tonight who would not notice her.

His body shot with heat. The light in her eyes was for him. Him.

And an answering emotion took him by surprise. It was pure possession, forceful and sharp, rising up from his feet to leave him tingling. *Sophie is mine.*

Since the night he'd laid her on the library divan and kissed her, something had been growing inside him. He had no doubt that Sophie wanted him. He even knew that she was ready to be his. These past days had served as ex-

quisite foreplay, days and evenings filled with glances
pregnant with meaning, emotion, even sensation.

If he'd wanted, he could have had her. The knowledge
thrilled him. It also struck him with fear. Sophie was not a
woman to seduce. She was a woman for a lifetime. And he
was a rake, poison to her reputation, and, yes, even unworthy of her.

But he was not a good enough man to walk away. So
he'd let her play out her little flirtation, let her roast him
alive with the heat of his own desire for her, wondering
how long the fast-failing myth of his honor would hold
out.

Michaela turned and made a playfully coquettish face at
the major. It was full of such familiarity, such volumes of
true emotion, Gideon felt like a voyeur watching it. But it
pierced him. He recognized something he wanted.

The dark gypsy foil to Sophie's golden beauty,
Michaela Khoury was a beautiful woman. More than that,
she was a lively, vivacious creature who for some reason
had offered Gideon unqualified friendship.

She gave Gideon a broad, warm smile and a lift of her
eyebrows, sending him a silent message of encouragement.

"May knows how to give a party," Khoury said, seeing
the interchange and obviously not objecting.

"She certainly does."

He should have known May would arrange a perfect
setting for a stylish get-together. Soft music played. The
room was lit with enough light to create an intimate mood.
The guests who had already arrived mingled easily.

There was a casual atmosphere tonight. He knew May's
circle was of the highest ton, and yet they were not stiff,
not pretentious, nothing he had anticipated.

"Sophie looks beautiful tonight," Khoury said. "She always does, of course, but especially so tonight. She has a
particular glow."

Gideon caught the smile before it could come to full

fruition. He would appear the gaping idiot if he let his pride and admiration show. He composed his face.

"And your wife as well," he countered. "Mrs. Khoury has been very kind to me, and she does not know me that well. She truly is a great lady."

Khoury got that soft, pleased look that came over him when Michaela was present. "I happen to agree."

"As do others," Gideon observed as an older gentleman approached their group, his gaze on Michaela.

Khoury made a sound, half pleased, half exasperated as Michaela smiled prettily at the man. "Which is why I must ever be on the watch for any admirers who might get carried away. There are those—"

He cut off abruptly and gave Gideon a strange look. It took him a moment to realize that he must be one of the "those" of whom the major was about to speak. Of course. Khoury was thinking of Gideon's penchant for bedding other men's wives.

"There are women who are vulnerable to wolves," Gideon said diplomatically, "and those who will never be touched. Mrs. Khoury is immune. Take it from me. A predator knows."

"You really are the most irreverent, unabashed man." The major shook his head in disbelief, but there was a hint of a smile about his face. "I do not know why Michaela thinks you amusing, but she does."

"Because she senses I am harmless."

"A harmless predator?"

"Some women wish to be caught." Gideon shot him a look and saw Khoury nod in approval. "And you are not really worried."

"But imagine how disappointed my wife would be if I did not at least pretend a concern."

They laughed, and the major excused himself. Gideon watched Sophie for a moment longer. Perhaps the major received some pleasure at watching his wife in a room, dazzling the company with her charm. He felt the same way looking at Sophie.

In his chest, his heart balled into a fist, then promptly relocated to his throat. Watching her brought an exquisite blend of pleasure and pain. Their clandestine attraction was too . . . clandestine. He wanted to march up to her right this minute and slip her arm in his. Claim her.

What a primitive notion. But *right*.

"Are you surviving?" May said, arriving at his side, rescuing him from the disturbing bent of his thoughts.

Lord Marcus Roberts was with her. "You seem to be holding up under the strain of having to make small talk and entertain the upper crust."

"I have hardly begun." He tried to look droll. His eyes scanned the room, touching on different faces, avoiding Sophie's.

"You must not hang back," May fussed, hooking her arm in his. "You really will like everyone. Give them an opportunity, Gideon."

He liked her little gestures of affection.

"It is not as bad as I anticipated, I admit. It took a bit of getting used to, having so many people look at me." He indicated his scars.

"Nonsense, Gideon. You can barely notice anything."

It wasn't that he was vain. But he felt as conspicuous as a branded bull. "How did you manage to get anyone to come?" He saw the steady flow of people filing in from the hall. "Are they all aware that the notorious Lord Ashford is in attendance or is that a surprise? I wonder if I should brace myself for an exodus when they realize they have a bona fide scoundrel in their midst."

"Gideon, no one thinks of you that way any longer. Or at least they will not before long." May gave him a conspiratorial glance. "And you cannot think you are the first among the ton to dally in disrepute. Come, now. Scandals come and go as quickly as the weather. Rakes reform and scoundrels settle down, and new misbehaviors arise to distract the rabid appetites for gossip. My friends are not mean-spirited. They are curious, of course, but they will give you a fair chance."

Roberts grinned proudly as he peered down at May. "Do not underestimate her, Ashford."

"I even managed to get Lady Viola to come and bring her niece," May crooned.

Gideon asked, "And why is that such a coup?"

"She and Sophie are friends—Margaux Milton, did she not speak of her?"

"Yes, actually. She likes her quite well. So why should it be such a great conquest that her friend has come?"

"Oh," May said with a start, casting an alarming glance to Roberts.

"Lady Viola is one of Lady May's oldest friends," Roberts explained. "However, she does have her niece's reputation to think of."

"Robert, please," May said. "It was not Lady Viola, but that wretched sister of hers who made the objection. But she is not objecting any longer. I can change the way things are with a few tricks."

"You cannot help a person change if they do not wish to," Roberts observed wryly. "Leading the horse to water and all of that."

"And I am the horse?" Gideon asked, pricking at the tone the man used.

"It's better than a jackass," Roberts replied, and strolled away.

"That man!" May shook her head and looked cross. "Oh, Gideon, do try to have a good time. I want so much for you to enjoy yourself."

But Roberts's needling was well placed, and well taken. To be a coward, to be afraid to try . . . well, then, one was a jackass, plain and simple.

May looked at him pleadingly, and Gideon suddenly thought how rewarding it would be to please this lady. Affection, ties of any sort—he'd avoided them for so long and they didn't come easy to him now.

He'd allowed his life to slip along, being irrelevant to humankind, his diversions eating up time until he found

himself nine and twenty and realizing that it was not at all
very diverting after all.

That was what had him tonight. He had the awful impulse to mean something to someone. To May.

And to Sophie. Yes. To Sophie. Not just a secret assignation, not just a lover.

May smiled up at him. "Do try," she said.

"I will," he said, and impulsively snatched her hand. He
brought it to his lips and kissed her fingers through her
gloves. "Thank you for doing so much for me."

She appeared touched. "Put some of that charm to good
use with the others," she said, and wandered off.

He felt . . . good. Deep down good. He loved May. He
needed her, and she needed him. They were family, by
God. Even after everything, the hurt and Reginald and the
dueling, he was her brother and she was the only person in
the world he could claim to care for him.

His gaze strayed to Sophie again. Desire was not the
same as love. Did Sophie care for him, too? Could she?

Beside her now was that . . . Sir Burton, Lord Burton.
Gideon recognized him from his visits to the house. He
never stayed to converse when callers came as a rule. It
was simply not within his powers of self-discipline to
make himself witness her courtships. But he was not above
a bit of spying.

Lord Burton was her favorite, he knew. Gideon despised him for no other reason than that.

Turning away, he drew in a breath. It was going to be a
long evening if he did nothing but moon over Sophie. He
was here to reestablish himself with good society. May
wished it. And suddenly he thought—why not?

The idea grabbed him like a fist around his gut. *Why
not?*

He was Lord Ashford, after all. A peer. He belonged
here. These people were not better than he . . . and hadn't
he only fooled himself into believing that because Reginald had convinced him he would never measure up? The
self-important snobs whose derision and back-biting had

turned him against the world of high society were worlds away from this gay crowd.

What the hell did that shriveled old man know, anyhow? Why had he ever allowed one single word of Reginald's poison to influence anything in his life? He'd had a family once, he'd had love. It had taken being reunited with May to remind him of all he had been once, all he had possessed.

And it had taken Sophie to want to defeat all he had let get in his way.

Sophie wanted a husband. A respectable husband. He could never give her the position she craved, but she wanted him.

And he loved her. He loved her madly.

Why didn't that frighten him? He loved her—of course he did.

And as he'd remembered lately, love counted for something. Everything, really. He'd had it all around him as a child. He'd believed in love. He'd known its power. He had foolishly thought when he'd lost it, that he'd been denied it because he had not deserved such gifts.

But that was crazy. Had he been a kind of insane for fifteen years? And now?

He wanted it all again. Damn him for a fool, but he was not going to give it all up again, not again. Surely God could only demand that of a person once.

Blast it, he was going to fight for her. *Why not?*

She was his. Sophie was already his, and he . . . he belonged to someone again. He was hers.

How Reginald would howl to see him like this, tucking his tail and pleading to the very society he'd scorned to take him back. For Sophie. He was going to fight for Sophie. He'd grovel if he needed to, learn to execute the smartest courtly bow to please anyone and everyone he had to, because he had to be what she needed him to be.

The mental image of his old nemesis changed. Reginald's sneer changed from gloating to displeasure. How had he forgotten that what had fed his guardian's dislike was his failure? Perhaps Reginald even thrived on it, liking the fact that Gideon fulfilled all his dire predictions.

Well, Reginald's forecasts might be borne out. It could all come to colossal failure, Gideon knew, but it was better than being, as Lord Roberts so acerbically observed, a jackass.

Chapter 19

Sophie felt Gideon's presence the moment he arrived at the
party. Knowing he was here had given the evening a luster
she felt in every bone, every tingling measure of skin. Excitement made her nerves jump. She was impatient to find
him, speak with him, but she had to share hostess duties.

May noticed the difference in her. "You are positively
sparkling tonight," she said.

Sophie grabbed her arm and stepped away from her
group of friends. "Have you seen Lord Ashford?"

"He is playing cards." May raised her eyebrows, a silent
question as to whether Sophie considered this a good or
bad development.

"He is in his element, then. It is far more what he is used
to doing than parlor dancing. But he is making the rounds.
I saw him speaking to Colonel Renshaw and Lord and
Lady Palmerston."

"Oh, my goodness!" May clapped her hands together.
"I half feared he'd have ducked out by now. Oh, this is
excellent!"

May flitted off and Sophie turned, smiling as pleasantly
as she could to Lord Burton, who arrived with a cup of
punch.

"Your aunt seems in high spirits," he commented.

"Well, it is a wonderful party!" she declared with un-controllable giddiness.

He laughed and inclined his head. "That it is."

Margaux approached and Sophie motioned her over. It was apparent that Lord Burton's presence gave her pause, but she was polite.

Margaux murmured, "Is this not just the loveliest party?"

There was general agreement that it was, and while Sophie tried not to make it too obvious that she was look-ing for Gideon, they exchanged absolutely insipid compliments on the floral arrangements, the music, the food, the décor.

Sophie's heart stopped when she spied Lord Farnsworth in the crowd. He gave her a smirk. To her horror, he headed straight for her.

How had he gotten invited? Had Gideon requested it? The man might have been instrumental in helping Gideon, but he was a social disaster, as Sophie knew quite acutely.

Sophie considered alerting Aunt May, but was aware that it would not do to make a scene. She braced herself.

He did not come to her, however. He paused next to Margaux and addressed himself to her. "Miss Milton, how excellent to see you."

Margaux could not hide her joy. "Lord Farnsworth. I am so glad you could come."

She cast a meaningful look to Sophie over her shoulder, who instantly understood that this was Margaux's beau, the one she had been talking about. Margaux was being courted by Farnsworth!

Sophie tried to calm the rush of displeasure that came over her. Perhaps she was mistaken, having seen the worst in him.

Her instincts screamed that she was not wrong. His smiles were oily, as if he were playacting. He took Mar-gaux to dance, and Lord Burton squinted at the two of them, as if he also did not quite approve.

"Miss Milton's friend . . . I do not believe I've met him before."

"I should have made the introduction."

"Is she . . . Are they well acquainted?" he asked. He hadn't taken his eyes off Margaux.

"I really do not know."

With an effort, he turned away. "Would you like some refreshment?" he asked.

She did not wish to linger with him. She wanted to find Gideon. "I best see to the other guests," she said as an excuse. Feeling guilty as she left him, she wondered if a woman should find the man she was considering marrying—should he ask—second in her interests?

In the dining room, where the chairs had been pulled away from the long table and lined up against the wall so that a buffet could be laid out, there was a line proceeding slowly past the array of fine foods. Sophie was astonished to see Gideon, standing in the middle of the queue with a plate in his hand, chatting with no less than a bona fide duchess.

She rushed to his side. "Lord Ashford. I have been looking all over for you. You did promise me that dance."

He covered his surprise and presented her to the duchess. "Her Grace, the Duchess of Longbourne," he intoned reverently.

Sophie held her breath, terrified he would slip into mocking tones, but he remained sincere.

"May I present Miss Sophie Kent, my sister-in-law's ward and niece."

The duchess lifted her lorgnette and peered at Sophie. "Charmed."

Sophie dipped a curtsy. "Your Grace. Are you having a pleasant evening?"

"Surprisingly, yes," she said with a tight smile at Gideon. "This young man is entertaining me with the most unusual stories."

Sophie relaxed. "I can well imagine."

The woman might have gray in her hair and lines on her

face, but she was not immune to Gideon's powers of charm. Sophie gave him a look of exasperation, and he returned a look, his thinly veiled with triumph and a shrug, as if he could not help himself from being irresistible, now could he?

"Could I ask you to wait upon that dance until after supper?" he said. He sounded as softly spoken and sincere as a poet. "I would like to sit with Her Grace." He paused, turned and inclined his head reverentially. "That is, if she will allow me to attend her."

"You are every bit the scamp you are reputed to be," Her Grace replied, but not with disapproval.

"Is that a no, then?" His smile was pure honey.

"My husband will be outraged," she declared. "And for that reason alone, I will permit you to entertain me. But I have my eye on you, Ashford. None of your antics."

"There, it is settled," Gideon said, satisfied, and to Sophie he said, leaning in so that only she could hear him, "You would not expect me to completely swear off the married women, would you?"

He straightened, looking so dignified and polished she wanted to reach up and kiss him then and there. "Would you pardon me?" He slipped around her. "Her Grace and I would like some of this excellent roast beef."

Sophie gaped as he and the duchess sauntered together down the buffet, piling their plates high with food and chatting as if they were old friends.

Admiration mingled with incredulity. He was astonishing.

She was distracted by Margaux entering with Farnsworth. She had his arm, and they were chatting. Margaux seemed so happy, unaware of the sly way her escort scanned the room. He caught Sophie watching him and smirked.

Was it only her dislike that made him seem so unpleasant?

She sought out Lady May. "Did you invite the Viscount

Farnsworth?" she asked her after drawing her away from a group of friends.

"But you were the one who asked me to invite Margaux's new beau. And, as he was so good a friend to Gideon, I did not think you would object."

Sophie remembered it was her suggestion to include him on the guest list. She felt a sense of responsibility. If she had her way, she would like to dissuade Margaux's interest in the man.

Tapping her finger to her lips, she considered the dilemma. Lord Burton passed close, smiling and bowing. She gave him a halfhearted smile and thought she must concentrate on making more of an effort with him. He really was a lovely man.

And, after all, she had no partner for the supper.

"Oh, Lord Burton," she called, going after him.

Margaux hated herself for the white-hot surge of jealousy that went through her when she saw Sophie calling after Lord Burton. She had no right to be jealous—Burton was Sophie's suitor, after all.

She concentrated on the man who stood beside her. He was talking with some friends, looking very urbane and dashing. He had them laughing over some story he was telling. Catching her eye, he winked.

Lord Farnsworth was just the kind of man for her. He was fair of face and outgoing, as she was. If he tended to overshadow her, she shouldn't mind so much. It was just . . . well, she wished he were not so outrageous sometimes.

He liked to be shocking, greedily observing her reaction when she blushed. It wasn't cruelty, exactly, it was just that her mother was so strict with her, she was a bit green. That was what he told her often enough, as if it delighted him.

Farnsworth was a worldly man, a swell whose exploits about Town were hilarious. These he loved to recount. He rather liked being the center of attention and everyone liked him.

She liked him, too. He was exciting.

Why did her eyes keep going to Burton's dark good looks, the way his hair fell in spiky points nearly to his eyes? His full lips and high cheekbones gave him a haughty, impossibly remote look that made her want him all the more. Burton was quiet, dignified. Farnsworth would say stuffy, and maybe he was correct. But she was attracted to Burton all the same, although it was an ill-fated attraction. He only had eyes for her best friend.

Oliver. His name was Oliver. She daydreamed about him sometimes, and it made her ashamed. If Sophie and Burton should marry, she would have lusted quite unpardonably after her best friend's husband.

He was ever polite to her when they met and had mentioned that Sophie had told him of her interest in Oriental artifacts. She'd quite lost herself in her enthusiasm.

She cringed at the memory of how she'd gushed, "My mother has friends who were invited to dinner at the Pavillion. They could not stop speaking of it. Great chandeliers shaped like coiled dragons with each light shielded with a delicate lotus. And the Egyptian motif in the after-dinner parlor was absolutely decadent."

He was fascinated, and they'd had a lively conversation. It was only after, when she'd remembered her mother's admonitions on going on so immodestly on the topic of her rather imprudent interests, that she wondered what he had made of her. No doubt he thought her a silly aspirant to intellectualism, which was best left to the masculine world.

"This is a stuffy party," Farnsworth said, turning to Margaux suddenly. He had a restless, cagy quality that made him, Margaux thought, a trifle frightening. "Let us go outside."

"It is chilly outside," she replied. Her mother would absolutely murder her if she slipped out of the party.

"Come, now," he said, pulling on her arm. "You cannot prefer this crowded room to a bit more . . . privacy." His eyes gleamed in a way that made her nervous.

He put a hand on the small of her back and began to guide her through the crowd. She felt a moment of panic. What was she supposed to do?

"I was hoping to be asked to dance." Her broad hint fell on deaf ears. He kept moving her forward.

"There must be an exit to the garden. Where could it be—do you know?"

"My mother will be angry with me if I leave," she admitted at last. "I dare not go with you."

He laughed. "My dear, if we always did what our mothers would have us do, what fun would we have? Come on, now, let us just take a walk. It clears the head. It is far too warm in here." He leaned closer, his eyes unnaturally bright. "And getting warmer. We'll just step outside, just a moment or two. It will be fine. You will see."

"Margaux!" Sophie said, stepping up to them just as they were passing through the library. There were French doors to the outside standing open on the other side of the hearth. "Where are you two off to?"

Farnsworth answered. "We were merely going outside for a moment. To take in a breath of fresh air." He paused and smiled at Sophie. "Miss Temple, did I say how good it is to see you again?"

Sophie froze. Her face went pale in an instant.

"It is Kent," Margaux said quietly, thinking Sophie was insulted that he had forgotten her name. It wasn't like Sophie to be so haughty over a mistake, but her reaction was unmistakable. Equally obvious was a spark of dislike as she all but glared at Farnsworth.

"Miss Kent? Are you certain? My, you bear an uncanny resemblance to a young lady I knew, a Miss Temple. A very interesting young woman."

Margaux stiffened. Was this another beau to fall at Sophie's feet?

"Are women so indistinguishable to you, my lord, that one face is the same as any other?" Sophie inquired, tartness in her tone.

"Indeed, there are some who stand out." Farnsworth

glanced at Margaux and shrugged. "But I have a very tepid memory. Miss Milton, shall we go outside as we planned? Good evening, Miss *Kent.*"

But Sophie stood firm. "Margaux's mother has asked me to find her. She wishes to see her." She spoke to Margaux rather firmly. "We should go right away."

"Oh." Margaux flushed. She was horribly embarrassed. Farnsworth must now think her a child. She hated the way her mother fussed so over her. She was far too over-bearing.

She felt Farnsworth's amused and scornful look. "Then you best run along, Miss Milton. *Mama* is calling."

Men like Farnsworth didn't give a fig about mothers' wishes. They were dangerous and daring. She wished she had the courage to tell her mother to wait. She wished she had the courage to go outside with him instead of trotting obediently to her mother's side.

She never could tell her mother no. She was afraid of her, and too eager to please and win her stingy approval.

"I will come right away," she told Sophie, casting one last look at Farnsworth. His expression of disappointment shamed her for the coward she was. Sophie tried to hurry her away, but Farnsworth called after her. "Goodbye. Miss *Kent.*"

Now he disliked Sophie just because she'd fetched her for Mama. Margaux saw the night that she had looked forward to so long, a night with Farnsworth and Sophie . . . and, yes, with Lord Oliver Burton, had turned into a disaster.

What made it all the worse was that when she arrived at Mother's side, she seemed puzzled to find her present and shooed her away.

Flushed and miserable, Margaux caught Lord Burton's eye once again. He inclined his head politely and came to ask her to dance.

That, at least, brought some brightness to the otherwise miserable evening. They fetched punch together afterward, but just as she was relaxing in his company, Sophie joined them.

Margaux imagined his attentions shifted to her friend and excused herself quickly. It was simply too difficult to see the two of them together, knowing that they would without a doubt be betrothed before long.

She swallowed her pride and went in search of Farnsworth, but she found he had left.

Farnsworth remembered her, now Sophie was sure of it. She was equally as sure he was going to use it.

The brief and disturbing interview was much on her mind as she continued circulating among the guests. Surely, he did not understand that she was not Millicent Kent's daughter. Sophie thought he would have been more direct if he completely fathomed the depth of her deceptions. No, it was more probable that he thought she had changed her name merely to hide her past so as to avoid censure from the ton.

His calling her "Miss Temple" had been a warning. He wanted her to keep her distance, to not interfere with his romancing Margaux.

If she thought Margaux would heed her, she would tell her about Farnsworth immediately. But was it decisively an indication of bad character to think a woman of the demimonde was available for assignation? It would take more than the sour feelings the man inspired in her to dissuade her friend from her romance.

She made up her mind to discuss the matter with May, as surreptitiously as possible. May always knew what to do.

She was waylaid by Gideon, who grabbed her elbow and swept her along with him.

"I am doing splendidly," he announced, leading her to the punch bowl. "Everyone loves me."

"No doubt your stunning humility has impressed them," she countered brightly. She felt her heartbeat quicken as she walked with him.

He looked very handsome in his tailcoat and embroidered waistcoat. His long legs flexed in the tightly-fit silk breeches that were the height of fashion. She had seen women casting long, sly glances at him from behind their fans and it maddened her.

"No. I rather think it is my vast wit." He nodded as if considering the matter deeply. "That combined with my good looks, of course."

She laughed softly. His presence brought forth a low thrum of excitement. "I must say, you are quite surprising me. I thought you would sit in a corner and glower the entire time."

"Oh, I've decided that I am going to allow May to rehabilitate me." He nodded to a passing couple, whom he seemed to know. They smiled back. "As a result, I have found that the stodgy old fusspots, otherwise known as the bon ton, are not as bad as I recall."

"How kind of you to notice. Did you think May's friends would be the same as Reginald's?"

His brows shot up as his lip curled in the corner. "Touché. But it is only part of it. I have had surprising ease at winning them over."

"May's doing. And do not discount the fact that you haven't dunked anyone in the pond as of yet."

"There is no pond."

She smiled as he handed her a cup of punch. "I trust you to improvise should the occasion arise."

"I actually think I've outgrown such measures. Maturity is dulling to one's sense of adventure. Are you disappointed?" He took a drink from his punch and winced. "Good God, what is this stuff?"

"It contains no liquor."

He put down the cup. "Then why on earth would you drink it?"

"You do not need spirits," she said, "as you are quite already intoxicated with your success. I wonder if you could handle a real challenge."

"You strike me to the quick! You doubt my charm?"

"Not at all." She sipped her drink, her eyes dancing. "It is merely that May has arranged a very forgiving crowd for this initiation. To build your confidence."

He gave her a dangerous look. "You taunt me, Miss Kent."

She jerked her head to her left, a mischievous look in her eye. "All but one. Margaux's mother, Mrs. Eugenia Milton, is, I am sorry to tell you, not at all pleased to be in the same company as a notorious rake. In fact, it took quite a bit of doing for her to allow Margaux to attend the soiree tonight."

"I'd heard about that. A stiff curmudgeon, is she?"

"The worst." She glanced to where the woman in question stood with her daughter and several others. "May only invited her because she is Lady Viola's sister, and Margaux's mother."

"But how can she dislike me? She has not even met me." He plucked her cup from her hand. "Which we must remedy immediately. Quickly, tell me something about her."

"She rules her daughter with an iron fist. Hmm. Let's see. She is partial to sweets."

"I can deduce that from her girth. What does she love? What does she talk about all the time?"

"What does she talk about all the time—other people. She is a dreadful gossip. And a braggart. She is forever going on and on over the superiority of her family. Let me see . . . I know she loves music. I have heard she is a very accomplished musician herself."

"The pianoforte?" He was rubbing his chin in contemplation. "She is an aficionado?"

"The harp, actually."

His face brightened. "Really, the harp? Oh, dear Miss Kent, have I never told you that I absolutely adore the harp?"

He gave her such a look that she couldn't hold back the giggles. He said, "You must present me. Quickly. She appears to be gathering her daughter to leave."

"What are you going to do?"

"Trust me. I am going to leave her limp with pleasure." He guided her toward his quarry. "Married women are, after all, my specialty. A woman never charms so easily as when she is neglected by a busy husband. I see no Mr. Milton at her elbow, and so she is fair game. In addition, a braggart always loves attention, even from a scamp."

"Gideon," Sophie warned, feeling a tingle of apprehension. She had goaded him into this. Gideon was capable of anything. She did not trust him at all.

But she could not wait to see what he would do.

Mrs. Milton's face pinched tightly when Sophie presented Lord Ashford to her. She barely inclined her head to him, while Gideon swept into a low bow.

"It is delightful to make your acquaintance," he said solemnly. "Lady May and Miss Kent speak so highly of you all the time."

She gave him a long, dry look without benefit of any response.

"Do you find the evening diverting?" he inquired. His smile would have charmed a miser out of a thousand pounds.

"It was lovely," Mrs. Milton said with a sniff. "I expected no less. Lady May Hayworth is a noteworthy hostess."

Margaux piped up. "Lady May always puts on such beautiful parties—"

"Margaux," Mrs. Milton said sharply, "it is late. It is time we are going."

Gideon looked stricken. "Ah, then good night. I am fortunate that I do not have to take my leave as I am in residence at the moment." His smile was absolute innocence. "This is my favorite part of the evening, when the crowd thins and the music still plays and I can enjoy it without all the noise of conversations to intrude. I thought the musicians were wonderful tonight. Did you like them, Miss Milton?"

Effectively stuck, Mrs. Milton and Margaux could not

leave while Gideon was addressing them so pointedly. Mrs. Milton resented this and let it show.

"I did indeed," Margaux said pleasantly, but the darting glance she shot to her mother betrayed her awareness of the mounting tension.

"I have only one complaint. I am partial in particular to the angelic strains of the harp, and there was no harpist in the orchestra. Would that have not been heavenly? Miss Kent, have you ever danced to music played on the harp?"

My Lord, he was as subtle as a lorry. "I have not," she murmured.

"Ah, it is the sweetest thing. I had the privilege at a house party the summer before last. I shall not forget it. The music made the dance seem that much grander, more dignified. It was quite an experience."

"Did you know, Lord Ashford," Sophie said with feigned diffidence, "that Mrs. Milton plays the harp?"

He looked stunned, but not too much so. And so pleased. Sophie almost giggled. He was absolutely perfect.

And Mrs. Milton's mouth was twitching, showing she was pleased to have this mentioned. "A long time ago," she said, waving her thick hand encased in expensive silk gloves. Ah, but she was no longer casting Margaux urgent looks to quit their company.

"Indeed, my admiration knows no bounds," Gideon declared. "It is such a difficult instrument. The skill required is so complex, quite beyond my imagining. I do applaud you, Mrs. Milton. Ah, but I am too bold. There it is, Miss Kent, that trait that is always getting me into so much trouble. Have I embarrassed you, Mrs. Milton? I do sincerely apologize if I have."

Her head bobbed a little, the way a hen's does when she's preening. "It gives me great pleasure to speak to a fellow admirer of all music, but I must confess, I am delighted to know of your appreciation of the harp. It is quite a singular instrument, and not many realize the superiority of it."

"She is an excellent harpist," Margaux chimed in. Her

mother feigned a quelling expression, but there was no disguising her secret pleasure at such complimentary attention.

"Do you play for company?" Gideon inquired. "How I should love to hear you sometime."

"I do not," she said, the stridency back in her voice. "I believe that younger talent should take precedent when at public gatherings. It is the young ladies who need to show off their accomplishments. My daughter shall play, when she is ready."

"But is it right to cheat your audience of talent, just because you are a respectable married woman?" He seemed appalled. "What a loss to all of us who so enjoy a skilled musician. It is not often one is privileged to hear a harpist. Now, the pianoforte, the cello, these are ordinary, but the harp . . ." He ended by shaking his head sadly. Then he appeared to remember something. "Ah, but I am keeping you. You were about to take your leave. So good to meet you, Miss Milton."

He bowed low over Margaux's hand, a gesture of reverence without a trace of sarcasm. Mrs. Milton's lips tightened, but the corners jerked upwards the tiniest bit.

"And Mrs. Milton, please forgive me for going on so. I only wish I could convince you to allow me to hear you play."

"Well," she said, and to Sophie's utter astonishment, she actually gave Gideon a look that on any other woman would have been flirtatious, "my sister is forever urging me to have a small dinner party and invite the friends I have made here in London. I've put it off, being so busy with my daughter's introduction into society. Perhaps it is a good idea after all. In such a small, intimate group, I do not think I would feel it untoward if I took a few moments to play a piece or two before the young people took over."

Gideon gave a stunning performance of subdued excitement. "Indeed, madam, I think that a most excellent plan! I know your guests will be the better for your relenting in your rule to keep your talent to yourself. How kind you are, by the way, to ordinarily think of others instead of putting yourself forward. But how pleased I am that you would make this exception."

"I will be inviting Lady May and Miss Kent, of course," Mrs. Milton said, adjusting her shawl. Her chest, puffed up as it was, took up much more of the expensively embroidered garment. "I will place your name upon the invitation as well, Lord Ashford, and you may judge my talent for yourself."

"It would be my most anticipated engagement," he said. He held her hand and bowed over it, again executing an impeccable performance of thunderstruck pleasure. "You are very kind to include me. I am overcome."

When they left, Sophie looked at him and groaned. "That was nauseating."

"But it worked." He was smug and not hiding a trace of it. "I tricked her into receiving me. Mrs. Milton, my chief detractor, is going to invite me into her home."

Sophie's jaw dropped. "You are frighteningly confident in your ability to charm any woman."

He grinned. "It worked for you, my most difficult challenge to date."

She looked about, nervous someone might have overheard them. When she turned back to him again, he was smiling, as if harboring some secret joke.

"I am going to win them all," he said, his voice low with solemnity. "And then I am going to win you, Sophie."

She drew in a sharp breath. Her heart pinched for a moment, and she felt a dizzying weakness peel away her composure.

His face, however, was perfectly sedate. He was not joking. He looked pleasant, congenial, almost benign in stark contrast to the stunning impact of what he was saying. "I am going to wheedle my unworthy self back into the good graces of high society. You see, it has struck me that not being regarded a reprobate any longer might have its advantages."

"But you hate society." Why would he want to change?

"Not so. True, I despised the people I knew before, as a younger man when I first came into the beau monde. Reginald's associates—I could not even call them his friends—were mere weasels who hated me before I stepped foot in the room because of all the bad he'd told them about me. All I could see at the time was to shock their pruned-up faces with the boldest, brashest, most outrageous things I could do or say. Then it got away from me. How do you turn back, once down that road? I am afraid I did the only thing I could do; I convinced myself it was fun. But it wasn't fun, Sophie. After a while, it was not even mildly amusing. Oh, it was diverting, it was numbing, but damn if it wasn't boring after a while. And it was lonely."

He saw the shock on her face, and nodded. "It was far from satisfactory to be hated by all but a bunch of drunken fools and imbeciles whose idea of brilliant entertainment was out-debauching the other. Although I would have never admitted so before, not on my life."

Her mouth worked for a moment, trying to generate sound. "I am glad. You should take your place—"

He made a sharp gesture with his hand. "I am not doing this to take my place in society or any other rubbish. I am not even doing it for May, though I owe her everything, before and now. She is the one to credit for anything good in me. She sowed it into my soul when I was a boy, and now as a man, she brought me here. To you.

"This is for you, Sophie. I am doing this only for you. Because I want you. All of you. Not just a quick *temporary* affair before you go into a stunted marriage with a man you marry on the sole recommendation that he is respectable. *I* want to be that man. And I will be. I will make myself all that you need me to be, because you are mine and only I will have you." He stepped forward, and now his eyes blazed. His breath fanned across her cheek, dragon's breath to fire her to her bones. "Tonight I knew you were meant to be mine. Only mine, and no other's."

She felt a wave of shock go through her. She was aware

that there were still people around, although they were all speaking among themselves and not paying her or Gideon any mind.

"Are you asking me to marry you?" she asked in barely a whisper.

"I will. Sophie, I want you. I want you for all of my life. I want to marry you. But I cannot ask yet. Give me time. Unless . . . you do have an ardent suitor in Lord Burton."

"I do not love Lord Burton," she blurted.

What remained unsaid was whether or not she loved Gideon.

Did she? She knew suddenly and without reservation that she did. Surely she did. Why else would her heart be hammering mercilessly in her chest like this, threatening to crack a rib? Why else would she feel so elated she could barely stand still while they spoke like this? It took all she had not to throw herself into his arms.

"That is good," he said with a smile. "Then you will wait?"

"Yes," she said, wishing she had not. She had to think! It was one thing to contemplate an affair, quite another to promise to hold her future in check for . . .

Oh, God, what was she thinking—of course she would wait.

"This is awkward," he said, glancing around. "What a stupid place for me to go into this. I have no worry that we will be overheard, but my dear Miss Kent, I would very much like to kiss you right now."

May appeared at Gideon's side, wearing a triumphant smile. "You are quite the man of the hour," she announced. "I am so proud of you."

"Did you doubt me?" he asked.

She raised her brows. "Every moment. I cannot make you behave yourself any longer, Gideon. You are far past the age when I could send you to your room with bread and water for supper."

"But you have provided everything I need to wish to behave." His eyes shifted momentarily to Sophie, then back to May. "I actually enjoyed myself. It was a fine affair."

"I do have a gift," she said with a satisfied sigh.

By the way she looked at Gideon and Sophie, it seemed she was quite pleased with the night's work.

Chapter 20

The whisper of Sophie's bare feet on the hardwood floor sounded impossibly loud. In the dead of night, noises were magnified, making clandestine creeping about in the night a nerve-jarring experience.

She did not wear her bedroom slippers because of the tiny wooden heel. The sharp clicking would be much more damning than the padding of her feet as she hurried to the staircase.

A shadow in front of her almost ripped a scream from her until she realized, just in time, who it was.

"Gideon!" she hissed.

He was as shocked to see her as she was him. "Miss Kent," he drawled. "What are you doing about at this hour of the night? Or morning, should I say?"

She blushed hotly. Damn him, damn him, he knew what she was about.

"I was going to the library," she stammered. "To find a book. I couldn't sleep. I . . ."

He stepped forward. His finger came up and sealed itself over her mouth. She felt a jolt at the contact, just that little touch.

He wore only his shirtsleeves, which she'd seen him in

enough times before that it shouldn't make her tremble like this, with anxiety . . . and anticipation.

"Were you now?"

She knew he could tell she was lying. And he did hate liars.

"I thought we might talk," she said, drumming up her courage. "What you said tonight . . ."

"I was standing here," he said softly, "thinking that I am mad. Each time I took a step toward your room, I told myself to turn back. And each time I made to turn back, my body would not obey my will." He grinned. "Thank goodness you happened along. It might have taken me three more hours to make my way to your door."

"You were coming to my room?"

"And you were going to mine."

She closed her eyes. "I . . . Yes."

He lifted her chin and she faced him. In the gloom, his face was dark planes and shadows.

His voice was barely a whisper. "The measure of a man is and always will be honor. If I lost most of myself in the years since living with May and Matthew, I did not lose that. But, Sophie . . . what I cannot decide is what that honor is. Is it staying away from you, driving us both mad, or is it sealing our fate together? If I trust every bone in my body, it is the latter. But I cannot tell any longer, Sophie, if this is so or just what I want to be so."

The muscles in his face twitched, and he smiled, but it was a smile full of emotion, full of moment.

"I am here not for a fashionable *affaire de coeur*. I am here as the man who loves you. What I've spent the last . . . God knows how long, deciding is whether that is an honorable enough reason to rap upon your door."

In the silence and the dark, the time seemed to extend forever. Then she was in his arms, a slight sob in her voice as she cried, "I love you, Gideon. I love you, I love you."

His hands trembled as they nestled into her hair. "How could you love me? How is it possible?"

"You are Lord Ashford, scandalous rapscallion and,

secretly, a man of the highest character that I have ever known. I love you so much."

She turned and kissed him, and the feeling was sweet and rough. The hardness of his body was welcome shelter, calming the roiling of nerves and stirring a new excitement deep at the core of her.

When they parted, he looked into her eyes. "Then we are betrothed. In our hearts, we are promised. In the days of Sir Walter Scott's noble ladies and knights, a betrothal was as good as married."

Laughing, she nodded. "Very well. We are betrothed."

He stroked her cheek. "Then I ask to be invited to your bedroom, my dear love."

She stepped back. Her eyes shone into his. He slipped his arm about her waist and held her close as they went inside and shut the door.

Gideon's eyes adjusted quickly. It was a small room, appointed lavishly. There was a dressing table, a chair, a chest, a wardrobe, a small table, and a canopied bed.

He held out his hand and she took it. He drew her close to kiss her. Her response was sweet, stirring. He braced his legs and slipped his hand to the small of her back.

Tremors wracked him and he struggled for control. He wanted so much for this night to be everything he wished it to be, but his body was betraying him. The throbbing insistence from his groin was driving him mad.

"Shall I undress?" she asked.

"I would like to assist you, if you do not mind."

Her eyes were wide, somewhat bewildered. "Very well," she agreed. She was intrigued, he could see.

He began with the long row of fasteners up the back of her gown. His fingers were fairly adept at this task, but their skill seemed to have deserted him. He fumbled with a few of them, but they eventually relinquished their grasp and he slipped the gown from her shoulders.

She turned, her eyes glowing like coals. "Shall I undress you?"

"If you like." He smiled. She was not shy. She did not

balk at standing in her undergarments in front of him, not even when he slipped his finger in the neckline of her chemise, just to feel the upper curve of her breast against his knuckle.

She was not skilled at the studs, but she managed. He forced himself to be patient. When she had them all undone, he shirked the garment and her hands reached out to touch his chest. Palms flat, fingers splayed, she studied the way he was formed.

This nearly sent him to the ceiling. She had a delicious, uncensored air of wonder about her. But she was a virgin, his first virgin. The first woman who made him feel like this, as if she were looking not just at his body, but at *him*. So, it was new for him, too, as new as if he'd been the most unschooled of lovers.

"Come," he said, and led her to the bed. He drew down the covers and sat her on the edge. Kneeling before her, he caressed each lithe limb.

He watched her as he did so, saw her eyelids go heavy at the silky glide of his fingertips over her flesh. She gave herself to every moment. He was aware of a growing knot of emotion gathering behind his Adam's apple.

"Are you warm? You are perspiring," she noted, touching the fine sheen of moisture that had collected on his brow.

He gave her fingertips a quick kiss. "It is merely because I am coming out of my skin."

She flashed a pleased smile, then caught her bottom lip in her teeth, uncertain. "Am I taking too long?"

"I am taking too long. But I want to. It is better . . . And I want to make it last as long as possible." He pressed her back onto the bed, leaning over her. "I want to make it good for you."

"You are good for me," she said, pulling him down to kiss her.

The rest of their clothing came off quickly, and when he lay next to her, skin to skin, his breath froze in his chest.

She was warm, soft, wrapped all around him with restless wanting as he kissed her soundly.

"Do not wait," she whispered. "Take me if you wish."

He would have liked to force himself to wait. It was the way he'd planned it, dreamed it, but when she uttered those words, nothing could stay the surge of unrestrained lust that grabbed hold of him.

He prepared her with deft strokes. When she was slick, he shifted and slowly sheathed himself in her body. She arched, her mouth forming a soft O. Fearful of hurting her, he stopped, but she slipped her hand to his hip and urged him on.

The feeling of her was unspeakably glorious. He watched her as she responded to his thrusts. There was no pain. This seemed to surprise her. The pleasure surprised her as well.

He . . . well, he was grateful. He would have been patient. He would have restrained himself to the brink of insanity before hurting her, but his body was demonstrating a curious and unforeseen proclivity for operating outside his will. He let himself go, and the rush of a punishing tide drove him to the edge.

His pleasure ripped through him like searing wind, a blast so pure and strong he nearly lost consciousness.

When it was over, he took a moment until he could breathe again, he slipped his hand between them, his fingers seeking her sensitive place. She was hot and wet, and she responded quickly to the deft pressure of his thumb. He was still inside her when she climaxed. He felt the rhythmic clenches of her inner muscles as she melted under him, and he was aroused again.

They were quiet, then, for quite a long time. They whispered softly in the dark. Then he lit a taper, and made love to her the way he had imagined. Slowly, savoring each touch, exploring her body, encouraging her curiosity to explore his. They occupied themselves for hours, long into the night.

In the morning, he awoke just as the first threads of daylight split the thinning night. Extricating himself from her warmth, he rose from the bed carefully and gathered his clothing. With a quick kiss and soft steps, he left her and returned to his own room.

He slept until noon, awaking with a feeling so full in his breast, he could not move for a long time. He lay on his back, with the sunshine ripe and strong coming through his window, and replayed the previous night's delights over and over in his mind.

That was what it was like to make love. He'd never really done that before. He'd called it that, but it had not been anything to do with love. Affection, at times, but that was so pale in comparison to this deep, soul-shattering thing that had his body buzzing even now, hours after their last caress.

Once, he'd imagined he was incapable of that kind of feeling. Only now did he realize that it had been a bitter tonic. He'd never imagined life could be so full.

When he walked into the drawing room, May and Sophie were already seated, chatting as they worked on their needlework. May looked up at his arrival and gave him a curious look. "You had a restless night?" she asked as he pressed a fond kiss to her cheek.

"Quite the contrary. It was extraordinarily pleasant," he said, inclining his head toward Sophie. "I had the most incredible dream. It followed me the entire night, and since it was so enjoyable, I was reluctant to awaken. I suppose it is the only excuse I have for being so lazy."

May, who was oblivious to the low undertone to his voice, or the answering flush that heated Sophie's cheeks, patted his hand. "Well, we all need a good lie-in every now and then. It is so restorative."

"I agree." His gaze caught Sophie's again, very quickly, before she ducked her head and stabbed her needle into her sewing. But there was a smile there, the sweetest curl of those sensuous lips.

He chuckled, not able to resist a little tease. "I feel more refreshed than I can remember being in a long time. How did you sleep, Sophie?"

She raised her eyes. Her expression was bold, completely unapologetic. He felt the bolt of it clear through his chest.

"I awoke early myself," she said. "It is simply too glorious a day to waste lying abed."

He had a difficult time finding his voice. "Well, I envy you your early start, for it is indeed a fine, fine day. The finest."

May frowned, peering at him as if he were daft. "Are you hungry? We already had luncheon."

"You are astute, as usual. I am utterly famished." He leaned back, cupping his hands behind his head as May rang for a servant.

As she was giving instructions for a plate of food to be brought into the drawing room for him, Sophie leaned back so that she could see him behind May's back. She directed a scolding glare at him and mouthed the word "Behave!" silently.

Behave.

Ah, but that woman sometimes expected too much from him.

෬ Chapter 21

In Lady May's drawing room, Margaux tried to cover her nerves. She'd come to call with her aunt and mother and found Lord Burton had had the same idea. His lean, dark aspect had nearly sent her into a faint.

It was becoming impossible to ignore her growing feelings for the man. Why could she not get him out of her head? She had Lord Farnsworth—*Viscount* Farnsworth! True, he was entirely a different sort than the noble, admirable Lord Burton, but that, she had decided, was exactly what she needed to rid herself of this hideous obsession with her best friend's chief suitor and, no doubt, soon-to-be husband.

She groaned at the hopeless bent of her thoughts, drawing stares. She gaped back in horror. She had just emitted the most unladylike noise! "Oh. I was just . . . I . . ."

"Margaux," Sophie said calmly, "I was hoping you would play something for us. It would brighten up the afternoon so much for us. The rain is dreadfully dreary, and we are cozy inside."

Lady Milton stiffened.

Margaux gave Sophie a scolding glance. Her friend should know better than to ask her to play or sing in public, not until she was good enough to draw the kind of admiration for which such exercises were meant. Her mother had made this abundantly clear.

She was about to refuse when Lord Burton turned his beautiful face toward her, and spoke. "I would be most gratified, Miss Milton. I am a great admirer of the musical arts. A bit of song might be just what we need."

Margaux was flustered. She wanted to refuse. How could she put herself on display, especially in front of him?

Her mother said, "Perhaps another time."

"But Mrs. Milton," Sophie insisted, "Margaux's gift is quite significant."

"But she has not yet conquered her nerves." Her mother stated this with enough disapproval to sting Margaux's pride.

It was true, of course, but to have herself exposed! What would Oliver think of her? A ninny, that was what— he would think her a ninny.

She felt a cold wash of misery, and then, suddenly, she caught Sophie's encouraging glance. She raised her eyebrows and set her jaw, as if to silently communicate: "Go on!"

She rose, suddenly infused with a wild impulse. This was her chance. If she were not to be overlooked, if she were to draw any sort of admiration from the man she herself admired, she would have to stop acting like such a damnable *ninny!*

In as composed a voice as she could muster, she asked, "Would you like to hear anything special?"

Her mother was shocked, but it was Lord Ashford's voice that thundered into the silence. "Hurrah! This is capital. I say, Mrs. Milton, it is ingenious of you to have your daughter make her debut among a group of intimate friends like ours. This way, she can have the experience of playing for others without being intimidated by a large crowd."

Aunt Viola clapped her hands gaily. "Oh, Margaux, dear, this is a surprise. Yes, yes, Eugenia, it is about time."

Whether Mrs. Milton was in agreement or merely unable to object after such an enthusiastic response, Margaux could not tell. She supposed she would find out later, at home.

But for now, Lord Burton had requested a song.

She began slowly, a classical piece, which was one of her favorites. Her fingers were stiff at first. To her utter humiliation, they stumbled over the notes a few places at the start. She closed her eyes, and blocked all thought out of her mind.

She imagined the music building towering trees around her, majestic mountains in the distance, the glittering sunlight thrown off from a fast-moving brook breaking light on everything around her. And the breeze, and the warmth. Her fingers found their place.

When she reached the allegro, her fingers flew. She opened her eyes, but she saw no one. This was how she played at home, when she was alone.

But now she was playing for Lord Burton. And she was playing for herself.

She slowed the piece, streaming artfully into the finish. There was a silence and suddenly Sophie exclaimed, "My goodness, Margaux! That was magnificent!"

They began to applaud and Margaux beamed at them. She dared a look at her mother and found her, for once, openmouthed. She, too, applauded, a half-smile of wonder on her face.

"My goodness, what a performance!" Lord Burton exclaimed, standing and beaming at her. "Please, perform something else."

"Yes, do," Sophie chimed. "And sing something. She has the most excellent voice, my lord."

"What would you like?"

"Something sweet," Lord Ashford interjected. "For it would suit you." He leaned back in his chair and gazed at her with warm appreciation. Sometimes it was difficult to remember when she'd been leery of him. His reputation was abominable, but he had always been utterly proper and so very kind to her.

She sang a folk ballad, a quiet song about unrequited love. She almost lost her courage, fearing she was being too transparent, but something made her look to Lord Ashford, knowing she would find the courage she needed.

He was a man of the world, a man who would be amused by her silly romanticism, and if she found censure there, she would know she was making a fool of herself. But his expression was rapt, caught in an emotion she herself felt in her breast. She finished her song, and was again rewarded with rapturous applause.

"Another, please," Sophie said.

Margaux was firm. "No, no. Enough music. Let us have a lively game of cards or something else."

She took her seat next to her mother. She felt her lean close, and reflexively braced herself.

But she said, "That was absolutely lovely, my dear. Absolutely lovely."

It was the most praise she'd gotten from her mother since she could remember.

They were not enough for two foursomes, so Margaux sat out, as did Lady May, who coached Sophie liberally from a chair set behind her, and Lord Burton.

She roamed the room, strolling deep in thought. Where had she found the courage to play today? And where had she found the means to play so well?

She was astonished when Lord Burton approached her.

"Allow me to congratulate you on your remarkable talent, Miss Milton." He bowed slightly.

She smiled back nervously. "Do you play as well?"

"No, no. I enjoy going to the symphony, of course. I am one of the only members of the audience who arrives on time. I do not speak during the performance, no matter if it is a duke or the Prince Regent himself who arrives at my box, and I do not leave until the last note is played."

"And does the prince often drop by your box at the theater?" she inquired.

"No, thank goodness. In fact, never."

"Ah. You and Lady May might have a long conversation on that score. I am afraid she is not an admirer of his either."

"Our king is mad. His son . . . well, he is no tribute to rational thought or temperate living. Our country needs a leader."

"Oh, but he does lead, my lord. In Brighton, he leads his orchestra in great fanfares and his Marine Pavillion is the leader of Chinese fashion. His court is the leading authority of excess and misuse of prestige."

He surprised her by laughing. "Your views mirror mine. But I must say, however, he has done quite a lot for the cultural arts. And you know I share your fascination with imports he had brought to England, so I suppose he has done some good."

"He has, it is true," she replied, excited. "Why, Lord Burton, I neglect to mention a wonderful new pamphlet making the rounds in some circles, on the wilds of the African jungle."

He appeared dumbstruck. "Dear Miss Milton, do not tell me you were present at the chilling presentation given by Mr. Wilheim Westerhaus detailing his journey to the dark continent."

"I was not!" she exclaimed. She had dearly wished to attend that one. "Were you?"

"I was, Miss Milton, and I must tell you it was fascinating, absolutely fascinating."

He proceeded to detail with thrilling exactitude all he recalled of the lecture. She interrupted him with rapidly fired questions from time to time, but he did not seem to mind. Instead, this seemed to ignite his enthusiasm, causing him to go into deeper detail.

The time passed quickly. Margaux found she lost her awkwardness and told him her thoughts on the native tribes and her disagreement that these "savages" were subhuman.

"I read a most persuasive argument indicating that although the customs and beliefs of these people are very different from ours, they contain the basic elements of honor and loyalty, adherence to the community, and many higher-order ideals."

He smiled, intrigued. "You must give me the name of this pamphlet."

"I will find it and have a footman bring it to you, if you would leave me your direction."

"Perhaps I will call on you tomorrow and save you the trouble."

She flushed, too pleased to contain herself, but it was quickly squelched by a rush of conscience. Of course, she wanted Lord Burton to call on her! But he was Sophie's romance.

With Sophie it was not romance, exactly, she knew, but still . . . still, it was wrong!

She'd loved Oliver for so long . . . *Loved* him. Maybe not the deep, true love, but the infatuated, heart-pounding, palm-sweating, tongue-tying love . . . yes, she loved him. And she had the strongest indication that this regard would only deepen. He was so sincere, so intense. His humor was subtle, very, very dry, but she liked it. She could love this man forever.

But she must not allow herself even friendship. She was far too vulnerable.

"I am afraid I am often not at home," she said with an apologetic look that she hoped belied the obvious rudeness of what she was saying. "I think sending my man with the pamphlet is best. I shall enjoy discussing it with you again when . . . when we meet again at some party or ball."

He took the hint. Bowing he said, "Your servant, Miss Milton. I am most grateful for your generosity. I will impose on you no more than I must."

She wanted to call him back. No. She had to stop this ridiculous infatuation. No matter that her heart pulsed wildly with so much joy, so much sadness, she thought it would burst.

Sophie won the rubber and Lady Milton made a sound of disgust and Lady May laughed in delight.

"Your first time to win!" she declared. "We will make an Ellinsworth of you, yet. You know, we all excel at cards!"

Sophie went stiff, looking very strange. But Margaux was too preoccupied watching Lord Burton drift over to the table to take much note. As usual, he positioned himself at Sophie's side.

"I love shopping." May sighed as she alighted from her carriage on Gideon's guiding hand and surveyed the posh shops lining Bond Street.

Gideon, who looked decidedly less pleased, reached in for Sophie. "I wonder if it will do my new efforts to refurbish my reputation good or ill to be seen with the two most beautiful women in all of London."

Sophie emerged, smiling brilliantly at him. He felt that sweet punch of pleasure to his solar plexis that came every time she looked at him like that.

"Bosh. It is Sophie they call the Beauty of Bond Street." May fluffed the pink feathers at her wrists. "Although if they knew how much she resisted every time I suggested a shopping trip, she would lose the title."

"But I do not need anything," Sophie protested. She lingered beside Gideon, her hand still in his.

He drank in the smell of her, wondering if he were giving all away to anyone who might glance at them. How impossible it was to act normally when she was this close. He found her intoxicating. Making love to her had not ameliorated his desire for her, but ignited it to new levels. He was so damnably besotted, he'd agreed to accompany the women on one of their famous shopping trips.

Sophie had begged him to go, actually. He found it curious that she disliked shopping. He had never met a female who did not enjoy strolling the most exclusive shops on Bond Street.

"I think we should stop at the perfumer's shop first,"

May said, starting in that direction. "I want to look at face powder."

Gideon winced. The perfumer's? What had he gotten himself into?

Yes, he was infatuated with Sophie, glad to be taking this step toward establishing himself as a gentleman worthy of asking for her hand in marriage . . . but the perfumer's?

As if reading his mind, Sophie chuckled. "No one said becoming respectable would be easy," she murmured as they walked down the street.

May, who never got very far when out in public without seeing someone she knew, paused to speak to a passerby. Gideon used the opportunity to bend close to Sophie. "When are you going to dismiss your other admirers?"

Sophie was taken aback. "What do you mean?"

"I mean Burton. You must break it off with him as soon as possible. It is driving me mad that he thinks you and he are in any sort of understanding."

"What has brought this on?" She laughed, her eyes sparkling in the sunlight. "Why, Lord Ashford, are you jealous?"

"I admit it freely. And you would not like it if the shoe were on the other foot."

She tapped his arm in gentle admonishment. "A gentleman does not mention body parts in front of a lady."

"I will do more than mention them . . ." He watched her face shift into a blend of sultry reaction and alarm. He loved being bold with her. She never quite summoned the arrogance she would have liked to put him in his place.

She glanced around self-consciously. "You are behaving like the scoundrel you are purported to be. I thought you meant to change."

"Well, these things do take time." He gave her a serious look that told her he was not joking. "Break it off with Burton, Sophie. The time will come soon when I have repaired my reputation enough to declare for you."

The thought thrilled her, and he smiled, understanding

her excitement. "I am determined no stain will be set upon our engagement. You wanted a respectable man, and I will be the most respectable damned man you could want."

"Gideon, not here."

"I am merely reminding you that I plan to move quickly. We have wasted too much time already. I have some apologies to make, some old wounds to heal. Some . . . er, music to face, as it were. But, I swear that as soon as the way is clear, I will be a member of good standing of the most prestigious echelons of London society," he declared with mock solemnity, setting her to quiet chuckles. He grabbed her hand and held it tight for a moment. "Until then, have some pity on me, relegated to the shadows while you are ferried about by Burton."

"He is merely a very good friend, Gideon. You know that."

"Whom you have considered marrying," he stated.

She nodded. "Yes, Gideon, but it was never a courtship, merely a convenience." At his uncompromising expression, she conceded. "He has asked me to the theater and I have accepted. This happened before the soiree, Gideon, so do not look so cross. I promise that I will use the opportunity to advise him that my affections are not engaged and that he and I will remain friends only."

"Very well. I know these things must be done with a certain protocol. One of the things, I now recall, that I hated most about society—so many damned rules. But I mean for him to understand that he has no chance with you. As he is a good man, I will be patient a bit longer, but keep in mind that I will not hesitate to inform him myself that his attentions are unwelcome."

"You wouldn't," she gasped.

He gave her a look that promised indeed he would. Lady May entered the perfumer's. They followed wordlessly.

He watched Sophie pretend to look at the array of cosmetics on display, but noted that every time May held something for her to try, she refused. When May wished to purchase a box of sachets for her, Sophie adamantly insisted she did not want it.

The door chime sounded and Gideon saw Mrs. Milton enter with her daughter and a man in tow. It was a shock to see Farnsworth.

His former friend gave him a sly leer behind the women's backs, and it took considerable effort not to make a cutting remark. The man had been encouraged since Gideon began circulating among the ton and was, apparently, following suit.

Farnsworth had always been a leech, Gideon thought sourly. It bothered him immensely that he was with Sophie's dearest friend. What the devil was the man doing with a respectable woman?

"I thought I saw you coming in here!" Margaux exclaimed. She and Sophie embraced.

Gideon greeted them, addressing himself to Mrs. Milton. "What on earth are you doing in a perfumer's shop?" he inquired. "I cannot imagine you or your daughter in need of any of these paltry enhancements."

She gave him a scathing look that shared his joke. "Every woman is in need of a touch now and then, Lord Ashford. Do not think to flatter me into thinking you find the Milton women so flawless."

She patted her hair and simpered like a woman half her age.

"You have caught me," he confessed. "My flattery is meant to convey my great admiration. Have I overdone it?"

Mrs. Milton was enjoying his teasing. She played her part in the game. "Immeasurably. Now stand aside. I must speak to Lady May. I must ask her if she will join us at the tea garden."

As she passed, Gideon exchanged a guarded greeting with Farnsworth.

"Fancy seeing infamous Lord Ashford at a perfumer's shop," Farnsworth purred, sidling alongside him to ogle the women companionably.

"And you." Gideon stepped away. He wanted no part of the man or any doubtful intentions he might harbor. "Do you not have other amusement you could be about? Drinking, gambling?"

"Nothing more worthy than attending Miss Milton."

"She seems above you," Gideon intoned. "I wonder why she allows you to scurry after her as you do."

"My charm," he replied. "It is difficult to resist a rake, as you surely have found out yourself, and since I was never as . . . open with my indiscretions as you, I am quite the catch. What fun this new diversion you and I have found." He bounced on his heels. "Innocent blood."

Had they been alone, Gideon would have set down the annoying fop quite forcibly. As it was, he was constrained by their company, and distracted by Sophie's reaction. She had been smiling, but the light faded when her gaze rested on Farnsworth.

"Miss . . . Kent, a pleasure," the man said, bowing low. Gideon's hackles rose, his instincts picking up on something undefined but unpleasant in his manner. Why did he hesitate like that before speaking her name? Was there some significance?

Sophie's face was cold, as rigid as stone. "Viscount Farnsworth."

Farnsworth was smirking, and while Gideon wondered at the ugly gleam in his eye, he bent low to speak to Margaux. "Allow me to show you something over here, my dear."

He led her away. Gideon saw Sophie's reaction flare raw for a moment. She was furious.

He was equally disturbed. A sense of something happening that he did not like vibrated along his nerves like a low growl. He made up his mind to have a strong word with Farnsworth at his earliest opportunity.

"Margaux!" Sophie called sharply and hurried to her, hooking her arm through hers. "I am not in the mood for shopping today. I will go to the tea garden with you and

Aunt May can join us when she is finished. I have to speak with you at once. Alone."

"I am afraid I cannot join you," Farnsworth said, as if he'd been asked.

Sophie's smile was wooden, and her sarcasm subtle. "Alas."

Farnsworth gave Margaux a melting look, which seemed to thrill her. "If I may call on you again, Miss Milton?"

Miss Milton said yes eagerly under the beaming smile of her mother, who had missed the near groping and came up now, a bit belatedly, to preside over her daughter.

Farnsworth turned toward Sophie. "Good to see you again, Miss Temple . . . ah . . ." He stopped, seeming abashed. "I mean Miss Kent. I keep getting you confused with that other young woman. Silly of me." He grinned as he passed her.

Sophie's reaction struck a coldness in Gidcon's breast. She seemed to go through a series of emotions. First fear. Unmistakably, her eyes flared and she swallowed hard. Then she glowered at Farnsworth, looking nothing at all like the lady she always held herself to be.

And something inside of him ignited as well. Curiosity. A faint feeling of unease.

He'd been worried over Burton, but this . . .

What was this?

✿ *Chapter 22*

Sophie fought against the overwhelming urge to haul her foot up and plant a nice, sound kick to Farnsworth's rear as he exited the shop.

She turned to Gideon to see he was watching her. She had to face the inescapable fact that she was on borrowed time.

Dread formed a tight knot in her chest. It had become comfortable, the life of Sophie Kent, so much so that she barely remembered that she was not. As Farnsworth delighted in reminding her, she was Sophie Temple.

How pleasant it had been to forget. To fall in love with Gideon, with this life, to have a family, a wonderful family, again.

They all thought she belonged, but she did not. They thought she was a good person, an honest person. And Gideon especially, he was rehabilitating himself for her — what irony, when she was the liar, the cheat, and deceiver.

He had to be told the truth. How would she find the words? The sheer terror of the task had made her push it away. In time, she'd told herself. If he did truly love her, it wouldn't make a difference. But . . .

Of course she could not marry him unless he knew who

she was, what she had done. She had always known that, she supposed. She'd just been a miserable coward about it.

Farnsworth was trying to use his knowledge to threaten her so that she would not interfere with his seduction of Margaux, this she understood. His manipulations might be what now forced her hand—for never would she even entertain the thought of remaining silent if Margaux's well-being were in danger—but it was time to face what she had done for many other reasons.

Aside from the fact that Gideon deserved to know the truth, she could not live the rest of her life quaking every time she was threatened with exposure. The more time went by, the worse it would be unless she cleared the slate now.

At her first opportunity, Sophie brought up the subject of Viscount Farnsworth to her friend.

"Do you think he is serious in his intentions?" she asked her.

"He has not said anything specific," Margaux admitted. "But he is of an amorous bent." She blushed. "He is very affectionate."

"I noticed. He can hardly keep his hands from you. Do . . . do you think that is wise, Margaux? I mean, an attentive suitor is one thing, but he does push the line."

"He tells me he cannot help himself. I . . . he . . ." She blushed profusely. "I have allowed him to kiss me."

Sophie remained nonplussed, although the mental image of Farnsworth's embrace disgusted her. "And did you find that pleasing?"

"You are so shocking! Why, yes, I suppose I did." Her forehead creased and she appeared thoughtful, as if she was not quite certain of this.

Sophie spoke with care. "I trust he is not pushing you toward anything that you are not absolutely at ease with."

"No . . ." Margaux's denial was weak. "You have Lord Burton, you see. Of course, he is of a different nature. Very reserved and dignified. But he is taken with you, that is obvious. And it is the same for me. With the viscount."

Sophie had the uncomfortable feeling Margaux was try-ing to talk herself into liking Farnsworth's attentions. She wondered why she would do this, for it was completely out of character. Her friend was not the silly type to run off with anyone who paid her a bit of attention. She'd had plenty of men interested, but had proven very particular.

She desperately wanted to warn her against Farnsworth, but she did not know what she could say.

The subject worried her so much, Gideon noticed her mood and commented on it. When she merely made an ex-cuse, he mentioned that the Viscount Farnsworth certainly seemed enamored of Miss Milton. He added, with a wicked twinkle in his eye, that any man who would accompany a woman to a *perfumer's* shop was certainly besotted.

She laughed, but the previous joy she had felt was lost. Gideon had to know the truth. The man who treasured hon-esty deserved that.

And May, dear, wonderful May. Her heart wrenched in her chest. They would both despise her. She would be cast out, and she would deserve every bit of their collective loathing.

With these troubled thoughts, she retired, making a point to mention that she thought she might have a megrim coming on. A glance at Gideon told her he had understood. He looked dark-eyed, thoughtful, and none too pleased, but at least he would not be coming to her in the night.

She needed time to think of what she should do.

"I believe we have come to a great understanding, Gideon and I," said May, smiling contentedly at Robert.

"But . . ." he prompted.

She put aside her sewing. "I am still so afraid he will leave me again."

"Is that why you have turned a blind eye to what is hap-pening with him and Sophie?" Robert queried.

"I am not blind. My goodness, of course it is obvious,

but I shall not make mention of it until one of them approaches me on the subject."

"But it pleases you."

"Of course, having Gideon married to Wooly's daughter definitely ensures he will always remain in my life. In any event, I can see that their affection is true. They belong together."

Robert pursed his lips. The gesture drew long hollows under the high points of his cheekbones. "We belong together," he said flatly. "How long are you going to make me wait?"

May rose and went to him. She held out her hand and he took it, raised it to his lips. The contact sent a tiny thrill up her arm. How could it be that after all this time, just his touch could do that to her?

"A little while longer. You understand, Robert, why this is so important. This is the one thing in my life I have to atone for. To see Gideon happy, settled in a good, rewarding life, and Sophie, whom I love and have always worried over . . . well, it is all I can think about at the moment."

"You have nothing to atone for," he said, but he did not press it.

He cut off and dropped her hand, looking behind her. May turned to find Sophie standing in the doorway.

She looked strange. Drawn, tired, tense. "Is something wrong, dear?"

"Could I speak with you, Aunt May?" Her voice was tight.

"Indeed, please sit." She waved her hand to a chair. Sophie hesitated, her eyes on Robert.

He rose. "If you will excuse me."

"Wait," Sophie said. She seemed to be in a state of extreme nervousness. "Forgive me if I am impertinent, but it has been obvious to me for some time that your friendship is a close one. I was always under the impression, Aunt May, that Lord Roberts is a very intimate confidant. No doubt you would discuss what I am about to tell you with him in the end. It would therefore be pointless to ask you to leave, Lord Roberts. Please sit down. That is, if you wish it, Aunt May."

May nodded to Robert. He took his seat again.

Sophie's face creased and took a long moment to draw in her breath. "I have something to tell you. Something very : . . wrong that I have done to you, Lady May."

Her hands moved spasmodically over the folds of her dress. Her chin quivered. "I should have the grace to look you in the eye when I tell you this, but I cannot," she said, her voice hitching.

May spoke gently. "Sophie, darling, you do not have to be so afraid. Just tell me what it is, and we will sort it out."

"I have no right to your understanding, or to ask anything from you. I want you to know firstly that I have not told anyone what I am about to tell you. I do owe Gideon this same explanation. But you are the one whom I have most wronged, and you must be the first to know."

She took a breath, closed her eyes. No. She opened them and steeled herself.

"Lady May, I am not Sophie Kent. My real name is Sophie Temple. My mother was Annabeth Temple and she never had an affair with your brother. Aunt Millicent bore his child, but that child died as a babe. I pretended to be her in order to come here and be the woman you were looking for so that I might advance myself in society and make a smart marriage."

May had not reacted other than the slight widening of her eyes. Sophie went on. "I cannot ask you to understand why I have done this, but I wish you to know it was not out of malice or mere greed. I did it because I had no other place to go."

May turned to Robert, who caught her eye and sighed. "Sophie . . ."

"I lied to you." Sophie rose, her voice growing stronger. "I want you to understand that I did not mean to hurt you, but I did. I looked you in the eye and I lied to you, that first day when I told you I was Sophie Kent, and every day since. I know what family means to you, Lady May, and I played on that for my advantage."

"And what about Gideon?" May asked quietly.

Sophie's mouth opened, then closed. "I will tell him."

"Sophie," Robert said, "please sit."

"I have had my bags packed. Only those things I came with. I have no way yet to repay you for the money you spent on me except that you might sell the clothing and other things and get at least some of the money back."

"I care nothing about the money!" May cried.

Robert stood, crossed the room, and grabbed Sophie's arm. May was grateful that he was taking charge. She seemed unable to move.

"Sophie, sit, please. We must discuss this."

"I intend to pay back every pound!" she said earnestly, resisting him.

"I agree with Lady May that there are matters of greater import right now than the financial settlement. Go ahead, then. Sit."

Sophie deflated at this gentle remonstrance. With an effort, she raised her gaze to May's.

"I wish to hear all of it," May said. Her voice was calm once again as she mastered her feelings of betrayal and anger.

"There is nothing to tell you but the facts. I pretended to be Millicent Kent's daughter. I am not. I will not make excuses."

"An explanation is not an excuse," Robert said, his voice gentle but firm, "and you owe Lady May at least some sort of accounting."

May waited. Her heart felt as if it had been shattered. Perhaps Sophie most of all among those children she'd found of her dear brother's had been closest to her. Sophie had been at her side in her own crisis with Gideon. She thought of how she had depended on her, and Sophie had never failed her, never faltered . . .

Gideon . . .

He loved this woman. And Sophie loved him. She'd

welcomed that because she wanted Gideon to be permanently in her life, a marriage to one of her brother's children to seal him to her. She herself had done some using. She herself had deceived.

And she'd never told him the truth about Matthew.

"My mother died several years ago," Sophie began. "She was a minor actress. Not like Aunt Millicent, although they were great friends. My father was a poor artist with whom I have no contact. He left us when I was young. That was the way of things with my mother and aunts.

"I remained in the care of my aunt Millicent until her death, after which I found myself quite alone in the world. Unlike other women who make grand careers out of finding a succession of wealthy protectors, my aunts were not ultrafashionable demimonde. They did not move in elite circles. Their friends were artists, aging actors, writers, people from the theater, musicians. No one was in a position to help me."

May knew her weakness was her deep sense of compassion. She fought the pull of it as she watched Sophie, her face bearing testament to her regret, her voice soft and trembling as she spoke.

"When Aunt Millicent died of influenza, her house was reclaimed by Lord Bonnington, who had given it to her to use as her settlement after their affair ended many years ago. But it was his, not Aunt Millicent's, and I found myself with no money, no prospects, not even a place to live."

May glanced at Robert. He was still, serious, listening attentively. He did not, however, appear as severe as May would have suspected.

"Your mother or aunts made no provisions for you?" she asked.

The laugh Sophie gave was short, curt. "You might not realize the kind of women they were, my aunts. Good women, but not wise. They were gay, artistic, wonderful dreamers. But they were irresponsible. The financial struggle they suffered in their later years was a result of their incapacity to plan for their own futures. My future was beyond their ability to foresee. To their credit, however, they never imagined that I would have any difficulty."

She looked away, blushing. Robert nodded. "They assumed you would find a protector."

Sophie swallowed hard. "They thought it a matter of course. And I nearly did do that. Lord Bonnington came to see me after Aunt Millicent died. He offered me . . . protection."

"The man is over three times your age," May said. It should not astonish her, but it did. The fact that it was Sophie prey to a lascivious old man struck an instinctive note of horror in her breast.

But that was because this was Sophie, whom May had grown to love. Was she merely fooled by a conniving schemer? How could she, such an excellent judge of people, be so taken in?

"It was a kind gesture on his part, nothing more. He wished to help me. He is not a lecher. He did not really desire me in that way, but he felt an obligation." Her breath drew in, labored and ragged. "But he would have availed himself of what he had bought. It was a business proposition, not charity. I understood that. And so . . . I think I went a bit mad then. And I almost . . ."

She shook her head sharply, then stopped. Tilting her chin up, she looked at May straight on. "I almost accepted. I did not have a choice. I thought . . . I thought, 'What does it matter?' But then I could not. I simply could not. At that moment, I beg you to understand my state of mind. I'd lived under the disapproval of society all my life, kept it from my aunts so as not to hurt them. I promised myself over and over that their life would not be mine." She made a helpless gesture with her hands. "But what I became was worse than a courtesan. At least that is honest."

She bowed her head. "Not two days after Lord Bonnington's visit, I found the letters from your solicitors. So I took them to his offices. And I told them I was the daughter of the Earl of Woolrich."

There was a long, protracted silence, broken by a rap

on the door. The maid stepped inside, bobbing a quick
curtsy. "Miss Sophie, your bags have been brought down."

"Take them back upstairs," May said, standing and
speaking to the servant. She saw there was only a pelisse
and the shabby trunk Sophie had arrived with set out in the
hall. Sophie was leaving as she had come.

Sophie seemed as if she were about to protest, but May
whirled on her. "We have only begun to sort this out."

Sophie had never been anything but pleasant, compliant, even a bit meek—this to May's sometime frustration—since her coming, but right now she looked as
adamant as May had ever seen a person look.

"Surely, you do not wish me to stay under the circumstances."

"I am only just beginning to be apprised of the circumstances," May countered. "I would appreciate it if you
would remain so that we might sort this out to everyone's
benefit."

Sophie blinked, clearly taken aback. "I will do whatever
you wish. But there is no cause to be mindful of my benefit, surely. I am at your disposal."

"Did you lie to me always?" May asked suddenly.
"How much of this was pretense, your patience and your
steady companionship?"

"It was not a lie that I came to care for you, that I
wished to be of aid when Gideon's arrival created difficul-
ties in the household. I lied about my mother, and my right
to Lord Woolrich's inheritance, that is much. But it is all. I
truly wished to ease my conscience by being as good a
friend to you as I could be. So much so, that I became convinced that we were friends, real friends."

"But it was only repayment," May said, knowing she
sounded bitter.

"Yes, at first. I desperately wanted to do something to
make myself think I was not only taking, but giving something back. And then, I simply enjoyed it. I enjoyed your
companionship, Lady May, and your family. Michaela,
and you, Lord Roberts, and the major and Gideon. I came

to care deeply for you all. My time here in this house has been so happy, marred only by the prodding of my conscience, but that came less and less. I think I wanted so much for it to be true that this was my family, I let myself believe it, and love it—every moment."

She smiled a weak smile, adding, "Except the embroidering."

"You must have thought me a fool, all the times I said this thing or that to liken you to the Ellinsworths."

"Never. It made me proud if some trait made me like your family. I wish I could claim heredity, and not for a single pound of inheritance but for all the true treasures this house holds."

May paused. Why was she angry? She'd been wronged, but she was not above her own deceptions. And worse.

She had been a desperate woman once. She'd lied. And she looked in the face of someone she loved very much, and lied to him still, every day, in not telling the truth.

It was not the same. But close enough to deflate her injured pride.

"Lady May wishes you to stay," Robert said, coming to May's side as they stood together, facing Sophie. "Will you?"

"I will." Sophie paused, releasing the tension in her jaw. "Do you mean to call the magistrate?"

"Lord no!" May exclaimed. "Why would I do that?"

"I've stolen from you. The dresses, the things you bought."

"What? Those things mean nothing."

Sophie gave May a strange look. "They mean nothing to you because you have them in abundance. To me, they cost more money than I could make doing honest work in a year. My debt to you is very great."

"I want to hear no more of debts," May said. "It cheapens what has occurred."

"What I did to you was cheap. It was tawdry. I—"

"Sophie Temple," May said, and this time her voice was as stern as a schoolmistress's, "you might think I am a brainless piece of fluff. I affect pink and feathers and love to shop. You might not think me a serious woman, but I, too, have known desperate times. I am not some shallow thing who floats high on my own morality. You have been a woman in a world without a friend. I have as well, years ago. Do you think you were the only one in this house to face a crisis in her life?"

Sophie was stunned. Robert laid a hand on May's arm, muttering her name in a low, warning tone. "We should talk later, after we've all had a moment to calm ourselves."

May nodded. Her heart was beating fast. There was no indignation any longer. She just did not wish to lose Sophie.

She did not wish to lose Gideon, either.

When she glanced at Robert, she could tell he knew what direction her thoughts were taking her. And he did not like it.

Chapter 23

Gideon slipped into Sophie's room. His eyes flashed, taking her in as she stood, braced for what she had to do.

"The servants said those were your bags in the hall," he said. "Are you going on a visit?"

His voice was low, threaded with the displeasure he was keeping in check.

Sophie's shoulders felt suddenly heavy. "You should not be here in the daytime with everyone awake. It is unseemly."

"I know. What is happening? Sophie, look at you." He came toward her but she skittered away from his grasp. If he touched her, she would melt into his arms.

"Those are my bags," she said. "I was leaving this house."

He froze. His expression was completely blank. "Is it because of me?"

"You? No. How could you think that? Don't you suspect? You heard Farnsworth, you know about the letters." The genuine confusion on his features brought a sigh of exasperation from her. "I thought you knew, or at least had surmised."

"That you have a secret? Of course. The great mystery of Sophie. Is that what this is about?"

"Don't you even care?" She was suddenly furious with him. With herself, really, but he was standing there, looking at her with an expression that made her want to run because it held nothing but consternation and concern. She was disgusted with herself, but he did not seem to be at all.

She told him everything. In sharp, biting words, she told him about her mother, her aunt Millicent, the lost baby, the proposition by Lord Bonnington, the stolen letters. She told him about each and every lie.

The only reaction he gave her was a series of blinks when she started. His mind worked behind a blank façade as it all came pouring out of her.

She told him much more than she had May. She found it was difficult to go into detail about the slurs she had endured, about the men and what they had tried when they thought she was of the same ilk as her aunts, but she pushed herself through it.

She told him of all the times she'd been treated like she was less than other *respectable* people. And she told him how deeply that had made her resolve to push her life into a different course, no matter what the cost.

"It made me hard," she admitted. "I did not think when I started this that it would hurt anyone. I knew it was wrong, but I thought it was only because of the money. I had a plan to pay it back, and I would have. I will. But May will not hear of it. I cannot understand her reaction, or yours. Even Lord Roberts was not truly angry."

He listened. He listened to everything. And when she was finished, he said, "What exactly has May said? Has she asked you to leave?"

"No. She is preventing me. Although I cannot imagine why she would wish me to stay after what I've done. She said she has to digest the news. She is hurt, of course. Shocked. Appalled, and deservedly so. She may hand me to the authorities yet after she's had a chance to think on it."

"No, she will not. That is not May. And may I ask what you are going to do?"

"Await her pleasure. Or displeasure."

"Sophie Kent . . . Temple—you never waited for anyone to hand you a thing. You once told me that you were a survivor. I understand more deeply now what you meant."

His lack of censure was maddening. "You do not seem at all overset by this."

He shrugged. "It is deeply troubling. It is not a pleasant story you depict. And it is not a nice thing to do to May, and I do care for her very much. But I do not judge others, an aversion I have resulting from being judged so harshly myself."

"You hate liars. How many times have you told me that the one true virtue you hold in absolute is honesty?"

"But I love you. I know your heart, Sophie. So perhaps I can understand how you were driven to desperate measures. I do not sanction it, mind. What you did was very wrong. But then, I used to sleep with other men's wives. This might be drastically perverse of me, but it comes as some relief to know that at least you have a flaw or two."

"Flaw or two? I impersonated a dead relative to steal the child's inheritance!"

Gideon nodded. "Indeed, it makes me look like a saint in comparison."

"Are you teasing me?" She was incredulous. "Are you even taking this seriously, Gideon, or are you going to turnabout now and remonstrate me when you have me off guard?"

"No. I am going to sneak you out into the folly, and we are going to discuss this. There is a good deal more to say between us than to have you list all of your evil machinations."

"Why do you want to listen to a word I have to say after I've lied?"

"Because you lied, yes, but you are not at heart a deceitful person. It would not weigh on you so much if it were otherwise. Tell me one thing before we adjourn. Why did you decide to come out with the truth now? Why all of a sudden, when you've successfully pulled off the ploy?"

"It was Farnsworth." She felt miserable thinking of the arrogant lout gloating over the hold he had on her. "He knew."

"He would reveal you? To what end?" His face clouded over like a fast-moving storm. "He did not try to extort you."

"He did, but not for any aim to harm me. I know what you are thinking, Gideon, but he has not tried to renew the acquaintance, as brief and unpleasant as it was, or use his knowledge to force me to his will. He did wish to warn me off from interfering with Margaux, however, and that is much worse. His veiled threats made it clear he would 'slip' on my name as many times as I attempted to interfere, or even go further. He has his mark set on her, and does not wish me to spoil his plans."

"And, of course, you have no intention of remaining silent." His smile seemed vaguely proud.

"I will not." Sophie felt passionately on this, that she must dissuade her friend from this fatal fascination. "The man has not a hint of good character. I am sorry to have to say something so unkind about a man you call friend, but it is true."

"I shudder to think of our friendship, and I quite agree with your assessment of his character."

"I have no idea why Margaux wishes to entertain his suit. She is of a romantic bent, but not foolish."

"I have a suspicion, but come, now, and walk outside with me."

She followed him into the hall and out of the house. "You are being much too kind to me."

"Kindness, Sophie, is something I can give you. When a man loves a woman and has as little to offer as I do, it is a pleasure to find he can be of some use."

He kissed her, then led her outside and sat with her in the folly. It was much later, when she had exhausted her self-recriminations and he had patiently waited them out, that she began to think of all she stood to lose.

"I made a new life and now I will have nothing." She felt the sting of tears. "I never got to meet Trista and Roman, nor their children. I feel as if I know them, but I might come across them one day and not even realize who they are."

"You will always have me," he said softly.

She moved into his arms. "The wisest thing I ever did was to fall in love with a scoundrel."

The warmth of his laughter was like a balm.

Michaela's unexpected and breathless arrival brought everyone into the drawing room for tea.

It was not a good day for visits, especially when Sophie saw the bright, anxious smile on Michaela's face. It brought a pang to her breast, for she had grown so fond of her, and she was keenly aware that she stood a good chance of losing this person with all the others of whom she'd grown so fond before long.

She would have liked to beg off, but she had her duty. May had asked her to stay, and it was clear she was to play the part a bit longer. She donned as pleasant an expression as possible and sat quietly as Michaela giggled with pent-up excitement.

Gideon, who had a fondness for the vivacious brunette, made much over her mood. "You are in exceptional spirits," he declared.

Michaela glanced at him almost flirtatiously. "It has been an exceptional day."

Gideon agreed dryly, causing May to cough delicately into her handkerchief.

"What is it?" Michaela asked. "You all seem rather dour. Sophie, you are so quiet!"

Gideon interrupted as Sophie was about to respond. "Miss Kent has not . . . ah, been herself."

May coughed again and shot Gideon a reproachful glance. "If you are going to be wicked, you may leave us ladies to speak in peace. Come back when the major arrives, that is if you can behave yourself."

Gideon bowed to her, kissing her hand. He murmured, "Do not mind me. Old habits and all that. But do not mistake that I mean to make light of what is no doubt quite a distressing situation. Forgive me."

When he left, Michaela stared after him. "What was that all about?"

May sighed. She slid her gaze to Sophie. Sophie understood. Michaela was not to be kept in the dark.

Sophie opened her mouth to make yet one more confession, but her words were cut off.

This time, it was Michaela who rushed into the breach. "I will hear of it in a moment, but while we are all alone, with no men, I have the opportunity to tell you my great news."

She stared at them in turn with expectant excitement. Then, in a rush, she declared, "I am with child. The physician confirmed it just yesterday. I am going to have a baby!"

May's exclamation was pure joy. Sophie followed suit, her troubles forgotten for the moment as they embraced.

"But tell us everything," May demanded, shooing Michaela into her chair. "When is the baby coming?"

"In seven months, I expect," Michaela said on a laugh, "for they do take the same time each and every one."

As they talked, Sophie felt her heart fill with a mingling of emotion. She had no illusions that this was her family, not any longer. It was a peculiar form of torture, sitting with these happy women, knowing she did not belong, and that their future—this baby, and the others that would follow—would not be a part of hers.

Their happy chatter was interrupted when Michaela observed the tears glistening in Sophie's eyes. "Why, Sophie, you are crying!"

Dashing at the moisture, Sophie shrugged. "I am only so happy for you."

"Oh, my, you are sweet." Michaela raised her eyebrows. "But I am not blind. There is something very wrong here. What is it? Tell me."

"We should not spoil your happy news," May said. "We can discuss other things later."

Michaela, however, would not be put off. "I will be most annoyed if you do not tell me what on earth is the matter. My imagination will take wing and I will become inconsolably overset, and as I am a mother-to-be, then I suggest you avoid this state and *tell me*."

May took a moment before speaking. "We have just found out, Sophie and I, that there was a mistake made by my solicitors. Sophie was contacted by them in error and came to me under the misapprehension that she was the child of your father's I had been looking for."

Michaela's eyes popped wide. "You mean . . . Oh, no! Oh, Sophie."

"She is not your sister. Not Wooly's daughter." May turned to Sophie and smiled. "We are trying to recover from the news, and to concentrate on what really matters, that we are dear to one another. That we have become family, despite our lack of blood. But it is still something of a shock, you see, and only just come about today. But, Michaela, dear, we mustn't worry ourselves now. You and Adrian have waited so very long, and this is the most joyous of days."

"But of course, Sophie, you must understand that you will always be part of us. We love you dearly, indeed we do. This mistake is not dreadful in the least. It has brought us a good fortune, for you have been such a comfort to Aunt May, and to me." Michaela looked around at them, her eyes shining. "How happy I was coming here today, anticipating that you would share in my delight so truly. That is a real friendship, truer than blood in so many instances."

Sophie's voice would not work for a moment. "You are so right. I have found something here with you and May, and Lord Roberts and Gideon and your dear, dear devoted husband that I never knew before. You have become my family in spirit, and in my heart."

May nodded approvingly. "See, there, it is all fine and well. Now, Michaela, we must think of names."

"Why May, of course, if she is a girl. I have already insisted, and Adrian agrees."

"Oh, no! It must be after your mother. She would be so put out."

"She has my sisters to name babies after her. Lilah is going to birth any day now. . . ."

The chatter faded into the background as Sophie's thoughts churned. What did May mean, making up this story? Was it only to avoid upsetting Michaela in her delicate condition, or did she mean to make this the official account?

She felt hopeful. If she did not exactly deserve to be granted this reprieve, she would not refuse it.

Margaux slipped out of the carriage and hurried to the figure awaiting her in the shadows.

"You are late," Lord Burton said, but his voice held no admonishment. His eyes, as they traveled over her nicely rounded figure, gleamed.

No doubt he was impatient to be inside, she figured, and that was why he was so happy to see her. "You could have gone ahead."

"But I wished to make certain you arrived. I was not sure your mother would give permission."

Margaux tried not to look guilty, but she had no talent at lying. Her mother thought she was spending the evening with Sophie while she and Aunt Viola played cards at Lady Woodbridge's house.

"How silly," she said, her voice so hollow in her own ears, she thought that surely he would detect how false she was.

"Then hurry. I have reserved two seats for us. I arrived early to make certain we were near the front and saw the array of exhibits being set up behind the curtain. They are simply *astonishing*, Miss Milton. How pleased I am that you have reconsidered attending this lecture series with me."

She ignored her conscience in the rush of excitement. So much for her good intentions to stay clear of Burton.

"I cannot wait," she said breathlessly, her feet moving rapidly as he rushed them to the seats he had retained.

She was soon caught up in the utterly captivating facts of the ancients, their lives, their monuments, and the strange things they had left behind to taunt the curious as to how they had lived thousands of years ago.

Lord Burton was overcome as well. His hand quite naturally slipped over hers and held tightly as the Egyptian artifacts were unveiled.

May came to Sophie's room that evening. "May I sit?" she inquired.

"Of course," said Sophie, trying to keep the quiver from her voice. Was this, then, to be the dressing-down she so richly deserved?

"I wish to know one thing, Sophie, and I wish only honesty from you. I need to know if you offered friendship only as a foil."

"Indeed not, my lady." Sophie took a step forward, her voice filled with vehemence. "I never lied in my affections. They are true, and it will be a just punishment for me to go without your treasured companionship if you deem we should part."

May nodded. "I am relieved. And, no, I do not deem we should part. The story I told Michaela is the one I will put out. You are to say the same if you are asked about the matter. Do this for me, will you?"

"I will do anything you ask," Sophie assured her.

"Sit, dear. This is not an interrogation. Come."

Since May had settled herself in the wing chair by the fireplace, Sophie perched on the edge of the bed.

May took out a bundle. "Thank you for returning

these," she said, untying the ribbon. "I would like very much for you to tell me about Millicent Kent."

Sophie paused, then spoke. "She was a woman of great personality. When she entered a room, everyone knew she was there. She was like that on stage, as well. You could not spare a glance at anyone else when she was playing her part."

Unfolding a letter, May said, "Let us read this one."

Shifting to a seat beside Sophie on the bed, they quietly perused the letter.

"See," Sophie said softly, pointing to a passage where Millicent responds coyly to his worries after she ignored him at a party, "she would often play that ploy when she was very interested in a man. It made them jealous, she said, and that set the stage for a very interesting . . . um . . . well . . ."

She smiled, obviously recollecting fond memories. "Yes. Wooly would love that passionate spirit. He would not even mind the game, as long as he got what he wanted in the end."

"But they were a pair, they understood each other. I recall Aunt Millicent speaking about their parting. Their love affair ended before the child was born, but he supported her until her confinement ended."

"Tell me about the child. How did she die?"

"It was quick, I was told, very soon after birth. She simply failed during the night. There was no explanation. Aunt Millicent did not speak of her, and I think part of the reason she was so kind to me was out of the enduring loss she felt. I do know that she and Lord Woolrich did not continue their friendship afterward, although she always spoke of him with respect."

"Poor Wooly. I wonder if he were distraught to lose his daughter."

Sophie gave her a strange look. May raised her eyebrows. "What is it?"

"Nothing. No." She bent over the letters. "Let us continue reading."

"I demand you speak, Sophie Temple."

There was no remonstrance, other than the demand to hear what was on her mind. Sophie said, "I should not say anything. I know you loved your brother very much."

"But you are thinking that perhaps too blindly. Oh, Wooly was wonderful, but I am not ignorant of his faults. He was good of heart, but not strong of character. When he loved, he loved fiercely, but it was always fleeting. And it was always shallow."

"But he had so many children he never spoke of."

"Indeed. I do not know if I can forgive him for that. Do not mistake his honor, he did support many, but only financially. He cared nothing for the family connection to these beautiful children, but he did know his duty."

"He did not claim them publicly?"

"Not once. He kept them secret even from me. I can guess much of it was out of discretion, for many of his off-spring were assumed into the marriage of the woman who was his lover, or else the woman did not wish the child to be recognized as his bastard for their own reasons. You can understand wanting to avoid the stigma."

Sophie nodded. She of all people understood how difficult it was to labor under the scathing regard of society.

May continued, "Others sought independence on their own and rejected his offer to help. I only know he helped all those who needed it and anyone who asked. His diaries are quite specific about that. His fault, Sophie, was not in being stingy or withholding, but in merely being as thoughtless and gay and unconcerned with the past or the future as a being can be. Wooly lived in the moment."

"You are a very understanding woman." Sophie cleared her throat. "I suppose I should be very grateful, as I have benefited the most from your forgiving nature."

May sighed. "Sophie, I find that I cannot fully condemn you. I am wounded, surely. It will take some time for this to mend. However, I do not wish to lose you. You are dear to me. You have been a great aid to me. I know you and

Gideon are in love, and that has pleased me. I trust you
have told him."

"Today, after I spoke with you and Lord Roberts."

"Very good. I suspected you would, and I think it was
wise. He is not put out. Trust Gideon to see to the heart of
the matter."

"But we must speak about my leaving. I simply cannot
continue to take your charity. It is bad enough I have already claimed what I did for as long as I did."

May waved her hand dismissively. "I will not hear of it.
If I paid you as a companion, someone to act as my confidant, I would have counted the days you spent at my side
well worth it. Could we say, then, that it is a fair trade?"

"That is too generous, Lady May."

Pulling a face, May said, "And as for that, I quite like
you calling me Aunt May. Your aunt Millicent and aunt
Linnie were not your blood kin, but the title was one of affection. Would you extend to me the same?"

This was too much. "But it would be wrong after what
happened."

May thought about this. "Then in time, perhaps, we will
address it again." She stood and paced to the window. "I
wish you to understand something very important, Sophie.
I am not stupid nor so besotted by sentiment that I am un-
troubled by what you have done. But I am a woman of the
world.

"I have seen good people do things that do not inspire
admiration, and yet I still view them as the best this world
has to offer. My own dear Robert had a scandal attached to
him, I am sure you have heard. His background is not pris-
tine. He was an accused murderer. I will confide in you
that these accusations were not ill-founded, and yet he did
what his conscience bade him to do, and I for one do not
fault him for the life he ended. And there is dear Gideon,
of course, a man of great worth who suffers most acutely
from appalling judgment in his choice of social companions, although it is my fervent prayer that this is in the
past."

She turned slightly, her smile very tight. "I myself, Sophie, I have made terrible mistakes in my life as well, ones that had deep and lasting consequences for those whom I loved."

Sophie was silent. She sensed May needed to tell her this, although she wanted to stop her. May owed her nothing, least of all such profound understanding.

"It is not a defect of character that caused you to be less than your ideal. It is merely the affliction of being human. We all of us fail. We all of us do things in our lives that make us ashamed.

"It does not matter to me at this moment how or why you came to be my family. Family is what we are now, and I would keep it so. I have come to ask you if you will stay, to simply be my friend as you have been. It is a friendship most precious to me."

"You can always trust me for that. I shall never fail you again, Lady May. I will endeavor—"

"No! Not gratitude, child! Friendship freely given or not at all."

Sophie stopped short, then sighed. "You have it most heartily."

"Good. We will speak again from time to time on this matter. There will be moments when I will have questions. Perhaps I might discover I am annoyed with you after all. But with it all is the love I have for you, and I hope you will bear it."

"I will bear it," Sophie vowed.

"Now unpack your bags. There is one last thing. If you ever wish to leave, I do not want you to stay for my sake. I am not above the taint of pride. I offer you friendship, but do not require it as a condition of my forgiveness. I will happily write a letter for you to achieve a position of your choosing, or whatever you would require from me."

"Since you will have me, I will most gratefully stay."

"Not just for my companionship, I imagine. Gideon, too, has your heart." May laughed at Sophie's expression.

"I've embarrassed you. Come, dear, you must know it has been obvious. He is a wonderful man."

Sophie nodded. "He is indeed."

"Now, tomorrow night we are to attend the ball at Hargrave House, in Kensington. We will begin to put out the story of the 'misunderstanding' then. Will you be ready?"

"I will. And Lady May . . . thank you."

"You are welcome, dear. Truly welcomed to my pardon. I only hope that in being so generous in giving it, I might one day be worthy of its reception."

She left Sophie with the question of that last enigmatic statement puzzling her brow.

When Robert asked May later that night why it was she was so quick to give Sophie her absolution, she told him this same thing. And she told him that it was time she was as brave as Sophie had been.

It was time to tell Gideon.

"I suppose you disapprove," she ventured, watching his reaction.

"Indeed." He was stoic as he came to her and wrapped his arms about her shoulders. "There are two truths I must face. The first is that I cannot protect you. And the second is that even if I could, you would not need me to. You do quite well on your own. I was wrong, I think, to ask you to keep the past to yourself. I see that. The silence I begged you to keep with Gideon is wearing at your heart. I only wanted what was best for you, May, but perhaps it is you and not I who knows exactly what that is."

"You are not angry?"

"I am frightened. I would not have anything harm you. But I do see that you must have peace."

"I didn't think you would understand. You've been so forceful."

"May, I will always stand beside you no matter what you do. Marriage would not change that. Nothing will."

"Would you still have me, with all of this mess my life has become?"

"I will have you this day or any day you call upon me.

I mean to marry you, and I will not relent. You are my life, May. Whatever happens with Gideon, whatever course this situation with Sophie takes . . . you will have me, always. Right here."

May took a deep breath. "Then be waiting for me for I mean to have this burden from me as soon as I get the opportunity to speak to Gideon in private."

❧ Chapter 24

The ball was a massive affair, spilling out of the Kensing-ton mansion and onto its well-tended lawns. The gardens were lit with colored lanterns, a style of night illumination borrowed from the fantastical decorations of the Vauxhall pleasure gardens, and flowers were in such abundance that the air hung heavy and moist with their perfume. It was lavish and loud, both of which grated immediately on Sophie's nerves as soon as they made their entrance.

"We must find Margaux immediately," she told Gideon. "I am free now to discuss Farnsworth with her. I must warn her off. She is here somewhere."

"And I will have that little discussion with Farnsworth that I have been looking forward to," Gideon replied, his jaw set in a hard line. "After you find her and do your good work, I wish to dance with you. I stuffed my pockets with coin to bribe the orchestra to play a waltz."

"You know I cannot dance. I will tread all over your feet."

He wagged his finger at her. "Ladies should not refer to body parts, Sophie."

"I am a courtesan's daughter, and no lady," she reminded him flippantly, making him chuckle.

He leaned close for a moment. "Which I find has too many advantages to name." His manner sobered as his gaze lifted. Sophie turned to see Lord Burton coming up to them.

"Here is your opportunity," he muttered under his breath. His smile disappeared and his eyelids lowered to half-mast. "Set the matter straight with him. I want no gossip when it is noticed that you and I dance a scandalous number of times tonight. The ton will know tomorrow that you and I are a pair."

"Good evening," Burton said, bowing to both. His manner was pleasant, but guarded. He eyed Gideon. "Lord Ashford. Miss Kent."

"Your servant," Gideon murmured, returning the gesture and giving Sophie a meaningful look. "I was just about to leave Miss Kent on an errand of utmost importance, so if you will excuse me, Burton, I will be off then to my mission."

He bade them farewell with a sardonic twist of his mouth and a sideways glance to punctuate his intention that she take advantage of this opportunity. As he walked away, she admired his tall, broad-shouldered frame. His clothing was good, fashionable and well-made, but he did not fuss. She liked that about him, that he was so easily himself. He'd managed to slip back into the fold of the polite world without compromising one whit.

He was still irreverent, but his charm was winning, even when it was performed for his audience with his tongue planted firmly in his cheek. Although still controversial, he was generally received and few were the times when a haughty snob saw fit to give him the cut.

He'd done it for her. But she rather thought he was glad for it. He seemed happy, in his element. That edge of bitterness in him had eased of late. He smiled more often. He had made some friendships and enjoyed the briskly paced social whirl May put him through.

She thought, then, that perhaps it was all going to happen just as she dreamed it. She and Gideon, her children respected and welcomed by their fellows. A happy life.

She felt as if this night was a beginning. Her secret was out. May had not despised her; Gideon had forgiven her.

A surge of freedom, of exhilaration buoyed her for a moment. They were here, in Kensington, at a ball, together. And nothing bound her to any path but the one she wished.

She was about to ask Lord Burton if they might speak in private, as there was no point in putting off the task, when he preempted her with the question, "Have you seen Miss Milton yet this evening?"

"Why no, my lord. I've only just arrived. But I was interested in speaking with her myself. Perhaps we could search her out together."

He crooked his elbow and she took it, bemused at this surprising turn of affairs.

Gideon had never been good at swallowing his pride. It was too big a morsel.

But as he spied Selwyn, he clenched his jaw and made straight for the man. Executing a respectful bow, he said, "Your servant."

They had not seen or exchanged a word since the duel. Now, confronted by the scarred visage of the man he had challenged over a matter of honor regarding his wife, Selwyn was dumbfounded at being accosted in so public a manner.

The men with whom he had been conversing also stared, all awaiting the explosion that was certain to follow.

Finally, one of them said, "What the devil are you doing here, Ashford?"

"I was invited," Gideon said simply, and turned to Selwyn. "I believe that an apology is in order. I offer my humblest request for such forgiveness and profoundly beg your pardon."

The other men looked at each other, shifting under the

gathering tensions. Selwyn remained still, his jaw working. "You . . . you beg my pardon?"

"Indeed, I do."

"I cannot believe your gall, Ashford," Selwyn muttered, his eyes glittering with malice.

"I cannot understand why it would fail to be obvious. I thought the matter of my gall was fairly well-known."

The self-deprecating comment caused a flicker of doubt in his adversary's eye. "And you do so publicly," he observed, his tone significantly less strident.

"It is what is called for. My apologies should be a matter of record."

The stunned men gaped. Gideon continued. "What is left now is for you to accept or . . . or do we adjourn for another 'interview.' It is up to you."

The covert term *interview* was how the *code duello* dictated any matter of honor be addressed, since dueling was illegal.

Selwyn took a long time to answer. "My satisfaction is met. I think you have more than compensated me for your insult to my family."

"Then we are settled on the matter."

It took a moment, but he inclined his head, slightly.

The gathering of men began to murmur. Gideon offered another bow. "Then I shall press my unwelcome presence upon you no longer. Good evening, Selwyn. Gentlemen."

When he turned, Farnsworth was there, livid red suffused across his face. Gideon went directly for him. "A word with you."

Farnsworth hung back. "How can you grovel like a dog, and in front of all?"

"It is what I should have done to begin with. I slept with his wife, Farnsworth, so do not act as if I have betrayed some great code in doing only what was right."

Farnsworth choked, his mouth working silently. Gideon fancied he could see steam rising off of him. "I actually admired you. You were the infamous Ashford. And now—

have my eyes deceived me, or did I actually see you *beg for pardon!*"

He didn't give a fig for Farnsworth's childish indignation. He extended a hand to the open French door, inviting him outside. "That word if you please."

"I think not," Farnsworth replied heatedly. "I do not believe you and I have much to say to one another any longer. Are you a coward, is that it? Did that injury steal your nerve? Selwyn would not have called you out again. You did not have to placate him like that. Good God, Ashford. I am ashamed of you."

"I shall take that as a compliment," Gideon said dryly. "As for what we have to say to one another, you are quite wrong. There is much on the subject of Miss Milton that we must get straight."

"Bugger off!" Farnsworth spat, and stalked off.

Gideon watched him through eyes narrowed with anger. He kept in mind those that might be watching and decided it was best to seek him out later.

Too bad. Now there was a fellow who deserved to find himself headfirst in a pond.

"Oh, Lord Farnsworth!" Margaux exclaimed when he appeared at her side. She was immediately puzzled by the intense, even angry look on his usually affable features.

"Come with me, please," he requested, his voice and manner as tight as a wound clock spring. "I need to have a word with you. It is most urgent."

"Why, what is it?"

"Come to the garden."

Again, he wanted to coax her outside. Margaux had decided that she'd had enough of his flirtation with propriety. She shook her head. "I do not feel the need for the night air, thank you."

She saw the irritation flash more deeply. Margaux stood firm.

It had become clear to her that she did not care for Farnsworth's company as much as she had thought at first.

She felt a bit guilty, realizing that she had used him to rid her mind of thinking so much about Lord Burton. But recently, Oliver and she had been speaking more and more. They'd attended a few lectures together—secretly on her part—and were trading pamphlets frequently, to her great enjoyment, and she realized that whether or not he was in love with Sophie, he *liked* her, and that knowledge gave her the confidence she had been lacking. Their friendship made her realize that she would not cheapen herself any longer with Farnsworth.

"I wish to speak to you about your friend," Farnsworth said. "Miss Kent."

That gave her pause. "What of Miss Kent?"

"I am afraid there is something of a scandal, and I think that you should know about it, being a good friend of hers. After all, we are judged by the company we keep."

He cast a sullen look behind him, back into the assembly. He was acting very odd, full of pent-up energy that frightened her.

"There can be no scandal attached to Miss Kent. She is in very good standing with her reputation."

"Come with me, and I will explain."

She could not refuse this evocative invitation. She stepped outside with him, trying to keep her distance.

The music was faint out here on the terrace. She felt very far away from the party, although there were plenty of people strolling the outdoors. She dared not venture any farther away from the house and down to the gardens, where Farnsworth was intent on taking her. "My mother would have my head upon a silver platter, my lord. I dare not take to the paths with you."

"What rubbish. She has you too cowed. Where is your sense of adventure, indeed, your spine? You know she thinks most highly of me, and would not mind in the least." He offered his most rakish countenance. "Besides, look at the garden. It is teeming with people. The lights make it quite safe. And what I have to say should not be overheard."

"I would rather not," Margaux said, flushing with embarrassment from his ridicule.

She was saved from her gathering tears when she turned away to find Lord Ashford standing in front of her.

His eyes were sharp as he took in the situation. "Miss Milton, I have been looking for you all over the party."

Farnsworth barked. "What is this? A rival for your affections? Ho, Ashford, have a care or I might be forced to call you out. You may have rid yourself of one challenge only to find another, and then you can beg *my* pardon."

Ashford did not give Farnsworth the favor of his attention. "Miss Kent was most anxious to speak with you," he continued. "And I was harboring the hope that you would consent to grant me a dance."

"Yes. I love to dance," Margaux said, relieved at Ashford's fortuitous arrival.

"Then let us head back into the ballroom," Ashford replied. "We shall find Miss Kent there with Lord Burton."

"She . . . She is with Lord Burton? He is here?"

"Yes. We only just arrived, you see, and spied him at the door. Miss Kent is probably still with him."

Of course, Burton would go right to Sophie as soon as she entered the ball. They were often together at parties. He was always calling on her.

A dizzying, draining feeling of despair overcame her.

What had she thought—that sharing a mutual interest meant he had fallen in love with her?

The reminder of Lord Burton's first interest hit harder than she could have imagined. Only now did she realize that she *had* harbored a hope that their companionable visits would come to be seen as something more in his eyes.

How could she think such a thing when Sophie was so beautiful, so graceful? She of all people appreciated her friend's fine qualities.

How could she ever compare, meek, so much less pretty?

And what was this gossip Farnsworth had to share? The thought hit like the broad side of a board. Was it news of an engagement? To Burton? Would it be announced tonight?

And perhaps that was why Sophie had sent Ashford to fetch her, to tell her this before it was touted before the rest of the guests.

She faced Ashford again. "If Sophie is occupied at present and well tended by Lord Burton, I should not like to interrupt them. I shall speak with her later." Margaux smiled at Farnsworth. "I do believe I am not in the mood to go inside after all. The night air is so pleasant and mild this time of year. Lord Farnsworth, I will take in the gardens if you still have a mind to do so."

"But Miss Milton," Ashford said, his pleasant smile tightening to betray his displeasure, "I think it best that you come with me. The matters we need to discuss are of some import."

"Surely there is no crucial need for us to run to the parquet floor this moment. You see, my lord, it is all fine and well. The gardens are quite a proper resort to bodies wishing to refresh themselves after the press of the crowd. Thank you for your concern, but I will be the better for the respite."

Ashford said nothing, not even when Farnsworth shot him a tasteless smirk. Margaux latched on to the man's arm and they walked quickly into the maze of formal gardens laid out on the flat terraces falling away from the house.

The mansion was nearly a palace. Margaux chattered about it as they went into the rows of yews. She wished she could stop herself from talking so much. She was nervous, but she did not turn back. She had to move away from this obsession with Burton. She could not wallow in this wretched state forever.

She stopped when Farnsworth directed her down a darkened path. "There are no lights, my lord," she protested. "We should stay upon the path."

"But where is the adventure in that? Do not be a prig, Miss Milton. Let us see where this serpentine leads."

She allowed him to direct her into the shadows. The high-growing hedges enveloped them within a few steps.

"This is quite intriguing," Farnsworth purred. "Are you chilled?" he murmured.

"No, my lord." She turned to face him. "Now what is this about Miss Kent that is so mysterious that we must speak of it in secret?"

"You are supposed to say yes, you are chilled," he instructed with a chuckle in his tone, "so that I may do this." He slipped his arms about her.

She tried to pull back.

"No, no," he urged. His hands went up her back, then down again, riding low on the rise of her derriere. She twisted, not liking that.

"Kiss me," he begged. "Come now. Do not deny me."

She did not wish to kiss him. But she said nothing as his mouth came over hers. Then he did something utterly shocking. His tongue touched her lips, and when she reacted with a small gasp, he slipped it inside her mouth. The hold he had on her tightened, preventing her from breaking away.

She twisted her head away, finally succeeding in ending the kiss. What a terrible mistake she'd made. Farnsworth could not help her forget her unrequited emotions. He was not the antidote to her broken heart.

"You toy with me most cruelly." He reached for her, but she slipped away.

"It is you, my lord, who are in error of your manners." Her words rang with sharp alarm.

"We are all alone, no one to stop us from enjoying ourselves." He moved quickly, capturing her face in his hands.

She yanked herself back suddenly, and his fingers, which he had dug into her coifed hair, ripped out several pins.

"I wish to go back now," she said as she wiped the wetness from her mouth.

"You are such a little prig," he said, mockery in his voice as he observed her attempt to make quick repairs to her hair. "Look at you. Do you not know how to conduct a simple flirtation?"

"Perhaps, my lord," she said, bite in her words, "if I felt the slightest inclination for your disgusting advances, I would be able to welcome them with more enthusiasm."

"You little baggage." He shook his head again, and she thought she might like to plant a sound slap squarely on his cheek. "Why have I wasted my time with you? You are always simpering about your bloody mama. You are the stupidest chit I have ever met."

A male voice startled the both of them.

Lord Ashford was standing a few steps away. "I suggest you have a care with your language, Farnsworth. You are in the company of a gently bred woman."

Margaux took the opportunity to flee to Ashford's side.

"Look who is talking," Farnsworth snorted. "As if you know anything about women of quality. You are known for the married strumpets you collect. Now you make pretensions of respectability—what a joke!"

"The discrepancy between us," Ashford said, his tone taking on a deadly quality, "is that I know the difference between a willing woman and an innocent who has made an error in trusting you and wishes to return to the party. I believe, Miss Milton, that you would like to go back inside now."

Margaux bit down on her quivering lips. "I cannot. I am in disarray."

He came to take her arm gently. "We shall find a cure. Let us be away."

Farnsworth was red in the face. "Be off with you, Ashford."

"We shall settle this at some point, Farnsworth. But at this moment, Miss Milton's present state of distress is what I am most concerned with."

He took one threatening step toward Farnsworth. "Do not repeat this ever again, or I will be the one issuing the challenge."

Farnsworth fell back. Perhaps he saw something in

Ashford's eye. Margaux could not tell, but the viscount melted away with a promising scowl, first to Ashford then to her.

"I am so humiliated," Margaux muttered. She saw her sleeve had been slightly torn in the scuffle and a small cry erupted from her lips. "I have been a terrible fool."

"You were deceived, and there is none of us who have not been at one time or another," Ashford said. He examined the sleeve. "It is ripped on the seam. You might make repairs if I can get you inside to the ladies' retiring room."

"But my hair," she cried.

He frowned at the thick hanks of curl coming loose from its pins. "That is a problem."

"I cannot go in there like this."

"Then I shall have to make away with you."

"But how? The house is full and there is no way to the carriage from here."

"No. No, please, Miss Milton, do not weep."

Gideon contained a groan. He detested when women wept. It always made him feel alarmed and utterly helpless.

Placing a comforting hand on her shoulder, he was stunned when she flew into his arms, her arms squeezing him tightly.

"There," he said, patting her gingerly on her back.

"I am such an idiot."

"No, you are not," he said, although he might have been more honest and agreed with her had he not been afraid of increased hysterics.

"I am. I . . . I think I might faint."

He pulled her tight against him to hold her against such a disaster. "You shall not. You are a brave girl."

His voice was not comforting now. It was sharp with the ring of command.

"I am not brave. I am . . ." The rest of what she said was lost, for she had turned her face into his coat and the sounds that came forth were muffled.

Gideon looked about him desperately. Where was Sophie? She was supposed to be searching for Margaux, was she not? What he would pay for her to arrive right now and take this poor sobbing wretch off his hands.

The sound of people approaching brought hope.

"Miss Milton," he said, pulling her away from his coat. Margaux looked up at him. The last of her hair came undone into a glossy tumble down her back. She sniffed, her arms still clutching his sleeves. His hands were on her shoulders and in the darkness, lit romantically by the softly glowing torches, they might have been just released from a kiss.

That is precisely the thought that went through his mind when five strangers walked in the clearing, their eyes wide and mouths open with shock.

He was acutely aware of the fact that he was holding this woman much too close. That her hair was down, her face flushed. Her lips were swollen and red from Farnsworth's rough kisses. Their hands were on each other in what would surely seem a lover's embrace.

It was exactly what the newly arrived five thought. He could see it in their shocked faces, the gleam of delight and interest in their rabid little eyes. They were a group of young people, three girls and two youths. They stood, locked in shock, until one of the girls yelped like a pup and ran off.

Miss Milton did not make matters any better when she whirled and gave a huge sob, her hands going to her hair in a frantic effort to gather it together.

It was strange what came over him. He felt as if he were falling backward, being sucked into something over which he had no control. Their stares were sharp and bright, filled with accusation and excitement.

They looked accusingly at Miss Milton. He put his arm about her shoulders to shield her.

"My companion is ill," Gideon began.

His finger caught on the slight tear in the sleeve of her gown. One of the girls flickered her gaze to it, her eyes widening. She clamped a hand over her mouth in shock.

"Well," one of the youths said, grinning and exchanging a knowing look with the other young man.

The little idiot who had fled returned, this time with a pair of older men. She pointed and cried, in a gratingly shrill voice, "There they are!"

"Ashford?" one of them said, peering into the darkness. "Is that Lord Ashford?"

Gideon's mind was working fast, but his heart felt as if it were shrinking. His world shrank with it. He was being trapped. He could feel it.

"Explain yourself," the other man demanded, taking in the situation and growing enraged.

"What is it? What is all this?" another voice said, and an elderly woman appeared on the scene. She stopped short at seeing Margaux and him standing together. "Oh. Oh, dear."

He had to take command. "Miss Milton is feeling ill. The air is quite close inside. She came outdoors to gather her strength."

It was a feeble excuse, but he had to say something.

The elderly woman stepped forward. Over her shoulder, she said, "Summon the girl's mother. Eugenia Milton is in the card room." To Margaux, she said, "Are you injured, gel?"

"No. I . . . came outside, as he said. I was upset. It is all just as he said." Margaux sniffed. She refused to let go of Gideon's coat, her eyes wild and helpless as she stared at the accusing faces of those who had surrounded them.

The one who had identified Gideon queried, "Has this man done you ill?"

"No. No, he helped me. I had come here with—"

"She was ill," Gideon said, cutting her off with authority. "I told you. I saw her leave and followed to make certain she was not in need of aid. I came upon her in a bad state and was about to summon aid."

"Gideon?" a voice said.

Sophie had arrived. Gideon looked at her in misery, his

chest aching. He understood what it was to be a man of honor, what was required of him.

Did she?

Several things happened at once. Behind Sophie was Mrs. Milton, who nearly pushed several people on their derrieres in her rush forward.

"What have you done?" she accused.

Gideon paused, thinking to allow Margaux to answer, then realized that the woman was staring at him. She was speaking to him.

"Mama, Lord Ashford helped me," Margaux said.

The woman's eyes flashed in a surge of rage. "Helped himself, I would say."

"Where is Lord Farnsworth?" Sophie said, stepping forward. "Is he behind—?"

"I followed Miss Milton outside when I saw her wander here to the garden by herself," Gideon said, flashing a warning look to shush her. Margaux's reputation was in jeopardy, surely enough, but if that reprobate's name were brought into it, she would be done in for good. He hoped Sophie would realize this quickly. "It seemed to me that she looked unwell and I wished to find out if she needed assistance. I keep explaining this."

"What happened to your hair, then?" one of the girls asked slyly, eliciting twitters from the other young people.

Mrs. Milton went ramrod straight, her face like a beet in the flash of an instant.

Gideon answered. "She lost her way and became overset. You must have fallen, did you not, Miss Milton? That must be the problem, and your pins fell out."

Margaux tried to smile. "It was silly of me to panic. I don't know why I did."

"I am afraid she made a muddle of her dress," Gideon said, making certain to address this to the boy who had noticed it. "It must have been torn on a shrub. Nasty, I hope you do not have a cut, my dear."

Mrs. Milton was having none of it. She glared at him.

Burton arrived on the scene then, and Margaux let out a

helpless wince. Gideon understood because he felt the same way, for the man moved to Sophie's side.

Gideon remained where he was. Miss Milton's reputation, her entire future without a doubt, was on the table right here, right now. Not only that, but it was his honor that was in debate as well. Honor and respectability were the two things he held of value, more precious than anything else, for it was what he needed to be worthy of Sophie.

Sophie. Did she understand what was happening?

His place was by Margaux Milton. If he abandoned her now, his honor would be nothing, and her life would be ruined.

"I just wish to go home," Margaux whispered to him. "Please. They are all staring at me."

"Come over here at once!" Mrs. Milton commanded, taking exception to the intimate way she had spoken to Gideon. Her daughter reluctantly left the shelter of his side and, with her head hung, slipped into her mother's shadow.

"Well, sir, what do you intend to do about this?" Mrs. Milton squared off at him, and the question sealed it.

He inclined his head respectfully. There was no use in any other course. "I will call upon you on the morrow."

The older woman's nostrils flared and she gave him a nod of satisfaction, but she was not pleased. He had a sudden apprehension, seeing her enraged, seeing Margaux shrinking in humiliation beside her. Why he felt responsible . . . but he was, whether it was fair or not, deserved or not. Good God, the girl was his responsibility now.

"I will expect that Miss Milton will receive me in good spirits." He spoke meaningfully, so that Mrs. Milton would know what he wanted her to know. She was not to take her temper out on her daughter.

"You will speak to *me,* you impertinent man!" she shot back, having none of his bossiness.

He narrowed his gaze and set his jaw. "I will speak to Miss Milton or I will not speak . . . at all."

They struck a silent bargain, the two of them, and Mrs. Milton understood clearly that she was to leave off haranguing her daughter. In return, Gideon would arrive at their home tomorrow and they would sort this matter out.

The gazes of those around him disgusted him. The young persons were wide-eyed, and the girl who had asked Margaux about her hair was smiling, loving the drama being played out, as if for her specific diversion. The elder woman took the scene in silently, regarding him with surprise and approval when he announced he would call on the Miltons tomorrow. She had not expected him to act honorably. The two older gentlemen turned away, disturbed still but mollified by the outcome.

And Sophie stood and looked at him. He returned her gaze for only a moment, then offered Margaux his arm. "Allow me to see you to your carriage."

Chapter 25

Sophie came to Gideon as soon as she and May arrived home.

She stood in the doorway to his room, and when he turned to her, she flew into his arms. It felt so good to hold her, to feel the familiar feeling of his arms around her.

"This is a disaster of my making," she said softly.

"Shall we not go into playing with blame?" His breath fanned the loose tendrils of gold-spun hair. His large palm smoothed across her cheek. He told himself to memorize this, each scent and sensation. They would not have many more moments like it. "I should think it would be utterly obvious that no one is culpable."

"Except that horrible man. Oh, if I'd only told Margaux about Farnsworth immediately." She broke away and paced the width of his room, then wheeled and retraced her steps. Her lips trembled. "Gideon, I cannot lose you."

"No. It is quite inconceivable, is it not?" He was still rather dazed, walking about feeling like a bit of dried wood, his mind frozen.

Sophie's shoulders slumped. "Margaux does not even know that I love you. I never told her. I was waiting until you had made your peace and we could let everyone know of our intentions. And she, she is enamored of Burton, you know. Oh, nothing is as it should be. We belong together, Gideon. And she belongs with him. I think even he is beginning to see that."

He gave her a dull look, devoid of emotion, and it was this that hit Sophie the hardest. He's lost hope, she thought.

"Are you suggesting that I not go to see the Miltons tomorrow?"

"I . . . No." The surge of hopelessness weakened her knees. She sank into the chair where she had sat so many hours, reading or sketching. "Of course not. It would be devastating to her. She would be left in utter disgrace, and she does not deserve that. Everyone is expecting you to do the proper thing and . . . and . . . Oh, why do you have to be a man of honor in the end?"

He knelt before her, placing gentle hands on her shoulder. "Look at me, Sophie."

She was slow to obey, tilting her head to look up at him.

His smile was lopsided, the way it always was when it held a generous portion of irony. "You made me the man I am."

"And what have I done? You are trapped, as you always feared you would be, and it is all my doing."

"No, no. That is not what I meant. Sophie, no matter how it came to pass, here I am, a gentleman of the first cut. I am proud of that. However, as such, I have no choice. To ignore Miss Milton's need would be cruel. It would consign her to something neither of us could face."

"I don't care," she flung, grasping his hands with her own. "I do not care if the entire world scorns us. I want you. I don't care about anything else. None of it matters anymore."

"What a romantic you have turned out to be. What happened to my practical Sophie?"

"If it were anyone else, I would demand you tell the truth. Oh, I would! But how could I hurt her?"

"You wouldn't. And you would not ask it of me."

"You were right all along. This is so stupid. Society has

the most insane ideas of men and women—it is a foolish, twisted institution. Why should we be punished because of what Farnsworth did? He escaped, completely unscathed in this when it was he who caused this disaster."

"But we cannot reveal that," he warned. "Do you remember what I told you of the debacle of my youth, the young woman who was ridiculed, the man whom I humiliated? Society is unforgiving, yes, and it is powerful. The only answer for this crisis is to contain it as soon as possible. I will get my revenge on Farnsworth in my own time."

She twisted away and rose, resuming her pacing. "I know it would do no good if he were brought into it. Even in the best of circumstances, it would be he, and not you, who would be forced to marry Margaux, and that is too miserable a fate for her. No, that cannot be borne. She is worth more than this horrible scandal. But, oh, all of our lives gone because of one small error? It is not fair. It is simply not fair."

"Sophie," he said, reaching for her. "No, love, it is not fair. I fear I may weep with you."

"What insanity this is." She came into his arms, his collar in her fists. "Why doesn't it matter if she's happy? No, as long as she's *respectable*. Well, she *is* respectable. She's the best, dearest, most admirable person, Gideon. And you—what of you? You rescue her and now you must marry her."

"Give me another solution, I beg you, and I will take it."

"We could speak to Mrs. Milton. Make her understand how it is, offer another possibility. . . ."

"Think, Sophie. Think of every possible idea, and I promise you I have already considered it."

She stood facing him, rigid, shivering in frustration. "But if you do not offer marriage, she will become an outcast. Yes, I know. I *know*, Gideon, that this is how it must be, but I cannot accept it."

"Find me another way, anything," he begged. "All I could come to think of is a mad wish to run away. We could run away, Sophie, forget them all. You and I, and we shall have all we need."

"Yes, yes, let's run." She sobbed, but she knew they were only pretending, knew he was speaking out of grief.

Run away—to what end? They would leave everyone they loved decimated in their wake. And how could they be happy then?

"Shhh," he said, catching her and not letting her go, even when she tried to twist away. "You once told me that I had spent my life being less than I am. Would you ask me to do that now?"

"No. I don't want—"

"I don't want it either. But it must be this way, Sophie. It is nothing any of us want, but we cannot change the world."

She suddenly went still. She began to sob, and the wildness left her and she was in his arms, limp and clinging. He held her tightly, closing his eyes.

He took her to bed. They lay, fully dressed, still wrapped tight until sleep came. But that was a long, long time.

Margaux sat in a stiff-backed chair in the center hall of her aunt Viola's town house and waited. She did not move, her eyes fixed on some point in middle space as her thoughts churned.

She did not see the footman as he walked past, paused. "May I get anything for you, Miss Margaux?" he asked.

Shaking her head, she barely registered his inquiry, or his hesitant retreat.

The voices that came from beyond the door to the drawing room, which had been raised only a moment ago, were quiet now.

Lord Ashford had arrived promptly this morning as promised, and her mother had ushered him into the drawing room with pursed lips and flashing eyes full of rage without a word. She'd closed the door, leaving Margaux locked outside of the room where her future was to be decided, and all Margaux could hear of what was being said was the soft muffle of conversation and the slightly sharper, louder tones of stridency from time to time.

The clip of footsteps sounded sharply on the marble flour and Aunt Viola appeared before her, wringing her hands. "Any word?"

Margaux shook her head. Aunt Viola reached for her, and she extended her hands. "What is to become of you, child?" she fretted. "Oh, poor dear."

It was hardly the bolstering sort of comment Margaux craved. She wished Sophie could be here, she would have dearly wished to have her friend at her side, but Mother had forbid Margaux sending any communication to her this morning.

"That gel—that *Sophie*—is where all the trouble came from!" Mama had insisted last night, lashing in her most ferocious voice all the way home from the ball. "And that dreadful woman with pink feathers! I rue the day I allowed my sister to persuade me she was good ton. Pink feathers— who ever heard of such a thing? But, truth be told, her reputation is impeccable, although I cannot see why people find her so charming. Ah, but true nature will out, and see what comes of her loose association with *that man*."

That man was Lord Ashford, although Margaux had tried repeatedly to explain what had really happened. Actually, she had not tried so hard. When Mama spoke over her in that loud voice of hers, she'd allowed her half-hearted efforts to flag, for she was too humiliated to press the matter.

She kept thinking of Oliver's face, standing in the crowd of everyone who stared and judged her. What must he think of her?

"What are they saying?" Aunt Viola said, going to the door. Her hand trembled, as if she considered knocking on it. Aunt Viola was not afraid of Mama, necessarily. In fact, Margaux had her to thank for the freedoms she enjoyed, for she challenged her sister's overbearing ways on Margaux's behalf. But one did not taunt a cornered wolf, and

Mama's mood right now was not one that would brook any interference, so Aunt Viola dropped her hand with an apologetic glance at her niece.

"I haven't heard a—" Margaux broke off with a start as the door was suddenly flung open. In the breach stood the magnificent form of Lord Ashford.

He was handsome, and imposing. He looked very angry.

He was startled to see Aunt Viola standing right there. Within a moment, he recovered himself and bowed. "Lady Viola," he said.

"Lord Ashford," Aunt Viola fluttered. She glanced anxiously at Margaux, who stood.

"May I speak with your niece, if you please?"

"Yes, indeed." She fluttered her hand at Margaux.

She felt like a lamb, all of a sudden. She slipped into the room. Lord Ashford, however, remained at the door.

He addressed Mrs. Milton, who sat glowering on the sofa. "I requested to speak to your daughter privately."

"You have seen enough of my daughter *privately*, my lord," Mother said, not budging.

"You do not expect me to speak to her without the dignity of some solitude," he said with tones of such disdain, it did not fail to shrivel Mama just a little. "I understand if you are ignorant of how things are done in the bon ton, being a first-time guest in Town, but this is not a cattle market, Mrs. Milton. We have courtesies here that elevate us above common bartering, and we do our best to observe them even in the most difficult of times."

Margaux bit her lips to keep from gasping, and Mama went as white as snow. Gray, sickly, week-old snow.

She rose without a word and marched from the room. Before Lord Ashford closed the door, however, Margaux glimpsed Aunt Viola's face. She wore an expression of surprise. And a bit less stricken than before, as if the shock were not unpleasant.

When they were alone, Lord Ashford slowly turned to face her.

"Miss Milton," he began.

"Lord Ashford," she replied.

They stared at one another until he heaved a labored sigh and indicated they sit. She did so, perching herself on the edge of the chair, her body charged with tension.

He had taken the chair directly opposite hers and pulled it closer.

"I did not mean to trap you," she blurted.

He took her hands in his. "I know you did not. You did nothing wrong, nothing to be ashamed of, and it pains me to see you like this."

She lowered her eyes. Her hands were ungloved, as were his. The size of his hands shocked her. They were big. Broad palms, long, lithe fingers.

Lord Burton had slender hands. Pale, though not as pale as hers. She had noticed when, while passing him a book she had taken from the lending library on the artifacts being imported by the East India Company, his hand had rested for the briefest moment over hers. She'd had gloves on, of course, but he had removed his, and the elegance of his naked hand had sent a thrill straight up her arm.

She closed her eyes. Thinking about Burton was much too difficult, and this moment was arduous enough.

Lord Ashford spoke. "You realize what must happen?"

She nodded.

"Margaux, please look at me." He waited patiently until she opened her eyes and raised her gaze to his. "You seem afraid. There is no need to be. I am not angry, if that is what you fear."

"But, my lord, you cannot be happy to be forced to this."

He paused, choosing his words. "It is not a *happy* time, for either of us. I cannot pretend that it is." He bowed his head, and seemed to be gathering his composure. "Miss Milton, I am ready to become your husband. Ah, do not look so sad. I am not nearly as bad as my reputation makes me out to be."

"You are very kind." She was going to weep again. "My lord, but I do not love you."

He grinned, but it was a sad smile. "I know. And it is a dreadful disappointment to a young woman's heart to lose the dream of love." His expression altered, shifted, and he looked for the briefest moment as bleak as she had ever seen another human being appear.

"You are very good, my lord, for a man who has such a black reputation."

"Well," he said with a shrug, "the thing about reputations is that they can often bear little resemblance to the character of the person."

"Like Viscount Farnsworth," she said bitterly. "He is held in the most elevated regard, being a viscount, but he is a horrible man."

"Indeed, but let us not think too much on that. What is done is . . . well, done, as they say. We shall make the best of it."

"I do not know how you can be so accepting of all of this. It is not what I expected."

"We should be friends, Margaux."

"I will try," she promised.

"So, then. I suppose I should be about the business of proposing to you." He rose and cleared away his chair, then sank on one knee. "Will you do me the honor of becoming my wife?"

Margaux was touched. "I will, indeed," she whispered.

"I am grateful," he said, and rose. It seemed to be something of an effort, as if a burden weighed on him and made it difficult to bear up. She glanced away, feeling a surge of guilt, sadness, uncertainty. It was all settled, then.

He opened the door quickly to reveal her mother and Aunt Viola standing just outside, listening.

They were startled. Mama's face immediately reverted to its scowl.

"She has accepted my offer," Lord Ashford said. "I will leave the arrangements to you. I think it best if we are seen together in public as soon as possible so as to establish the courtship, so I will escort Miss Milton to the theater the day after tomorrow. I will call at seven o'clock, if that is convenient."

Mrs. Milton gave a jerky nod.

✑ Chapter 26

When Gideon arrived home at May's house, he was grate-
ful to find her alone in the drawing room.

She came to him and offered an embrace. His eyelids
were heavy, giving him a weary look. "You seem tired,"
she said.

He shook his head. He was distracted, distant. May
peered up at him, not letting him go. "Sophie is resting upstairs. Come and sit."

The look of pain that came across his face was fleeting,
but her eager eyes saw it, saw everything.

"She knows where I was today?"

"Of course."

"Good," he murmured. "I must speak with you alone."

She did not like the sound of his tone. Immediately, her
apprehension rose.

He seemed sad, but so very noble as he wandered to the
window and faced the glass. He was not looking outside,
she could tell, but inward. She had never seen a man appear more alone.

"You thought I have lived a dissolute life, and I admit,
there was plenty that I did that I was not proud of. But the
past was always there, May, like a seed. Those days with

you and Matthew. They were like a compass for me, they kept me from being completely soulless. If there is good in me, it is because of you."

"I believe Sophie had more to do with it than I."

"Sophie . . . Yes, Sophie, too." He made a thoughtful face and closed his eyes. "Sophie is . . . Oh, God, May. I am lost."

May held him, and they stayed locked together for a good while, after which she went to the sideboard and poured him a scotch whiskey. He took it from her without a word, but he did not drink. He simply cradled it in his hand and stared into space.

May drew her petite frame up and took in a long breath. "If you are indeed leaving, Gideon, then I must do something I have been putting off for far too long."

He gave her a measured look, clearly curious.

"This is a horrible moment to tell you, but time has run out and I have waited far too long. There are things you do not know, about me. And about Matthew. About how he died, and about why I could not be part of your life."

"It was Reginald."

"Yes, but I should have fought him, and I would have. With all the love I had in my heart for you, I would have never allowed him to take you away from me, but for the one thing that could stop me."

She paced to the other side of the room, suddenly feeling warm, closed in. "I am to blame for your unhappiness, all of it. And every moment that you have been here, I have suffered knowing that nothing would be right until you knew."

"May?" He took a few steps toward her and she turned, holding her hand up for him to come no farther.

"I know what you are facing now is enough sorrow for anyone, but I am losing you all over again. The future is so unpredictable, as we have seen, and you will soon be a married man. I may never have a chance like this again to explain."

His eyes narrowed and he was suddenly cautious.

"What did you mean, you have to tell me how Matthew died? He killed himself. He was ill."

"He was ill, yes, it is true. But he did not die at his own hand."

And she told him.

The sound of furniture being shoved about, and all other manner of clanking and thumping resounded as Sophie neared the doorway to Gideon's bedchamber.

"What is it, what has happened?" she asked, entering the room.

Gideon whirled. "Don't you knock?"

Sophie recoiled. He had never spoken sharply to her like this before.

He seemed to regret it immediately. He frowned and turned back to what he was doing.

Which was, she saw, putting clothing into a valise.

"I am leaving," he said, his voice jerking in rhythm to the hard shoves he gave his clothing. "I just need a few things, and I can send my man for the rest."

"You are leaving," she repeated numbly.

"You cannot expect me to stay in this house when I am engaged to another woman, do you?"

He was almost shouting at her. Sophie stood mutely, watching him. Thank goodness she felt nothing. Shock, blessed shock, held her still and silent.

"What am I supposed to do, I ask you? Walk about this place and ignore you?" He shot her an angry look. "It was all just a stupid, stupid illusion, did you know that?"

"Gideon, what was an illusion? You are not making sense."

He threw his head back and made a harsh sound. "Of course I am not making sense. I am the epitome of the ridiculous, Sophie."

Glancing at her, he stopped. She saw the hard swallow convulse his throat. "Oh, God, don't look like that," he pleaded. "Say good-bye to me, Sophie."

He came to stand in front of her. "I love you," he whispered. "I will love you until the moment I draw my last breath. But I shall never speak to you again, and I shall endeavor not to be in the same room as you. I am too weak for that sort of temptation. So, say good-bye to me now."

Tears slipped rapidly onto her cheeks. "I love you with all my heart. My every thought is of you, and it will be that way always."

He snatched her to him and kissed her, and she cried out softly, grasping him so that he would not end the kiss too soon.

But he did. Her mouth ached and her throat, jammed with unspent sobs, throbbed, and still he left her.

"I told him," May said as soon as Robert entered the house.

"Gideon?"

She nodded.

His eyes were hard. "What did he say?"

May pressed her lips together. She could not speak.

"He . . . is he going to reveal what happened?"

"No, no, Robert. Gideon would never do that."

He took her by the hand and pulled her into the library, then closed the door. "May, please, love, tell me. What did he say?"

"He said nothing. He just listened. Then he asked me if I loved Matthew. I don't know what he meant . . . I tried to explain."

"Did you tell him the circumstance, how Matthew threatened you?"

"I did. He did not question me—"

"Was he angry? Did he seem vengeful? Dear God, please, tell me that he did not threaten you. He is not going to the authorities, is he?"

Gideon stood at the door. "Have no worry on that score, Lord Roberts."

Robert whirled.

"I intend to leave," Gideon continued. "I am going tonight, May. I think it best. I need . . . I need some time. To think. Everything is all around me here."

He appeared cold, remote. He was the polite stranger again.

"I will send for the rest of my things in the morning," he said, then turned to Robert. "And if your anxiety for May is the reason you are looking as if you will lay me on the floor, then let me assure you I have no intention to ever tell anyone what May told me this afternoon. You should know I would never speak a word against her."

Robert relaxed. "I beg your pardon. A reflex, merely. You see, I worry . . ."

Gideon clamped his hand on the other man's shoulder. "How glad I am that you do. It gives me a great deal of peace."

"Should we not talk about this?" Robert ventured. "It cannot have been easy to learn what you did today."

"Actually, I cannot remember a worse day in my life."

"Gideon, please talk to me," May pleaded.

"About what? The past?" His smile flashed quickly, then was gone. It wasn't a pleasant one, though. "I think we have spent enough time today visiting the past. I thank you, Lady May, for your generous hospitality to me all these many weeks. Your kindness is much appreciated."

Robert said, "You cannot leave, not without some kind of resolution."

"But there is resolution, it is all quite neat. Or . . . do you mean forgiveness?" His voice was sharp again. There was an edge to him, a wildness that was roiling beneath the civilized exterior he projected. "Well, then, you have it. It is not difficult to give. After all, who am I to throw stones?"

"You are very angry, Gideon. I should not have told you. It was a very bad time for you right now, for all of us, with everything else that has happened."

"On the contrary. It was excellent timing. It helps sever the ties. Ties that must be severed, after all. It was sweet, all this hominess and reminiscence, but it, like all good things, must end. This, you know, of course. You and

Matthew did not last. Does anything?" He suddenly appeared unbearably bitter.

Robert looked combative again. He took a step toward Gideon. "You know what she did. She had no other choice."

"Robert!" May grasped him and tried to pull him back.

Gideon seemed to snarl. "I do not blame her for killing Matthew." He looked from May to Robert, then back again. "You don't understand at all, do you? She gave me hope. Dastardly thing, hope. I'd almost gotten used to living without it."

"I love you, Gideon," May whispered.

He gave her a long, steady look. "And I you. Always. Good evening."

When he was gone, May let out a small cry of frustration. "He is an idiot!"

Robert turned to stare at her, amazed. "I would have thought you would be in a puddle of tears by now."

"I have cried them, and perhaps shall shed more before this is done. But he is taking this all the wrong way. He . . . he is not angry with me because I killed Matthew—"

"You did not kill him. It is different, May, than murder, a distinction we must have a care to draw . . ." Robert stopped. "He is not?"

She stuck her index finger into the air. "It was most peculiar. Did you hear what he said just now, about hope? Robert, I told you that the only thing he asked me when I told him about the accident was 'Did you love Matthew?' And I told him that I had, once. And then he said the strangest thing. He said that it was true. That it all comes to an end and that Sophie was right. What do you think he meant? In any event, that was all that mattered, and it was that which sent him storming out."

"That fellow is damned peculiar."

May wheeled on him. "Do not judge him, Robert."

Robert threw up his hands. "You were the one who called him an idiot."

"Well, he is one. But he is hurt. He loves Sophie, but he

offered for Margaux today, and that was difficult. And I have just told him that the death that took his brother, his whole life, to be thrown to a bastard who treated him deplorably was at my hand. He is a decent man, and his world has just come asunder."

Robert paused, then relaxed. "I tend to judge him harshly because he has always had the power to wound you." He sighed, taking her into his arms. "He is a better man than I gave him credit for, I do admit it."

"I should not have told him tonight. But I have been meaning to for so long, telling myself each time I was set to do it that another opportunity would come, a better one, and then I suddenly realized I'd run out of time."

"No. It is best the thing is done, as much as I dreaded it myself. There is a relief to having it behind us. He is a grown man, not the child you remember. You cannot coddle him any longer. And he is not the cad he is purported to be. Gideon will shoulder this with all else he must. It is best to take it all at once. Give him time, May."

"Time, time, I've wasted too much time. Would that I had the courage to do it all differently."

"Would we all could undo our mistakes. But I am not sorry for anything. You are safe, and that is all I care about."

"Can you be so selfish? What about Gideon?"

"He is a man of some substance. Trust in that, May. He loves you."

"I wish he would stay. I wish . . . oh, so many things."

Gideon sulked. It was not attractive, nor was he particularly proud of it, but he did it nonetheless, actually threw himself into it. He felt he was entitled.

The news that May had been the one to put the ball in his brother was indeed shocking. He was not certain yet what his reaction was. He remembered Matthew's rages, his depression, his long lassitude and despondency. As a child, he had seen things the adults would have liked to have kept him sheltered from, and May had succeeded to

some degree. Enough so that he could block out that particular unpleasantness from his memory, and that is exactly
what he had done.

He had chosen to remember the good times, but there
was no escaping the truth that Matthew had been deeply
ill. Homicidal? As difficult as it was, he believed it. He
knew May would not have done murder in cold blood. If
she said she killed Matthew in order to save her own life,
Gideon knew in his heart this had to be so.

What had him by the throat was the idea that their great
love, the idolized vision he'd always held in the back of his
mind, the happiness, the pure adulation that he'd grown up
with, all around them, as natural as air, had been *false*.

He had been fooled. The belief in that one thing, so pure
and shining and real—he had *felt* it, hadn't he?—had been
an anchor and a beacon, even when he pretended he didn't
give a fig for such things.

The truth was he'd always been waiting.

Yet it had been untrue all along, ill-fated, corrupt. What
a foul lie, for it had hooked him into falling in love with
Sophie. What disaster he'd come to because of that.

Is that all love was, a temporary flare, just desire
dressed up prettily for the moment, like a gorgeous blos-
som dazzling the eye only to rot into a shriveled brown
twig? Matthew had been a sick, violent man. And May had
been ready to run for her life. A more degrading situation
he could not have imagined. That was his secret, hidden
dream? That was the legendary "Matthew and May"? It
shook the very foundations of his world.

What was left, then? What of his life, and the fate of the
girl he was now bound to marry?

Would he grow to hate the sight of her, always compar-
ing Margaux's dark prettiness with the incomparably fair
beauty that was indelibly in his heart? Would he see Sophie ten years from now, riding in the Park or coming out
of church after Sunday services with a cluster of children
around her and a husband—what unnamed fiend with no

face or form would that being be, to torment him without ever knowing it?

Would his breath still hitch, would his heart stop? Would this pain, so sharp and throbbing now, have faded, or would it flare to life over and over again?

Why had he ever opened himself up to such dismal anguish? Oh, it was May's doing, it was the seed she had planted with her playfulness and lovely laughter, and the doting way he remembered her looking when her gaze rested on his brother.

Once. Once, but not always. Her love had died. God, that his would. That he would forget that winsome face and never be tormented with the desire to know a lifetime with her.

If only May had never told him. Better to be ignorant, deluded. It was May's fault, all her fault, every last misery he'd endured in his life. He felt bruised, ill-used.

He was not so sullen that reason left him, and in a moment, the cold anger subsided. He did not blame her, not really. He would like to. It would be sublimely pleasing to hold *someone* accountable, for God's sake.

Never had he felt more muddled in the head. It occurred to him that he had not really assessed the pain of losing his brother, then losing May. Englishmen didn't ponder these things—stiff upper lip and all of that. Yet he had to admit it had left a hole inside of him, one he'd thought he'd been on the way to mending these last months. He'd come home at last, to May and then, to Sophie.

But he must leave again.

Surely, he was not meant to always be driven from the ones he loved? Why did it keep happening to him?

A cold face emerged in his memory. A curling sneer, a glittering eye. He remembered Reginald's hard words. He was worthless, a cur, a blight.

He'd fought against believing it his whole life, but that sort of thing got under one's skin if one wasn't careful.

It was pricking his flesh even now.

Chapter 27

In the room Gideon had recently vacated, Sophie wan-
dered, touching the corner of his chest of drawers, smoothing her hand over the coverlet.

She could feel his presence still. It was comforting, as
if he might come in through the door any moment.

The realization that he would not hit her like tiny darts,
small increments that deepened her understanding, her realization that Gideon was gone.

He was gone forever.

"I was afraid I would find you here," May said as she
entered.

Sophie whirled. May looked smaller than she'd ever
seen her. The pale pink dress she wore was in the mode of
the sketch she had done for her, the current style altered to
more flattering lines for May's petite frame.

That day seemed so long ago.

"Do not look so sad," May said. Her gaze drifted
around the empty room. "I can hardly bear it myself. I
wanted for things to be very different from this."

"Have you noticed that things have a way of occurring
quite independent of our intentions?" Sophie inquired.

"Indeed, it makes a trial of life sometimes." She crossed

the room, seeming to be moving aimlessly, then stopped. "Sophie, Lord Roberts and I are going to be wed."

Sophie was taken aback. She was happy, yes, but it seemed like a strange time. "Let me congratulate you. When?"

"He is procuring a special license. We wish to have a quiet ceremony at our neighborhood church. The timing might seem odd to you, with all that has happened, but in truth, it comes at just the right time. I have kept him waiting too long."

"I know you and he will be very happy."

"Robert is the man I've waited for all my life. It is time, now. Things are changing. First Gideon . . . and I know you will leave me soon." It wasn't a question. May seemed to know already that had been foremost in Sophie's mind.

"I think I should."

"But the season . . ."

"I cannot stay, Aunt May, surely you understand. I would still like to marry, yes. I want children. But for now, I think I need to just recover from all that has happened." She grew thoughtful. "It is difficult, when you have thought of your life as one way, and then must settle. And after such a grand dream as I once had, it seems rather lackluster."

"Do not settle," May said sternly.

"In any event, I do not think I can continue here. You are going to be a married woman again. You should have your house to yourself. And Gideon will wish to visit you. I should not be there for that."

"I do not know what Gideon will choose to do." May bowed her head. "It could be that he will never wish to see me again."

"Surely, not!"

"Dear, that is his choice. I have done all I can. But for you, please do not think of leaving. Robert is very fond of you. He does not mind in the least if you stay."

"No, please, do not ask it of me. I do have some pride

remaining, after all I've done to compromise it. I vow, however, that our friendship shall not end."

May seemed to wish to continue the debate, but rolled her lips and nodded. "We shall make sense of all of this later. I'll go and change now. Robert and I have an appointment to speak to the reverend to make the arrangements for the ceremony. Will you be there?"

"Most certainly. I have no doubt, Aunt May, that you and Lord Roberts will be perfectly blissful together. I am very happy for you."

Alone with her thoughts once again after May left, she reflected how swiftly things were changing. Gideon was marrying Margaux, May and Lord Marcus Roberts were sealing their long-standing love with the blessing of the church. Michaela's child would arrive within the year. . . .

It was time for her to look to make a change as well.

She turned herself in a circle, taking in the room one last time. On the table by the bed was a volume she recognized. She laughed softly. *Hours of Idleness.*

She recollected how Gideon had come to love it. He hadn't at first.

"What the devil is he talking about?" he'd groused after a particularly convoluted line. "The fellow is quite incapable of plain speech."

"It is poetry," she had reminded him gently.

"It is rubbish."

"You are a Philistine."

He'd harrumphed, but his smile had been there, tucked into the corners of his mouth.

Images of him filled her mind. This room created a flood of them. She could see him in the bed, his ravaged face swathed in gauze and linen, the scent of liniment and salves pungent in the air. That bleary first meeting when he'd shocked and fascinated her.

With the patch over his eye, worried he'd look ridiculous, not realizing how the rakish affectation had made her blood pump faster every time she looked at him. And later, stretched on the coverlet, his bare skin bathed in the moonlight that poured in through the window, his eyes ravenous as she disrobed for him.

She picked up the volume and sat in his chair. She smiled as she read over familiar verses, recalling when she'd read them to him, and the comments he'd made. Irreverent, irrepressible man.

> *Remembrance only can remain,*
> *But that, will make us weep the more.*

She almost closed the book. She did not come here to grieve, but to say farewell. She had nothing to resent. She'd stolen a life, and she'd known love.

What complaint could she have that things had not turned out better for her? She had deserved nothing when she came to this house. If she left with nothing, it was only right.

Perhaps she would ask May to find a position for her, if she knew a kind family in the country somewhere. She would like that. After the wedding, she would see to it.

She glanced down at the book again, her teeth sinking painfully into her bottom lip.

> *Again, thou best belov'd, adieu!*
> *Ah! If thou canst, o'ercome regret,*
> *Nor let thy mind past joys review,*
> *Our only hope is, to forget!*

Good advice, she thought. She closed the book, placed it on the table, and left the room.

*Vincent Biggs's house was a shambles. This was not un-*usual. This place where Gideon had come often in the past with his friends to carouse had not borne up under the misuse of countless nights of high jinks. The single-minded dedication of an energetic group of miscreants had wreaked havoc with the man's home that no team of servants, let alone Biggs's apathetic staff, could right.

Biggs didn't mind. He was either drunk or nursing a sore head. Gideon had never minded, either, yet he felt a repulsion overtake him now as he entered the place.

He'd grown used to May's comfortable home, the soft mélange of fabrics and bric-a-brac collected over the course of an active life. This place seemed a tomb in comparison.

"Good to have you back," Biggs declared as he rushed into the room. His hair was rumpled. It was four o'clock in the afternoon, and the man had no doubt been napping.

Rushing to grab a bottle of whiskey, he added, "Have a drink."

"No, thank you." Gideon eyed the filthy glasses. "Is Farnsworth here?"

Splashing a liberal amount of whiskey into a glass, Biggs jerked his shoulder to the ceiling. "Still sleeping."

"It's nearly time for tea."

At the mention of that genteel meal, Biggs was startled. He gave a short, surprised laugh, as if Gideon were joking.

He said, "Yes, well, we didn't get in last night until well past dawn." He grinned at Gideon. "Sorry you missed it."

"I am not. Which room?"

"What?"

"Which room is he in?"

Biggs told him, then downed half his glass before following Gideon out into the hallway and up the stairs.

After a knock at the indicated bedroom door, Gideon entered without waiting to be invited, requested in a calm voice that the surprised young lady in bed with Farnsworth take herself off as he had urgent business with the viscount, and ordered his former friend to dress.

Back downstairs in the drawing room, Biggs rushed for the whiskey. "What the devil are you about, Ashford?"

"When Farnsworth comes in, stay. I want to have a witness."

"What's he done?" His eyes bulged as an appalling thought occurred to him. "You aren't going to shoot him, are you?"

"That would be too quick. As to the subject of shootings, I wanted your opinion, Biggs. Do you suppose I should hold him to be at fault for the fact that he overloaded the pistol? It could have killed me. It nearly did."

"It was an accident," Farnsworth called from the door. He strode in dressed in trousers, bare feet, a shirt that was not fastened either at the wrists or the neck, and strands of hair standing straight up. "I was drinking. We all were. Besides, I saved your life. I brought you to the loving arms of your relatives. That should count for something."

Gideon faced him. "I shall give you credit for that, Farnsworth. And I must say, such independent thinking shocks me. You were never good at acting on your own. You always fell into someone's shadow, usually mine. That is why you courted Miss Milton, isn't it? You thought it a lark. What was it you called her . . . ? Oh, of course. Innocent blood."

"It was you who gave me the idea. I figured it was some new game of yours. The way you were slinking about, cozying up to that Kent woman."

His gut tightened at the mention of Sophie. "Your small mind could not possibly understand what it was I was doing with Miss Kent."

"Besides, I was tired of women who made it too easy. I looked at you and thought, Ashford's found some sport. Seducing debutantes." He shrugged. "I was only doing the same thing you were."

"As a result, you almost ruined a good woman's reputation."

Biggs jerked his glass toward Gideon, splashing some of the liquid onto his hand. "I say, is it true you are going to wed this girl? I heard a rumor."

"It has not been announced yet, but yes, I will be taking Miss Milton as a wife." Turning back to Farnsworth, he added, "I had no choice."

"God, Ashford, what a sop you've become. Why should you sacrifice yourself because the girl behaved like a stupid chit? I was just having some fun. She changed her mind at the last minute, got wild over just a little kiss. Who asked you to play hero?"

For one moment, Gideon's rage got away from him. He took a step forward, then forced himself to stop. The urge to do violence was difficult to control. Every part of him trembled with the desire to feel Farnsworth's neck under his fingers.

He was not here for Margaux as much as for Sophie. Farnsworth, damn him, had cost him Sophie.

"I did not come here to discuss my wedding plans. I wanted to give you notice, Farnsworth." He drew from his breast pocket a packet of papers. "I wanted to serve these to you myself. Sort of a nod to the fact that we'd once been friends. And, you'd saved my life, after all."

Farnsworth was wary as took them. As he flipped through them, his brow furrowed in confusion. "What the . . . How did you get these?"

"It took a bit of doing, but it was nothing more than leg-work." Gideon shrugged. He was staying very still, not trusting himself to stray too far from the steely control he held over his emotions. He wanted to physically hurt this man, vent the rage and the grief that roiled inside him.

"No one gave me any trouble. They were glad to get payment at last. Farnsworth, you are a disgrace at paying your debts."

"You bought them up?" Farnsworth's bravado deflated swiftly.

Gideon nodded. For the first time since coming here, he began to feel good. Farnsworth's face was stupefied, and there was fear glimmering in his dark, close-set eyes. "You plan to ruin me, don't you? Oh, God."

Gideon said nothing. The silence was more effective than anything he could have said.

Farnsworth flew into a panic. "I saved your life, Ashford. I took you to May Hayworth's house. Remember that."

"I have. As I mentioned. That is why I am going to give you one chance."

"What? What are you talking about? What chance?"

"I want payment on these debts. In full. Every last ha'penny."

"I can't make payment. You know I cannot afford this."

"Yes, you can. You just have to apply some of the vile ingenuity you used to such effectiveness in seducing Miss Milton. And here is something to motivate you to be brilliant. If you cannot pay your debts, you will be subject to the action of your creditor. That is me. And I do not plan to be kind."

Farnsworth's breath quivered out of him.

"Make the payments, Farnsworth," Gideon continued, his voice like steel. "Here is how you are going to do it. You are returning to your country house, and you are going to either manage your estates into profit or you are going to sell off everything that is not entailed. In either case, the settlement should keep you gainfully occupied *outside* of London. I want you away from this city, away from the people I love."

"You want me to go back to Southerton? The place is a tomb!" Farnsworth looked to Biggs, as if appealing for aid. "There is nothing I can do there. I can't manage the estates, you know that. I am appalling at that sort of thing."

Gideon remained silent. Farnsworth's color deepened as he grew more desperate. "It's horribly dull there, Ashford. The people, God, you cannot believe what they are like. It isn't like Town, they . . . Come on, man! I'll pay, I'll make good. But I have to stay here, give me a chance to win at the gaming tables. One good streak, and I can give you a fourth of what I owe."

Gideon studied him, unfazed. "Farnsworth, do not think you have the option of remaining in London as a free man. The only residence that awaits you here is debtor's prison. Now, I believe I have been kindness itself in my generous offer. I will only make it once. It is Southerton or Newgate. Your choice."

Biggs spoke up. "Come now, we used to be friends. Surely we can work something out."

The words echoed in Gideon's head. They used to be friends. Yes, it was true. To his utter and eternal shame . . . they used to be friends.

Farnsworth showed his teeth. It was his best attempt at a smile. In his eyes, tears brimmed. "What the hell happened to you, Ashford?"

Gideon looked at him, then took a deep breath. "I woke up."

He left them puzzled and enraged, exiting the den of pleasures with his heart no lighter than when he had entered.

The wedding was a quiet affair. Sophie was touched by the happiness she saw on Lord Roberts's face when May repeated her vows. She rather thought there was a gleam of a tear in his eye, but she could not swear to it.

Michaela, who stood next to her during the ceremony, wept loudly during the entire procedure, from the moment Aunt May entered (or even a few minutes before her arrival, in anticipation) to long after the final pronouncement was given by the reverend.

Her husband was very kind to her, patting her hand, enclosed in his, and putting his arm about her shoulder, but the suffering look he shot to Sophie made her want to giggle. Women who were in a delicate condition were sometimes strange in their moods. It was, however, incredibly touching that the major was so patient with her.

As they filed out of the pews to go and congratulate May and Lord Roberts, she saw a familiar figure move into her line of vision. It felt as if the bottom dropped out of her world.

When had *he* arrived?

On his arm was Margaux. Suddenly Sophie felt a wave of weakness nearly take her down.

She watched as May moved forward, an expression of pure rapture on her face. He could have taken her hand, bowed, inclined his head—any of the acceptable things that gentlemen did to posture suitably in public. Instead he wrapped his arms around her slight shoulders and May was enveloped, almost disappearing against the great bulk of Gideon's height.

He held her like a child, for she was so slight and petite. And he laid his cheek against the top of her head, his eyes closed. Sophie saw his mouth was moving and May was giving little nods in acknowledgment of what he was saying.

Margaux appeared at Sophie's side. "He was so quiet on the way. He told me all week that he did not wish to come but showed up at my house this morning and said he would accompany us."

It hurt to hear Margaux speak of Gideon like this. Yes, it was one thing to realize that Gideon was Margaux's fiancé, or would be as soon as they had established themselves enough as a couple to make the announcement of their engagement seemly. It would probably take place in a week or so.

It was quite another to be confronted with it. She said quietly, "Gideon always surprises you."

Margaux gave her a strange look. After a moment, she stammered, "Did . . . have you spoken to Lord Burton?"

"He is here. Over there somewhere, I imagine, waiting to congratulate the groom. Ah, there he is, just as I suspected, with Lord Roberts."

She saw the expression on Margaux's face as she looked for Burton. Poor Margaux, no better off than Gideon or herself. None had gotten what they desired.

Margaux might have been thinking the same thing, for a somber expression fell on her face. She moved away to offer her congratulations to May and Lord Roberts.

Sophie was relieved to be left alone. She desperately wanted to excuse herself. There Margaux was again, perched on the arm of Gideon, and he had not so much as looked Sophie's way, not once.

Perhaps he didn't trust himself. Or her. And perhaps he was correct not to do so, for she did not know what she would do if he did acknowledge her.

She closed these thoughts out of her mind and felt a gentle hand close over her arm. She looked up and saw May before her. She flung herself into the woman's arms. "Congratulations, I am so happy for you!" she cried. To her horror, she sounded a bit hysterical.

"Sophie, what is it?" May's gaze was sharp as she held her at arm's length to examine her face.

"Nothing, nothing. I am just being sentimental. I suppose Michaela's emotionalism has been a bit contagious."

May's knowing glance at Gideon told Sophie she was not fooled.

"He came." May's voice was filled with happiness.

"I knew he would."

"He said the sweetest things to me. Sophie, I have not lost him."

"I am so pleased." She slid a baleful glance at the couple mingling among the other guests.

May groaned. "Oh, dear, how thoughtless of me to go on so when you must be so unhappy. I am very sorry."

Sophie shook her head. "No, please. This is your day, and you should not apologize to me." She sighed prophetically. "The situation is what it is, and it is certainly not of your doing."

"How I wish I could do something to mend it."

Sophie gave her a quick hug. "Aunt May, you always want to mend the lives of those you love. But sometimes, you just cannot. Please, please do not let this spoil your wedding. I should not have said anything!"

It was wrong of her to be maudlin when this was such a happy day for May, and Sophie was very angry with herself. "You and Lord Roberts deserve this happiness. And I must get used to seeing him with Margaux, after all. I will, in time."

"How will you ever get used to that, darling?" May cooed sympathetically.

"Well, I must, mustn't I? And I can take inspiration from her. She was so kind to me when I was being squired by Lord Burton, before he noticed her, and she was always hopelessly in love with him, right from the beginning. I can at least return the favor in kind. I must, no matter how difficult."

May froze. Her eyes widened and the slightest hint of a smile touched her mouth. "Margaux and . . . and Burton?"

Sophie nodded sadly. The waste of all these broken hearts was almost too much to bear. "I think it might have been a match if he had spoken. It was for him she promenaded with Farnsworth, you know. All the while, I suspect poor Burton harbored a growing tendre for her he was reluctant to acknowledge because he was afraid of hurting *my* feelings. He had made such a point of establishing his suit with me and then his feelings began to change. . . . Oh, what a mess it all is."

"Margaux and Burton . . . you and Gideon!"

"Why are we discussing all of this unhappiness? I am an ungrateful wretch to burden you with this. I think I should leave before I spoil everything."

"Nonsense, you silly girl. You have made my day all the happier. And as for your troubles, do not fret a moment longer. I think I just might have a solution."

Sophie was stunned. "A solution? To what?"

"To all of this! As you so aptly observed, I like nothing better than to meddle benignly in the lives of those I love. Therefore, what greater happiness on my blissful day than to find the perfect resolution to an unsolvable dilemma? Oh, my dear, but it is so simple. And obvious. Why, I am surprised you did not think of it yourself!"

Chapter 28

The news that Margaux had a caller waiting in the draw-ing room was not a surprise. Lord Ashford—she simply could not think of him as Gideon, it was too much to ask— had been meticulously courteous about calling on her reg-ularly. He was, it appeared, determined to keep up appearances so there would be little stir when their en-gagement was announced.

But when she walked into the room, it was not her soon-to-be fiancé who had come to pay her a visit. Lord Oliver Burton stood in the center of the room.

She immediately felt her temperature rise, and her stomach began to hurt.

He seemed a tad nervous, too.

"Good day, Miss Milton," he said, executing a bow.

"Lord Burton, it is a delightful surprise." Her voice held the faintest tremor. "Please, sit. Would you care for some refreshment?"

"Nothing, thank you." He held up a parcel wrapped in brown paper and tied with twine. "I am returning the read-ing materials you so generously lent to me. I found them of the utmost interest, as we already discussed."

"You did not have to do that," she said, then winced. She sounded ungracious.

He ignored this as he laid the parcel on a table and folded his lanky frame gracefully into a chair. Margaux hurried to do the same before her knees gave out.

Folding his hands before him, he gave her a level look. "It was good to see you at Lady May's wedding. I had not had the pleasure of your company at any gatherings of late," he said. "I hope you are not feeling unwell."

"No. Thank you. I am quite well. I have been rather busy."

His right eyebrow jerked up. "With Lord Ashford."

Margaux ducked her head, not knowing what to say in reply.

"I was not aware that you and Ashford were so well acquainted."

She ventured a glance at him without lifting her head. "He is a very kind man."

His sharp cheekbones with the long hollows underneath them seemed gaunt, as if he were the one who was unwell. "The ton has been the worse for not having your charming presence."

She flushed. "That is a kind thing to say, although I cannot help but believe that for many, my absence is a relief. I am afraid I am not in favor at the moment."

It was a broad acknowledgment of what had happened with Farnsworth—but of course he did not know it was Farnsworth. Everyone had assumed she had been caught with Ashford.

Oh, it was all such an awkward mess.

And no doubt Oliver was convinced that she was of loose morals, a disgrace. Her mother had pounded it into her head that her "indiscretion" would be the ruination of her unless she married quickly. It had made her feel like spoiled goods, pawned off on a kind man too honorable to fling her to the wolves, which is perhaps what she deserved.

She should be grateful. She was, truly, but she could not

be *happy* about all of it. And neither, she well knew, was Ashford.

"I was visited by Lady May recently," he said slowly and with care. "She had some interesting thoughts I would discuss with you."

She opened her mouth, and out came, "I am going to announce my engagement to Lord Ashford next week at Lady Bonningham's rout."

He froze, his expression inscrutable. After a moment, he seemed to remember himself. "Then allow me to offer my congratulations and wishes for happiness."

Margaux was not certain, but she thought she detected a shift in his manner, as if he were forcing the words out. "Thank you," she murmured. She wondered what he had been about to say.

His lashes lowered over his eyes. They were long, delicate, and dark. His masculine beauty was so astonishing sometimes, a contrast of symmetry and gracefulness melded with the hard lines and planes of an aristocratic male.

"I trust it is not rash," he said, his voice soft. "Indeed, marriage is a great responsibility. It should be undertaken with measured consideration."

He raised his gaze and she felt a tremor go through her. She would have broken down right then and there, confessed everything but for the further humiliation it would cause.

He spoke again, his voice lower. "The consequences are deep and abiding. One should be certain."

"I do believe I am making the correct choice." The only choice. Did that make it right?

She was feeling a bit dizzy. Lord Burton rose and came to her, taking her hand and drawing her to her feet.

When she stood, he did not release her hand. His voice was softer.

"One must examine all the implications," he said. His gaze seemed to have fastened on her lips.

They were dry all of a sudden. She ran her tongue over them and saw his eyes twitch, narrow . . .

Her body tingled in response. She was aware of a wicked sensitivity of her skin, as if the fine lawn of her chemise were as rough as sackcloth.

"I trust he did not . . . force this issue. The night of the ball, there was some"—he paused, his mouth tightening — "to-do involving his treatment of you."

She flinched at the mention of the debacle that was her fault. "I will tell you the truth, sir, though I trust you will not mention this to another soul."

His gaze burned into her, flashing with excitement, and she had to fight not to moisten her lips again. "You know indeed that you can trust me with your secrets."

"I had made the mistake of strolling in the gardens with a gentleman who . . . who . . ." She faltered, then forced herself to finish. "Who was no gentleman, as it turned out."

"Farnsworth," Burton said irritably. "I suspected he was not what he seemed."

"He was beastly," Margaux said. It humiliated her to have to confess her stupidity, but she wanted him to understand. "And it was Lord Ashford who came upon us when I wished to quit the man."

Burton's eyes widened. "He did not detain you by force, did he?"

Margaux drew a steadying breath. "He was trying his best to persuade me. Lord Ashford convinced him he should desist."

It was unnecessary to go into details. Burton would understand.

"I was a bit . . . overset after the confrontation, and it was then, when Ashford was comforting me, that we were discovered by a group of youngsters. They raised the alarm, and things got quite out of hand."

Burton was shocked. "And it looked as if Ashford had been the one . . . But why did neither of you set the matter to rights?"

"He insisted and I was too confused and upset to do anything at the time but take his lead. As he later explained to me, he has some familiarity with the fact that the ton would be no more forgiving if they knew the truth. Farnsworth might be blamed, but I would seem the worse for my part. He saw no cure for the situation other than the one he has taken, and my mother agreed . . . and it seemed quite decided."

She thought he might touch her, reach out and put his arms about her, for there was that sort of look on his face. But surely that was only wishful thinking, an aching heart seeing what it would in innocent friendship.

"And what did you think of the matter, Margaux?"

It was the first time he had ever used her name. It fell on her ears sweetly. "I thought I should get what I deserved for being so foolish."

"Were you heartsick over Farnsworth?"

"No. Not at all. I realized very soon after making the dreadful mistake to go with him that my affection for him was more of a wish than a reality."

"A wish?" His expression was keen. "Why should you wish to harbor an affection for him when you did not?"

"Because . . ." She wrung her hands. Should she speak? What good would it do? "Because the season was running longer and longer, and I had no one else to interest me."

"Was it your mother? Did she pressure you to marriage?"

"Partly," Margaux conceded. "But it was more to do with other things."

"Other things being what?"

"My lord, this is far too personal—"

He moved quickly. Suddenly his hands were on her arms, holding her tightly as he peered intently into her face. "What were the other things?"

She bit her lips, fighting with the urge to tell him. Why did one always have to pretend—were appearances so important? Would it be humiliating for him to know that she loved him? Didn't love take courage, after all?

Heat crawled over her skin. The place where his hands held her burned.

"May I assume, Margaux, that I might not be exhibiting too much conceit to think that I could be the 'other thing' to which you refer?" he asked softly.

"My lord, I cannot think you do not already know the answer to that question."

He frowned fiercely, his grip tightening on her shoulders. It was vaguely painful, but she did not wish for him to release her.

"Do you care for Lord Ashford?"

"He is a good, good man. He has treated me with unimaginable kindness, my lord. I hold him in deep affection and regard."

"Margaux," he said steadily, "you know what I am asking. Do you love him?"

I love you, she wanted to cry. Opening her mouth, she felt her courage leave her. She merely shook her head.

"Do you wish to marry him?"

"I accepted his proposal."

He made a hissing sound, full of impatience. "By God, woman, will you speak plainly to me for once. Do you wish to marry the man?"

"No!" she exclaimed. "I always dreamed of marrying for love."

He hesitated, nodding slowly. "I never thought to marry for love."

"Yes. That is not the way things are done, I realize. I am foolish—"

"But I like the idea now. I do not wish to marry merely a suitable woman. I find the idea of some woman whose sole recommendation for the position is her pedigree utterly distasteful. Isn't that curious? I suppose I'd never given it much thought before, but I find myself pondering little else these days, and I've concluded that I would always regret not having made a more satisfying choice in partners."

Margaux was speechless. Lord Burton was a romantic?

"I think," he said, his gaze locking on to hers, "that I would very much like you to be my wife."

She was still, her body frozen. She felt the pressure of his hands lessen. They slid down her arms to capture her fingers.

"Do you think there is a way," he said carefully, "that you would consider breaking off with Lord Ashford and consider an offer of marriage from me instead?"

She felt stupefied, dazed. A part of her was cautioning that she could not possibly have heard what she had. "But, what of Sophie? I always thought you were enamored with her."

"I regard Miss Kent with the highest esteem, and we are great friends. However, she does not have my heart. I find with you, Miss Milton, that there never seems to be enough time to say everything there is to say. You seem to understand the strange course of my thoughts, my interests. I have never been able to speak as freely with anyone else as I do with you. I think about you all the time, look forward to seeing you. I believe those are the symptoms of love, are they not?"

He touched her face. The contact sent an immediate jolt through Margaux's body. He loved her! "I have been in love with you since the moment I spied you across the room at my first ball," she said in a rush. "Of course I wish to marry you. Yes, yes! I will marry you."

Burton smiled, beamed actually. His solemn face wore the expression of joy well, Margaux thought, and they both began to laugh with happiness.

"But what of Ashford?"

"I cannot help but to think he will be relieved," Margaux told him. "He was only being a gentleman, after all."

"You have made me so happy," he declared. He snatched her to him and without asking permission and with a rather rakish disregard for the fact that she had not yet unattached herself from her previous fiancé, kissed her soundly.

"Margaux!"

Her mother's voice was like a bucket of freezing water

being dumped upon her. Margaux let out a small yelp and leaped backward.

"It is quite all right, Mrs. Milton," Burton said. He was acting almost frivolous, not like his usual self at all. "Margaux and I are to be married."

"She is marrying Ashford," Mrs. Milton said, striding into the room and taking firm hold of Margaux's wrist.

"I am afraid there has been a change of plans," Burton said with an edge to his voice that was actually—it sent a jagged little thrill down Margaux's spine—a touch threatening.

"There certainly is not. I will not risk any more scandal. Margaux knows her duty. The engagement will be announced in two days' time, the banns will be read, and the wedding will take place as soon as is seemly after the proper observances have taken place."

"No, Mama," Margaux said.

Her mother turned to glare at her, the surprise on her face almost as great as Margaux's own.

She had never actually defied her mother before, not in private and certainly not in front of company.

"I love Lord Burton, and he loves me," she explained calmly. "We have been meeting secretly, actually."

Mrs. Milton was scandalized. "What?"

"No, no, not like that at all. We had a very firm friendship, based on mutual interests. We went to lectures, and some exhibits at the Royal Academy. We were friends. I thought he was interested in Sophie, you see."

"And I thought her enamored of Farnsworth," Burton put in.

Yes, it suddenly seemed so silly. She laughed and continued, "It was all quite respectable."

"Good lord, no one saw you did they? Now everyone will consider you a bluestocking—those dreadful women."

Margaux exchanged a look with Burton and sighed. "Mama, I do not care. If it is a bluestocking I am, then I will not hide it and pretend otherwise. I *do* enjoy intellec-

tually stimulating conversations and, quite frankly, I fail to
see why that is such a sin."

The room was silent. Mrs. Milton actually took a step
back, as if Margaux had slapped her.

Margaux was not sorry. She said it again. "I do not care
a whit what anyone thinks. I possess intelligence, and opinions, and interests. Lord Burton thinks I am interesting."

Burton stepped in. "Mrs. Milton, I admire your daughter a great deal. Had the circumstances been different, I
would have observed all the usual courtesies and approached you first. But they are not ordinary. Margaux has
confided that her engagement to Lord Ashford is to be
announced in short order, and I simply had to speak before
she made that mistake."

"But this is quite unseemly!"

"But I am happy, Mama!"

Mrs. Milton frowned. "I shall have to think on this.
Lord Ashford—"

Margaux shook her head. "There is nothing for you to
think upon. I am going to marry Oliver."

"Do not grow a spine at this late date," Mrs. Milton said
with authority. "I have done quite well looking out for your
best interests thus far. I do not appreciate your ingratitude,
nor your disrespect, especially in front of a gentleman."

"I am grateful to you, Mama, and I love you very much.
You do mean well, I know, but I am ready to take on that
responsibility. I am quite convinced that I am doing the
right thing. And the *gentleman* to whom you refer is going
to be a part of our family very soon, so I suppose it is not
untoward that he should witness our discussion."

Eugenia Milton gaped at her daughter. "What has gotten into you?"

Margaux smiled and gazed at Oliver. "Love, Mama.
Isn't it miraculous?"

 *Chapter 29*

Sophie was alone.

She stood in the center of the bedroom that had been hers since coming to May's Park Lane town house, and took everything in. The room looked barren without her belongings.

Her trunks were packed with the clothing she had arrived with and a few of the less extravagant gowns May had bought for her. She had left behind the fine silks and elaborately embroidered ball gowns, the satin slippers, the costume jewelry and pelisses, the reticules, everything May had insisted she needed to be "all the crack" in the ton.

She would not need them where she was going. Country life was much less formal. She thought she might like the country. It would be quiet, restful.

And far away from Gideon.

The sound of heels clicking in the hallway brought her attention to the door. Michaela appeared. "May I come in?" she asked.

"Do," Sophie said.

Michaela entered, glancing about the room. "This is where I stayed, too, when I came to May's. It brings back wonderful memories being here again." She sat on the edge of the bed. "You are all packed."

"I think I should have my things out before May and Robert return."

Michaela said, "The house will seem empty. First Gideon left, now you."

"Lord Roberts will be here with her. And you and Adrian will be close by. Your child will be here soon, and the house will be very busy again whenever you come to visit, which I daresay will be often."

Michaela smiled sweetly. "It will not be the same without you here." She rose with a long sigh. "I did not come to beg you to stay, although I dearly would love it if you did. I actually came to see May."

Sophie was confused. "But you know she is on her wedding trip. She left immediately after the ceremony yesterday."

"Yet I thought I saw her equipage on the road earlier this morning. It happened quickly, in passing, but I am certain it was hers. I thought something might have gone amiss and she changed her plans." Michaela frowned. "Odd. And what is even more strange is that although I did not see her inside, I did see the figure of a man. And not Lord Roberts. He looked like . . . and this is completely preposterous, I realize, but he looked like Lord Burton."

"How peculiar. Where was this?"

"Eton square."

Sophie frowned. "Why, that is close to Lady Viola's house. She resides at number eleven Holcolm Street, which is just behind the square. Perhaps May lent her carriage to the Miltons for some reason."

Michaela frowned, thinking. "Or perhaps it was Gideon who was using it. She could have lent it to him. I believe he made a lovely reconciliation with her. It was the best wedding present she could have wished for." She grew doubtful, then shook off her dismay. "Ah, well, it could be the fancy of a woman in a delicate state. Lord knows my brain is doing odd things these days. I thought I would flood the wedding with all of my weeping, to my utmost embarrassment."

Sophie laughed with her. "Will you stay to tea?" she inquired.

"No, really, I will not keep you. I have errands to run. I just wished to see if there was anything amiss. How odd— well, the mystery of the errant carriage will be solved soon enough when May returns in a week. Good day, Sophie."

They kissed and Michaela left. The house seemed so quiet when she was gone. She returned to her packing.

It was not a quarter of an hour later when the silence was shattered but the explosive sound of the front door being thrown open. The crash echoed all throughout the house.

Sophie started, listening closely. The sound of footsteps on the stairs thundered closer.

Her heart began to beat. She told herself it was silly. There was some logical explanation, no doubt, for this terrible ruckus, and it likely had nothing to do with her—

The door to her room burst open and Gideon stood there.

She nearly fainted.

He was out of breath, his face beaming with excitement. He said, "I'm free."

Sophie blinked.

"I'm free, Sophie. Margaux has declined my offer of marriage." He began to laugh, walking toward her with his arms outstretched. "May did it. Damn if that woman isn't the fairy godmother everyone says she is."

Sophie reached out with shaking hands and he caught them, kissed them. "Can you believe Burton arrived on the scene and took her away from me?"

He laughed again, and Sophie, who finally began to comprehend what was happening, joined him in tentative spurts. "I suppose," she told him, "you will have to settle for me."

"Indeed, I shall have you, and without delay. Ah, you have packed your bags. All the better for our swift departure to Gretna Greene. And then to Ashford Manor. Do you like the country?"

"I don't give a fig where we are!" she exclaimed happily.

"Well, that is a blessing because the place is going to need a monstrous amount of renovation. I trust you've learned a thing or two about interior fashion from May in your time here. Of course, we could get her to come visit and put her to work. We need a home, Sophie."

"Stop. Stop, you are moving too fast." She cupped his face in her hands and gazed at him with an irrepressible smile. "You are delirious."

"Just so," he agreed. He bent his head, murmuring, "Just so," and kissed her deeply. She pressed into him, but he grabbed her shoulders firmly and set her back. "You can wilt later. As a matter of fact, I am looking forward to it. But for now, we must away. We have a carriage waiting. I am going to get leg-shackled to you as quickly as possible before anything else can go wrong. Come, hurry."

"You are insane!"

"I am worried for your virtue," he growled as he slung a pelisse in one hand and another satchel in the other. "If we stay here much longer, I claim no responsibility for what might happen."

As for her virtue, it did not survive as far as Yorkshire.

 *Epilogue*

Sophie read to Gideon as he lazed in the sun.

"Do you see him?" she asked, laying the book down.

"He is romping with the girls. They are taking great care with him."

Sophie scanned the field in front of them. Caroline and Catherine were always patient with their "cousin." Whenever Michaela and Adrian visited, their daughters, the eldest six years old and the younger three, doted on the toddler.

Sophie smiled at her cherubic son. His giggles filled the soft summer air. He was chattering in his unique language, his face screwed up earnestly. At two years of age, Joshua was a charming child, quite the prettiest male child Sophie had ever seen. But perhaps she was biased. Gideon, however, heartily agreed with her. But then, he was rather pie-eyed about his little son, as well.

"What the devil does he think he is saying?" Gideon mused in wonder, chuckling as the child launched into another tirade, sending the little girls into shrieks of delighted laughter.

Sophie laughed. The mew of her baby daughter drew her attention.

"Let me," Gideon said, picking up the infant. Miranda squirmed, her small fists working loose of her bundling and waving in the air. "Hello, darling," he cooed softly. The child stilled, listening. He kept talking until she gave him the smile he sought.

She settled back to nap a bit longer, and Sophie exchanged a smile with her husband. He was always ridiculously triumphant when he charmed his daughter.

"It is good to know your talents extend beyond married women," she commented. "As I recall, they were something of an expertise of yours."

He shot a cocky grin at her. "There is only one married woman I am interested in at present."

She leaned toward him, kissing him lightly, then gazing down at the baby in his arms. She smoothed her palm over Miranda's fuzzy head. "I have always heard that reformed rakes make the best husbands. And it is so very true."

The Khoury girls began to shout, and Sophie turned to see their parents were coming down the sloped lawn from the house. "Ah. Here are Adrian and Michaela to join us," Sophie said.

"Halloo!" Caroline called, waving madly. Adrian trotted to her and swung her up on his arm. Then he had to perform the same trick for Catherine. Joshua, who never liked to be left out either, raised his chubby little arms to his uncle.

"May sent me to fetch you," called Michaela. "She says she will not venture out in this sun for fear of her complexion. She wants you all to come up for tea."

"She manages to take charge, even in my own home." Gideon shook his head.

"Do not pretend you mind." Sophie rose. "It is time to go inside, anyway. The baby needs to be changed and fed."

They walked back to the house and assembled in the large drawing room. The buzz of conversation was loud, but Miranda did not mind. She woke pleasant and fascinated with the goings on around her. Sophie did not hand her off to her nurse. May, then Michaela took turns holding her. Joshua, who had a fascination with Lord Roberts, snuggled on the man's lap.

The tea came in. Sophie laughed at the silly story Lord Roberts was making up to entertain her son, when her eye caught her husband's gaze. He had a strange expression on his face, of peace, and contentment.

He looked at all the faces of the people crowded in his house, talking, laughing, cooing, whispering. Then he gazed back at Sophie, a soft smile on his face.

He mouthed, "I love you."

She nodded, and silently returned the message.

Then she poured out the tea. Everyone was hungry.